Righteous Rogue

A Hound Series Novel

Righteous Rogue

A Hound Series Novel

JD McIntire

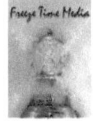

Acknowledgments

I would like to thank Debbie Sadowski, Di Freeze, Dr. Charlie Weiner, Gary Schueman, Gjelard Karrica, Emily Crutchfield and Carla Crutchfield for their help in making this book a reality.

1

It was early Saturday morning during the first week of May 1980. Hound and Pardner, a Bloodhound pup given him by Dobi, were fishing for trout in the river a hundred feet from the rear of a small log cabin that had recently became their new home.

Hound was hoping to catch enough fish for supper that evening. His first day as foreman of the ranch would begin on Monday. He planned to fish for a couple of hours, then drive into town with his new boss Dobi to get outfitted with the clothes and other items he would need for his new job.

Hound had been on the road for some time, exploring areas of the country. He was looking for a place to rest and heal emotionally from the mistakes and tragedies of the past. He hoped to find some peace of mind in a new life. His old one had been nefarious, filled with extreme demands, responsibilities and danger. He was filled with countless untold regrets.

Dobi was the nickname of Debbie Dobson, veterinarian and owner of the ranch located south of Great Falls, Montana. She was in need of a foreman and hired Hound for the job. He didn't have the required experience, but her instinct told her he would learn quickly and soon become a valuable asset to her ranch. She sensed he concealed a troubled past and didn't want to reveal or share information about it to her or anyone else. She decided to accept him at face value and allow the privacy he required.

When Hound was introduced to the six hired hands he would oversee, they became instantly angry that he had been hired as foreman. They expected the position to be filled by one of them. Cole Hanson was senior member of the ranch hands. He was well liked by his coworker cowboys, who all expected he would be their new supervisor and welcomed the prospect. He was tough, but fair, hardworking and honest. He was a real cowboy who followed the code adhered to by all true cowboys.

While he sat with his back to a tree and his dog lying close to him, Hound voiced conformation to Pardner that he had never intended to be a ranch foreman. He was confident in his ability to be the best at it, but he knew he needed the freedom to travel on short notice. All he really wanted was to live in the cabin and do as he pleased. The cabin was perfect as a place to rest in the quiet of nature, but it was reserved as living quarters for the ranch foreman. He would decline the position after going to great lengths to get it. However, he intended to continue his residence in the cabin. He had already devised a plan to get what he wanted. He would make an offer to Dobi and Cole Hanson. Hound knew he would be her second choice for foreman and that they wouldn't refuse.

Hound knew that enough money would buy him anything he wanted, but he would have to be careful not to give the impression he wasn't the vagabond of moderate means he wanted everyone to believe. His desire to maintain that image could be interrupted should anyone become suspicious and take the time and effort needed to discover his true identity, history and financial worth.

Hound was still fishing when Dobi arrived to drive with him into town.

"You're not ready," she said. "Did you forget the time and our plan to go shopping?"

"No. I'd still like to do some shopping, but I need to talk to you first."

Dobi sat next to him beneath the tree.

"OK," she said. "What's on your mind?"

It was cold that morning and his breath could be seen as he began to speak.

"Dobi, I have a confession to make," Hound told her. "I never had any desire to be your foreman. Cole should have the job. I only wanted to live in the cabin. It's the perfect place I've been searching for since I began traveling the country."

"You're probably right about Cole being the right choice for foreman, but he'll expect to live in the cabin. It's a major benefit of the job. I'm sure you understand that. Besides, why would you expect me to allow you to stay in the cabin and give nothing in return?"

"Well, to be honest, I have some money saved and want to simply rest and enjoy myself for a time. Dobi, I'd like to buy the cabin and a portion of land surrounding it, if you'd consider selling at a fair price."

"Hound, I could use some extra money right now, but I'm not ready to sell any portion of the ranch to get it at this time."

"OK, how do you feel about me paying a fair amount of rent to live here?"

Dobi paused as she considered Hound's proposal.

"Well, having some extra money coming in would help, but a fair price you'd pay for rent would only be of little help."

"Dobi, it's none of my business, but are you having financial difficulties?"

Dobi paused again to consider if she would answer.

"Hound, I could lose the ranch if I can't catch up on all the bills," she said.

"Dobi, again it's none of my business, but how bad is your financial position?"

"My mom died during my first year of vet school. The ranch was already in deep debt to the bank. I wanted to drop out of school, but Dad said things would work out and insisted I finish. I graduated last year and started to build a practice, hoping it would grow fast enough to catch up on the payments due. Dad died a month after my graduation. It's been a day-to-day battle to keep the bank from foreclosing on the ranch and my practice."

"How much do you need to get current with all you owe?"

"A lot!"

"How much?"

"The bank must be paid one hundred fifty thousand dollars within ninety days to bring the mortgage up to date for the next twelve months. Half that amount is interest. I've resigned myself to losing the ranch. There's no way I can acquire that much money in three months."

"How large is your ranch? How much land?"

"A few acres over three thousand."

"I had no idea it was that big. How much livestock do you have?"

"Five hundred head of cattle and around fifty horses."

"The land I've seen looks to be covered in rich pasture. Is it all like that?"

"Yes, over ninety percent of the land is. The rest is mountain and timber."

"Why don't you have a larger herd of cattle?"

"I've been selling livestock to pay bills. Originally the ranch had a heard of almost two thousand five hundred Hereford cattle and two hundred horses. All the livestock were the highest quality to be found anywhere."

"You need a plan to get your ranch out of debt and earning a profit again."

"I know. However, I'd need to have enough money to catch up on the bills and replenish my livestock."

"Well, you could sell enough land to allow you to continue operating on a bit smaller scale."

"I know, but like I said, I'm not ready to do that. This ranch has been in my family four generations. I'm the fourth. I keep praying for a miracle that will allow me to keep it all together."

"Do you believe in miracles?"

"Yes, but it's hard to keep the faith at this stage of what's happening."

"You only have seven hired hands including a foreman. How is that enough to maintain a ranch this size?"

"It's not, but that's all I can afford. They don't make enough money as it is. If it weren't for Cole agreeing to keep working, the others would have taken jobs elsewhere by now."

"It seems Cole is a popular and influential figure with the other men."

"Yes, he was with all the hands, but especially with the ones who remained here with him after all the others found better paying jobs."

"Why would Cole stay? With his experience and track record, he surely could have bettered himself."

"Hound, Cole has hope that he and I can form a committed relationship sometime sooner or later. That's why he hangs around."

"Is that why you weren't concerned about him leaving if I was made foreman?"

"Maybe, but to tell the truth, I would likely have felt relieved if he had left. I have no interest in him other than he is a good hand."

"Why would he think a romantic relationship was possible?"

"I suppose he was encouraged to a point. I didn't want to lose all my help."

"Why would you risk losing him and the others by giving me the position of foreman?"

"Hound, I don't have a reason other than my gut told me you could be a great asset in a time of dire need. Besides, you're hard to resist. I suspect you're accustomed to getting what you want. I also suspect there's more to you than meets the eye, or what you're willing to disclose. Am I right?"

Hound stared at her while he considered how he'd answer. His instinct about her was like hers regarding him. He felt she could be trusted with some personal information about him, but certainly not everything. She'd decided it was necessary to know more. He was sure of that.

"Dobi, I want to tell you something about myself, but I need to know you'll keep it between us. Do I have your word?"

"Yes. What do you want to tell me?"

"Well, I'm not a man without means. My financial worth is substantial, enough to buy any mortgages against the ranch, loan you the money needed to catch up on your bills, replenish your livestock, restore whatever is in need of repair, hire additional workers and pay them a fair wage. I'm willing to do that if you want it. We can establish terms of repayment that you can afford and will not put you in any future financial problems. There will be no interest charged for the loans. What do you say?"

Dobi was clearly shocked and surprised at all she'd heard, but greatly relieved by the prospect. However, her expression offered evidence of undisclosed concerns.

"Hound, why would you be willing to do that?" she asked. "It would be a lot of money, maybe more than you've considered."

"How much are we talking about?"

"At least a million, to cover all you mentioned. Maybe even more. Do you have that much money to loan, especially interest free and at a slow payback?"

"It wouldn't be a problem."

"When a deal sounds too good to be true, it usually is. What's the catch? Tell me everything you expect from me if I accept your offer."

"Dobi, I would expect to live in the cabin rent free until all money is repaid."

"What else?"

"That's all. Nothing else."

She was clearly not convinced he was stating all that would be required of her.

6

"What's on your mind?" he asked. "Tell me what you're worried about."

"Hound, I think you're the most handsome man I've ever met. I'm sure you have no problem getting women into bed, but I want you to know that sleeping with you as a condition of your offer is not something I would do."

"That's understandable and I agree. Anything else?"

"OK, but most men would expect that. I guess you find me unattractive."

"Dobi, I find you very attractive, but I'm not like most men. I would never sleep with a woman unless we both wanted to for the right reason. I don't have to pay for the company of a woman. Besides, the money is not being paid; it's a loan."

"Why would you loan me the money under terms that offered no return on your investment?"

"Dobi, you're a decent woman in need of help. I'm happy to help you. All I expect is to be repaid, live in the cabin and fish in the river whenever I want, and that only you and I know where the loan came from."

"Hound, I need to know you're not a criminal and the money isn't dirty."

"The money is clean, and I'm not wanted by the law. I don't care to discuss my personal history any further. Give my offer some thought and let me know what you decide. I'm sure Cole will understand my living in the cabin. Just tell him I'm paying a premium amount of rent to do so."

2

Hound and Dobi drove to town. He didn't buy clothes and other items needed by a foreman, but Hound did purchase things needed to begin his residence at the cabin. During the drive into town, Dobi made the decision to accept his loan offer. She had become even more curious about Hound's history. She felt he could be trusted to keep to the terms regarding the loan and to be truthful in all things, but some questions and topics of conversation were off limits unless initiated by him. Dobi would never have given a stranger such a broad benefit of the doubt regarding the current relationship they had formed so quickly. However, there was just something about Hound that convinced her she had nothing to fear from him.

They were walking down an aisle of the local supermarket enjoying some casual conversation while Hound shopped for a week's supply of groceries. Dobi was anxious to know when to expect the money to be loaned to her and how she'd receive it. Hound was happy to satisfy her curiosity.

"First thing Monday morning I'll contact one of my banks out of state," he told her. "Your money will be wired to your bank as soon as we sign the contract specifying the terms of the loan and get it notarized by your attorney."

"I don't have an attorney. I've never needed one."

"OK. Do you know a decent attorney in town?"

"There are two. I know them both, but I don't know how good they are."

"Which is the biggest, does the most business?"

"That would be Ben Thompson."

"Who's the other one?"

"Beth Weaver. She's only been in town a few months. Beth is having difficulty getting her practice going."

"Well, it's tough to get a new business going in a new town. We'll use her. I might have need of a lawyer at some point. I'll check her out to see if we're a fit."

"I'm happy to help her get new business. Beth seems like a nice person. Besides, she's in a wheelchair and I feel sorry for her. I think that may be a major reason her practice is slow to grow."

"Well, now I know she's my choice. Beth will be willing to work harder than a lawyer without a handicap."

"Hound, I'd guess you'll require my ranch as collateral for the loan."

"At least enough of it to cover the amount you borrow. That doesn't surprise you, does it?"

"Of course not. I know you need to be assured of a way to get your money back if something should happen that I couldn't meet the terms of our agreement."

"Based on the terms, I don't think that would happen, but I do have to protect myself."

"Indeed, it would be most unlikely."

"Dobi, I'm happy to help you out with the loan and its generous terms. I sense you haven't told me the complete story regarding your fear of losing the ranch. If you want to tell me, I'd like to know."

"Your sense is keen. If you hadn't come along, it was certain the bank would foreclose and take the ranch in ninety days. The owner and president of the bank, Jack Long, has wanted to own the ranch for more years than I can remember. When I mortgaged it, he set me up to be foreclosed on. I was desperate and no other bank would give me assistance, so I was forced to agree to terms that I knew would be hard to meet and he knew would be impossible."

"Jack is the classical prick. I've known and dealt with a few like him. Won't he be surprised when you pay off your mortgage, he loses and you're free of his plan."

"It's for sure he'll be surprised, but I'm a bit concerned about how angry it will make him. He wanted the ranch very much and is used to getting what he wants. It's been rumored that in the past he's done some bad things to good people to get their property."

"What kind of bad things?"

"Jack is a very wealthy man. Not only does he own the bank, but he also has controlling interest in most of the business in town that he doesn't own out right. He's also the largest landowner in the area. All the property that surrounds my ranch belongs to him. He's always wanted mine to join his together and because of its rich pasture and abundant water. With wealth comes the power to hire bad men to do bad things. I believe Jack employs such men."

"Are you as concerned about him as you seem?"

"Well, I guess I am."

"OK, but let him know you have a new mortgage agreement with another lender. That will take his focus off you. He'll assume the lender is an out of town bank. He'll want to know which one. Don't tell him a damn thing. He'll spend a long time trying to find out information that doesn't exist."

"When that time arrives, he might use some type of persuasion to get the information from me."

"I don't think so."

"Why not?"

"Dobi, you worry too much. Trust me to be right and stop worrying about Jack."

"You have a plan to deal with Jack, don't you?"

"You give me too much credit. There's no plan other than to let him know he no longer will be able to foreclose on the ranch, or your vet practice. Now, stop asking foolish questions. I have no more answers for you."

"What if Beth tells him you're the lender?"

"She won't. He'll never know about her. Besides, it's privileged information between attorney and clients."

Hound was in his cabin by the river, seated at the small dining table eating supper that evening. Pardner was close by eating his. Hound looked at the dog and began to think out loud.

"Son of a bitch!" Hound said loudly. "I've been here only a couple of days, in a place I intended to be peaceful, with nothing to concern myself with but rest and relaxation. I've already managed to involve myself in a situation that could defeat the purpose of my being here. Well, what the hell! Dobi is a person in need of help, deserves to be helped, and I'm able to provide what she needs. Besides, if Jack Long is the bully Dobi says he is, then dealing with him will be enjoyable and relaxing. Pardner, you don't know this yet, but I have a strong dislike for bullies. The more dangerous they are, the greater is my disdain for them."

The dog looked intensely at Hound as if he understood and agreed with all that was said. Maybe in some unexplainable way he did.

The next morning, as agreed upon, Hound and Dobi met with Cole at the ranch house for breakfast. Cole was delighted to learn he would get the job as foreman. He wasn't pleased to learn that Hound would continue to live in the cabin. However, his feelings became positive when he learned the large sum of rent Hound paid would be added to the pot containing handsome pay raises for all the hired hands and what the pay increases would be.

Cole had a concern he showed in cues but didn't voice. Hound was a very handsome man. Cole felt his chance for a personal relationship with Dobi could be threatened. Dobi didn't pick up on the cues, but Hound saw and understood them immediately. He smiled and said nothing. He would address Cole's concern if and when it should ever become necessary.

"Hound, I like your nickname," Cole commented during breakfast. "How did you come by it?"

"I had a dog as a best friend when I was a kid."

"How long do you plan on staying?"

"I'm not sure, but I'll be away from time to time. There are still some parts of the country I want to visit."

"Do you plan to get a job at some point?"

"I have some money saved. When it's gone, I'll get a job. However, for now I just want to kick back and enjoy myself."

"Hound, I don't want to seem rude, or nosy, but Dobi told me that she knows very little about you. Your nickname is Hound, real name is Jim Hobbs, and you've been traveling around the country for some time. I mean no offense and it's really none of my business, but I think Dobi needs to know more about you if you're going to be renting the cabin and living on the ranch."

"Cole, no offense is taken, but you're right, it's none of your business."

Hound's response angered Cole. He tried not to show it, but he felt put down in the presence of Dobi. Cole saw himself as the alpha male, proud, tough and not to be challenged by a recently arrived outsider.

"Well, I've been looking out for Dobi's best interest for a long time. I think that makes it my business."

Dobi realized Cole intended to get what he wanted or become physical.

"Cole, I appreciate your concern, but I know all of Hound's history needed for me to feel he is no threat to the ranch or me personally," Dobi said. "He's agreed to pay more money as rent on the cabin than it's worth. I've agreed to let him live there and that's the way things are. While he is here, I want him to be treated as a guest. We'll mind our business, and he'll mind his."

"Well, OK! Hell, whatever, you're the boss!"

Saying nothing more, Cole took a final sip of coffee from his full cup, stood from the table and left. Hound and Dobi sat silent looking at each other for a moment, each wondering what the other thought about what had happened.

"Dobi, I'm sure you realize Cole's behavior was motivated to some degree by his stated concern," Hound told her, "but mostly by jealousy. I think he truly cares for you."

"I have to agree with you on both counts. Cole has been there for me during some tough times. I owe him a lot, but I could never care for him the way he does for me."

"Are you sure about that?"

"Yes, very sure. I know I should have told him that long ago."

"If you're so sure, then why haven't you?"

"Honestly, I didn't want to risk him leaving and taking the other hands with him. I couldn't have worked the ranch by myself."

"How far have you carried your charade to keep him hanging around?"

"What do you mean? If you're asking am I sleeping with him, it's none of your business."

Hound knew she was or had in the past. He smiled and nodded.

"Of course you're right, it's none of my business," Hound replied apologetically.

"Hound, you should make every effort to avoid contact with Cole," said Dobi. "You've insulted him and hurt his pride. He's slow to forgive and never forgets. He's been fighting since he was in first grade and is known to have never lost a fight, or left an opponent standing without significant injury."

"I appreciate knowing that. Thanks for telling me."

"You know, Cole was right about what he said."

"What?"

"I really don't know enough about you to verify your character. In the two days I've known you, I've agreed to let you loan me an unbelievable amount of money. The terms of the loan are equally unbelievable. I've agreed to you living on my ranch and trust you like family that has always been in my life and have proven trust-worthy. My decisions haven't been rational."

"I have to agree with everything you said, but I thought you had a good gut feeling about me and trusted your instinct. If you're having second thoughts, there's still time to change your mind. Pardner and I can be gone by tomorrow morning if you like."

"Hound, keeping my ranch and being able to continue building my vet practice are my first and second priorities in life at this time. I'm sure my quick acceptance of your offer to loan me such a sum of money clearly shows how desperate I am. I do have a reliable instinct and it tells me you can be trusted. However, I also choose to trust you because I have no other choice. The fact remains that you drifted into town, giving the impression of bumming around the country in search of a place to stop and enjoy for a time. However, you're not what you want to appear. The fact that you have enough money to make me the loan under such liberal terms of repayment and not hesitate is proof of that. It also makes me question if I'm confusing my instinct with my desire to save my ranch. I mean no insult or disrespect, but surely you can understand my concern."

"Dobi, I completely understand, but the way I see it you have only two choices regarding my offer to help. Trust that my intentions are good and I have no hidden motives, or decline my offer and send me on my way. I know you're dying to know more about me, but I'm not going to tell you any more than I already have, at least not at this time. I will honor my word to you at all times. I expect the same from you, no more, no less. If you refuse my offer, then you lose for sure, but if you elect to trust me and it's well placed, then you win. I may be a huge gamble, but God damn, Dobi! What have you got to lose?"

Dobi realized Hound was right, she had nothing to lose.

"Hound, you're right. I have nothing to lose that I wouldn't lose without your help," Dobi replied loudly, with confidence. "I will have faith that you're the kind of man my instinct tells me you are."

"Good for you!"

3

O n Monday morning, Hound and Dobi were having lunch
in town before attending the 1 p.m. appointment they had
scheduled with the attorney, Beth Weaver. Hound had hand-
written the terms he and Dobi had agreed upon regarding the loan
to present to the attorney.

When they arrived at Beth's small office at the end of main
street, she was waiting anxiously to greet them. The office was
comprised of one medium size room with a bathroom located down
a short hallway to the side. The furnishings were adequate, but
clearly modest in value. Beth rolled in her wheelchair from behind
her desk to great her clients when they entered. Beth had met Dobi
after arriving in town. They seemed happy to see each other.

"Beth, this gentleman is Jim Hobbs," said Dobi, "but he prefers
to be called Hound, his nickname."

"It's a pleasure to meet you, Hound. You're hanging out with a
darn fine young lady."

"I think so too, and it's nice to meet you as well."

"I'm sure Dobi has told you that my practice in the area is new, so I'm thrilled at the prospect of having you both as new clients. As you probably suspect from the size and condition of my office and lack of staff, I need as many new clients as possible that are willing to give a handicapped gal a chance to prove she's a capable attorney."

"Are you capable?"

"Give me a chance to prove it and I will."

"Fair enough, Beth. I've agreed to loan Dobi a substantial amount of money. I was hoping you could draft the necessary terms of our agreement and become our attorney of record regarding any future needs we might have. I've written the terms of our agreement for your review."

Hound handed what he had written to Beth. She rolled back behind her desk to read it while he and Dobi took a seat in chairs. Beth's review of what he'd presented didn't take long. It was precise, but rather short.

Hound, if you decide to retain me, as your attorney I would feel it my obligation to make sure, even though I would be representing her as well, that you understand this agreement is very one-sided in favor of Dobi," said Beth.

"How so?"

"Well, you're agreeing to loan an initial sum of one million dollars to her with very modest terms of payback at no interest. You'll be losing whatever interest you're currently earning on the money, failing to replace any of it through this loan. All you're asking that resembles any type gain is to live in a cabin until all monies loaned are repaid in full."

"I'm aware of all that. Naturally, if Dobi doesn't repay the monies in accordance with the terms, then I can foreclose and recover my money by taking ownership of all or an appropriate portion of her ranch and vet practice."

"Hound, the modest payments and generous grace period you've agreed to will make it close to impossible for Dobi to lose anything through foreclosure."

"I agree. That's what we both wanted."

Beth smiled as indication she was certain the relationship between Hound and Dobi was more than one of only business, even more than business and just good friends.

"Beth, I know what you're thinking," Hound said, returning the smile. "I would think the same thing, but Dobi and I are friends, nothing more. I wouldn't want word to get out otherwise. As a matter of fact, I don't want anyone to know I'm responsible for Dobi getting the money, or that you are our attorney and know anything about how she acquired it either."

"I can guarantee that. Are you hiring me?"

"Damn right, if you plan to charge us a fair price for the work you do."

"How does fifty dollars an hour sound?"

"I don't think that's fair."

Beth looked surprised.

"Well, I need your business," she replied. "What do you feel is fair?"

"One hundred dollars an hour sounds fair to me. How does it sound to you?"

Beth offered another smile.

"Thank you, Hound. That sounds good to me."

"Great, when will you have the paperwork ready for signing?"

"As simple as this is, I can have it ready by 4 p.m. today."

"Good. We'll sign everything this afternoon, and I'll have the money wired to at least four separate banks out of town as soon as Dobi can get the accounts opened."

All the paperwork was signed Monday afternoon. Dobi was able to close her vet clinic the next day and travel to four small towns within a reasonable driving distance and open a bank account in each. Hound went with her. The next day he had two hundred fifty thousand dollars wired to each of the accounts.

4

On Thursday morning, Dobi had an appointment to meet with Jack Long, the owner and president of the bank that held the mortgages on her ranch and vet practice. Jack was certain she wanted to negotiate for an extension on the large mortgage payments due to be paid within less than three months. He would be kind and sympathetic to her coming in early to report she would not be able to meet the deadline, but he would confirm his intention to foreclose. He greeted her in a friendly but business manner and asked her to be seated in the most comfortable chair in his office.

"Well, Miss Dobson, what can I do for you this fine morning?" Jack asked like the wolf in sheep's clothing that he was.

"I'm here to pay in full all that is owed your bank on my ranch and vet practice."

The look that came to Jack's face was one indicative of surprise and less than certainty she was joking.

"I believe the full amount required to pay my debt in full at this time is $378,427.77. Is that correct?" asked Dobi.

"Well, that sounds right. I'll pull the paperwork and see."

Jack called for the paperwork, now realizing she wasn't joking. While they waited for the paperwork to be delivered, he wasted no time in asking questions.

"Dobi, I see you're serious about paying off your debts, but where in the world did you get the money needed to do it? The amount is substantial."

"Where I got it is of no concern to you, Mr. Long. I have it and that's all that matters."

"Of course I'm happy you have the money, but it's only natural for me to be curious where it came from. I can only assume you took a mortgage with another bank, but that would have been difficult."

"I don't care to disclose where it came from, but I will state it was obtained by legal means, just in case you think otherwise."

"Dobi, that thought never crossed my mind."

Dobi wrote checks from her accounts in all four banks and her business with Jack Long was concluded. She could clearly see he was trying hard to conceal his anger over losing the power to take her ranch. After she left, he cursed loudly as he picked up items from his desk and violently threw them on the floor and against the walls of his office.

When his tantrum had ended, Jack wasted no time in contacting the banks Dobi had her accounts in. He was certain she'd been given a loan. However, given the fact her current collateral and credit rating was poor, he was convinced a loan of such an amount was unlikely to have been authorized by any bank. The money must have been loaned by an individual, probably someone other than he who wanted an opportunity to foreclose and obtain the ranch. If he could find out who, then he might be able to buy the mortgage and once again find a way to foreclose on the property.

Jack had been projecting himself as a rancher for a long time. His initial goal was to acquire large scale pieces of select properties to one day be the largest ranch owner in the state. However, at some time in the past he discreetly had all his current lands surveyed for the prospect of oil and natural gas. The results were positive. As promising as they were, he was informed that the land comprising the Dobson ranch likely held beneath the ground an inexhaustible supply of both.

The presidents and/or general managers of the banks Dobi had her money in were friends of Jack. His relationship with them included business that was at least unethical, if not in some cases dishonest. He would have no difficulty finding out all they knew about where Dobi got her money.

The money had been wired to the four banks by four banks, each in different states. Each wire was in the amount of $250,000. When Jack called each of the out of state banks, he was unable to obtain the name or any information about the lender. Jack could only assume at that point that the lender considered Dobi's likely inability to repay the loan as the reason for giving it. He became convinced the lender also knew the truth regarding the hidden value of the ranch. Jack was determined to discover who the lender was, what he knew and if he would be a serious adversary in the competition to gain ownership of the ranch. He wanted to know if the mineral rights were included in the loan agreement should the lender foreclose. If not, then the lender knew nothing of the oil.

Hound was an intelligent man. He had included mineral rights in the loan contract. He may not have known or even considered the possibility that oil or natural gas might be present, but he would leave nothing to chance in any of his business dealings. Besides, his only goal was to help Dobi. To do it properly meant covering all bases.

A month had passed. It was the first week of July. Dobi had been busy building her vet and ranching business. Cattle had been purchased and the herd was now twelve hundred in number. Fences, barns, the bunkhouse and the ranch house had been restored to a proper condition. Dobi was now showing a profit and had made her first payment to Hound. Hound had been spending most of his time fishing, making phone calls to check on his businesses and completing an extensive physical fitness workout each morning. Dobi had allowed him to construct a primitive gym in the large storage barn located near his cabin. He had avoided going into town as much as possible. Monthly trips to the barber shop and food store was as much interaction with local citizens as he wished to have at that tenure of his residence in the community. Dobi called him by phone occasionally to say a brief hello and check on him.

Dobi had hired enough new ranch hands to handle all the work required. Cole was given the final say on all new hires and terminations. Living quarters separate from the regular bunkhouse were built for him, as was appropriate for his position and status. Cole was becoming more comfortable with Hound living on the ranch. He knew Hound was keeping to himself more than he considered normal, but that included staying away from Dobi as well. Cole was happy about that.

During the last week of July, Hound had completed his morning workout in the barn and was about to begin his standard, five-mile run. Cole was on horseback close by inspecting fence repairs that had been completed by some of his men the day before. When Cole saw Hound exit the barn, he joined him for a short visit. The two men had talked only once for a short time since their less than friendly conversation a month before during breakfast with Dobi at the ranch house.

"Good morning, Cole," Hound said in a friendly manner. "How have you been?"

"Not bad. Been staying busy. Lots of work is required to keep the ranch running like it should."

"I can believe that. You and your cowboys have a hard job, from sun up until dark much of the time. Right?"

"Yep. That's why me and all the ranch hands enjoy and look forward to Saturday nights."

"I guess on Saturday nights you fellas like to play as hard as you work."

"Damn right. That's why we need Sunday to recover and be ready for work Monday." Cole paused for a moment, considering if he should ask about Hound's current life of solitude. He decided to introduce it into the conversation.

"Hound, I don't want to get into your business, but you don't get out much, do you? I mean to have some fun, maybe spark the ladies a bit."

"That's true. I've been keeping to myself since I got here. Why, are you worried about me?"

Cole smiled and got off his horse to visit longer than he first intended.

"Well, since you asked, I don't think a night on the town from time to time would hurt you. It's not healthy for a young feller like you to live like a hermit. If nothing else, you need to get laid on a regular basis. You're not opposed to that, are you? Shit! I know you're not queer!"

Cole suddenly realized there was a possibility he might have asked a question that was too personal. It was asked in jest, but if Hound chose to answer, he hoped it wouldn't be in the affirmative.

Hound saw Cole was in distress and laughed.

"Cole, do you have a problem with homosexuals?" Hound asked in a serious tone, after he stopped laughing.

"Well, I don't think so, but I've never met or been around any. If you swing that way, then I guess it's your business. Just don't let the wrong folks know about it."

"What do you mean? Why not?"

"Shit! Hound, this is cowboy country. Most of the folks around here are good people and believe in minding their own business. However, queers and dykes would find it difficult to live around these parts, if you know what I mean. If a man or woman were different that way, then they sure as hell would be wise to keep it a secret."

"I understand, and I'm sure all the men and women who live in cowboy country and are different in that way understand it as well. Cole, put your mind at ease about me being one of them. I'm not, but I'm also not going to judge a man or woman if they are."

"Well, I'm not either, but it's good to know you don't swing that way!"

Hound had come to like Cole a bit better during their conversation. He had always known Cole was tough and could be abrasive in his behavior toward others. His instinct now was telling him Cole was a decent man in all the ways that mattered.

"Cole, I'm going to trust you with some personal information about me that I don't want anyone else to know unless I tell them," said Hound. "Will you keep it between us?"

"If that's what you want, then you have my word on it."

"I was married to a beautiful woman and had two infant twin sons. I loved them more than life. My wife and boys died together in a horrible way a few months ago. That's why I began traveling around the country. I was looking for a place where I could begin to heal from that. When I arrived here, saw the cabin and experienced the peace, quiet and beauty of the scenery, I knew this was the place for me. I haven't been interested in getting to know folks around here, and the company of a woman is the least of my needs or desires. Knowing at least that much might help you better understand me."

Cole looked at Hound for a moment. His eyes were misty when he responded.

"Hound, thanks for sharing with me. I only wish you had told me sooner. I'm so sorry for your loss. Why haven't you told Dobi?"

"I didn't want to share it with her at this time and didn't have to."

"Why did you tell me?"

"I feel you would be a true friend. That's something I'd like and telling you would be a good way to start building that friendship, if you're willing to have me as a friend. I sense you're a man to be trusted and counted on to be the kind of friend I want. I had the same feeling about another man some time ago. We are and always will remain the best of friends."

"Hound, I'm willing to take a chance on you. What is your friend's name?"

"Bear is his nickname. That's all I've ever called him."

"I'd bet Hound is all he ever calls you."

"Right, but that's all anyone ever calls me."

"Good, that's all I'll ever call you, unless you piss me off!"

"Sounds good, Cole."

"Say, would you like to see a good rodeo?"

"Well, sure, I guess so. I haven't been to one since I was a kid, but I enjoyed it. Why?"

"Next Saturday, July 31, is the annual county rodeo. It's held at the arena north of town. Maybe you'd like to come and hang out at the chutes with me. All of us cowboys who are entered in events help others when it's time for their ride. You're welcome to be there with me in case you'd like to get away from the solitude for a while. After the rodeo, we go to the Broken Spur to celebrate our winnings or drink and dance away the disappointment of not winning."

"I saw posters and billboards advertising the rodeo. It must be a big one."

"It's the biggest county rodeo in the state. A lot of contestants, cowboys and girls, compete for good money. The stands are always full of spectators from all over the state."

"What are your events?"

"Bull, bareback and saddle bronc riding, calf roping and steer wrestling. I'm pretty good at all of them and usually place in the money in at least one, but not always."

"What's the Broken Spur?"

"It's a big bar and dance hall outside of town. That's where most of the locals go to have a good time."

"Cole, I greatly appreciate your offer, but I'll respectfully decline it. Maybe some other time."

"Sure, some other time, but you're going to miss a lot of fun."

"Sounds like it."

"Hound, guess I best get back to work. I'm damn glad we had this talk. I see you in a different way now."

"I feel the same way. See you later."

"Why don't you drop by the bunkhouse at 6:30 this evening? I'll introduce you to the five new hired hands. You're welcome to join us for supper. We're having steak with all the trimmings tonight."

"Sounds great. I'll be there. Do you want me to bring anything?"

"Hell no! Just your appetite. The grub is good and there's always lots of it."

Cole got back on his horse and rode away. Hound began his run. He hoped it had been a good idea to tell Cole about Rita and the boys. It seemed like it had been.

5

Hound arrived at the bunkhouse that evening and was greeted by Cole as if they had been good friends for a long time. Supper was ready and Cole told Hound to grab a plate and eating utensils from those stacked on the table and get in the self-service line that quickly formed.

After each man filled his plate, he took his usual seat at the large dining table. Cole showed Hound where to sit. Nobody began eating until all were seated and had poured either milk, tea or coffee to drink.

After everyone began to eat, Cole introduced Hound to each of the cowboys. The ones he had met briefly about two months earlier were included. Hound was made to feel welcome by them all. It was apparent Cole had told the thirteen men to behave in a respectful manner toward their dinner guest, and before supper was over the cowboys had come to view Hound as a man worthy to be among them. Hound was interested in the work and life of a real cowboy. He gave each man equal attention, asking questions and showing admiration and respect for their abilities and profession.

Hud Fletcher was forty and the oldest of the group. He had been working as a cowboy for twenty-four years. He had a history and reputation of being among the best. Hud was well known and respected in the world of rodeo. In his younger days he was a consistent money maker in the bull, bronc riding and calf roping events.

"Hound, Hud is my nickname," he said. "It's short for my real name, Hudson. I like your nickname. How did you come by it?"

"I had a Bloodhound for a best friend when I was a kid. The name was given me by my parents because of the dog."

"I hear Dobi gave you a Bloodhound pup. I'd guess that brought back some fond memories of your childhood pal."

"His name was Hunter. He was about two when I got him. I think Pardner will look like him when he grows a little."

"I understand you were traveling around when you arrived in town and decided to stay."

"That's right. It's nice here. This part of the country is beautiful. The folks who live here seem to be fine people."

"Most are, but there are assholes anywhere you go."

"Six of the men here served in the military. Harry, Billy, Carl, Bart, Lee and Cole were drafted into the Army and served a tour in Nam. I was never in the military. Did you serve?"

Hound wasn't sure it would be in his best interest to answer truthfully, but he decided it would assist in furthering his friendship with the men.

"I was drafted into the Army in 1968 and did a tour as well."

"I hear that place was a real hell hole!"

"Yes, it was."

"How bad did it fuck you up?"

"Well, I suppose less than some and as much as many. I try not to think about it, but sometimes memories just occur."

"Did you see much combat?"

"My fair share, I suppose."

"What part of Nam were you in?"

"Central."

Hound noticed Lee Foster leaning close to Cole and whispering into his ear. Cole gave a gesture to Lee indicating they would talk at another time.

Hound visited for an hour after eating and then excused himself and went to his cabin. The cowboys sat around a bit longer talking. Cole asked Lee to explain further what he had whispered in his ear earlier.

"From January 30 through February 2, 1970, Base Camp Bravo 127 in Nam was under siege by a massive force of enemy troops," Lee began. "The camp was overrun by the enemy and out of the hundreds of American soldiers defending the camp only twenty-five survived. A lieutenant, called by the nickname Hound, called for napalm to be dropped on his position inside the perimeter as he led the last of the survivors, fighting their way out. They cleared the perimeter a split second before the napalm was delivered. This Hound guy was to receive the Medal of Honor for what he did all through the siege but especially at the end. He turned defeat into a victory. I wonder if the Hound living here on the ranch could be the lieutenant from Bravo 127?"

"How did you hear about all that?" asked Hud.

"I was among the replacements sent to the base shortly after the battle ended. That's all anybody talked about for some time after we heard the story."

"You know, I recall hearing something about that fight from a guy I rodeoed with in the past," said Cole. "He told me a similar story while we were drinking a beer about a year ago."

"Do you think Hound, the mysterious drifter, is the hero from Nam?" asked Hud.

"Hell, I don't know, but it would be a big coincidence if he were."

"There's one sure way to find out. Let's ask him."

"No, we won't do that."

"Why the hell not?"

"He may not want us to know."

"Why not?"

"If the story I heard is true, the lieutenant was promoted to captain and put in command of his own base camp after he was recommended for the medal. He damn near beat a superior officer to death for not sending backup during a similar battle at the new base. He was to receive the medal, but as the consequence for the beating the medal was denied him. He was demoted back to lieutenant. Nobody heard anything about him after that until rumor got out that he had received an honorable discharge for a medical condition and sent home. He was on his second tour at that time."

"Shit! How did he avoid a court-martial and prison term?"

"I don't know. Hell, what I was told may have been pure bullshit. However, just on the slim chance Hound the drifter and Hound from Nam are the same fella, he deserves his privacy. I don't want any of you bastards asking him about it. I mean it! Do you all understand?"

All the cowboys agreed to mind their own business.

The next morning, Hound had just completed a five-mile run when Dobi arrived at the cabin riding a horse and leading another.

"Good morning, Hound," said Dobi, smiling.

"Good morning to you. It's nice to see you on this beautiful day. What brings you here?"

"Would you like to take a ride with me? I brought a gentle horse for you."

"Well, that sounds nice, but I was planning on taking a shower and fixing some breakfast."

"Come on, ride with me. We won't be gone long. You can shower and eat when we get back. I want to talk to you."

"Thanks for the invite, but I'll have to pass. Maybe some other time."

"OK. I heard you had supper with the boys at the bunkhouse last night."

"That's right. News travels fast around here."

"I saw Cole this morning. He told me."

"It's still early. When did you see him?"

"He stopped by the ranch house on his way to a ranch about

an hour drive from here. He's going to take a look at a bull for sale there." She paused before continuing. "Hound, is Cole the reason you won't ride with me?"

"Well, I wouldn't want him to think our relationship might be more than that of landlord and renter."

"Why?"

"Dobi, you know Cole has feelings for you."

"Yes, but I've tried to make it clear I don't share those feelings."

"Well, maybe you haven't tried hard enough because I think he feels he has a chance with you."

"Hound, I've told him to stop pursuing me, but he just won't give up. Every man around here knows how he feels about me and won't ask me out for fear of what he will do to them if I accept. I need him as foreman, so I can't fire him. Besides, if I did, he'd take all the hands with him."

"Is that the whole truth or is there another reason you don't want to fire him?"

"What other reason could there be?"

"Maybe you're afraid of him."

"Why would I be afraid?"

"Maybe you feel he'd be mad and hurt to the point he'd seek some kind of payback."

Dobi was clearly shaken by Hound's statement. She got down from her horse and stood face to face with him.

"Hound, the truth is I am a bit concerned what he might do beyond leaving and taking all the hands with him."

"So, you haven't made it clear he should stop his pursuit, that he has no hope of a future with you?"

"Hell, I hate to admit it, but you're right."

"You told me you slept with him once. You're still sleeping with him, aren't you?"

Dobi hated to answer truthfully, but she felt Hound would lose even more respect for her if she lied.

"Yes, but not on a regular basis."

"Just enough to keep him from knowing how you really feel so he won't leave and seek some other type retribution."

"Yes, that's the truth. I suppose you see me in a different light now."

"Dobi, I don't judge you for what you do, but if you're telling the truth about all this, then you need to take a stand and deal with whatever comes. Continuing to deceive a man like Cole will only increase the degree of wrath he'll have when he's finally confronted with the truth of how you really feel and why you've been leading him on."

"Can ... will you help me?"

"Make it clear to him how you feel. Let's see what happens. If Cole is the type man I hope he is, then he'll accept your decision. He may find it impossible to continue working for you but will do no more than leave. If the other hands follow him, then I'll help you find more. Don't worry about that."

"What if he seeks greater satisfaction?"

"That would make him a bully."

"What will I do if you're wrong about him?"

"Don't worry about crossing any bridges you may not have to cross."

"What will I do if I do have to cross that bridge?"

"Like I said, that would make Cole a bully. I don't care much for bullies."

"What are you saying?"

"Dobi, just do what you have to do and let's see what happens. That's what I'm saying."

"I guess you're right. I hope so! I got myself into this mess. I'll have to be the one to get myself out."

"I think you're right. By the way, the thirty-first is my birthday. If you've set Cole straight by then, maybe you'd consider having dinner to help me celebrate."

"I'd like that. Why didn't you tell me sooner it was your birthday?"

"I never thought about it."

"How old will you be?"

"Thirty-one."

"That is a good age — young enough to have the will and energy to enjoy all life has to offer and mature enough to make the right decisions."

"I feel older than my years."

"Why is that?"

"I suppose for many reasons."

"Actually, you look younger than your age."

"That's funny. When I was younger, I looked older than my age. Maybe that curse has been replaced by a new one."

"Why would you feel either to be a curse?"

"It doesn't matter. I'm just thinking out loud."

"Hound, do you want to get married and have some kids before you're too old?"

Hound's thoughts went instantly to Rita and his sons. Dobi saw the pain and regret in his expression.

"I've still got time for that," he replied. "A few more years to decide. Hey, I hope you didn't accept my dinner invitation due to a feeling of obligation because of the money I loaned you?"

"Of course not. You've proven that such would never be expected. I've been hoping you'd ask me out. If not, then I planned to ask you."

"Really, why?"

"Hound, there's not a single woman around here who has met you that didn't want to date you. I'm in that group, now that I know you're a decent guy."

"Dobi, I've been decent to you, but in the past, others have experienced me in a much different way. You need to know that."

"Hound, we've all done things in our past that we wish could be changed. I wish I'd never become so involved with Cole. All I can do now is end it and learn from my mistake, become wiser, and never make the same mistake again."

"I feel the same way, but some mistakes may be necessary to repeat in order to exist."

"I don't understand. What do you mean?"

"Nothing. I was just thinking out loud again."

"Where are you taking me for dinner?"

"When are you planning to settle things with Cole?"

"I'll take care of that as soon as he gets back from looking at the bull."

"OK, then I'll take you to the best restaurant around here. Where would that be?"

"There's a couple of good ones in town, but one in the next town to the north is the best for us to celebrate your birthday. Well, I mean it's fancy and the food is wonderful. I assume you're not concerned with the prices."

"Not really."

"That's what I thought. Hound, you must know that curiosity is killing me to know where you got the money to loan me."

"Yep, that's only natural. I'd bet you'd like to know how much I have."

"Well, hell yes! That's only natural too!

Hound laughed.

"I know," he said, "but all that should concern you now is that I have enough to buy you dinner at the best restaurant in the area. OK?"

"Of course. Fair enough."

"Are you expecting to sleep with me?"

Hound laughed again, loudly.

"No Dobi," he replied. "I don't expect anything but your company at dinner on my birthday."

Dobi laughed even louder.

"Shucks! That's not what I wanted to hear!"

"Yes, it was."

"You're right, it was. Thank you, Hound."

"You're welcome, Dobi. Have you had breakfast?"

"No."

"Let me take a quick shower, and then I'll cook some for us."

"How about you take a shower while I cook?"

"Sounds like a plan."

When Hound arrived in the kitchen after taking his shower and dressing, breakfast was ready.

"I hope you like bacon and eggs," said Dobi. "I would have made biscuits, but you didn't have flour."

"Yep, I need to buy groceries. I'd bet you're a good cook."

"Yes. I'll cook dinner for you sometime, if you'd like."

"I'd like."

Hound and Dobi enjoyed casual conversation while they ate and after eating, as they washed the dishes. After she left, he drove into town to buy groceries. While pushing a shopping cart in an aisle of the market, Hound encountered Jack Long. Jack was accompanying his wife, Casey, while she shopped. Casey was a pretty, sultry blonde, twenty years younger than her husband. Hound's first impression of her was that she had married Jack for his money and he had purchased a trophy wife.

Jack had seen Hound around town a few times and made inquiries as to who the stranger was. He had wanted to meet him since learning Hound had been renting the cabin on Dobi's ranch for the past couple of months.

"Excuse me," Jack said as he passed alongside Hound in the aisle. "Are you the young man called Hound?"

Hound knew who Jack was and looked at him briefly before answering.

"That's right. How did you know?" asked Hound. "We've never met."

"I've seen you in town before and asked who you were."

"OK."

"My name is Jack Long. I own the bank here."

"Nice to meet you, Mr. Long."

"You too. This is my wife, Casey."

"It's nice to meet you as well, Mrs. Long."

Casey had been looking Hound over thoroughly from head to toe and smiling. Naturally, she made sure her husband didn't see her doing all she could to flirt. Hound learned much about Casey from the way she looked and smiled at him. She was beautiful, but far from being a faithful wife.

"It's a pleasure to meet you, Hound," said Casey as she dropped her smile and stepped from behind Jack to shake Hound's hand.

"Thank you."

"I hear you're renting a cabin on the Dobson ranch," said Jack.

"Yes, that's right."

"Well, Hound, how long do to you plan on staying in our community?"

"I don't know yet, maybe for some time. I like it here. The scenery is beautiful and the people that I've met so far have been welcoming."

"Are you working on the ranch?"

"No, just renting the cabin."

"Are you working anywhere?"

"Not yet, why?"

"I don't want to seem nosy; I just thought I might help you find work if you needed it."

"I don't need a job right now, but when I do, then I'll call on you if I need your help."

"Hound might be wealthy and doesn't need to work," said Casey, smiling again.

Casey had no idea how much truth was in that remark she'd made in jest.

"I sure wish that were true," replied Hound, returning her smile.

"What kind of work will you be looking for when you need a job?" asked Jack. "I assume you've experience working on a ranch. Dobi will likely be happy to put you to work."

"She said that very thing."

"How did you come by the name Hound?" asked Casey. "I'm sure it's only a nickname."

"That's right. My parents gave it to me when I was a small boy. It stuck."

"What is your real name?"

"Jim, Jim Hobbs, but nobody ever calls me by that name. Hound is what I prefer."

Hound excused himself and continued his shopping.

6

Cole arrived back at the ranch around noon that day. He stopped by the ranch house to talk to Dobi about the bull he'd gone to see. When she chose to sit on the front porch rather than inside, he sensed she needed to discuss something besides the bull, something he would like.

"Is the bull worth buying?" asked Dobi in a businesslike manner.

"He's well worth the asking price. He'll produce some damn fine calves."

"Great, then I'll call the owner and tell him we'll pick the bull up later this afternoon."

"I've already told him we would. I knew you'd want the bull, so I closed the deal. I'll hitch up a stock trailer and go back to pick him up after I get some lunch."

"OK, I'll have a check ready to send with you, if you still want to work for me after I talk to you about something else."

"What could you say to me that would make me not want to work for you?"

"Cole, I've changed my mind about going to the Broken Spur with you after the rodeo on Saturday. It's past the time to end what's been going on between us. It should have never started in the first place. You're a great guy, but you'll never be the guy I want to spend the rest of my life with. I'm sorry, the last thing I ever wanted was to hurt you."

Cole wasn't prepared to hear such news. He stood from the chair and found it hard to respond.

"Bullshit, Dobi!" Cole shouted. "What the hell are you saying? You can't be serious!"

"I'm serious, Cole. My decision is final on the matter."

Cole's shock turned to hurt, and then quickly to anger.

"You know if I quit and leave, the rest of the hands will go too!" he shouted. "If you're serious, you know I won't stay here. Maybe you should take some time and reconsider your decision and make sure it's what you really want, what's really best for you and the future of the ranch."

"Cole, I want you to stay on as foreman. I want all the hands to stay, but my mind about us is made up and won't change."

"Are you fucking someone else? You are, aren't you? That's the reason you don't want me anymore!"

"That's just not true, Cole, but I do plan to start seeing other people. I want you to let me get on with my life and not cause any problems for me or anyone that I decide to date."

"Tell me who you're fucking! Tell me now!"

"I told you, nobody, Cole! That's the truth."

Cole couldn't control the rage building inside him. Dobi, concerned about what he might do, stood and started to go inside the house. He grabbed both her arms and threw her from the porch. She landed hard on her back, the wind being knocked out of her. Cole picked her up and began to shake her as a dog would a rag doll. She managed to regain enough breath to scream out in pain and terror. He stood her up and hit her hard in the face with his fist. She fell to her back on the ground, unconscious. Cole stopped his assault, saw she was breathing, walked to his truck, got in, and drove hurriedly from the ranch.

Joe Sparks, one of the ranch hands, drove past the ranch house a few minutes later, on his way to a barn to pick up more barbed wire for fence repair. When he saw Dobi lying on the ground, he stopped and rushed to her side, arriving just as she began to regain consciousness.

"My God, Dobi! What happened?" Joe shouted. "Are you badly hurt?"

"I don't know, Joe. Please get me to the hospital."

The right side of Dobi's face was badly bruised and swollen. Blood was dripping from her nose and mouth. Joe picked her up and laid her on her side in the seat of his truck.

They arrived at the small hospital in town within a half hour. Joe carried Dobi into the emergency room where evaluation of her injuries and treatment quickly began. He took a seat and waited to hear a report on Dobi's condition. Over an hour passed, and then a nurse arrived to report Dobi and her doctor wanted him to join them in the exam room.

When Joe entered the room, Dobi was lying in bed, hooked up to a variety of medical equipment. She asked the doctor to speak to him about her condition.

"How bad is she?" Joe asked the doctor.

"She has a concussion and broken jaw, but she'll have a full recovery."

"What the hell happened to her?"

"She was able to state that Cole Hanson did this to her. The sheriff has been called. He or a deputy should be here at any time."

"Shouldn't she be in surgery for the broken jaw?"

"Not until we know how bad the concussion is."

"Can she talk at all?"

"A bit, but it's very painful. She wants to speak to you."

Joe walked and stood beside Dobi's bed.

"What do you want to say to me, Dobi?" Joe asked her.

In garbled verbiage, she told Joe to find Hound and tell him to get there as soon as possible.

Joe found Hound sitting with Pardner under the tree at the river. Hound hurried to the hospital. Dobi hadn't been moved from the emergency room.

"How do you feel?" Hound asked her.

"Like shit," she said in the same garbled verbiage. "How do I look?"

"Exactly like you feel, darlin! Joe told me you said Cole did this to you. Why did he do it?"

Dobi struggled but was able to tell Hound everything that had happened.

The sheriff arrived and obtained Dobi's statement. Two hours later, Cole was arrested at the Broken Spur. He was drinking whiskey, intoxicated and talking to friends as though nothing had happened.

Cole had begun to sober up a bit by the time supper was served at the jail. Shortly after finishing his meal, he was taken to the visitor area to see someone who'd been allowed to visit long after regular visiting hours were over.

Cole didn't know why Jack Long was seated at the table waiting to speak with him.

"Hi, Cole," Jack said, smiling. "Looks like you've gotten yourself in some real deep shit."

"What are you doing here, Jack? What the hell do you want?"

"I want to help you out of the deep shit you're in."

"We've never been friends. Why would you want to help me?"

"Because if I do, you'll have to do something for me."

"Well, there it is! I figured something like that would be required. What would I owe you?"

"It's for certain you won't be working as foreman for Dobi any longer. I want you to come work for me as foreman, but you'll be doing other things that we'll keep a secret."

"What would I be doing?"

"Whatever I need you to do. That's why we'd need to keep certain aspects of your employment a secret. As far as anyone else is concerned, you'll just be my new foreman. Only a select few who work for me on my properties will know about your special duties. Like you, they have similar duties."

"That means the job could involve things that could land me in prison."

"Maybe, but not if you don't get caught. Besides, what you did to Dobi will for sure get you at least twenty-five years, given the fact you've been there before for a similar crime. So, if I help you to never get caught, then what have you got to lose by accepting my offer? You can expect to be paid a generous salary, more than you could ever earn as a ranch hand or foreman. You're soon going to be too old for that kind of work anyway. Think about your future."

"Even if I accept your offer, how are you able to help me get out of my current situation? The evidence against me is cut and dry."

"I have influence with the right people to make it happen; the prosecutor and the judge are among them. Do we have a deal?"

"Hell, you know we do!"

"Good, but you should know that to double-cross me in any way would result in severe consequences. After all, I have other bad boys working for me secretly. Do you understand my meaning?"

"Yes, I understand."

"Excellent!"

Cole spent the night in jail. The next morning, he was arraigned in court on the serious charges Dobi had alleged and the prosecutor had filed against him. Ben Thomson, the local attorney and longtime associate of Jack Long, stood at his side to represent him.

Cole pled not guilty. With no objection from the prosecutor, the judge released Cole on his own recognizance and a trial date was set for September 24 to begin at 9 a.m. Cole left the courthouse. A deputy sheriff accompanied him to The Double D ranch so he could pack and remove all his personal belongings. He was waiting in the bunkhouse to talk to the hands when they came in for lunch. He sat at his regular place at the table and had lunch with them. Joe had told the other hands what Dobi said happened. Cole wanted to tell his side of the story. Everyone was anxious to hear it.

"I told Dobi I was quitting," Cole began. "She became very upset and tried everything to change my mind. As you all know, or at least suspect, she and I have been in a romantic relationship for some time, one that she wanted to keep secret until she thought the time was right. I decided to break it off with her and knew it would be impossible to continue working here. She became so enraged, I felt it was best to leave and let her cool down, so I did. When I left, that newly broken stud she bought was tied to the hitching rail in front of the ranch house. I figure after I left, she tried to ride him again, and he sensed her rage and threw her. If that didn't cause her injuries, then the horse must have kicked her after she was thrown."

"That sounds reasonable," said Joe, "but why would Dobi blame you for her injuries, and where did the horse go?"

"Shit! You know hell has no fury like a woman scorned. She wanted revenge because I was dumping her and wasn't going to be her foreman any longer. Dobi isn't the sweet, meek and innocent little lady she wants everybody to think she is. The horse likely ran off. I figured one or more of you guys would have found it and returned it to a pasture or stall in the barn."

"The horse you're talking about was in a stall, but none of us found and put him there."

"What about Hound? Where was he?"

"After I got her to the hospital, Dobi sent me to find Hound and send him to her."

"Hound may have looked for, found the horse, and put him in the stall. I hate to think it, but maybe Dobi convinced him to do that and keep quiet about it to support her accusation about me. There's no telling what she offered him to help her. I thought Hound might be a decent guy, but maybe I was wrong. After all, we really don't know much about him."

"That's right, Cole," said Hound as he stepped from a short hallway leading from the front door into the bunkhouse, where he had been standing out of sight, listening. "But I know a couple of things about you."

Cole was surprised by Hound's presence but not at all concerned. He ignored Hound's remarks and continued to talk to the cowboys.

"Anyway, boys, I want you all to know I've accepted a job as foreman for Jack Long. He's agreed to hire all of you as hands and pay you a much better wage than you're making here. I'd like all of you to take his offer and continue to work with me. How about it?"

"When would we start?" asked Hud.

"As soon as you can get your belongings together and move into the newer, more modern bunkhouse Jack says he'll reserve for only you boys. Naturally, I'll be living in a house of my own."

"Can we give Dobi some time to hire new hands? Regardless of what's going on between you and Dobi, it wouldn't be fair to her to do otherwise."

Hound allowed Cole to complete what he wanted to say and then spoke again.

"Cole, don't you want to hear the couple of things I've learned about you?" said Hound in a soft but clear voice. "It seems I was wrong about the kind of man you are. Maybe the rest of you may want to consider what I have to say."

Cole stood from his chair and looked at Hound.

"Sure, Hound, say what's on your mind," said Cole angrily.

"You're a low-life, Cole, a bully and a God-damned liar. Dobi would never accuse you of something you didn't do. She said she didn't want any more to do with you. Your pride and ego couldn't take that. You lost your temper and viciously beat her, a dear, sweet little lady who was helpless to defend herself. None of these men are going anywhere, at least not until new hands can be hired."

"Is there some kind of threat somewhere in what you're saying?"

"No! Just facts. You're pretty good at beating defenseless women. How well can you do with a man?"

"I've always done damn well with men, any and all who have ever challenged me."

"Well, you son of a bitch, that's about to change."

"Are you planning to change it?"

"No, mother fucker, I'm going to change it."

Everyone, especially Cole, paid close attention to the soft tone of Hound's voice and how calm he remained despite the things he was saying and the words he used. They all saw his determination and confidence, but most of all his lack of fear.

"There's not going to be any trouble here, boys," declared the deputy. "I'm here to keep the peace. The man who starts anything will be arrested and taken to jail. Cole, you've done everything you came for. It's time for you to get out of here and off the ranch."

"OK, deputy. You're the boss for now, but Hound, I'll be seeing you at another time and place."

"I'll look forward to that, Cole."

After Cole left, Hound spoke with the hands.

"Gentlemen, Cole is a piece of shit, but he was right about one thing. You don't know much about me. I don't care to share things about myself with other people that I consider to be personal and none of their business. However, I will share with you that I am a man of my word and I never break it. Dobi has asked me to take care of things for her until she's up and around again. I've given her my word to do that. She's relying on me to do whatever is needed to protect what is hers. How many of you cowboys are willing to pledge your loyalty to me in my endeavor? If you help me, then I'll make it well worth your decision. You have my word on that."

"I speak only for myself," said Hud. "I'll stay on here, at least until Dobi is back and has hired enough new hands to run the ranch. However, under one condition."

"What's the condition?"

"That you truthfully answer a question all of us want answered."

"OK, but only if all the men agree to do what you've agreed to."

"They need to know what the question is before they can decide."

"I suppose so. Ask your question."

"Are you the Hound who was the hero and Medal of Honor winner for bravery above and beyond the call of duty for his performance during the siege at Base Camp Bravo 127 during the Vietnam War?"

Hound was silent for a few seconds, considering how he'd respond.

"Well, gentlemen, do you want me to answer?" asked Hound. "Are you all going to make the same agreement as Hud?"

It only took a brief moment for all of the cowboys to say yes.

"Fair enough. Yes, I am that Hound who fought during the siege at Base Camp Bravo 127 in 1970. I don't want to further discuss anything about that fucking war."

7

It was in the early evening on July 31. Hound entered Dobi's hospital room. She was recovering from the surgery required to repair her broken jaw. Fortunately, her concussion had been mild and was no longer a concern. The ranch hands were working hard to maintain the ranch at a proper level. Hound had made an agreement with a veterinarian in a neighboring community clinic to fill in for Dobi until she had recovered. Hound had offered the vet a generous amount of money, one that couldn't be refused. The ranch hands were pleased with the profit-sharing plan he had provided to them, one he felt certain Dobi would agree was a wise business move.

Hound had spent most of his time on the ranch, leaving only to buy groceries and visit Dobi. The ranch hands had reported seeing Cole occasionally but never having conversation with him. He was angry they had decided to continue working for Dobi and wanted nothing more to do with any of them.

When Dobi saw Hound had come again to visit, she smiled. He carried a vase containing three colors of roses, eight each of red, yellow and salmon. He placed them on the stand next to her bed and then sat in a chair.

"What are you doing here on your birthday, Hound?" she asked. "You should be out celebrating."

"We have a date for dinner tonight. Remember?"

"Of course I remember, but looks like I won't be able to make it. I hope you'll give me a rain check."

"As soon as you get those wires out of your mouth, we're going out for the best steak to be had around here."

"You have no idea how much I look forward to that! I'm so tired of a liquid diet. However, I won't let you be seen out with me until I look decent again."

"The doctor says after you've fully recovered that no will be able to tell you were ever injured."

"That makes me very lucky. It seems like I've been lucky ever since I met you. Hound, I'll never be able to thank you enough for everything you've done for me since you got here. I'm so grateful, but I still don't understand why you've done so much and asked for so little in return."

"I'm just a sucker for a lady in trouble."

"Have you seen Cole lately?"

"No."

"I can't believe that bastard got out of jail, especially without having to post any bail. He's probably run off to keep from going to trial."

"He's still here. Jack Long hired him as foreman."

"Why would Jack do that? Cole will be going to prison for what he did to me. Right?"

"If justice is served, he will, but I'm not sure it will be."

"What do you mean?"

"I think Jack is convinced Cole will win in court. Most likely Jack will be a key player in making it happen. The fact Jack hired him is evidence of that. if I'm right, then Jack is going to get something in return from Cole."

"Do you think that something might involve getting my ranch?"

"Jack would have to be prepared to do some heavy things, illegal things, to get your ranch now."

"Yes, or have Cole and others like him who work for Jack do those things."

"Do you think Jack has the balls to play that kind of hardball?"

"Not the balls, the contacts."

"Do you think he has that much influence with the right individuals?"

"What individuals do you mean?"

"Law enforcement, judges, prosecutors, those type people."

"I don't know, but it wouldn't surprise me if he did."

"Well, let's wait and see what happens at Cole's trial. That might tell us what we need to know."

"What if we're right and Jack is able to get Cole off the hook? Even worse, what if he plans to get really dangerous in an effort to get my ranch?"

"Don't start worrying about problems that may not occur."

"I know, don't cross any bridges until you get to them. Right?"

"Absolutely."

Hound didn't want to worry Dobi, but he was more than certain Cole was going to walk and would be obligated to do anything Jack, the man he would owe for his freedom, would ask him to do. Beth Weaver, the attorney in a wheelchair, had been at the jail and saw Jack as he was sneaking in to have his secret visit with Cole. She had a secret meeting of her own with Hound to tell him what she had seen.

8

At 9 a.m. on September 24, Hound was seated in the rear of the courtroom when Cole's trial began. Dobi, now out of the hospital, sat next to George Wisnewski, the prosecuting attorney, at a table on the left in front of the judge. Cole sat with his attorney, Ben Thompson, at the other table on the right. Each of the attorneys gave their opening statements. The first witness called for the prosecution was Dobi.

"Miss Dobson, please tell the court what happened to you in the early afternoon on July 26 of this year," said the prosecutor. Dobi was almost fully recovered from the brutal beating she received from Cole, but she still suffered from a degree of discomfort when she spoke. As a result, her verbal delivery was cautious and a little slower than it would be when her recovery was fully completed. She offered a precise, detailed and accurate account of what Cole had done to her and why.

Under cross-examination by the defense, the attempt was made to show that her injuries resulted from something other than an assault by Cole. The likelihood she had been kicked by a horse was quickly introduced.

When Joe was called to the stand, he testified to finding Dobi shortly after she'd been injured. He told what he knew and did, but said he never saw a horse. He never saw Cole in the area either. When the doctor who attended to Dobi in the emergency room and the one who performed the surgery to repair her broken jaw were called to testify, neither could rule out that the injuries were caused by being kicked by a horse.

Hound wasn't surprised to learn he would be called by the defense. He was pressured intensely to confirm he had found the horse roaming after the accident and returned it to a stall in the barn. The badgering continued to imply that at the request of Dobi he was lying about finding the horse, that she had offered him some type of desirable compensation for helping her send Cole to prison. During the time Hound was on the stand, the prosecutor made no objections to ways the defense was trying to lead, intimidate and badger him. The judge couldn't have cared less. He knew things weren't kosher but did nothing to intervene. This and the way Dobi had been treated in a similar fashion further convinced Hound that the trial was rigged in favor of Cole.

Cole testified that Dobi and he had been involved in an intense sexual affair for some time. He said she wanted to keep their relationship a secret for the purpose of appearance. She'd decided she wanted to end the secrecy and get married as soon as possible. He stated that he wasn't ready to get married and refused being pressured to do so by quitting his job as foreman on her ranch and becoming foreman for Jack Long. He said he had decided to tell her all of this on the day she was injured. When he did, she became highly angry and told him to reconsider or she would make him pay.

Cole stressed that Dobi was angry due to his refusal to marry her, remain her foreman, and because he was going to be Jack Long's foreman. She had a morbid hatred for Jack that was totally unfounded. He said she became physically aggressive and tried to hit him in the face, that he hurried to his truck and left the ranch to escape what she might do next. Cole concluded by saying there was a newly purchased stud horse tied to the hitching rail in front of Dobi's ranch house when he left. The stud wasn't yet fully broken to ride.

The trial only lasted one day. The jury was ready to return their verdict the next morning. Hound and Dobi were sitting on a bench in a hallway, waiting for the courtroom to open at 8:45 a.m.

"The trial was much shorter than I thought it would be, Hound," said Dobi. "Is that good or bad?"

"Honestly, I think it's good for Cole, bad for you."

"What makes you think that?"

"The prosecution didn't try to make a case against Cole. The defense did most of the talking, both during opening and closing statements, and sure as shit during the trial. The judge didn't do his job at all."

"You and I were painted to look bad, weren't we? Me worse than you."

"Let's hope the jury saw the same things I did about how the judge allowed so much improper behavior by the defense and even the prosecutor to proceed. All of them clearly favored Cole. Do you know if Jack has close ties to any of the jury members?"

"Jack has ties to everyone in town, but I don't know how close with any of the jury. My God! Do you think he may have influenced some, maybe all, the members?"

"I wouldn't be surprised."

"I know you're acquainted with all the members, but the defense made sure you were only casually acquainted. No such care was taken by the prosecutor regarding Cole, or Jack."

"Hound, you really believe the trial was rigged, don't you?"

"I've thought it would be ever since Beth told me she saw Jack at the jail the same day Cole was arrested."

"I will just die if Cole gets away with what he did to me!"

"I understand."

Hound was conflicted. He'd been running from an old way of life, one in which he'd inflicted his personal standards of justice on those he judged deserving of it. However, now he was on a mission to see if that dark side of him could be changed or at least be kept dormant. He knew it would be extremely difficult, perhaps impossible, to keep that dark side subdued if Cole wasn't found guilty and punished accordingly under the law. Hound felt a term in prison was inadequate for what a fucking bully did to Dobi, but at least society considered it justice. If Dobi would feel it was enough, then so would he.

At 9:15, the jury rendered a verdict of not guilty. The judge thanked and dismissed them, and then looked at Cole and told him he was free to leave. Most, if not all, the spectators in the courtroom seemed surprised, but not the prosecutor, defense attorney, judge, Cole and especially Jack.

Hound and Dobi left the courtroom and again sat on the bench in the hallway outside. Beth had been present to hear the verdict. She rolled in her wheelchair and joined them.

Cole and Jack emerged from the courtroom. Cole was wearing an expensive western style suit, hat and pair of boots he'd purchased with a portion of the money he'd won at the July rodeo. On his new belt was the silver buckle for winning the title of all-around cowboy. When he saw Hound with Dobi, he couldn't resist going to speak with them.

"Dobi, I just want you to know that I have no hard feelings about any of this," said Cole. "The same goes for you, Hound. I hope we can all just put everything that's happened in the past and move on."

Hound looked at Cole and said nothing, but Dobi had no such control.

"Get out of my sight, you piece of shit!" she yelled, drawing attention from others in the hallway. "I'm going to put what you did to me in the past, but I sure as hell won't forget it!"

"How do you feel about it, Hound? What do you have to say?"

"Get away from us, Cole," Hound replied in a soft, calm voice.

"Come on, Cole," Jack called from down the hall. "It's time to leave. You've got a lot of work to do today."

Cole smiled and did as Jack told him.

Hound sat with Dobi and Beth until he felt Cole was well away.

"I haven't had breakfast," said Hound. "I'm going to the café down the street and get ham and eggs. Will you ladies join me? I'm buying."

Dobi had to be at her vet clinic to treat some animals. Beth had work to do as well. They both declined Hound's invitation but asked for a raincheck.

Hound told the waitress who greeted him at the café that he'd like to be seated at a window. He ordered his breakfast and sipped a cup of coffee while he waited for his ham and eggs to arrive. He looked out the window at the vehicles passing on the street and the people walking on the sidewalks. He didn't know many of the community citizens yet. After all, he had been keeping to himself, spending most of his time alone with Pardner on the ranch.

While he was eating, Hound noticed a short, dumpy man had stopped at a window of the café and was looking inside. He didn't appear to be looking at anything in particular, just looking. The stranger looked to be in his mid-fifties. He was dressed in jeans and a western shirt and wore a cowboy hat. All he was wearing appeared to be old, dirty and in poor repair. Hound wondered if the man might be hungry. When the waitress arrived to refill his coffee, Hound asked her who the man was.

"That's old Boots," she said. "His name is Henry Slusher, but everybody calls him Boots."

"How did he come by the nickname?"

"He tried to steal an expensive pair of cowboy boots when he was just a kid. After that, people started calling him Boots. He was born mildly retarded. He's lived here all his life."

"I wonder if he's hungry."

"I wouldn't be surprised. He lives on the street. During winter, when it's raining, the fire chief lets him stay at the fire station. He takes a bath there, when someone makes him. I think the chief feeds him whenever he shows up hungry and it's mealtime at the station."

"Does Boots have any family?"

"No, his parents were killed in a fire when he was about twenty. He was an only child, has no siblings."

"Do you know him well?"

"As well as everyone else, I guess."

"Go tell him I want to buy him a meal and get acquainted."

"Boots won't hang around strangers. He's pretty shy."

"If he's hungry, he might make me an exception."

Boots hadn't eaten in two days, and he made the decision to accept Hound's offer. When he sat down at the table, Hound realized Boots was long overdue for a bath. People sitting at other tables close by got up and left. The owner of the café informed Hound that Boots would have to leave.

"I understand," Hound told the owner, "but fix my friend a couple of cheeseburgers to go and a large order of fries as well. We'll wait outside until the order is ready."

Hound paid for his breakfast and the burgers, and then he and Boots waited on the sidewalk outside until they were brought by the waitress, who also gave Hound her phone number written on a napkin.

"I hope you'll call," she said, smiling.

"Boots, how would you like to come home with me?" asked Hound. "You can eat the cheeseburgers on the way."

Boots hadn't said anything until now.

"Why do you want me to come home with you?" asked Boots, using better grammar than expected.

"You need a bath, some new clothes and a place to stay until I can find you a place of your own."

"Why would you do all that for me?"

"You need help to get on your feet and I need a good friend. Will you be my friend?"

"I don't know. Are you a nice man, a man worthy of a friend like me?"

The question made Hound pause. It seemed somehow profound.

"I try hard to be a nice man," he told Boots. "How about you spend time with me and decide if I'm good enough to be your friend?"

"OK, I guess so. Where do you live?"

"I live in a cabin on The Double D Ranch. Do you know where it is?"

Boots became excited in a happy way.

"Sure, I know where it is," Boots said, laughing and clapping his hands. "Doctor Dobi owns The Double D. I like her! She's a real nice lady and helps animals. She sometimes lets me feed the animals she has at her clinic. Does Doctor Dobi like you?"

"Yes, she and I are good friends."

"I thought you wanted me to be your good friend."

"I do, but can't I have two good friends?"

"I guess so, and if Doctor Dobi thinks you're a nice man, then I do too."

Boots quickly ate his food while Hound drove him to a vacant building where Boots said his spare clothes were. The clothes consisted of two shirts and a pair of jeans, both in the same condition as those Boots was wearing. Hound was able to determine the sizes from the labels. He then drove to a clothing store.

"What are we doing here?" asked Boots.

"You need some new clothes."

"I ain't got any money to buy clothes."

"I'll loan you the money."

"I ain't got no way to pay you back."

"You're going to work at the ranch. You can pay me back after you earn a couple of paychecks. You can do ranch work, can't you?"

"Well, I ain't a real good cowboy."

"There's other work you can do."

"What?"

"Hell, I don't know, something."

"I want to learn how to be a real cowboy."

"OK, maybe you can."

When they arrived at the clothing store, Boots started to get out of the truck, expecting to help with the shopping. Hound told him in the nicest way possible that he should stay away from other people until he had a long hot bath, using lots of soap. Boots nodded his agreement. Hound bought seven pairs of jeans, seven shirts, socks and the same number of underwear, a jacket for when the weather turned cooler and a heavy one for winter. As Hound was at the counter paying for the clothes, he heard a store employee asking in a loud and determined voice for someone to leave the store.

"I only wanted to look at them pretty boots and that pretty hat over there," Boots told the store clerk in a respectful manner.

Hound understood that Boots was bad for business because of the way he looked and smelled. The store owner was ringing up Hound's purchase on the cash register. He saw Boots and agreed with the clerk's desire to get him out of there. They knew Boots had no money to buy anything.

"Hold up," Hound told the owner. "That gentleman is with me. I'm buying him some new clothes. Fit him in a pair of good work boots and also in the fancy boots and hat he's looking at."

"Sir, those boots cost five hundred dollars and the hat is one twenty five," replied the owner.

"Well, then make damn sure both fit him perfectly. Say, while you're at it, fit him in a nice western suit to go with the boots and hat."

"Well, OK, sir. How much to you want to spend on the suit?"

"How much is the best you have, including a shirt and belt?"

"As much as the boots."

"Shit! They must be good boots."

It took about an hour to complete everything. The store owner personally handled the fitting of the suit, boots and hat. Somehow Boots became less offensive in his appearance and smell. The total of Hound's bill was close to two thousand dollars. He paid cash. During his time in the store, Boots behaved like a kid at Christmas after Santa had brought him everything he ever wanted. Hound enjoyed the time as much as Boots. During the drive to the ranch, Boots talked to Hound as if they'd been lifelong friends.

"You spent a lot of money to buy me clothes, Hound," said Boots. "I'll have to work a long time to pay you back, won't I?"

"Yes, a long time, but that's because you'll pay me back only a little of your money each time you get paid."

"Will I be working for you or Doctor Dobi?"

"I don't know yet, Boots. I'll have to check with her on that. Who do you want to be your boss?"

"If I work for her, then I'll have to do what the foreman says. Right?"

"I think so. She'll make that decision."

"Do you think I could work for you and you could tell me what to do?"

"Maybe she'll make me your foreman."

"Yes, that would be good."

When they arrived at Hound's cabin, Boots was directed to the bathroom and told to take a shower and give himself a good scrubbing. Hound burned all the clothes Boots was wearing, except his old hat. He said it was good enough to wear for work. After Boots was dressed in a set of his new clothes, he and Hound sat outside under the tree by the river. Boots was introduced to Pardner. The dog took an instant liking to him. Boots felt an immediate affection for Pardner as well. He had never seen a Bloodhound before. Hound was happy that Boots and Pardner hit it off so well, but surprised. Pardner had never been friendly and accepting of anyone other than Dobi. He guarded Hound, the cabin and the area around it, offering a convincing warning to strangers that trespassing was not allowed.

At noon, the cowboys came to the bunkhouse for lunch. Hound decided that he and Boots would join them. The hands recognized Boots. Not many people in town, or the immediate surrounding area, didn't know him. Hud had been promoted to foreman. He welcomed Hound and Boots to join him and the hands for lunch.

"I had a late breakfast in town this morning," said Hound. "I'm not hungry, but thanks anyway."

"I could eat a bite or two," Boots said.

"Boots, are you really hungry after eating those cheeseburgers and fries a couple of hours ago?" Hound asked, smiling.

"Not really, but I never pass any chance to eat. I never know how long it will be before I eat again." The smile left Hound's face.

"Boots, my friend, you'll be eating three times a day as long as you work on the ranch," Hound said."

"So, Hound, Boots is going to work for Dobi?" Hud asked.

"Yep, he his."

"Does Dobi know that?"

"Nope, not yet, but she'll like the idea."

"OK. I'm sure she will, but what will he do? He can't do the work of a regular ranch hand."

"I'll have to discuss that with Dobi."

"I suppose you want Boots to move into the bunkhouse?"

"Why not? You have to hire another cowboy, but you'll still have a bunk available."

"I don't want to stay in the bunkhouse, Hound," said Boots. "I want to stay alone somewhere. Where I stay don't have to be much. I ain't used to much."

"Hound, how about the barn where you do your workouts?" suggested Hud. "Boots could sleep in the room off the back of the barn. It's heated in the winter. He could take his meals here with us, showers too.

"That might work; let's give it some thought. I may talk to Dobi about building a bathroom in the barn so Boots will only have to take his meals at the bunkhouse."

"Hound, Dobi will go along with anything you want, you know that. Joe told us that Cole beat the charge Dobi brought against him. How did she take the verdict?"

"Like any woman in her situation would be, she was very angry and hurt."

"Hound, all of us changed our opinion of Cole for what he did to her. I just thought you'd be interested to know that."

"You're right. Dobi will be too."

When Dobi arrived at the ranch late that afternoon, Hound and Boots were waiting at the ranch house to see her. She was surprised to see Boots there and hear that Hound wanted him to live and work on the ranch. Naturally, she agreed, but she invited Hound to her house for supper that night to discuss what work he had in mind for Boots to do.

"Hound, what possessed you to adopt poor old Boots?" asked Dobi.

"My instinct told me it was the right thing to do."

"Your instinct, or the fact you just felt sorry for him?"

"Hell, maybe a little of both."

"OK, but what work did you have in mind for him to do? He's retarded, Hound."

"I thought he could take care of feeding livestock in the barns, keeping the stalls clean and maybe learn to do other things."

"Like what?"

"Well, maybe he could help you out at your clinic. He probably wouldn't be much help with the cattle and horses, but he could be a lot of help with the small animals that stay there, feeding and walking them, cleaning cages, mopping floors, things like that."

"Hound, you know I already have people hired to help me with everything I do."

"I know, but as your practice grows, you'll need to hire more. Besides, I plan to pay Boots until such time it becomes necessary to hire another hand to do what he does on the ranch and at your clinic."

"Oh, you do, huh?"

"Absolutely!"

Dobi smiled and agreed, but she said Boots would be working for her, so she would pay him. However, she did allow Hound to pay for enlarging the room in the barn and adding a bathroom and shower.

9

It was the middle of October. The weather was getting colder and the first snow of the year was forecast to begin that Monday morning. Hound had suggested that Dobi move her clinic to the ranch. She had done so and now her job as a vet and ranch owner were easier to balance. Boots was doing a good day's work helping her with the clinic animals and completing daily chores he was capable of around the ranch.

Hound had just returned from a two-week trip to meet with all the people in charge of his businesses. He was making more money than ever. Boots had been left in charge of caring for Pardner. They stayed together in Boot's living quarters at the barn. Hound had it enlarged and made modern. Nobody knew where Hound had been, but they were curious, especially Dobi. However, everyone minded their own business and hadn't asked any questions. They knew Hound didn't like others prying into his personal affairs.

Jack Long had become very curious about Hound, who had been living on the ranch for five months. Jack invited Cole to have break-fast with him at his home that morning. He had some things to discuss with him. Cole had told Jack about the death of Hound's wife and children and the story about Camp Bravo 127 in Vietnam. Jack had tried to use the information to find out as much as possible about Hound, but none of his sources could uncover any information about Jim Hobbs, alias Hound.

"Cole, have you told me everything you know about Hound?" asked Jack. "I haven't been able to track down any history on him."

"You know everything about him that I do, at least all he told me."

"I'd bet Dobi knows a lot more about him than anyone around here. Otherwise, I don't think she'd allow him to live on her ranch and have become so friendly with him in such a short time."

"Maybe, but I don't think she knows the things he told me and the other hands about the death of his wife and kids, or his tour in Vietnam."

"Well, if you're right, then there is another reason for her behavior toward him."

"He must have a fair amount of money saved. He's been here five months and still doesn't have a job. I'm told he's spent a lot of money around town. He spent a couple thousand bucks on new clothes for old Boots."

"Yes, and convinced Dobi to let Boots live and work on the ranch. I don't think she would have agreed to that if Hound didn't have a great deal of influence over her."

"I don't know what he has to offer, or what he could have possibly done for her that would give him such influence."

"If he's in a romantic relationship with her, then that might explain it. It's a rumor around town that they're a couple, but Dobi denies it."

"If it were true, then why would she deny it? I don't believe there's anything like that going on."

"She wanted to keep the relationship with you a secret, didn't she, but I suppose you're right about her and Hound. She'd likely want it known if it were true. Hound is a handsome man. Hell, all the single and probably a lot of the married women want to bed him. Dobi wouldn't want them competing with her."

"Are you saying she kept me a secret because she didn't care?"

"Shit! She told you that, Cole. Isn't that the reason you beat the hell out of her?"

"I suppose that's true."

"Did you care a great deal for her, or was she just a beautiful woman with a great piece of ass?"

"I would have to say both are true."

"Well, if you still have feelings for her, then you best get over them. It's for certain she hates you now. Besides, you're going to help me get her ranch. There's no telling what you might have to do to help make that happen."

"What do you mean?"

Jack didn't answer as he considered a thought that suddenly came to mind.

"God damn!" said Jack. "Is it possible that Hound gave Dobi the money she came up with to save her ranch and vet practice? He's been spending a lot of money, doesn't seem to need a job, and Dobi goes along with things he wants. Maybe that's the influence he has over her. If that's what happened, then he for sure is fucking her. Is it possible Hound is a very wealthy man, who wants to keep it a secret, and if so, then why?"

"Dobi would never compromise herself like that for money."

"Bullshit! She slept with you just to keep you around as her foreman. She would do anything to keep from losing her precious family ranch."

Cole wouldn't confide in Jack that he remained deeply in love with Dobi and had intense regret for what he'd done to her. The thought of Hound or any other man sharing her bed enraged him. He knew Jack was prepared to do whatever was necessary to get Dobi's ranch. He also knew Jack would use him as a tool in that endeavor. Cole was now feeling caught between a big rock and hard place. He only had three major desires. Gain Dobi's forgiveness, a chance to win her respect again and possibly her affection, and to be free of the tight hold Jack had on him. The longer he did nefarious deeds for Jack, the tighter the hold would become. However, at this time he felt there was no other choice available to him.

"Do you really think Hound could be more than he wants to appear?" asked Cole. "Secretly a wealthy man, wealthy enough to loan Dobi that much money?"

"Stranger things have happened. Dobi didn't have the credit rating needed to borrow the money from any bank. I made sure of that. So, it makes sense she got it from an individual. Nobody that I know of around here that had that much money would loan it to her."

"How can you find out if he did?"

"I was told that Hound and Dobi were seen visiting Beth Weaver at her office a short time before Dobi showed up to pay off all she owed to me. They have all been seen together many times since then. If Hound loaned the money, he'd want a legal agreement with Dobi to safeguard his investment. A lawyer would be needed to prepare the contract. Shit! I'd bet Beth is that attorney."

"Well, even if you're right, Beth would never admit it because of attorney-client privilege."

"Of course not, but she'd have a copy of the contract in her files. Looks like someone needs to get into her files and see if my suspicion is correct. After midnight tonight will be a good time for you to do that."

"You want me to break into an attorney's office?"

"That's right."

"You know what will happen to me if I get caught."

"Don't get caught, but if you do, then I'll take care of you. Don't worry. You can get away with anything in this town."

"If I don't find anything, then what?"

"Then nothing is there, but if I'm right, bring the paperwork to me, so I can see what the agreement is and know what I need to offer Hound to buy the contract."

"He'll wonder how you found out about the contract. He'll assume you had the file taken."

"Let him. Nobody can prove I was behind the break-in. Nobody will give a shit and try."

At 3 a.m. the next morning, Cole broke into Beth's office through the rear entrance. He forced her file cabinet open with a crowbar and found the file with Hound and Dobi's name on it. At 7 a.m., the file was delivered to Jack at his home. He was having breakfast with his wife, Casey. Cole waited a short time in the living room. Jack sent for him after Casey had finished her meal and left the house to run some errands.

"Was there a file, a contract?" Jack asked Cole, anxiously.

"Yes, you were right, Jack. Hound did loan Dobi the money."

Jack smiled and quickly opened the file and began to read its contents.

"Let me see how much I should offer Hound to sell me the contract," said Jack. "One he won't refuse."

As he continued to read, the smile on Jack's face vanished. He became angry.

"God damn it!" he roared. "Cole, this contract is of no use to me at any price!"

"Why not?"

"Fuck! Hound is allowing Dobi to repay the loan at no interest and at monthly payments a minimum wage employee could afford! There's no fucking way she'd ever have to worry about a foreclosure! I'm sure of two things now!"

"What?"

"Hound is fucking Dobi anytime he wants, and I have to come up with another plan to get the ranch! Son of a bitch!"

Cole grew extremely angry at the thought of Hound having sex with Dobi. His anger was apparent to Jack, who was happy to see it.

"What's next?" asked Cole.

"I have to somehow convince Dobi to sell me her ranch."

"She won't. Why would she?"

"She must be convinced it's in her best interest if she wants to remain healthy."

"I don't think threats of violence will work on her."

"Maybe not, but acts of violence might!"

"What do you mean?"

"Never mind for now. I need some time to figure out a plan. Whatever it turns out to be, rest assured you'll help me carry it out."

"Are you thinking about hurting her?"

"I don't want it to come to that. I hope other things can be done that will convince her to sell the ranch to me."

"What kind of things are you thinking about doing?"

"She needs to realize that severe, unwanted consequences will result if she doesn't."

"Hound and Dobi are going to assume it was you that had the file stolen from Beth's office, since nothing else was taken."

"Good, I want them to, and nobody can prove I had anything to do with it."

"Would it concern you if they could? You seem to control the law around here."

"That's true, but I want to maintain the best image to the general population as I can."

"What's your next move?"

"I'll set a meeting with Dobi and Hound and make her a very generous offer to buy her ranch."

"She won't accept it."

"Well, then things will start happening to help change her mind."

"Why would you want Hound at the meeting?"

"Why not? Dobi will tell him about it anyway. Besides, at the first opportunity before I schedule the meeting, I want you to pick a fight with Hound and beat the shit out of him. That should send the proper message to him and Dobi before I meet with them. Are you up to the task?"

"Hell yes. I'll enjoy messing up the face of that pretty boy."

"I thought you would."

When Beth arrived at her office and determined only Hound and Dobi's file had been taken, she called Hound. He and Dobi arrived at her office a short time later.

"Who would break into my office to steal your file?" Beth asked them both.

"Jack Long was behind it," replied Hound."

"How can you be sure it was Jack?" asked Dobi.

"He became suspicious that I was the one who loaned you the money and wanted to verify it. He assumed correctly that Beth would likely have been the attorney to draft the agreement. Beth, do you agree with my thinking?"

"Yes, I do."

"Why would he want to know what was in the file?"

"He still wants to get your ranch," said Hound. "He wanted to know the terms of our agreement so he could make me an offer to buy the contract. He wanted to get the mortgage on your ranch back."

"Why would he want to buy the contract? Its terms wouldn't give him the leverage he had over me before."

"He didn't know that, but he knows it now, and I'm sure he doesn't like it."

"Do you think he'll give up, now that he knows the terms?"

"No, I think he'll make you a very attractive offer to buy the ranch. Attractive enough that you'll accept it."

"Hound, I wouldn't sell the ranch to Jack at any price!"

"I know, but he's shown how much he wants it. The ranch is a beautiful property and I know his land borders it on all sides. He'd like to join all his land together. However, I suspect there might be another reason for him wanting your ranch so badly. Do you have any idea what that might be?"

"No, but when I make it clear to him that I won't sell, then he should give up."

"Maybe. I hope so. Beth, have you called the sheriff to report the break in?"

"Yes, but he or any deputy hasn't been here yet. Shoot! Nothing will be done about it anyway!"

"You're probably right, Beth."

Hound and Dobi left the office and returned to the ranch. During the drive back, they discussed what had happened. Hound was now convinced there was more than met the eye about Jack's obsession with owning the ranch. He kept his thoughts to himself, but he was determined to find out what was motivating Jack so fiercely.

"What's on your mind, Hound?" asked Dobi. "You've been quiet since we left town."

"I was just thinking that we still haven't been out for the dinner we planned for my birthday. How about we take care of that next Saturday night?"

"I was hoping you'd get around to asking me that. Sure, I'd love to go."

10

When Saturday night arrived, the first snow of the year had been falling for about an hour. The roads were still drivable, but it was uncertain how long that would last. Hound arrived at Dobi's house at the agreed upon time to pick her up for their dinner date.

"Hound, the weather tonight is uncertain," said Dobi. "This snow may not present a problem for us going out of town for dinner, but if it gets heavier and continues, then the roads could become difficult to navigate."

"I agree. What do you suggest?"

"Well, the Broken Spur serves a pretty good steak. The band on Saturday night is usually good, if you like country music. At least we can get home if the weather worsens."

"OK, but we still have to visit the restaurant out of town soon as possible."

"Naturally!"

Hound and Dobi reached The Broken Spur at 7 p.m. They were seated in the dining room of the club and each ordered a rib steak with all the trimmings. They looked forward to pleasant conversation during their meal and until the band started playing at 9. They could see a large part of the dance hall area to the right of the dining room from where they were seated.

Hound noticed that Hud and all the other ranch hands were seated at tables they had pushed together to accommodate the thirteen cowboys. In a moment he saw Cole standing beside Hud, talking to all of them. Dobi was tempted to find out what Cole had to say, but Hound convinced her to wait and ask Hud later. He felt certain that nothing good would come from Dobi confronting Cole.

"It might not have been a good idea for us to come here, Hound," said Dobi. "I didn't consider the likelihood that son of a bitch would be here."

"Calm down, Dobi. We're not going to bother Cole, and he's not going to interfere with our evening."

"You just don't know how much I hate that asshole!"

"I think I do, Dobi, but don't let it ruin your dinner."

"You're right, Hound. I'm sorry."

They talked during dinner and after until the band started.

"Do you like to dance, Hound?" asked Dobi.

"Absolutely, but it's been a while since I did. Would you like to dance?"

"Yes, I love to dance any time I can."

They left the dining area and selected a table in the now crowded dance hall. They put their coats on the back of their chairs, and then made their way to the large dance floor in the center of the room. Hud and the other cowboys saw them dancing and waved. Both Hound and Dobi returned a wave as they were dancing to a slow, cuddle song. Cole soon noticed them and how Dobi was holding Hound close to her. He quickly felt his anger grow strong. He remembered the order Jack had given him to give Hound a good beating at the first opportunity. The opportunity was at hand.

Cole saw several single women he knew sitting at a table. He promptly asked one of them to dance. Once he was on the dance floor, Cole moved into position next to Hound and Dobi.

"What did you say about this lady, Hound?" Cole shouted, indicating the woman he was dancing with had been insulted.

Hound looked at Cole, and then at the woman.

"I didn't say anything," replied Hound.

"I didn't hear him say anything," said the woman. "What did he say, Cole?"

Hound turned and started to dance himself and Dobi away from Cole. As he turned his back, Cole moved quickly and hit him hard on the side of his face. Dobi was forced backward as the blow connected. Hound fell to the floor on his side and rolled to his back. He was dazed and out of focus as Cole moved and stood over him. Dobi hurried to see how badly he might be hurt. Cole blocked her attempt and told her to move away.

"You rotten bastard!" Dobi screamed. "Hound never said a word to or about you or the woman you were dancing with! You are a real piece of shit!"

"Move back, Dobi," Hound told her as he gained focus and got up. "Move out of the way now."

Dobi saw that Hound's face was bruised and swollen, but he didn't act as though he was seriously hurt. She walked from the dance floor as Hound had requested. The other couples dancing did the same. Everyone knew Cole's reputation. They were certain he wasn't finished with Hound. He'd never lost a fight, and nobody wanted to intervene and calm the situation for fear of becoming a target of Cole's apparent anger. Besides, many of his friends were there and would come to his assistance should more than one at a time confront him.

Hud and the other Double D hands sat waiting to see what would happen next.

"Maybe we should do something to help Hound get out of the shit he's in, Hud," said Harry Casper, one of the hands. "Cole for sure ain't through beating him."

"Maybe, maybe not. Let's see what Hound does. I want to know what he's made of."

"God damn, Hud! Hound is a fit guy, but no match for Cole! Cole will hurt him bad!"

"Maybe, maybe not."

Hound now stood a short distance from Cole, looking in his eyes. The club was quiet as all the patrons watched and waited.

"You made two big mistakes tonight, Cole," said Hound in a soft, calm voice as he wiped blood from the side of his face and corner of his mouth.

"Is that right. What might they be, pretty boy?"

"The first mistake was hitting and knocking me down. The second and biggest was letting me get up."

Just as he finished his statement, Hound moved quickly to a position at Cole's right side. With unbelievable speed and accuracy, he delivered a power side kick to Cole's leg. A loud pop and snapping noise were heard as the leg broke at the knee. Bone was exposed above and below the knee joint. Cole shouted out in pain as he fell to the floor, no longer able to stand. Hound delivered a kick to the right side of his face, and then another to the left side. He sat on Cole's chest and began beating his face until it began to look like a pile of raw, bleeding meat. He stopped, leaving Cole unconscious on the floor. He stood over Cole, waiting for him to gain consciousness.

Several of Cole's friends, all employed by Jack Long, were moving in Hound's direction to finish what Cole couldn't. Hud and the cowboys arrived first. Seeing Hound wasn't alone to defend against them, Cole's associates decided to stand down.

"I was afraid you weren't going to stop before killing him," Hud told Hound. "It might be a good idea if you got out of here now, before the law arrives."

Dobi had returned and was standing at Hound's side.

"It's not time to leave yet," said Hound, still speaking in a soft, calm voice. "This cocksucker still owes a debt. When he wakes, he's going to pay it."

"What the fuck are you talking about, Hound?" asked Hud.

"He owes Dobi some fair justice."

Hound walked to a table close by and retrieved a full pitcher of beer that was sitting on it. He returned and poured it all on Cole's face. Cole regained consciousness. He began to utter moans and other sounds of pain.

"He's all yours now, Dobi," Hound told her. "Do what you feel will even the score for what he did to you."

"Hound, you've more than evened the score. Look at Cole; he's in bad shape."

"Are you sure the justice you need has been served?"

"Yes, it's over. I'm satisfied. Now, let's get out of here!"

Hound bent down to speak with Cole.

"Why did you come at me, Cole?" asked Hound. "I want to know. Will you tell me, and truthfully?"

Cole, still moaning from the pain, looked at Hound.

"This ain't over, mother fucker!" Cole uttered. "I'll settle with you for this!"

Hound drew closer to Cole, so only he could hear.

"Cole, know that if you, Jack, or any of his other hired thugs ever come at me again, or at Dobi, directly or indirectly, I will kill all of you stone, God-damned dead," Hound whispered. "I'm convinced Jack told you to give me a good ass kicking. I hoped there was still enough man in you to say so, but I guess you lost all of it when you beat Dobi. Don't fuck with me, Cole. I'm not a man you want to fuck with. Tell Jack that applies to him too."

Hound rose and using his right foot he pushed Cole's legs apart and stood at his feet between them. Cole again lost consciousness on the second of six brutal kicks Hound delivered to his groin. All eyes were on Hound as he and Dobi walked toward the entrance to leave. The thought on everyone's mind was that Hound was the first to ever best Cole in a fight. Instantly, that had earned him a reputation that would be respected in and around the community and everywhere else where Cole was known.

Emergency medical service arrived just as Hound and Dobi were driving off the parking lot. Cole was stabilized and then transported to the emergency room at the local hospital. Soon after, he was taken to surgery to repair his broken leg, nose, facial bones and the hernia resulting from the kicks to his groin.

Hound and Dobi said little to each other on the drive back to the ranch. Dobi didn't know what to say and Hound was busy thinking. The snowfall had become heavy by the time they arrived at Dobi's house.

"It looks like we made the right decision not to go out of town for dinner," Hound said as he offered a big smile. "This snow will likely be knee deep to a tall Indian in a short time."

Dobi busted out laughing uncontrollably at the remark.

"Yep! We could have run into some real trouble if we hadn't gone to The Broken Spur instead," she managed to reply through her laughter. "Your face is pretty swollen and bruised, Hound. How do you feel?"

"I guess like my face is swollen and bruised."

Hound walked Dobi to her front door and told her good night.

"Would you like to come in for a while?" she asked him. "I have something I can treat your face with that will help the pain and swelling."

"Sure, why not? I've never been treated by a vet with animal medicine before."

"It might interest you to know that many medicines used to treat animals can also be used on humans and vice versa."

Dobi sat Hound in a chair at her kitchen table. She obtained the things needed and then began treating his injuries.

"Hound, you're the first man to ever beat Cole in a fight," said Dobi. "Did you know that?"

"I heard he'd never been beaten, but I didn't know if it were true."

"Well, it is, as far as I or anybody else around here knows."

"Dobi, it doesn't matter how big, tough or mean a person is, there is always someone, maybe not bigger, but tougher and meaner, around somewhere. It's not the size of the dog in the fight that determines the winner; it's the size of the fight in the dog."

"You sure proved that to be true tonight."

"Maybe."

"Hound, I'm afraid Cole, on the insistence and with the support of Jack, will bring some serious charges against you for what you did tonight. It won't matter that Cole started it. You know how the law and court here can be rigged by Jack."

"Why would Jack get involved?"

"Don't you think he would, just to do Cole a favor?"

"Well, I think he now believes you and I are more than just friends. He may want me out of the way so I can't help you in any way when he makes his next move to get your ranch. I think what Cole tried tonight was ordered by Jack to either test my resolve or simply disable me for a time. Maybe it was both."

"How far do you think Jack would go to get my ranch? He'll never convince me to sell."

"I think he wants the ranch bad enough to do anything necessary to get it."

"What could he do if I won't sell?"

Hound knew the answer to Dobi's question but didn't want to tell her. Jack would first make a final attempt to buy the ranch for an amount that exceeded its worth. When that failed, he would likely try to frighten and intimidate her into selling by removing her ability to make a profit. Running off her hired hands and destroying property, equipment and livestock would be logical choices.

However, the quickest, most sure way would be to have her meet with a fatal accident. He would then use his corrupt friends in the right places to help him get the ranch at auction or by paying accumulating back taxes. However, Hound knew if Jack decided to win that way, then he would plan to kill him first. Hound wasn't going to let Jack succeed, but first he'd be sure of Jack's intentions.

"Don't concern yourself now with what Jack might or might not do," Hound told her.

"I know, don't cross bridges until you have to."

"Right!"

Dobi continued to administer first aid to him. When she finished, his injuries felt better. He thanked her and announced it was time for him to go home, check on Pardner and get some sleep.

"Would you like to spend the night here with me, Hound?" asked Dobi in a shy manner.

Hound looked at her, saying nothing for a brief time.

"Dobi, I think you are a beautiful, intelligent and very desirable woman, but I'm not the man you need. You still know very little about me. If you knew more, your opinion of me might be different."

"I know you're a nice, honest, trustworthy man who has done a great deal for me and asked nothing in return except to live in an old cabin down by the river. You're a good and decent man. Also, you're the most handsome, sexually desirable man I've ever known. I want you in my bed with me all night. Damn! I never dreamed of saying that to any man before you. I know you have a past, one that you're obviously not proud of. I don't care about that. All I care about is the kind of man you've been to me. I know you may not feel like having sex because of your injuries. Well, I understand that! Just be with and hold me. Will you do that?"

"Dobi, I think it's time I told you something about me that you need to know. It will help you better understand my reluctance to be with you or any woman intimately."

"OK, but please don't tell me you're a homosexual."

Hound smiled softly at her remark.

"You know, Cole wondered about that until I explained why I wasn't interested in meeting any women here. I'm going to tell you what I told him."

"OK, but why would you tell Cole and not me?"

"I thought he and I might be good friends, that he was a decent guy. I wanted him to know why I wasn't interested in dating, so he wouldn't worry about me making a play for you, and I sure as hell didn't want him to suspect that I was a homosexual!"

"OK, but you still haven't said why you told him and not me. We're close friends, aren't we?"

"Yes, we are, and I'm going to tell you now."

"Please do. Tell me."

Hound told Dobi about his marriage to Rita, his twin sons and how they died in a tragic accident. Naturally he lied and told her that Rita and the twins had been at the wrong place at the wrong time and died from gunshot wounds during a sudden and unexpected shootout between a group of criminals and law enforcement. It was the same story he'd told to Cole. Dobi was saddened by the story.

"Oh, Hound, I'm so sorry for your loss," said Dobi as tears began to fill her eyes. "It must be very hard for you to talk about."

"Yes, it is."

"I know you must have loved your wife and sons very much."

"I still love them very much. I always will."

"Of course. Hound, your story is so sad."

Dobi couldn't hold back the tears and began to cry.

"I'm sorry for breaking down, Hound," said Dobi, "but I feel so sorry for you."

"Thank you, Dobi, for caring and understanding. Your tears are evidence of both. You know, when I told Cole, he teared a little too. That led me to believe he might be a decent person. I don't misread people often, but I sure made a mistake about him."

"So did I. Hound, I'm here for you if you need me."

"Thanks."

Hound left and walked to his cabin. As always, Pardner was waiting and happy to see him. He hadn't been home long when Boots payed him a visit. Boots became concerned when he saw Hound's face.

"Gosh darn, Hound! What happened to you?" Boots asked anxiously.

"I'm fine, Boots, just had a little trouble with Cole Hanson tonight at The Broken Spur."

"I bet he looks worse than you do, don't he?"

"Actually, he does, Boots, but why would you think so?"

"Hound, my gut just tells me so, that's why."

"I'm surprised to hear you say that, Boots. I'm sure you know Cole's reputation of never losing a fight."

"Now that you've kicked his ass, you have a reputation, right?"

"I wish that wasn't true, Boots, but I guess it is, or soon will be."

"I'll bet nobody will mess with you now, right?"

"That's something I'd welcome, Boots. How's your house? Is it warm enough?"

"Yep. But I'm lonesome and came to see you."

"I'm glad to see you, Boots, but I'm feeling bad tonight and need to get some rest. Can we visit later?"

"OK, but can Pardner come stay with me tonight and keep me company?"

"Sure, if he wants to."

Boots was Pardner's pal, second of course to his best pal, Hound. Pardner was happy to go with Boots, but only after sensing Hound's approval.

"Hound, you're the only friend I've ever had, you and Pardner. You really do like me and want me as your friend, right?"

"Sure, I do, Boots, but you know that Dobi and all the cowboys here at the ranch like you and are your friend too."

"I know, but they ain't my friend like you are. You won't ever stop liking me and being my best friend, will you?"

"No, Boots, I won't. Pardner won't stop liking you either."

"Thanks, Hound. I love you."

Boot's parting words had a profound impact on Hound. He went outside and watched the simple man with limited intelligence walking away with Pardner until they disappeared into the night and falling snow.

11

By 4 p.m. the next afternoon, almost twenty-four inches of snow covered the ground. Cole was just waking up in his hospital room when Jack arrived to visit him.

"How are you feeling, Cole?" asked Jack, trying to appear concerned.

"I feel like the remains of a grizzly bear fight."

"Shit, man! You look even worse. I hear Hound opened up a big can of whoop ass on you last night."

"Ya! I guess so. I was in surgery for almost four hours to fix a broken leg, nose fractures in my face and a fucking rupture. The doctor said I almost lost my balls!"

"How in hell did Hound manage to do all of that to you? I was sure he'd be the one to wind up in the hospital."

"That son of a bitch had fighting skills I didn't expect. On top of that, the cocksucker moved like a lightning fast ninja, a fucking puff of smoke in a strong wind."

"Well, you'll have your chance to get even when the time comes, but first I need to meet with Dobi and make her an offer on her ranch. I'll invite Hound to the meeting. I'm sure he'll come."

"What happens if she turns your offer down?"

"Well, then I'll have to use unpleasant means to change her mind."

"Jack, there's something Hound told me before he smashed my nuts until I passed out."

"What did he say?"

"He said if you, me, or anybody else that worked for you, directly or indirectly, ever fucked with him, or Dobi again, that he would kill all of us stone, God-damned dead."

"You didn't take his threat seriously, did you?"

"Honestly, yes, I did! I'm convinced he's a man that tells it like it is. I don't think he'd make idle threats."

"So, you think one man could kill all the men I could send after him? Don't be absurd."

"Jack, we have no way of knowing what he's capable of or what contacts he might have that would help him. Shit! We still don't know enough about him to determine what he's capable of. Fuck! Last night I never thought for a second things would turn out the way they did and look at me now."

"I don't share your concern, Cole. If Dobi refuses my offer, then I'll show you that I'm right. Hound may have money, but he wouldn't be here, living in Dobi's cabin, if had the contacts and power you think he has. True, as an individual he may be a handful in a one-on-one fair fight, but I don't plan to fight fair or one-on-one."

The next morning Jack made a phone call to Dobi and invited her and Hound to come to his office to discuss some important business. Hound had told her Jack would extend the invitation and for her to accept. She agreed to meet at 4 p.m. the following Wednesday.

Hound and Dobi arrived a few minutes early for the meeting. Jack was out of his office in a meeting with the mayor but arrived on time to meet with them. They were invited into his office and offered seats in the two chairs in front of Jack's desk.

"Hello to both of you," said Jack in a friendly, welcoming manner. "Thanks for coming."

"Why did you want to see us, Jack?" replied Hound in a less friendly manner.

"I think you know why. I think you both do. I want to make Dobi my final offer to buy her ranch. Be assured the offer will be generous and most attractive."

"Mr. Long, I came to this meeting as a courtesy, but I have no intention of selling my ranch."

"Well, Dobi, at least listen to the man's offer," said Hound. "Anything is for sale if the price is right."

Jack looked at Hound and smiled.

"Hound, I appreciate the comment," said Jack. "I think the offer I'm going to propose to Dobi will prove you are right."

Jack wrote the offer on a piece of paper and then handed it to Dobi. She looked at it before passing it to Hound for review.

"Well, what do you think, Dobi?" asked Jack. "I'm sure you'll agree the price exceeds the value of your ranch."

Dobi thought for a moment before responding.

"Yes, it does," she replied. "What do you think, Hound?"

"It's a lot of money, for sure. Jack, why did you invite me here?"

"Well, I believe Dobi would have asked you to come, so I wanted to make her feel comfortable in doing so."

"Why would you believe that, Jack?"

Jack took a second to consider an answer.

"It's my understanding that you and Dobi have become close friends," he replied, "that she has grown to value your advice in business matters."

"Really. Why would you think that?"

"Am I wrong, Hound?"

"You didn't answer my question, Jack. Why would you think Dobi would seek my counsel regarding the sale of her ranch? Maybe it's because you learned that I loaned her the money to pay off the mortgage you had on her ranch and vet practice, the one you were going to foreclose on."

"So, you loaned her the money. I had no idea. Who would have ever thought it could be you? I had no idea you had that much money to loan, Hound, that you were wealthy. Why did you want everyone to think you were just a drifter who came to town and decided to stay for a while?"

"I didn't give a damn what everyone thought — still don't. Jack, did you get to look at the contract agreement between Dobi and me?"

"What are you talking about, Hound?"

"I'm talking about the file that was stolen from Beth Weaver's office, the one containing the terms Dobi and I agreed on for me to loan her the money?"

"Why would I have access to such a file? Are you suggesting I had something to do with stealing your file?"

"Did you?"

"Of course not! Your question offends me!"

Hound watched Jack's body and verbal cues and knew he was lying.

"I guess you didn't order Cole to give me a good beating either, did you?"

"Why would I do that?"

Again, Hound knew Jack was lying.

"Indeed, why would you?"

"Look, Hound, I heard what you did to Cole the morning after you did it. That's the first time I knew anything about the altercation. You sure kicked the shit out of my foreman. He sure as hell won't be back to work or competing in any rodeos for some time."

"He won't be bullying anyone for some time either."

"Well, enough about all that bullshit. Dobi, do you accept my offer?"

"Mr. Long, your offer is very generous, but I'm going to decline it."

"Dobi, I wish you'd reconsider."

"I won't sell my ranch at any price."

"Jack, why do you want the ranch so badly?" asked Hound. "Is there something about the ranch you know, but Dobi doesn't? I believe there is, and I'm going to find out what it is."

Hound and Dobi left Jack's office. He was furious.

"Jack is madder than a wet hen, Hound," Dobi said during the drive back to the ranch. "I enjoyed making him mad."

"Jack isn't a nice guy when he's in a good mood. I expect we'll get a taste of the real asshole he can be now."

"Should we be afraid?"

"We don't cross bridges until we have to, remember?"

"OK. I guess so."

The snow that had fallen in October was gone by the first week in November. This was a welcome thing by Dobi and the other ranchers. The weather forecast was predicting snow by the end of the week and lots of it. At the suggestion of Hound, Dobi had taken advantage of an opportunity to sell most of her cattle at a good profit. She was certain Hound's advice was motivated by his good business judgement, but she also knew it was a way to minimize the risk of loss should Jack target the cattle as a way to hurt Dobi financially. A minimum profit level had to be maintained on a consistent basis if all the bills were to be paid. About a fourth the number of cattle usually maintained through the winter remained. Most were prime breeding stock including a bull that had cost a healthy sum.

Everyone was on constant lookout for any threat, at any time. All the cattle had been moved to an area that offered the easiest and quickest access for feeding and security inspection of the herd. This area included the barn where Boots had his living quarters.

Hound was convinced Jack had something planned but was surprised he hadn't acted by now. It had been almost three weeks since Dobi had refused Jack's offer, making it clear the ranch was not for sale. The cowboys were required to carry a firearm with them at all times while working and be able to obtain one quickly if needed during the night. At least one of the cowboys was on duty 24/7, patrolling the area where the livestock were, and another kept an eye on the ranch house. Boots pulled more security duty than anyone. He liked doing it and it made him feel worthwhile. Hound kept his matching pair of Colt 45 pistols within reach at all times, day or night.

After three weeks, everyone was starting to think Jack might have decided to do nothing. Hound hoped they were right, but his experience with men like Jack in the past made him less optimistic than the others. In the not so distant past, Hound wouldn't have taken a chance on Jack not using violence against Dobi. Jack and all that were likely to be involved in the violence would have already disappeared. However, Hound was conflicted. He was torn between his determination to reform the man he used to be and his desire to make sure no harm came to Dobi. It was one thing to injure or even kill another person in self-defense, but another altogether to kill others for something they might do.

It was cold on Saturday night, the first one in November. It had started to snow around suppertime. The cowboys planned to have some end of week fun at The Broken Spur after they had eaten. Four of them would be staying on the ranch to take their turn at weekend security duty.

It was to be a special night at the honkytonk. It was Hud's forty-first birthday. The cowboys had planned a party for him. When Dobi learned about it, she appeared at the bunkhouse during supper and insisted they all go.

"Doctor Dobi, Hound said at least four of us should be at the ranch on weekends," said Boots, very sincerely.

"I know, Boots, but I think everything will be all right, just for tonight."

"Hound won't like it!"

"Boots, how about we don't tell Hound? Besides, you're invited to the party. Don't you want to go? After all, you're among the four whose turn it is to stay on the ranch tonight."

"Well, yes, I do, but I'm gonna stay and do security patrol like Hound said."

"OK, Boots, but I don't want you to tell Hound the others are in town. Promise me you won't."

"OK, I promise."

Snow began to fall shortly after midnight. Dobi was asleep in the ranch house, Hound was asleep in his cabin, and Pardner was lying on his rug in front of the fireplace. Boots had just started on another security tour to check the cattle in the pasture close to his living quarters at the barn. Several horses and a select few head of prime breeding cattle, including a prize bull, had been stalled in the barn until hopefully the temperature would begin to warm the next day. It was now fifteen degrees outside. A moderate wind was blowing from the north. The temperature was expected to drop below zero before morning.

Pardner suddenly let go a loud bark, and then another. Hound knew the bark was a signal of warning and jumped to his feet. As he quickly began to dress, he heard sounds of gunfire from the direction where the cattle were pastured. Grabbing his Colts, he rushed from the cabin and got in his truck, with Pardner at his side. He began to drive toward the pasture. When he saw that the barn where the livestock were was on fire, he changed course and headed for the barn. As he did, the cabin exploded in a fireball behind him. To his left, he saw another fire appearing as lightning in the sky. He instantly realized Dobi's house was now ablaze as well. He again changed course and headed for the ranch house.

Driving as fast as his truck would travel toward the ranch house, Hound saw the silhouettes of two men vanish into the darkness and falling snow. When he reached the ranch house, Dobi was standing a distance from the front of the house, barefoot and wearing only a robe. He was relieved she'd escaped the house, which was now an inferno.

Hound stopped his truck and rushed to her side.

"Dobi! Are you all right?" he yelled.

"Yes, I think so."

He saw that she was turning blue from the cold and quickly put her in his truck and turned up the heater.

"Oh my God, Hound! I see fires burning as far as my eyes can see. Is the big barn on fire?"

"Yes."

"Jesus! We have to rescue the livestock inside!"

"If any of the hands haven't done that by now, then it's too late."

"Boots is the only one here. Oh, Hound! Do you think he's OK? What if he's still in the barn?"

Hound sped his truck toward the barn. There was no way to save any living thing inside. The barn was completely engulfed in flames. The roof collapsed along with the rest of the structure seconds later. Hound heard a noise approaching from behind him. He turned quickly, prepared to fire the Colt he held in each hand. The noise was the horse Boots had been riding. It was returning to the barn.

"Was Boots riding this horse, Dobi?" Hound asked hopefully."

"He must have been. He insisted on riding security rounds tonight."

Hound and Dobi drove to the area where the remainder of her cattle were being kept. That was probably where Boots was when the trouble started. The headlights of his truck shining through the falling snow revealed a partial view of what Hound had expected to see. Dead cattle were lying everywhere. Hound drove slowly onward, calling out to Boots. They soon found him. He had been severely beaten, and then a rope had been used to hang him upside down from a tree. Hound cut him down. Boots was nearly dead from the ordeal. Hound put him in his truck and rushed him to the hospital emergency room. He was allowed to stay with Boots while a doctor examined him. Dobi was escorted to the nurse's lounge, where she put on surgical clothing to wear beneath her robe.

Boots regained consciousness briefly and saw Hound standing at his side.

"Boots, did you see the men who did this to you? Did you recognize any of them?"

"It was too dark to tell for sure who they were, but there were a lot of them."

It was then that Boots told Hound he wanted to share a secret with him. There was no rhyme or reason for telling it at that time, but Boots felt the need to share it with Hound at that moment.

"OK, tell me, Boots," said Hound. "What's the secret?"

"There's a lot of oil and natural gas under Doctor Dobi's ranch."

"What? Boots, where did you hear that?"

"I heard Jack Long talking about it one time with a man I ain't never seen before. They didn't know I was around and heard them. Hound, am I gonna die?"

"No, Boots. The doctors here are going to make sure that doesn't happen. How do you feel?"

"I don't feel good or bad, Hound. I don't feel nothing."

"What do you mean?"

"I can't feel my arms, legs or nothing else. Hound, I'm scared."

"You're going to be just fine, Boots."

The doctor told Hound Boots needed to be in surgery right away. It appeared the bullet wound to his back had shattered his spine in the area below the base of his neck. His spinal cord had been severed and bone fragments were lodged within the mass of blood vessels. Internal bleeding was slow but expected to become severe at any time. While Boots was being prepared for transport to surgery, Hound pulled the doctor aside to speak to him further.

"Is my friend going to survive?" asked Hound.

"He's in bad shape. At best, he'll be paralyzed from the neck down. However, the damage done to his body from the beating he received after he was shot is most traumatic. My God, after being shot, and then beat, the poor man was hung from a tree! I don't know how he survived this long!"

Hound went to the surgery waiting room. Dobi soon joined him.

"Is Boots going to be all right?" she asked as she began to sob.

"It doesn't look good. Let's hope for the best, but prepare for the worst."

"This is all my fault, Hound! I should have never insisted on all the hands leaving the ranch tonight."

"Why did you?"

"It's Hud's birthday. The other cowboys wanted to help him celebrate. I should have never gone against your advice to keep at least some of them on the ranch at all times."

"Well, what's done is done. If more of us had been there, then maybe more of us would have been hurt."

"Jack was behind it, wasn't he?"

"God damn right he was!"

"If his intention was to get my attention by scarring the shit out of me, then he succeeded."

"The plan was to kill us both. If that failed, then he sure as hell wanted to let you know he intended for you to change your mind about selling the ranch."

"Why kill us both?"

"Kill you to get the ranch, and kill me so I couldn't foreclose on it after you were out of the way."

"We need to call the sheriff and get that son of a bitch arrested."

"The sheriff won't arrest Jack; you have no proof. Besides, Jack owns the sheriff, the prosecutor and the judge."

"We can't just do nothing!"

"Dobi, do you know if there's oil and natural gas on your property?"

"I don't know. Why do you ask?"

"Boots said he heard Jack say there was during a conversation with a stranger. We need to find out. If it's true, then that would explain why Jack wanted your ranch bad enough to kill for it. You could be worth a fortune and don't know it."

"Do you believe it?"

"Yes. After what happened, I sure as hell do! I hope you have insurance to cover all loss."

"I do, but where is everyone going to live until I get everything rebuilt? The bunkhouse was destroyed along with all the other structures. Rebuilding everything is going to take some time. Will the cowboys be able to find work until I can get the ranch up and running again? What about Jack? He'll try something again, won't he? Shit! Maybe I should sell to protect both of us!"

"You're not going to do that."

"Really! What choice do I have?"

"Dobi, there's a solution to any problem. It's just going to take some thought to find the solution to this one. Let me worry about Jack. For now, we need to rebuild your ranch and get it operating again. I know how to expedite that. I figure Jack found out all your hired hands were in town. He must have known they were providing armed security at the ranch. That was slowing his plans to wage an assault on you. He couldn't afford for any of his men to be injured or killed during a raid. That would connect him to it."

"How did Jack know my men were gone? Do you think any of my cowboys told him?"

"No. I think they were all seen at The Broken Spur by one or more of his men. They reported it to him, and he took advantage of the opportunity he'd been waiting for."

"He's going to try something again, isn't he?"

"We aren't going to give him another easy opportunity to do that."

"Leave that to me. Dobi, if there is oil and gas on your land, will you consider letting it be drilled?"

"I don't know, Hound. I'd have to make a choice between preserving the tradition of the ranch or changing the land forever. What would you do?"

"That doesn't matter, Dobi. It's your ranch, your life, your decision to make."

"I suppose the first thing to do is find out if what Boots said is true."

"Yep, but not until I get a few things in place on the ranch. When Jack finds out you're looking into the oil and gas situation, then he'll be forced to give up or move against you as soon as possible."

"He really plans to kill us, doesn't he?"

"I told you he did."

The cowboys had no idea of the tragedy that had happened until they returned to the ranch after 2 a.m. the next morning. The fires had all been extinguished and the firefighters were completing the final mop up of their work. The fire chief told the cowboys all he knew about what had happened. There were no human casualties, but it seemed like all the livestock had been destroyed. If anyone had been injured, they were likely at the hospital.

The cowboys hurried to the hospital and found Hound and Dobi sitting in the surgery waiting room. They all assumed Jack was behind what had been done.

"Oh Lord, Dobi! All of us should have never been away from the ranch," said Hud. "We're all so very sorry! We should have done as Hound said!"

"Nobody is to blame but me, Hud. I should have done as he said."

"Where's Boots? Was he hurt?"

"Yes, he's in bad shape. They have him in surgery now."

"Will he be all right?"

"We don't know."

"Hound, I hope you can forgive us for being so stupid and careless."

"We all make mistakes, Hud. Did you guys invite Boots to celebrate with you?"

"Yes, of course."

"Why didn't he go with you?"

"Well, he said you would've wanted him to stay on security duty, so he did."

"You know, Boots is mentally challenged, but he's pretty damn smart in some ways. He's loyal to me, Dobi, and all of you. We're his family, the only one he ever had. He's a better person than any of us in some respects."

"I'd have to agree with you on that, Hound."

"I'm glad you do."

Two hours later, the surgeon arrived in the waiting room to inform everyone that Boots had died from a massive hemorrhage during the operation. Hound didn't say anything. He stood and left the waiting room to be alone for a time. His thoughts began to focus on an overall plan to end what had begun. He knew it was time to check on Pardner, who had been allowed to stay in a janitorial supply room. When he opened the door, the dog rushed to greet him. Pardner must have sensed the sadness Hound was feeling. He seemed to join Hound in grieving the loss of Boots when he stood at his side and began a moaning howl that was loud enough to be heard over a large area of the hospital. Hound and Pardner walked from the hospital into the cold, early morning to get a breath of fresh air. It had stopped snowing. Stars could be seen as they began to emerge in the sky that was clearing.

12

When the stores in town opened later that morning, Dobi and the cowboys joined Hound in buying clothes and essential items lost in the fires. Rooms were rented as temporary living quarters for them. Hound declared that the cowboys would continue to receive their regular wages and would help in the rebuilding of the ranch as soon as it began, which he said would be soon.

By noon that day, Hound was on a pay phone making the calls necessary to put the plan he'd devised into action. The first call he made was to Maggie Mitchell in Phoenix.

"Holy shit! Hound, it's great to hear from you!" said Maggie. "Where in the hell are you? Are you OK?"

"Maggie, I'm in Montana, but I only want certain people to know that."

"OK, I'm glad to be one of those people. Why am I?"

"Maggie, I've been living on a ranch here. As much as I wanted to keep a low profile and have some peace in my life, I find myself in a bad situation."

"A ranch! No shit! You bought a ranch! So, are you a fucking cowboy now?"

"I didn't buy a ranch. I've been living in a little cabin on a ranch owned by a very nice young woman."

"Well, all right! I'm glad you're starting to live life again. Is she good in bed?"

"I wouldn't know. I'm not sleeping with her."

"If that's true, I know it's your decision, not hers, if she's known you longer than a day."

"Maggie, are you ready to hear about my situation? I need a favor from you to help save my ass."

"OK! Sorry. Tell me what's going on."

Hound explained his problem to Maggie. She listened without interrupting to ask questions or offer any comments.

"Son of a bitch! Hound, you'll never stay out of trouble until you learn to fear it. You know I'll do anything you ask. What do you need?"

"I need 20 of the meanest, toughest, most deadly members of the biker club that are reliable. Go nationwide to get them if you have to. Get them to Phoenix as soon as you can. I'll send Bobbi and Robbi in a private jet from California to pick them up and fly them here. Tell them to respect the pilots and not scare the shit out of them. Make sure they bring automatic rifles and plenty of ammunition. I also need you to contact Uncle Mike O'Malley in Baton Rouge. Get a truck, trailer and driver to transport to me at least twenty large drums of acid, the kind that dissolves bodies."

"God damn! That's a lot of acid! How many mother fuckers are you planning to kill?"

"Several, but I don't know yet how many. I just need to make sure I have enough acid."

"Do you want me to send some chainsaws and other items needed for cutting up the bodies before they're put in the acid?"

"Oh, hell yes! Why not? Good idea."

"What do you plan to do with the drums of acid after the bodies have been added?"

"I want them transported out of Montana and disposed of. Can you arrange that?"

"Well, why not, Hound! God damn! Is there anything else you need?"

"Yes. Send me enough pure heroin to kill a horse."

"Are you going to kill a horse?"

"No, but I want to make sure I have enough."

"Right! By the way, you're going to owe me!"

"What do you want?"

"Get your ass to Phoenix or New Orleans as soon as you can and buy me dinner."

"Anything else?"

"I'll let you know during dinner."

"How's Bear doing?"

"He's still in Bogota, shipping drugs to the States."

"How are things going for you now that you're the big boss in the States?"

"I can't come up with enough ways to spend the money I'm making. Naturally, I travel a lot, but as you know, most of my time is spent in Phoenix and New Orleans."

"Do you find time to practice law?"

"Fuck yes. There's constantly some mother fucker associated with the biker club with his or her ass in a legal crack. From time to time, I take on some big shot corporate crook as a client."

"How do find time for all you do?"

"Shit, Hound, I have a lot of assistants, including attorneys."

Hound's next call was to Tim and Randy Sanders, father and son that were his partners in the now nationwide construction company. They agreed to send a construction crew large enough to rebuild all the structures on the ranch that had been destroyed. This would be completed within a month, despite the weather. Hound also told them to keep his whereabouts unknown to others. They agreed.

After he was finished with his phone calls, Hound paid a visit to Cole, who was feeling better but still recuperating in the hospital.

Cole was alarmed when Hound entered his room, not knowing the purpose of the visit or what to expect.

"What the hell are you doing here, Hound?" Cole blurted out loudly. "What do you want?"

"Relax, Cole, I only want to talk."

Hound pulled a chair to the side of Cole's bed and sat in it.

"Have you heard about what happened in the wee hours this morning at The Double D Ranch, Cole?" Hound asked in his usual calm, soft voice.

"Yes, but you must know that I didn't have a part in it!"

"Cole, I never thought you did, but I think you know who did."

"I don't know any such thing."

"Cole, several men came to the ranch to kill me and Dobi and to do as much destruction as possible to decrease the value of her ranch's property. You weren't there. Neither was the son of a bitch that gave the order. I know it was Jack, but I don't know the low life cocksuckers who carried out that order. I'd bet you do and that you're going to tell me."

"I don't know anything, Hound, but if I did, you know I wouldn't tell you."

"Why not, Cole?"

"You have no idea what would happen to me if I did."

"That leads me to believe that you do know, Cole. Even if you weren't told and didn't participate, you know who came to the ranch. You're right, I don't know what Jack would do to you if you told me, but I know what I'm going to do to you if you don't."

"What?"

"Cole, you work for Jack as one of several men who do dirty deeds for him. I told you what was going to happen to Jack and all the thugs involved if anything was attempted to harm me or Dobi, directly or indirectly. You were lucky not to have been directly or indirectly involved this time. You're off the hook for now. However, if you refuse to tell me what I want to know, that will put you in the indirectly category."

"Are you threatening to kill me?"

"No, I will kill you, Cole. I promise that I won't fail to get it done. What you now have to decide is if I can pull it off or not. You have about sixty seconds to decide, because that's when I'm going to leave. I won't make you the same offer again after I do. What's your decision?"

"God damn it, Hound! I would never have done anything to hurt you or Dobi ever again! I'll regret beating her until the day I die! I would've never picked a fight with you if Jack didn't have me by my balls. Hell, Hound, I liked you and felt we were beginning a good friendship. He would've done worse to me than you did if I refused to do as he said. However, I would've suffered whatever he did to me before I'd harm Dobi! Jesus! I would never have anything to do with what happened at the ranch!"

"For what it's worth, Cole, I believe you, but you still need to tell me what I want to know, then get the hell out of Montana and stay out."

"Where would I go? This has been my home all my life. I don't have the money needed to leave Montana and start over."

Hound paused to consider his thoughts. He was able to empathize with Cole's situation. The damage done to Cole as a result of the beating Hound gave him had satisfied Dobi's need for justice for what he'd done to her. Perhaps Cole didn't deserve anything more to happen to him. Hound's plan for retribution was set, but his instinct was telling him that Cole wasn't deserving of the full measure of that retribution.

"When are you due to be released from the hospital, Cole?" asked Hound.

"My doctor says at least by Thanksgiving. Why?"

"Cole, when you're recovered, I'm going to give you enough money to leave Montana and start a new life somewhere far away from here. For doing that, I will want the names of all the men who took part in the attack on the ranch."

"What if I refuse your offer?"

"Cole, you've been behaving like a prick, but I don't feel you deserve the fate that will befall those men and Jack for sending them. You will, if you refuse my offer. You've paid enough for what you've done up to now. The beating I gave you evened the score for what you did to Dobi. She agrees."

"Hound, you can't take on Jack and win. He has everything at his disposal to beat you at anything you try. God damn it! He controls the town and maybe a large part, if not all, the county."

"I know that, but he's the one who can't win. You need to believe that, Cole."

"What are you going to do?"

"Cole, your time is up! Do you accept my offer or not?"

Cole had been confronted by many men who had attempted to run a bluff on him. He somehow knew Hound wasn't such a man.

"If Jack finds out that I took your offer, he'll kill me, sure as hell!" Cole said loudly.

"He won't find out in time to do anything to you."

Cole wrote the names of a dozen men on a piece of paper and gave it to Hound.

"Hound, all the men work as muscle for Jack," said Cole, "but I don't know if they were all sent to the ranch."

"That won't matter. None of them were in the hospital when it happened."

"Hound, Jack is planning to have me file charges against you as soon as I get out of here. I don't know why he wanted to wait."

"He wants to wait and see if it will be necessary. I'm sure he has another plan to try before any charges are filed. As soon as you're released, come find me. I'll get you paid and on a private jet that will take you anywhere you want to go. Cole, don't ever think about breaking our agreement."

"I won't, believe me!"

"OK."

Hound left the hospital and returned to the motel where he,

Dobi and the hired hands would be staying until all the housing on the ranch had been rebuilt.

Within three days a private jet landed at a private airport near a neighboring town. Hound was there to greet the pilots and passengers. He had rented enough four-wheel drive vehicles to transport the pilots and twelve members of the biker club. Robbi and Bobbi were the first to get off the plane and greet Hound.

"Hello, sweet baby!" said Robbi.

"Sweet Jesus, it's good to see you again!" added Bobbi.

"It's good to see you both as well. How was the flight here?"

"Smooth as a baby's butt until we got over Wyoming. Then it got bumpy," replied Robbi.

"How did your passengers behave?"

"Quiet as church mice all the way. Golly, it's cold here. I'm glad you told us exactly what kind of clothing to bring. It was 80 degrees when we left Phoenix. It's close to zero here. What are you doing in a place this cold?"

"I've been asking myself the same question."

In a short time, the twelve passengers, carrying all the gear they were told to bring, stood in a group around Hound and the pilots. Hound took a moment to look at each one of them before speaking. If their overall appearance defined the type men they were, then Maggie had sent the type of crew he'd requested. One man seemed to stand a bit forward of the others. All of the men presented a first impression of having an evil nature, but this individual could be cast in a horror movie as Satan himself.

"You must be Hound," said the large bearded man.

"That's right. Who might you be?"

"I might be the fucking Pope, but I'm not. My name is Sam."

"Nice to meet you, Sam. I assume you're the leader of these men."

"Why would you say that?"

"You just look like it. The toughest and smartest always leads the pack."

"All of us are tough and smart. That's why Maggie sent us, but yes, I'm the leader. Maggie has told me a lot about you, Hound. She said you weren't a man to fuck with."

"Well, Sam, I guess that means there are two of us standing here that are men not to fuck with."

"Nope, there are thirteen such men standing here."

"OK, Sam, I have no reason to think otherwise."

Robbi and Bobbi rode with Hound in his truck back to the motel where rooms had been secured for everyone. Sam and his crew followed in the three vehicles provided for them.

"I don't suppose you're going to tell us what's going on, Hound?" said Bobbi."

"Girl, you know better than to ask that," remarked Robbi. "Hound will tell us what we need to know. Shit! I don't want to know any more than what is necessary."

"You ladies will be in town until it's time for you to fly your passengers and maybe one more out of here. Until then, just hang around and enjoy your stay as much as possible."

"What kind of nightlife goes on in town?" asked Robbi.

"The Broken Spur is the main club where everybody goes."

"Do any black folks go there?"

"Sure. You'd be surprised at the number of black cowboys that live and work around here."

"We don't know any black cowboys in L.A."

"No, I wouldn't think so."

"Hound, the men we brought here are far from being choirboys. Are you sure they can be trusted with whatever you need them for?"

"I'm sure. By the way, I want to expand our business in California. We have a successful charter service, flight school and aircraft service department. Now, how do you ladies feel about selling a full range of top of the line aircraft?"

Robbi and Bobbi were excited to hear Hound's plan. They knew anything he took on as a new business would be successful.

"Hound, when are you going to step back into society again?"

asked Bobbi. "It's just not the same with you absent. We need to see you more often."

"I don't know. When and if the time is right, I suppose. Anyway, our business and all my others are doing fine with me just checking in from time to time. I have terrific people, just like you and Robbi, taking care of business in my absence."

After the new arrivals were settled in their rooms, Hound gathered them, Dobi and the cowboys together in a private conference room. He completed the necessary introductions. Dobi and the cowboys were surprised at the appearance of the bikers, that Hound would know their caliber of persons and what their purpose was for being there. They were surprised to learn Hound was the major stockholder in a California-based company being ran successfully by two black women.

"Well, folks, it's time to let everyone know what's going to happen next around here," began Hound. "The men I brought here will be responsible to provide security on site and off for all of us and our property during the rebuilding of all that was destroyed at the ranch. Sam will be the man on the ground in charge of that under my direction. I've offered to form a partnership in the ranch with Dobi. She's accepted my offer to buy fifty-one percent controlling interest in the ranch. I have enough men and equipment from a construction company I control coming here to have all rebuilding complete by early December, regardless the weather. When that is complete, Sam, his men, Robbi and Bobbi will go home. All the ranch hands will remain employed as construction workers and/or security personnel until that time comes. I don't think those who attacked the ranch are satisfied with the total outcome of their actions. We have to be ready for anything they might try to finish that they started. We'll stay here at the motel until we can move back into quarters at the ranch. Boots will be buried on the ranch tomorrow at 10 a.m. I'll expect everyone here to attend. Hud, after the service I want you and the cowboys to give Sam and his men a complete tour of the ranch. He'll be in charge of the cowboys pulling security duty. Are there any questions?"

There were none. The group went out for supper together that evening. After supper, Hound had a private meeting in his room with Sam and his crew of eleven men.

"Hound, Maggie told us that you'd pay each of us one hundred thousand dollars plus expenses to come help you complete some business," said Sam.

"Yes. Is that satisfactory?"

"Hell yes."

"Did you bring the heroin?"

"Yes, enough pure, uncut shit to kill two horses. Maggie wanted to make sure you had enough."

"Good!"

"Besides what we already know, what else do you want us to do?"

Hound disclosed the plan he'd devised.

The sun was shining the next day and the temperature had risen a fair amount. The weather was more agreeable for Boot's funeral. The ground on the ranch was frozen, making the digging of a grave difficult. However, it was done. The pastor of a local church who knew Boots preached at the graveside service. Hound's thoughts were on how and why Boots had died. Pardner sat still and quiet at Hound's side throughout the entire service.

The next afternoon, a caravan of construction workers and equipment arrived to begin replacing all the structures that had been destroyed on the ranch. The following morning, a single semi and trailer arrived. The trailer carried the twenty large drums of acid Hound had requested. The two men delivering the cargo were from the New Orleans chapter of the biker club and would be under Sam's command until it was time for them to leave.

The semi and trailer would be kept a secret from everyone except Sam and his crew. It was driven to and hidden in an abandoned warehouse just beyond the town's city limits. Hound had learned of the warehouse from Boots, who had used it for shelter in the past.

Cole was discharged from the hospital a week before Thanksgiving. Jack had visited him on a regular basis after he was admitted but never found out about Hound's visit. Cole was waiting in a wheelchair at the main entrance when Jack arrived to personally drive him home. Jack had kept Cole informed about the large amount of activity going on at The Double D ranch. They discussed it as they drove.

"Damn it!" said Jack. "Everything that was destroyed on that fucking property will be restored by Thanksgiving or a short time after. Armed security is everywhere 24/7 there!"

"What are you going to do now, Jack?"

"Wait until things calm down and then try again. I've decided it's time you filed charges against Hound. We've got to get him in jail and out of the way. That son of a bitch has got more juice than any of us thought. He's the only thing standing in my way to get that damn land. Unfortunately for him, his juice won't be worth much once we get him in jail and the judge won't allow him bail."

"Don't you figure he'll get the best out of town lawyer money can buy and get his case reviewed by a judge you don't control?"

"He won't be alive long enough, once we get him in the town jail!"

When Cole arrived home, he was welcomed by his twelve counterparts that were Jack's special team of thugs. He visited with them a short time and then went to his living quarters. He wasn't expected to return to his regular work duties for at least another week. When he was in his quarters, his first task was to call Hound.

13

At 10 a.m. the next morning, Hound met with Cole at a safe
location not far from town. Cole knew from their visit in the
hospital that Hound would give him instructions required
to be carried out as a condition of their agreement.

"Hound, I'm fucked if Jack finds out about our meeting!" Cole
stated loudly. "He has eyes everywhere. It won't be long until he
sees us together, if we continue to meet."

"We'll meet only one more time, and Jack will be joining us."

"Joining us! What the fuck are you talking about, Hound?"

"We're going to a pay phone. You're going to call Jack and tell
him to meet you at the old warehouse just outside of town at 1 p.m.
today."

"What do I say is the reason for asking him to meet me?"

"Tell him Hud ran into you in town and said he'd been fired for
allowing all the cowboys to be off the ranch during the time of the
raid. Tell Jack that Hud wants a job and additional compensation
to provide him with valuable information about what Hound and
Dobi are planning to do about the oil and natural gas on the ranch

and to pay him back for all he's done to acquire ownership of The Double D. "

"Oil and natural gas! So, that's the real reason Jack is willing to do anything to get the land! Is it really true, is there oil and gas on the ranch?"

"I've confirmed that there is and lots of it."

"What are you going to do when Jack shows up, if he does? He might assume it's a set up."

"My instinct tells me he'll show up, that is if he trusts you. I believe he feels the hold he has on you is solid. He sure as hell wouldn't think you and I are allies after what you did to Dobi and our personal history. However, I don't know if he'll trust Hud's motive."

"Well, then if he doesn't trust Hud, why do you think he'll show up?"

"He won't risk not getting the information if Hud is genuine."

"If you're right, then Jack will bring plenty of backup. He'll likely bring all his hired thugs."

"Do you think he'll bring all the bastards he sent to trash the ranch and kill me and Dobi, if possible?"

"I'd bet he would bring most, if not all of them."

"So would I."

"Damn, Hound! That's what you're counting on, isn't it?"

"Yep."

"Son of a bitch! Hound, what are you planning to do?"

"What I told you to tell Jack I'd do if he directly or indirectly came at Dobi or me."

"Is it really your plan to kill him and all his men?"

"Absolutely. Be glad that you aren't going to be one of them. Be grateful that the beating I gave you kept you from taking part in the raid on The Double D, the attempted murder of Dobi and me, and Boot's torture and murder. You're a very lucky man, Cole."

"Hound, why are you so sure you can trust me?"

"Because you won't be away from my presence until I complete my plan."

"What happens to me after you do?"

"I give you one hundred thousand dollars cash and put you on a private jet that will take you anywhere in the U.S. you want to go — just never come back to Montana."

"I'm afraid you won't be comfortable knowing that I know what happened to Jack and his men. I would always be a threat, a loose end that could tell what you did."

"I don't think you'd ever tell anyone that you were an accessory to the massacre of Jack and his men. Does that ease your fear?"

"I didn't consider that. Well, yes, I guess it does."

"Cole, I only kill to protect my life or the lives of innocent people. You no longer deserve to die. All you need to worry about now is where you want to make your new home."

"Hound, can I ask you a personal question and not offend you?"

"Why not. What do you want to know?"

"You have a lot of experience killing, don't you?"

"Yes, Cole, I suppose I do."

"When did you begin? When did you kill your first man?"

"It was in the time of my life before I knew better. I was only twelve when I first killed. He was just sixteen, hardly a man."

"I guess he deserved it."

"No, actually he didn't, but I thought he did at the time."

"How many men have you killed since?"

"A lot."

"Did you ever kill a woman?"

The look that appeared on Hound's face caused Cole to regret asking the question.

"Only one," answered Hound.

"I guess she tried to kill you first."

"No, she was responsible for the death of my wife and children."

Hound drove Cole to a pay phone. Jack agreed to meet with Hud at the warehouse.

It was exactly 1 p.m. when Jack drove into the parking lot of the warehouse. Four trucks transporting the twelve men that were expected to accompany him followed close behind. Jack and the men, all armed, got out of their vehicles and walked past the only other two vehicles at the site. Jack recognized one to be Cole's and accepted the other to be Hud's. The twelve men entered the warehouse first. Jack walked in cautiously after the last man was inside. Cole was standing near the door of an office.

"Where's Hud?" shouted Jack as he and his men stopped walking.

"He's in the office waiting for you."

"Tell him to get his ass out here and tell me what I came to hear!"

At that moment, twelve automatic rifles opened fire from the shadows at strategic positions. Within two blinks of an eye all the men except Jack were lying dead or dying on the concrete floor. Blood was everywhere. Jack ran to the entrance and to the outside where he was tackled hard from the side by Hound. The pistol he was carrying flew out of his hand as he hit the ground.

Hound forced Jack back inside where he was bound in a chair and gagged. The trailer housing the drums of acid had been concealed behind a large wall in the center of the warehouse. The doors of the trailer were swung open and the lids carefully removed from the drums of acid. Guards were posted outside to give warning of any unexpected visitors.

The sound was almost deafening as three of the bikers started chainsaws and quickly began cutting the legs, arms and heads from the dead bodies. These were carried and placed in drums separate from those used for the torsos. Hound walked to Cole, who was still standing at the office door. He seemed to be in shock from seeing all that had happened and was continuing to happen. He started to speak when Hound reached him. Hound spoke first.

"I never leave an enemy at my back, Cole," said Hound in a cool, calm voice.

Before Cole could respond, Hound raised his right arm. In his hand he held Jack's .357 revolver. He quickly aimed it at Cole's forehead and pulled the trigger twice. Cole's body flew back hard against the door and then dropped. He was dead before his body hit the floor.

Within a half hour all the drums had been tightly resealed, and the truck driver and his co-driver pulled the tractor-trailer from the warehouse onto the main road. They drove away from town and eventually out of Montana.

Hound went to have a chat with Jack, who had been forced to witness the butchery of his men. The gag was removed from his mouth so he could participate in the conversation.

"Well, Jack, what do you think about all of this shit?" Hound asked in his usual cool, calm manner.

"Dear God! Oh, sweet Jesus! Hound, what are you going to do to me? I'll do anything! I'll give you anything! Just please don't hurt me!"

"Come on, Jack, you know neither God nor Jesus gives a shit about you. Besides, they're not here. Anyway, I'm not going to hurt you, Jack. However, I am going to kill you, but I promise it won't hurt. You're going to stay here until later tonight. Around midnight, you're going to be injected with a hot dose of pure heroin. You'll be dead shortly after. Your car will be driven and left in the parking lot of The Broken Spur. At some point, someone will find you dead, sitting at the steering wheel. The trucks your men drove here will be driven into town and left at various locations. The body parts of your men will never be found and your pretty young wife, who has been cheating on you, will become owner of all you have. I plan to purchase all your land from her and add it to The Double D. Naturally, I'll make her an offer she won't hesitate to accept. In case you don't know it yet, I now own fifty-one percent of Dobi's ranch. I haven't decided when I'll start selling the oil and natural gas that's under the ground.

"Please, Hound! Have mercy! Surely you know you'll never get away with all this!"

Hound replaced the gag and walked away.

Around midnight, numerous gallons of gasoline were poured

onto the wooden walls and concrete floors of the warehouse. The structure exploded into a huge ball of fire that could be seen from miles around.

Jack's body was discovered in the parking lot of The Broken Spur at closing time by a couple of drunk hired hands that were in his employ.

14

The drums of acid containing the body parts were delivered to the Nevada chapter of the biker club that had its headquarters in Las Vegas. The drums were stored in a secure facility. Within a few hours after being stored, the acid had completed its task. It would be kept there in the special product proof drums for later use as needed for a variety of purposes.

Later, on the morning Jack was found, his body lay in a cooler at the town's hospital morgue. The sheriff was waiting for Casey Long to arrive and formally identify the body of her husband. When Casey entered the morgue, it was apparent to the sheriff and the coroner that she wasn't a grieving widow. She showed a calm resolve regarding the death of her husband. Jack's body was pulled from the cooler and identified by her.

"What happened to him, sheriff?" asked Casey, now trying to show some degree of sorrow.

"We don't know for sure yet. Most likely a heart attack."

"Maybe, but Jack's regular checkups never found any heart problems. I want an autopsy performed."

"That has already been scheduled, Casey, but we wanted you to see Jack before it was performed."

"I appreciate that, sheriff."

Casey left the hospital and went directly to see Ben Thompson, the attorney who had prepared Jack's will after they were married. She knew he'd left everything to her in the will, which included what he owned before their marriage and what was acquired after. Casey had demanded the will as a condition of marrying him.

"Hello, Casey," Ben said as she entered his office and sat in a chair. "I'm so sorry for your loss."

"Thanks, Ben. Jack will be missed."

"Indeed, greatly missed by everyone around here. How can I be of service during this terrible time for you?"

"Ben, I want to get everything taken care of as soon as possible regarding my assuming legal ownership of all mine and Jack's monies, properties and businesses."

Ben looked at Casey in a way that made her instantly anxious. He found it difficult finding the best way to respond.

"What's going on, Ben?" Casey asked in an uncomfortable manner. "Shit! What's wrong? I'll become sole owner of everything, won't I?"

"Well, yes you will, Casey, but that includes all debts as well."

"God damn it! Ben, what in hell are you talking about? What debts?"

"Casey, Jack has borrowed a lot of money from his bank and several others in and out of state. Everything he owns has been used as collateral and is mortgaged to the hilt."

"What did he use the money for?"

"I don't know everything, Casey, but his actions in part were to protect his property and assets in the event you and he got a divorce."

"Do you mean he secured the money so I couldn't get my share?"

"Well, yes, that's it, Casey. If you and he got divorced, then whatever you were awarded would also include the debt owed on it."

"That dirty son of a bitch! He was planning to divorce me, wasn't he?"

"Well, yes, at least that's what he said."

"He was going to pay me off in peanuts, then use the hidden money to pay off all the debts after I was out of the picture. Is that right?"

"I assume so."

"Assume my ass! You knew what he was doing and why. You likely helped him with any needed legal matters! Why the hell didn't you tell me what was going on, Ben? I was just as much your client as Jack was!"

"Casey, actually you weren't. Besides, you know what Jack was capable of if I had betrayed him in that way. He wasn't above doing to you whatever was necessary to save his empire. Don't you know that?"

"I never knew if any of the rumors about him were true, but I suspected they were. Fuck! Is there anything I can do to get anything out of being married to that piece of shit?"

"The best way is if you could find a buyer for all of Jack's holdings that had the money to get them by paying off all the mortgages. In that way, perhaps you could negotiate a reasonable sum for yourself."

"How would I get started to find such a buyer? Do you know any possible prospects? Surely some big rancher would be interested in all the land."

"Jack was the biggest landowner in the county, maybe even the state. I don't know anyone who would be willing or even able to spend the amount of money needed to by all of Jack's land and businesses, especially the bank. If you don't find a buyer for everything, you'd still be stuck with the debts on what didn't sell. I suppose the best way to start is to advertise in town, the county, around the state and out of state. If an individual can't be found, maybe a corporate group might be interested. I'm sorry, Casey. I wish you the best of luck in this."

The day after Jack's death was busy as usual at The Double D. The bunkhouse was planned to be bigger and more modern. A few additional, larger and more modern barns were nearing completion. Dobi's ranch house also would be bigger and more modern. Hound had specified his new cabin to have seven large bedrooms. The master was the largest, with a full bath in each. There would be an additional bath in the long hall for visitors, a laundry room and den. The living, dining and kitchen areas would all be a huge open floor plan, which composed half of the forty-eight-hundred-square-foot log structure. A covered porch surrounded the entire home. Self-entrance dog panels would be on all exterior doors, so Pardner could enter and exit as he pleased. The number of construction workers busy getting everything completed in the most expedient time possible resembled a colony of ants at work. Their work would be completed the second week of December, despite inclement weather.

Two days later, the autopsy on Jack had been completed and the cause of death established. It changed from a suspected heart attack to one of murder. The disappearance of Cole and the twelve other men employed by Jack, the three trucks found abandoned around town, Hound's confidence that Jack was behind the raid on the ranch, and the known fact that Cole was planning to bring serious legal charges against him started the sheriff, prosecutor, Ben Thompson and the judge to thinking about what likely had happened. The sheriff and a half dozen of his deputies paid Hound a visit at the ranch. They arrived at lunchtime on a Wednesday.

"Sheriff, I was just on my way to the new bunkhouse to have lunch with all the workers," said Hound. "Would you and your deputies care to join me? Are you hungry? Please join me; the cooks always prepare plenty to eat. Also, the food is splendid."

The sheriff and his deputies walked with Hound to the bunkhouse. It had been the first structure to be completed. Sam and his crew of bikers joined Hound in the walk.

"These guys look like members of some kind of gang or

something," remarked the sheriff in a low voice so only Hound could hear. "Pretty rough and shady boys."

"They're only part of the construction crew, sheriff. I thought the same thing when they first showed up, but they've proven to be damn good workers. They have a way of looking better the longer you're around them."

The sheriff and deputies sat at a table with Hound, Sam and Dobi, who decided to join everyone for lunch. Pardner sat quietly on the floor beside Hound's chair. He didn't seem to like the sheriff as evidenced by his growling. He stopped at Hound's command.

"Your dog doesn't seem to like me very much, Hound," said the sheriff.

"Pardner doesn't like anybody until he gets to know them and determines if they're worth a shit or not."

"Hound, after lunch I'd like to talk to you about some things. You might prefer to go somewhere private so I can ask you a few questions."

"Ask them now. Why would I want it to be private?"

"I wanted to extend to you the courtesy due to the nature of the questions."

"Thanks, but that won't be necessary. Go ahead and ask me now."

"I'm sure you're aware that Jack Long was found dead in his car at The Broken Spur."

"Yep, I heard."

"Jack's death is being investigated as a murder."

"Well, I didn't know that. Someone said it was a heart attack."

"How did you hear about his death?"

"Our cook heard about it while he was at the market buying groceries. He said it was being talked about all over town. If it wasn't a heart attack, then what killed Jack?"

"Somebody gave him an overdose of heroin — pure heroin."

"No shit! What if Jack was a user and accidently overdosed himself? That's always a possibility, isn't it?"

"Jack had no history of using drugs."

"How do you know? A lot of addicts are able to keep it a secret, especially the wealthy ones."

"That wasn't the case with Jack. Hound, where were you from around 9 p.m. until Jack's body was found around 2 a.m. the next morning?"

"Well, let me think. OK, sure. I was playing poker with Sam, and let's see, six others from his crew in my motel room. We had two games going. The other five guys were playing at the other table. We had both tables sent to the room by the manager."

"You played poker until 2 a.m.?"

"No, we didn't quit until around 4 a.m."

"Did you hear about the big explosion at a warehouse near town?"

"Nope. What about it?"

"Someone saturated it with gas and set fire to it. I think it was done to destroy evidence of what happened there."

"OK, what do you think happened there?"

"I'm not sure yet, but I suspect it was somehow connected with Jack's death and the disappearance of Cole Hanson and twelve other men who worked for Jack."

"That's very interesting, sheriff, but what does all this have to do with me?"

"You felt certain Jack was behind the attack on Dobi's ranch and we know you and Cole had problems. Hound, you're the only suspect at this time. It was Dobi's ranch that was destroyed, so she may be involved as well."

"Sheriff, do you really think that Dobi and I were the only people who knew Jack or Cole that have ever been mistreated by them?"

"You and she are the only ones who we believe have been hurt enough to kill Jack."

"Sheriff, I can't help what you think and I really don't give a shit. Here's what I think. You, the judge, prosecutor and Ben Thompson were Jack's puppets and are corrupt as hell. It's time you and your deputies got the hell off The Double D. I've got things to do. Don't bother me or Dobi about your suspicions again unless you have some kind of proof."

"This is Dobi's ranch, Hound She hasn't asked us to leave. She hasn't said anything; maybe she wants to."

Dobi decided to speak.

"Sheriff, Hound now owns fifty-one percent of the ranch," she said. "Also, I support everything he has said."

"Why would you sell controlling interest of the ranch, Dobi?"

"It's really none of your business, but it was only fair after all Hound has done to keep me from losing the ranch."

"What do you mean?"

Dobi realized she may have said too much. She looked at Hound for some indication of what to say next.

"Go ahead and tell him the truth, Dobi," Hound said, smiling. "I've decided to let everyone around here know more about me than I had initially intended."

"Hound, I'd like you to tell him. After all, you're the boss now."

"OK. Well, sheriff, I'm a very wealthy man, a legitimate businessman. I needed a rest from my responsibilities and hit the road to travel incognito around the country for a time and rest from my hectic life. I was passing through this community, met Dobi, and liked her and the area, so I decided to stay a while. I found out Jack was about to foreclose on The Double D and decided to loan Dobi the money to pay off all her mortgages. It was enough to provide her with enough working capital to make needed improvements at the ranch, keep her hired hands paid and working, and to buy needed livestock. I must admit it was a large loan. When the raid occurred, the ranch was destroyed and the livestock killed, I agreed to furnish the money to rebuild it to a level much better than before. Instead of loaning her more money to do that, Dobi asked if I would accept fifty-one percent ownership in the ranch as full payment for all the money I'd invested. I accepted her offer, with the condition she could buy me out at any time she could pay the full amount of the money I've invested plus eight percent interest on the principle, compounded annually. She insisted on the interest, saying it was only fair."

"What kind of businessman are you?"

"All I'll say is a damn good one. If you're going to ask me how much money I have, then don't. That's nobody's business but mine. However, I do have enough to help Jack's widow solve her problem."

"When did you find out about that?"

"I'm told she's telling everyone she wants to sell all of Jack's land and businesses. That means she has to sell for some reason. I'll be contacting her today. After I make a deal with her, I want to schedule a meeting with you, the judge, the prosecutor and Ben Thompson. I have important business to discuss with all of you."

"What kind of business?"

"I want to discuss if all of you want to keep your jobs and maybe stay out of jail."

"What in the hell are you talking about?"

"I'll explain everything at the meeting. Now, like I said, I need to get to work and you need to leave. Have a nice afternoon, sheriff."

Hound had managed to turn the purpose of the sheriff's visit away from its initial intent. The sheriff realized this as he got up from the table and left.

"That young man is one slick son of a bitch!" the sheriff told his deputies as the walked to their vehicles.

"What's next in the investigation, sheriff?" asked the chief deputy.

"Hell, I don't know!"

"Do you think that Hound character had anything to do with Jack's death and the disappearance of his men?"

"You're damn right I do. I got the idea Hound wants me to think it. However, he was right, we have no evidence, no proof and likely may never have. I'm convinced he knows that."

"Maybe we should bring him to the office and swear him some."

"Maybe we do nothing right now and just wait."

"What did he mean about that meeting to see if you and the

others he mentioned wanted to keep your jobs and maybe stay out of jail?"

"That was just bullshit, but I'm interested to hear what he has to say."

"So, the meeting will take place?"

"Sure, maybe he'll say something that will help in the investigation."

The sheriff regretted allowing the chief and other deputies to hear what Hound had inferred about corruption in the court, sheriff's and prosecutor's office. He made a joke of it and indicated it was a ploy used by Hound to change the discussion from him being a major suspect to the topic of corruption within the legal system. The sheriff said this had been temporarily effective but was ridiculous and without merit.

After the sheriff had left, Dobi asked Hound to take a walk so she could talk with him in private.

"Hound, you've done everything to help and take care of me and everyone else on the ranch," said Dobi. "I'm ashamed, but I have to ask you a question, one that is awkward and difficult."

"You need to ask if the sheriff's suspicions about me are correct?"

"I'm so sorry, but yes."

"If the answer was yes, I wouldn't tell you. If it was no, I would be offended and refuse to dignify the question. You'll just have to think and believe what you will."

Hound smiled and then excused himself. He returned to the bunkhouse where a phone had recently been installed. He placed a call to Casey Long at her home. She was happy that he was calling but surprised. She hadn't yet learned that he was the only suspect so far in the murder of her husband and the disappearance of Cole and the other twelve men.

"It's nice to hear from you, Hound," she said, cheerfully. "Why are you calling? What can I do for you?"

"I'm calling because of what I can do for you, Mrs. Long, but first allow me to offer my condolence regarding the death of your husband."

"Thank you. What is it that you could possibly do for me?"

"It's my understanding that you wish to sell all of the land and businesses owned by Jack. I'll give you a fair price for everything."

Casey became angry. She hadn't heard the news that Hound was much more than a drifter with meager and limited finances.

"Mister, I'm not in the mood for that kind of sick humor!"

"I'm certain of what you mean, but you should never judge a book by its cover. It's content may be worth reading. I know you haven't gotten the word on me yet."

"What word?"

"That I'm not the guy everyone has believed me to be since I arrived here."

"What kind of guy might that be?"

"A semi bum with no means, prospects, ambition, a pot to piss in, or a window to throw it out of. However, I assure you I'm more than able to pay a fair price for all you wish to sell. You can verify that with Dobi Dobson or the sheriff. He was enlightened just today. However, you should know before you speak to him that I'm currently the only suspect in the murder of your husband. I was told that by the sheriff over lunch today. I wanted you to hear that from me first. I assume by the way you greeted me on the phone that you're hearing it from me first."

Casey was rendered speechless by Hound's disclosures.

"Is the sheriff right, Hound? Did you have something to do with Jack's murder?" she asked.

"Of course not! Are you interested in selling to me or not?"

Casey had a strong feeling that Hound was telling the truth about his financial status, but she wasn't sure if it was large enough to buy what she had to sell. She couldn't have cared less if he'd been involved in Jack's death. Hound knew this. He also knew she'd quickly verify all he'd said. With that completed, she'd be anxious to close a deal and get paid before he was arrested, just in case he would be.

"Do you have any idea how much it would cost you to buy everything?" she asked him.

"Not really. Would you care to tell me."

"I don't yet know the exact amount, but I'm told it will be huge."

"Who does know?"

"My attorney, Ben Thompson, is getting that information together as soon as possible. He should have it by late tomorrow morning."

"Call me when you have the figures. We can discuss things more seriously then."

"OK, but I'm not sure you'll have enough money."

"Mrs. Long, I assure you that I'm more than capable of paying a fair price, but only if it's fair."

"Fine, but please call me Casey. Mrs. Long is too formal to suit either of us."

"I agree, Casey. By the way, please come up with a reasonable figure you want to personally walk away with after I help you get free of your dilemma."

"What dilemma?"

"You have to pay off all the mortgages Jack created or lose everything through foreclosures."

"How do you know that? It's private information. Ben and the creditors are the only individuals privy to that information."

"I didn't know it for sure until now. I'm sorry. I was fishing and you took the bait."

Maggie Mitchell had obtained the information for Hound through a chain of well-connected contacts. However, he didn't wish for Casey to know that.

It was late morning the next day when Hound received the call that he expected sometime that day from Casey. He accepted an invitation to meet with her and Ben Thompson in Ben's office at 1 p.m. Hound informed her that Beth Weaver would be with him at the meeting. Should an agreement be reached, she'd handle all the legalities required.

"Hound, you seem convinced we'll reach an agreement," said Casey.

"If you're reasonable, then I'm certain we will."

Everyone was seated in Ben's office a little after 1 p.m. Ben provided an accurate accounting regarding the sum of money Hound would have to pay in order to acquire what had been offered for sale. Everyone was in awe when Hound, with no hesitation, declared the sum to be acceptable.

"Casey, what figure did you arrive at as your separate personal compensation for electing to do business with me?" asked Hound.

"Does seven hundred fifty thousand dollars sound reasonable?"

"Of course. Mr. Thompson, how long before the final papers will be ready for signing?"

"Actually, I can have them ready for you to review with Beth in a couple of days. The signing can take place at any time after."

"Sounds good."

When the purpose of the meeting had been served, everyone prepared to leave. Ben asked Hound if he'd please stay for a private conversation. He agreed.

"Is it OK if I call you Hound?" asked Ben.

It was clear Ben was a tad nervous. He had been since Hound first arrived.

"I prefer to be called by my nickname," answered Hound. "You've been using it during the meeting, so why would you ask if it's OK now? Anyway, what do you want to talk about?"

"The sheriff said you wanted to meet with him, me, the prosecutor and the judge. Is that right?"

"Yep, in the near future."

"What for?"

"I'll let all of you know when we meet."

"Do you have a date and time in mind?"

"Why don't you touch base with everyone invited and decide that? I'm free anytime during the next couple of days. Can you arrange things in that time frame?"

"Maybe, but everyone will want to know what the meeting is about."

"Ask the sheriff; he can tell you the basics. By the way, did the sheriff tell you that I was suspect in Jack's death and the disappearance of Cole Hanson along with twelve of his other hired hands?"

"Well, as a matter of fact, he did."

"Did he tell you and the others I want to meet with at the same time?"

Ben wasn't sure if he should answer truthfully but did.

"Yes, we all were told," replied Ben.

Hound turned and left without saying anything else. When he arrived at his truck in the parking lot, Casey was waiting for him. It was cold outside, so she was sitting in her car with the motor running and the heater turned up. She rolled the driver's side window down far enough to shout and get his attention. He walked to the open window.

"What do you want, Casey?" he asked in a friendly manner.

"Can I talk to you for a couple of minutes?"

"Of course."

"Get in the car with me where it's warm."

He walked to the passenger side of the car and got in.

"What's on your mind, Casey?" he asked.

"I was wondering if you'd like to come to my home for dinner tonight. I'm a fair cook."

"Don't you think it's a bit soon after your husband's death to invite a man to your home for dinner, especially one who is suspected of killing him?"

"Well, maybe. I just want to get to know you better. I also thought it would be a way for me to start showing my gratitude for what you did to help me."

"You don't owe me anything. Besides, seven hundred fifty thousand dollars isn't even peanuts compared to what you would have gotten if Jack hadn't arranged things so you wouldn't get anything.

I assume you're going to try and find where Jack secured the money and try to get it."

"You're damn right! Ben is working on that now."

"Well, I wish you luck with that. How much is Ben charging as a fee to try and find the money and then return it to you if he does?"

"Thirty-five percent of all money found and returned. He assured me the odds of finding all the accounts were very good."

"I'm sure they are. What are your plans now? What's next for you?"

"I guess just hang around until I get my money. How long do I have to vacate my home? You'll soon own it along with everything else."

"You can live in the home as long as you need to, but I'll require something in return."

"What?"

"Are all the current hired hands good people?"

"They've always kept everything running smoothly."

"Do they consider you their boss as much as Jack?"

"Sure, they like me better too. Why?"

"I'd like you to tell all of them that their jobs will be secure under my ownership. Also, I'd like you to remain as my second-in-command boss over them until you get your money back and decide what you want to do. Naturally, you'll be paid well for your work."

"Well, I'm very familiar with ranch operations, so I likely could help keep things on a proper course. OK, you've got yourself a second-in-command. By the way, I may have the reputation of an unfaithful wife, but I've never shunned my fair share of the work needed to keep operations profitable. Will you need any help with any of the other businesses? I have a handle on them as well."

"Yep, you'll be my second-in-command regarding everything."

Hound shook hands with Casey as a gesture to seal the work agreement. He got out of her car and began walking toward his truck. She again rolled down her window to shout a final question before driving away.

"By the way, Hound, how long has it been since you had any extraordinary sex?" she shouted and then smiled.

"Not since an extraordinary woman rocked my world."

"How long ago was that?"

"Not long enough for me to have forgotten."

Casey realized he was talking about a very special woman.

"May I ask her name?" Casey shouted in an apologetic way.

"Rita. Her name was Rita."

Two days later the required paperwork to finalize the sale of all property owned by Jack was reviewed and signed by both parties. Hound was now the owner of the land, bank and several of the businesses in town, including The Broken Spur.

After his business with Casey had been transacted, Hound went to the courthouse for the meeting he'd requested with Ben, the sheriff, the prosecutor and the judge. The meeting was held in the judge's chamber. Hound positioned himself in a chair to the right of all the others.

"Ben, thanks for arranging this meeting," Hound said in a friendly way. "I'd like to thank all of you gentlemen for agreeing to meet with me."

"All right, all right. Let's cut through the bullshit and get to the reason for this meeting," barked the judge. "We've all got work to do, especially me. Besides, I don't much like meeting with a man who may soon be tried in my court for the murder of one of our most prominent citizens."

Hound's eyes widened as his anger became apparent in his total expression.

"OK, you pompous, arrogant son of a bitch, I'll make the meeting short and to the point," Hound began. "I will never be tried in your court, or any other. I don't give a good God damn that Jack Long was murdered, but there will never be any proof that I had anything to do with it. When this meeting is over, I'll expect to no longer be considered a suspect or hear it rumored ever again by any of you corrupt cocksuckers. There's a new stud duck in these parts and I'm him. Jack put all of you in office, but I can change that faster than a mouse can fart. If all of you turds want to keep your jobs, reputations and not risk going to jail, you best know now to never fuck with me. I'll leave it to your judgement to decide if I'm bluffing or the most powerful man you shit kickers will ever meet. If you want to test me, then you'll soon regret it. I won't tell you what I know about your business dealings with Jack. It's enough just to say I know all of them, that they were illegal and I have all the proof I need to bury all of you under the prison. You all work for me now, or you'll all suffer serious consequences. Now, each of you fuckers, one at a time, give me your decision."

All of the three men were shocked and surprised at what Hound had said, the judge most of all. It took each of them only a moment to decide what they had been told was the truth. When they all agreed to Hound's terms, he knew his plan had succeeded.

"I'm happy with your decision, gentlemen. I'll look forward to a lasting and trusting friendship with each of you. Ben, you've known all along where Jack hid his money. Get it returned to his widow as soon as possible. You'll pay me twenty-five percent of the thirty-five percent of the money the widow has agreed to pay you. She'll never know you paid it to me. Are we in agreement?"

"We are."

"Good. Do any of you gentlemen want to ask any questions or say anything?"

They all remained silent.

"Very well, but I have one final thing to say. If by chance any or all of you are willing to make an attempt on my life, I want you to know Jack was willing to make such an attempt. Remember that."

Hound left the courthouse and returned to The Double D. The construction of Dodi's new home had been completed. She'd insisted that Robbi and Bobbi live there with her for the duration of their stay in Montana. Hound met with them and said they were free to fly back to California the next day. He told them to service a new jet, that he was ready to buy one. His charade as a common drifter had been revealed. It would no longer serve any purpose. He drove to the bunkhouse to meet with Sam.

"Sam, the pilots will be leaving tomorrow," said Hound. "You and your crew are free to go with them if it suits all of you. However, you and as many of your crew that wants to stay and work for me an indefinite time longer are invited to do so. The pay is one hundred twenty-five thousand dollars a year for you as their leader and one hundred thousand dollars for each of the other men who elect to take my offer. You and the crew can live rent free in the separate bunkhouse I had built or provide housing for yourselves off the ranch. If you live on the ranch, three meals a day will be provided, but you'll have to obey the rules. Also, the cowboys must think you make the same wages as they do. When any of you aren't handling a job for me, you'll be doing ranch work under the supervision of Hud."

"Fuck! Hound, me and the boys don't know shit about being a cowboy. Hell, as far as I know none of us have ever rode a horse before. We're bikers; Harleys are what we ride."

"You all could learn to be cowboys. I think you'd all make damn good ones."

"Maybe, but we'd have to get Maggie's OK, or we couldn't do it."

"I've already asked Maggie. She said it was up to you and each of your men to decide what you wanted to do. How much per year do you make back home?"

"Honestly, more than what you're offering."

"Your bonuses working for me will earn you a paycheck substantially more than you earn back home."

"We all have women waiting back home. Can we bring them here?"

"Sure, but you'd have to live with them off the ranch."

"That's fine. Hell, we wouldn't live on the ranch anyway. We'd be breaking rules all the time."

"OK."

"Well, shit! Let's get the boys together and see what they say. We're all close. We all have to agree to stay, or none of us will."

"Sam, would you stay if it was up to you?"

"Fuck yes. I'd like to be a cowboy, at least for a while."

"Good, then convince all the guys to stay. I'd bet where you go, they'll follow."

"Probably so. We have to have our Harleys to ride from time to time if we decide to stay."

"I'll have them shipped here by truck as soon as winter is over. I don't think you'll be wanting to ride them until then."

"You're sure as hell right about that."

Sam called all the men in his crew together, presented Hound's offer, offered his opinion and then called for a vote. The men voted unanimously to stay.

Hound was in his new log home later that evening. Pardner sounded a loud bark, signaling that company was about to arrive. When Hound answered the knock on his front door, he found the company to be Dobi.

"May I come in?" Dobi asked with a warm smile.

"Of course, come in out of the cold."

Hound took her coat and invited her to sit in the living room close to the warm fire crackling in the large fireplace.

"I'm glad to see you, Dobi," he said. "What's up?"

"Hound, I just want to talk to you about some things that I've wanted to discuss for some time."

"OK, what's your mind?"

"I hope I can be candid and not offend you, Hound. Can I?"

"Dobi, you're one of the few people I know who can be as candid as they want with me."

"Thank you."

Hound suspected that he knew what Dobi wanted to talk about.

"Can I get you something to eat, or drink, Dobi?" Hound asked.

"Maybe something to drink."

"I have coffee, juices, sodas, tea, wine, and I think a couple of beers left in the fridge."

"Anything stronger?"

"I keep scotch and bourbon on hand."

"I'll have three fingers of bourbon, straight, no ice."

"I didn't know you drank hard liquor, Dobi."

"I do, but only when I need extra courage to talk about something."

Hound poured and handed Dobi the bourbon. He poured a cup of coffee for himself.

"Aren't you going to have a whiskey with me, Hound?" she asked.

"No. I very seldom drink whiskey. Besides, I don't need any extra courage. What's on your mind, Dobi?"

She looked intently at him for an instant, took a long sip from her glass and then a deep breath.

"Hound, did you have anything to do with Jack's death and the disappearance of Cole and those other twelve men?" she asked.

"I can see why you needed extra courage, Dobi. If the answer to your question happened to be yes, I would never give that answer to you, or anyone else. However, if the answer was no, then I wouldn't say that either. I guess you'll just have to make up your mind as to what you think about me without my saying yes or no."

"All of the ranch hands and people in town want to hear what you have to say. The word has spread like wildfire that you're the only suspect."

"Well, they'll all have to decide for themselves, just like you."

"Hound, surely you can understand how much you've surprised me, the hands and everyone else. When you first came to town, you were thought to be just a common drifter. You were thought to be a young man with limited finances and no plans for the future other than to loaf until your money ran out. We all knew you weren't what you seemed when you loaned me the money to save the ranch the first time. Now, you've rebuilt The Double D and own fifty-one percent of it. In addition, you're the only suspect in Jack's murder and the disappearance of his men. The fact that you now own everything that Jack owned before his death is beyond mind-boggling."

"I can see how it would be."

"Hound, you need to be more transparent with people. They need to know who you are — really are."

"Dobi, I don't owe an explanation to anyone regarding anything about me. They'll choose to accept me or not regardless."

"How about me, Hound? Don't you feel I deserve to know more about you, or am I just another face in the crowd?"

"Why is it so important for you to know more than you do? Surely you know by now that I'm on your side, a man you can trust."

"It's important because I love you, Hound. I have for some time. I know your feelings for me aren't love, but I want to do all I can to change that. I'm going to try hard to win your heart, no matter what you do to discourage me. I don't think there's anything you could do, or have done in the past, that could change my mind about you, as long as I know the past would never be repeated. Won't you please drop the barrier you've built around yourself and let me in, if only long enough to give me a reasonable chance to make you happy?"

Dobi's words somehow touched something deep inside Hound. He looked at her with a warm smile and a feeling of affection that he'd never felt for her before then.

"All right, Dobi, I'll confide in you," Hound told her," but only if I can trust you to keep it between us."

"I swear on my life to do that."

"I was born in Louisiana, at a home for unwed mothers, the bastard son of a sixteen-year-old preacher's daughter from Arkansas. I was conceived as the result of rape and the identity of my father was never discovered. I've never met my real mother. Shortly after my birth, I was adopted by a young Christian couple who owned a farm north of Baton Rouge. I was raised on that farm by my adopted parents, John and Linda Smith. My true legal name is John William Smith Jr. When I was four, my parents nick-named me Hound. This was because of the special friendship I formed with a stray Bloodhound I convinced mom and dad to let me keep. The dog's name was Hunter. He's the reason I wanted to adopt Pardner.

"I have a high IQ and a photographic memory. I earned a graduate degree in business from LSU by the age of eighteen. Joanne O'Malley was my high school math teacher. We were married after I returned home from Vietnam. Jo and I divorced before having any children. I was driven to be successful and own a diversity of businesses. I'm now worth over several billion dollars, not including the value of all the ranch and farming land, real estate, land development and national construction company I own. In addition, I currently own 10 of the largest and most elegant nightclubs in the world. They're located in different areas of the country.

"I also own controlling interest in a flight school and worldwide air charter company. I just recently decided to add an aircraft sales and service division to that company. We'll be selling a variety of top of the line private aircraft including jets, prop aircraft and helicopters. As you know, I've added fifty-one percent of your three-thousand acre ranch along with fifteen thousand acres, a bank and several other businesses formally owned by Jack to my list of companies and properties. I was among the first to invest in ideas others have had about building new companies and corporations. My instinct told me they were all sound investment choices, so I bought as much initial stock as was possible in all of them.

"With all that said, I still haven't told you what you most need to know. I married a second time. Her name was Rita. She was my first true love. We had twin boys together. Last December, Rita and my boys were killed in a tragic accident. When I first arrived here, I had been traveling around the country looking for a place where I could begin to recover from the loss of my family. To do that, for a time I needed to separate myself from the man I was, and the life I was living."

Dobi didn't know what to say when Hound concluded telling his story. She drank more of the bourbon from her glass and sat silently, considering all he'd said.

"My goodness, you're certainly not the man I thought you were when we first met, Hound," she said.

"Dobi, I'm the same man. You just know more about me."

"I know you could never be happy with a simple woman like me, even if you were able to someday get over the loss of your family. It seems that will take a long time. Maybe you never will."

"Time will heal my wounds, Dobi, but there will always be scars on my heart."

"I understand, Hound. Thanks for being honest with me about everything, especially your family. I'm so sorry for your loss. Is there anything else you want to tell me?"

"No."

"OK, but I'm sure there's more."

"Nothing you need or would want to know, Dobi."

"I believe that. What's the next step in your plan here?"

Hound thought for a moment and then laughed.

"Hud and the hands need to start teaching Sam and his crew how to be cowboys," Hound said before again laughing.

"Sam and his buddies are rough characters, aren't they?"

"I suppose so."

"Why did you bring them here, Hound? Why did you have Robbi and Bobbi fly them here early?"

"For security, Dobi. You know that."

"Is security part of the reason you're keeping them around? I can't believe they're staying just to become cowboys."

"Dobi, don't concern yourself with them. They'll stay as long as they earn what they're paid."

"All right, Hound. What do you plan to do with all your new properties and businesses here?"

"Make them as profitable as possible."

Dobi gave Hound a soft kiss on the cheek. She put her arms around him and held him close for a time. Then she told him good night and left.

15

Thanksgiving had passed with very little time spent celebrating. A dinner was served in the new bunkhouse to all
the construction workers and ranch hands. A few went to
the Broken Spur after dinner, but everyone was in their beds by
midnight. Work resumed on the ranch at the usual time the next
morning. All the construction on the ranch had been completed by
the third week of December. The weather had delayed the targeted
completion date.

When Christmas arrived, Hound made sure that all the
construction workers' families and those of Sam and his men had
joined them. He held a dinner and party Christmas evening at The
Broken Spur for all of them. Generous cash bonuses were handed
out as Christmas presents.

On the day after Christmas, Hound began getting to better know
the employees of all his new businesses. He was particularly interested in the bank and The Broken Spur. He would soon learn that
the mortgages the bank held on a majority of the businesses in town
had high payments and interest assigned to them. He quickly set a

goal to lessen the burden on those struggling with them. He made it easier for the smaller businesses and ranchers to acquire a loan at a more reasonable rate.

The town would begin to see civic improvements occur quicker as a result of his support. He personally funded the building of a homeless shelter. Naturally, a shelter to house all types of animals was also built. He utilized his construction company to build them. Dobi donated her time and that of her growing staff to provide the medical services.

This instantly began to grow Hound's popularity in the town and dispel the rumors that had been circulating about his character since the death of Jack Long. The sheriff and prosecutor aided in this by spreading the word that he'd been completely cleared of any suspicion regarding the death of Jack and the disappearance of Cole and the other men.

Hound decided to enlarge and improve The Broken Spur. The dancehall was doubled in size and the dining area by half. This was the last work his construction company completed before leaving in the spring of 1981.

On New Year's Eve, Hound invited his ranch hands and employees from the bank to a party at The Broken Spur. Dobi included those she employed at her vet practice. Sam and his crew had gotten their hair and beards cut and shaped, giving them a more conservative, cowboy appearance. They looked like an entirely different group of men in their jeans, boots and western hats. Also, Hound had made it clear that they should present a more appropriate style of language and social behavior to the public. Sam would see that this was done on a consistent basis. However, Hound knew that the heart of a very dangerous, antisocial man continued to beat in each of them and likely always would.

Casey was doing a good job overseeing Hound's interests on his fifteen thousand acres of new ranch property. Hound made sure he showed up on a regular basis to interact with the ranch hands. They had come to like and respect him. They were all pleased with the profit-sharing plan, which helped to increase their earnings. Hud became foreman over all ranch operations and was allowed to select a second and third in command.

Hound was determined to help Beth grow her law practice. Ben wasn't happy about this but offered no objection. By March of 1981, Beth had already moved to a bigger office and hired personnel to assist her with her growing clientele. She invited Hound to have lunch with her. She was seated in her wheelchair at a table in the restaurant when Hound arrived a little before 1 p.m. on a Wednesday.

"Hi there, Beth," Hound said, smiling as he sat down. "It's not every day that I get invited to lunch by a pretty lawyer. Did you invite me here to discuss business?"

"No. Actually my reason is personal, Hound."

"Do you have some kind of a problem, Beth?"

"No, I invited you here as a way to start showing my appreciation for everything you've done to help me. I'm not the only one; you've helped the town and its individual citizens in so many ways."

"I appreciate the thought, Beth, but you don't owe me anything. I enjoy helping decent, deserving people."

"I know that, Hound, but you at least deserve a word of thanks from everyone you've been so kind and generous to."

"OK, Beth, you're welcome. How are things with you?"

"I couldn't be more pleased with the way my practice is growing. I always wanted to be an attorney, but I was beginning to think I'd never be successful, at least here."

"Why would you think that? It takes time to be successful at any career."

"Seems like it didn't take you very long. You're only a year older than me and already a very wealthy man."

Hound grinned and then offered a short chuckle.

"Beth, I suppose I was luckier than most," said Hound," but I wasn't a new law graduate trying to build a law practice in cowboy country Montana either."

"If you had been, I don't doubt your practice would be huge by now. I'm certain you'd be very successful at anything you do. Hound, why did you want to keep who you really are a secret from everyone when you came here?"

"I wanted to be accepted for just me, not how much money I had. Money gives a rich man a better chance at acceptance than a poor man."

"Money does have that effect on people. However, you kept to yourself most of the time. In addition to me, only a very few ever got to meet you. Why were you so private and seclusive?"

"I guess I needed some time to rest and relax. I came here to get away from the constant interaction with people my work demanded."

"Why did you decide to reveal your secret? You must have known by giving the large loan to Dobi it was eventually going to get out. There was no hiding it for certain when you started doing all the other things that cost so much money."

"I felt it was necessary. Helping Dobi and then many others was simply the right thing to do."

"Why did you feel helping me was the right thing to do? Was it because of my handicap? Did you feel sorry for me?"

"Beth, I've always admired you, but never have I felt sorry for you."

"Is this the first time you've ever had a lunch, or any kind of date, with a woman in a wheelchair?"

Hound sensed Beth was approaching another topic of conversation.

"Oh, is this a date?" he asked, smiling again.

Beth realized she had embarrassed herself.

"I'm sorry, Hound," she said as her face turned red. "I didn't mean to imply we were having a lunch date."

"Well, I feel like it's kind of a date."

"You avoided my question, Hound. Have you ever been on any kind of date with a woman in a wheelchair?"

"Honestly, no, Beth, I never have. Why?"

"May I be honest and you be the same with me?"

"Of course."

"Hound, you must know that you're a very attractive man. I'm sure all the women in town think that. I'm in this chair, but I'm still a woman. I see the same things as women who aren't and have the same needs and desires. Would you ever consider going on a real date with me, maybe one for dinner? That is if you aren't seriously involved with someone."

"Beth, I'm not seeing anyone. I haven't wanted to date for some time. The reason is personal and I won't discuss it. However, if things were different, I would enjoy a date with you."

"Dobi told me that you weren't interested in dating her. She said you gave the same reason as you gave me."

"Why did Dobi tell you?"

"Well, most people around here think you and Dobi are an item, but I had some doubt, so I asked her, just in case I was wrong. I really like her and would never have talked to you about dating if she was seeing you. Besides, if she was, I wouldn't have a chance anyway."

"Beth, part of the reason for my avoiding women is because I don't want to hurt anyone. If I should sleep with someone now, then it would only be to satisfy my physical needs. I have nothing else to offer at this time."

"Sometimes all a woman might want is to satisfy her physical needs. I'm such a woman."

Hound looked at Beth and smiled again. He knew what she was hinting at.

"You might be surprised at how I can perform in bed," she stated boldly. "I need this chair to get around, but I have full feeling in my lower body. I can't walk, but I have no handicap in bed."

"Well, that's good to know, Beth. I'll keep that in mind."

"Also, I would never kiss and tell."

"Nor would I. What exactly are you saying, Beth?"

"I want you to have sex with me. If it's only one time, then I'll be satisfied knowing I made love to the most handsome man I'll likely ever know."

"I don't know that I've ever received so nice a compliment, Beth. Now, can I be a bit forward in my language?"

"Please! I wish you would."

"I would like to fuck you in every way possible. When and where shall I do that?"

Beth's smile was evidence of her satisfaction with what he said and how he said it.

"Would you like to come for dinner tonight, Hound?" she asked.

"What time?"

"How's seven sound?"

"I'll be there."

Beth had a nice dinner waiting when Hound arrived that evening. She greeted him at the door looking very attractive in the attire she had chosen to wear. He kissed her on the cheek and then handed her a dozen roses. She asked him to put them in water and led him to the vase she wanted to use.

"You look lovely, Beth," Hound said sincerely. "I should have dressed more appropriately."

"You look just the way I want, in your jeans, western shirt and boots. Dinner is ready. Are you hungry?"

"Absolutely."

"I hope you like it."

"I don't think there's any kind of healthy food that I don't enjoy."

They sat down at the dining table and began their meal. At first their conversation focused on casual topics, mostly Beth's practice and a variety of things about the town, its businesses and the people who operated them. Beth had nothing to say negative about anyone until the sheriff, prosecutor, judge and Ben Thompson were discussed.

"I don't like or respect any of them, Hound," Beth said in a matter of fact way.

"Why not?"

"Hound, you know they're corrupt. I know you do."

"I suppose they used to be, when Jack controlled them."

"So, you knew that too."

"Didn't everybody?"

"I think they did, or at least suspected it."

"Well, with Jack gone maybe they'll change."

"Hound, a leopard can't change its spots. They're associated with several powerful men in the county and around the state. Jack was just a tie that bound them together. They'll find a new tie and the legal system here will return to business as usual."

"Explain what you mean about the legal system returning to business as usual."

"Justice won't be the same for everyone. Some will be above the law, just like Jack was."

Hound knew what she was saying was true. He had known for some time. However, he wanted to listen more than talk about it.

"Why don't you campaign for the judgeship, Beth?" Hound asked. "It would be a major step in correcting the problem if you were elected."

"I wouldn't stand a chance of being elected."

"Why not?"

"The big money in the state is in the hands of a select few men. The power of their money controls who's elected to the offices they want to control."

"I understand."

After dinner, Hound helped Beth with the dishes. Then they sat next to each other on the sofa in her living room and had a glass of wine.

"Where's your bedroom, Beth?" Hound asked when they finished their wine.

Beth pointed to the hallway leading to the bedroom.

"Hound, we don't have to go there if you're having second thoughts."

"Why would I be having second thoughts?"

"I just thought you might."

"Tell me what you're thinking, Beth. Be honest."

"I don't want you sleeping with me if you really don't want to. I don't want your pity."

"Beth, I never do anything unless I want to, but there's more on your mind. What else is bothering you?"

"Well, I know that it would be wonderful to experience you in bed, but the truth is that I have a strong affection for you. I know your feelings aren't the same. It's not likely they ever will be. We would probably never be intimate again. Am I right?"

"I would have to say it's a high probability that you are."

"I guess I'd rather know I could have slept with you and didn't, imagining what it would have been like, than to experience you and never have that pleasure again. I'm very fond of and attracted to you now. I can't afford falling in love with you. That's what I fear would happen. Do you understand, Hound?"

He smiled at her.

"Yes, I understand completely, Beth," he replied.

"I'll always consider you a very special man."

"I'll always be a true friend to you, Beth."

"So, you'll never forget me?"

"How could I ever forget the first beautiful woman to refuse my invitation for sex!"

"I believe that's true. Is it?"

"It is!"

Beth began to laugh. Hound joined her. They had another glass of wine and then he thanked her for the evening and started to leave.

"I know as soon as you leave, I'll regret my decision, Hound," Beth said as he walked to the door.

"No, I don't think you will, my friend."

During his drive home to the ranch, Hound's thoughts were on the evening he'd enjoyed with a remarkable woman. At the ranch, he drove past Dobi's house on the way to his. A truck unfamiliar to him was parked out front. He concluded she was entertaining a male visitor. As he passed, he saw the lights turn off in the front of her house. He smiled and knew it was due to happen sooner than later.

When he walked toward the front door of his new log home, Hound heard Pardner barking a loud welcome. He entered and was received affectionately.

"Pardner, it's good to see you, pal!" Hound said to the dog, as if Pardner could understand the words.

Pardner reared and put his front paws on Hound's chest. He offered a series of whines as though he was trying to confirm his understanding. Hound petted the dog for a time and then got comfortable in his easy chair to watch the news on TV. Pardner barked, signaling the arrival of a visitor. Hound was cautious due to the late hour. The first knock on the door was immediately followed by Dobi's voice to identify herself. Hound felt something was wrong and quickly opened the door.

"Is everything OK, Dobi?" Hound asked in a concerned way.

"No, not really. I'm just feeling lonesome. I was going to bed and saw the headlights of your truck when you drove past my house. I was hoping we might visit, if you're going to be up awhile."

"I thought you had company."

"I didn't. Why did you think so?"

"I saw a strange truck in front of your house and figured you were entertaining a guest."

"The truck is mine. It's new; I bought it today."

"Nice truck. I like the color."

"Did you think I had a male visitor?"

"I assumed so."

Hound invited Dobi to have a seat in another easy chair close to his.

"Did it bother you, even a little, to think I was with a man?"

Hound did feel strange about it, but he didn't know if he should admit it. His sudden realization of these feelings confused him.

"Are you going to answer my question, Hound?" Dobi asked.

"I don't see that your personal life is my business."

"OK, then let me tell you that I would be sorry to find out you were alone with a woman here, or anywhere. I care for you and want to be the woman you're with. Damn it! I understand how the loss of your family has hurt you, but the time has to come when you accept that life goes on. I sense that you have some feelings for me. I just wish you'd be honest and tell me why you're not willing to admit it."

"I don't want you to get hurt if we start something and it doesn't work out."

"Neither of us can guarantee the other anything, Hound, but it would be a shame not to at least give us a chance."

Hound realized what she had said made sense.

"I'm going to take a shower and then go to bed, Dobi," Hound said. "Would you care to join me for either, or both?"

Dobi looked at him.

"Both, if I can spend the night," she replied, smiling.

The shower was brief, interrupted by passion and desire they both had been holding at bay for a long time. Hound pushed Dobi gently to her back on the bed. He took a moment to view her nude body from head to toe. He had imagined many times what it would look like, but his imagination hadn't done her justice. He felt his penis become fully erect. She was hot, wet and ready for him as he entered and pushed deep inside her. She moaned with pleasure. He began with slow thrusts that gradually became faster.

"Oh my God!" she yelled as she began to orgasm.

He waited until she was finished, and then he pulled from her and began performing oral sex. He continued until she reached another orgasm and then rolled her to her side and entered her again. After her third orgasm, he lay on his back and she positioned herself atop him.

"Fuck me, Dobi!" he said loudly. "I need you to fuck me!"

She made her movements fast as she moved up and down his large cock. Each time she made an effort to place him as deep inside her as possible. When he reached a climax, she joined him as she felt the months of depriving himself begin to fill her and run down her inner thighs.

As she slowed her movement, he pulled her close to him and kissed her passionately. He rolled her to her back and continued with deep thrusts until he achieved another climax. She pulled him close and held him tenderly. As his body tensed from the pleasure he was experiencing, she explored his hard, muscular body with both her hands and legs.

When the urgency of their needs had been satisfied, they fell asleep holding each other. It was after 8 the next morning when they awoke, still in an embrace.

"Good morning, big boy," Dobi said in a soft endearing voice. "Did you sleep well?"

"Better than I have in a very long time."

"Me too."

"I'm hungry. Are you?"

"I'm so hungry I could eat a horse."

"I don't have any horse, but I can fix us some ham, eggs and hash browns."

"I think that will do. How about I whip up some biscuits and gravy?"

"Absolutely."

During breakfast they didn't say much about their night together, except that it wouldn't be their last. Each of them knew the other was well pleased with the outcome. It was Saturday. Dobi had planned to travel to the neighboring county. She was interested in taking a look at a bull and a few heifers for breeding that a rancher had for sale. She asked Hound to come along.

"I don't know much about top quality breeding stock," he told her, "but I suppose I need to learn."

"I think you might know more than you realize, Hound."

"What do you mean?"

Dobi grinned and then laughed. He got the jest of her comment.

"You sure have a way of making a fellow feel good, Dobi," said Hound, "in more ways than the things you say."

"I'm only being honest with you. I always will, in all things. Will you?"

Hound knew he could never be honest with her about all things, but she wanted an answer.

"I will always tell you the truth, if I tell you anything," he answered.

"Do you mean you won't answer if it's none of my business?"

"Maybe, sometimes. Surely you would reserve that right as well."

"I know there are things in your past that you want to keep private, so I promise to not pressure you about such things."

"I appreciate that, Dobi."

The drive to the ranch in the next county took two and a half hours. Jim Mooney owned the five-thousand-acre ranch and raised quality cattle. He greeted Hound and Dobi in a friendly manner when they arrived. He was proud of his livestock and always proud to show them off. He seldom wanted to sell any of his breeding stock. However, he had found himself with a prize bull and heifers that he didn't need. The price he was asking for them was high, but understandable based on their pedigree.

Jim escorted his guests to the area where he had the stock waiting for inspection. Hound remained silent while Dobi talked business with Jim. After they arrived at an agreement and Dobi had purchased the livestock, Jim focused his attention on Hound for some conversation.

"So, you're the young man called Hound that I've heard about," said Jim.

"Well, sir, that's the name I go by. What have you heard about me?"

"Honestly, some good things, some not so good."

"OK, tell me the good. I'll say if it's true or not."

"I hear you're a wealthy young man, one who has done a lot for the citizens of your town and throughout the county. In addition, that you've purchased everything formally owned by Jack Long."

"That is all true. Where did you get the information?"

"Hell, a lot of folks have heard about you, son. Word gets around in this part of the country."

"Tell me what you've heard that was bad?"

"Oh, hell, son, I didn't mean to say anything about the bad things, the rumors about you. Forget it."

"What rumors have you heard? The good things about me were rumors too. I'd like to hear the bad ones."

Jim really had let his tongue slip regarding the negative gossip. He didn't want to answer the question. However, he knew Hound expected an answer.

"OK. Shit! Well, it's been said you were suspect in the murder of Jack Long and the disappearance of several of his employees."

"Jim, I hope you've also heard that I'm no longer a suspect in any of that. I haven't been for some time."

"Yes, sir, I heard that too."

"I suppose some people might continue to wonder about me."

"I reckon some people are like that."

"Yep, I reckon. Did you know Jack?"

"We sold and bought livestock from each other a few times. I didn't know him well, but he struck me as a fellow not to be trusted too far."

"I heard a lot of folks felt that way about him, but I never judge a man on rumors."

"That's a good policy, son."

"Yep. It is."

Jim agreed to deliver the purchased livestock to The Double D on the following day. Hound and Dobi began their drive home.

"Do the rumors that you were a suspect bother you, Hound?" asked Dobi.

"People are going to talk about me for some time. They'll believe what they choose to. I'm not concerned one way or the other. I care about what you believe, but you're the only one."

"Hound, I've already said that I don't believe you had anything to do with that, but can I be honest about something?"

"Absolutely."

"I wouldn't care if you did. Jack was a piece of shit! We both know he was behind the raid on the ranch and the attempt on both our lives. I'm glad he's dead and no longer a threat, but I'm also glad you were cleared as a suspect."

Hound knew at that moment Dobi believed he was responsible for Jack's death and the disappearance of Cole and the other men. He was satisfied that she was comfortable with her belief, but he would never confirm it.

Hound and Dobi started going out together at least one night per week, usually on Saturday, and spent their nights together at the ranch. They were seen together in town shopping for groceries, feed for livestock and other items. It didn't take long for residents of the community to learn they were now formally a couple.

16

In March of 1980, Robbi and Bobbi picked up Hound and flew him to Los Angeles where he began flight training. He felt it was time to fly his own aircraft and not have to rely on hired pilots. It was no surprise to anyone how quickly and easily he earned a license to fly his jet and a variety of other fixed wing, prop aircraft. Naturally, his high intelligence and photographic memory were an asset.

During his time away, he would return to Montana on a monthly basis to spend the weekend with Dobi. He also made time to visit the corporate offices of all his businesses and meet with the CEO of each. He spent Thursday through Sunday of one week visiting his parents on the family farm in Louisiana. They were happy that he had come.

Things were beginning to settle down around the community. Talk about the disappearance of Judge Thibodaux and his daughter, detective Karen Thibodaux, along with her fiancé was no longer the major topic of gossip. The judge's wife and granddaughter were the only citizens who seemingly cared to keep the rumor alive that Hound was responsible.

The church that Hound had built on a large tract of land was now filled to capacity on Wednesday nights and during Sunday school and the two services on Sunday mornings. It was the same for the Sunday evening service.

After dinner on the first night of his visit, Hound sat in the living room with his parents and continued their conversation to catch up since he had been away.

"I don't suppose you'd care to tell us where you've been living for the past several months?" asked Linda.

"Honey, don't start asking questions," said John. "Hound will tell us everything he wants us to know."

"It's OK," said Hound. "I've been living on a ranch in Montana. I had planned to keep a low profile there. I did for as long as I could, but unforeseen circumstances made it impossible after a time."

"Did you buy a ranch?" asked John.

"Not at first, but now I own fifty-one percent of one that is three thousand acres and all of another that is fifteen thousand acres."

"Wow! That's a lot of ranch land. Do you plan to add the property to your current farming and ranching corporation?"

"Not now. For the time being, I'm going to operate everything under a separate corporation and oversee it personally."

"Is there a particular reason for that? You've always put specific people in charge of your enterprises. You always wanted the freedom to come and go as you please, to never be tied down with responsibilities."

Hound smiled.

"Yes, I've been dating a remarkable young lady. I never thought I would so soon after losing Rita and my boys."

"That's wonderful, Hound! What's her name? Tell us about her."

"Her name is Debbie Dobson. Dobi is her nickname. She prefers to be called by it."

"Prefers her nickname, huh? Like you."

"Yep."

"I'm sure you have more than that in common."

"Absolutely."

"Go ahead, tell us more."

"Dobi is a Doctor of Veterinary Medicine and is building a successful small and large animal practice. She has forty-nine percent of the three-thousand-acre Double D Ranch that we own together."

"Do you love this woman, Hound?"

"Well, I'm very fond of her."

"Well, when do your mother and I get to meet her? Shall we come to Montana, or will she come here?"

"We can do it either way, if and when the time comes."

"What does that mean?"

"Dobi and I haven't been dating long. I want time to see where our current relationship will lead before you meet her."

"Son, you don't have to have plans to marry before we would want to meet her. I'm sure Dobi is an exceptional woman, or you wouldn't be dating her. I'd bet she's very pretty too."

"She's exceptional in every way that matters. Dobi is beyond simply pretty' she's beautiful."

"Is Dobi from Montana? Has she always lived there?"

"She was born there and grew up on The Double D Ranch.

"How did you meet her?"

"I had just arrived in town. Dobi was parked under a tree, trying to find homes for stray pets, when she caught my eye. I went over and introduced myself."

"That's fine. Did you adopt a pet?"

"Actually, I did. It's hard to believe, but she had a Bloodhound pup that I instinctively knew would grow to look just like Hunter, so I adopted him."

"No kidding! What's his name?"

"I named him Pardner."

"That's a good name, but why not Hunter?"

"There will never be another Hunter, but Pardner and I have a similar relationship."

Hound continued to visit with his parents until it was well past their bedtime. Finally, John said it would be a busy day tomorrow. Everyone went to bed. Nothing in Hound's bedroom had been changed since he was a boy growing up on the farm.

Hound lay in bed that night looking up at the ceiling. A full moon was shining through his window, it's light almost bright enough to read by. As he waited for sleep, memories of days long past began to occupy his thoughts. In his mind, he revisited events and experiences of the past, both good and bad. As he had done many times, he wished it were possible to live his life over knowing what he knew now. Life would be very different in many ways for him if that were possible. He reconciled himself to the fact that such a wish was born in the soul of those with regrets, never come true. However, when sleep came, he dreamed his wish was granted. It was a wonderful dream indeed.

The next morning after breakfast, Hound decided he would drive into town and see what was going on. John told him to be aware that even though he hadn't been the topic of malicious gossip for some time, it could begin again if certain people saw him during his visit.

Hound told his parents that he only planned to drive around, not to visit any places where citizens were gathered. He knew his parents didn't want to contend with the problems they'd faced in the past due to what people were thinking and saying about him. However, he wasn't going to hide out as if he feared anything. John suggested he drive to the church he'd built and say hello to Pastor Brogan, who would most likely be there. John said the pastor was doing an outstanding job in service of the Lord.

Hound made the church his first stop that morning. He found Pastor Brogan busy at work in his office. The pastor greeted him with a warm smile and embrace.

"My oh my, it's good to see you again, Hound," said the pastor. "It's been some time since your last visit."

"Yes, sir, at least a year."

"What have you been doing? I hope life has been getting better for you."

"I think so, pastor. Finally. I've been traveling around the country, seeing some new places."

"Are you going to stay here for a while?"

"Only a couple of days. I still have things to do elsewhere."

"I hope you'll attend church with your parents on Sunday."

"Maybe."

"You should come and worship at the church you built and own. I'm sure the Lord would be pleased if you did."

"It might be best if I kept a low profile while I'm here. Dad said everything has improved with my absence and the church is overflowing with members."

"Yes, that's true. We need to enlarge the church, or soon we won't be able to accommodate the growing membership."

"Why haven't you already done that? I'm sure the church can afford it."

"We've approved the plans, but we wanted your approval."

"I appreciate that, but you don't need my approval, just my dad's."

"I know, but he wanted to include you. I assume he hasn't told you yet."

"No, I assume he wanted you to tell me. I'm happy to hear the membership is growing so quickly."

"Quickly indeed! I wish it was because the members were as interested in serving the Lord as they are in the golf course, gym, indoor/outdoor swimming pools and all the other attractions."

"Well, pastor, I guess it's your job to change their priorities."

The pastor smiled and shook his head.

"You're right, Hound," he said. "I'm trying to do that very thing!"

It was then that the pastor's daughter, Carol, entered her father's office. She didn't know the pastor had a guest, but she was delighted it was Hound. She was happy to see him again.

"It's wonderful to see you again, Hound!" Carol said in an excited and sincere fashion. "Am I interrupting an important meeting?"

"Not at all, Carol. I just stopped by to say hello to your dad and visit a few minutes. I was just about ready to leave."

"Don't leave on my account. I just stopped by to tell my dad hello too. I haven't seen him in a few days. Mom and I just got back from a trip to visit relatives in Atlanta. We drove by your nightclub there. Hound, it's a big, beautiful piece of architecture."

"Did you see the interior?"

Carol laughed.

"No, it was 9 in the morning and you know my mother would never patron a nightclub," she said. "Not even one of yours."

"Nor would you," remarked the pastor.

"I know, Dad, nor would I."

"How's Tim these days?" asked Hound.

"My husband is well, but being partners with you in the construction business keeps him away from home a lot. He's in New York now, starting a new project. His dad is in Florida on a job."

"I suppose you travel to see Tim when he's away too long."

"When I can, but working on my doctorate degree ties me down."

"Indeed, it would. Well, I'm planning to drive into town a see what's going on, so I'll say good bye to you both and be on my way."

"I hope to see you in church on Sunday, Hound," said the pastor.

"We'll see."

Hound left and drove into town. Carol left shortly after and drove toward town. Hound stopped at a gas station to fill up. When he emerged from the station after paying, Carol was refueling her car at the pump closest to his.

"Fancy meeting you here, Hound," she said. "I didn't think I would see you again so soon."

"Yep, a small town is a small world."

"Actually, I hoped to find you in town, Hound. There's something of a private nature I'd like to discuss with you."

"Really, what?"

"It's about Tim and me. I know you can be trusted not to say anything to anyone."

"How do you know?"

"Come on, Hound! I just know. Tell me if I'm wrong."

"OK, you're not wrong. What's going on with you and Tim?"

"Not here. Is there someplace private we can go to talk, a place where nobody will see us?"

"No place where that can be guaranteed. Why can't we just get a cup of coffee at the café and talk there? Tim is my business partner. It wouldn't look inappropriate for us to be seen talking and having coffee."

Carol hesitated before she responded.

"Hound, I'm planning to divorce Tim. I don't want to be seen in public with any man, especially you. You know how people like to start gossip. I don't want either of our reputations to be soiled."

Hound couldn't keep from laughing.

"I don't think there's a way to soil my reputation worse than it already is," he told her, "but I can understand how being seen with me, under any circumstance, could hurt yours. Why would you want to divorce Tim? He's a decent guy who loves you very much. Besides, he's become a wealthy man. That makes you a wealthy wife."

"Tim is hardly ever home anymore. Neither of us are the same high school sweethearts who likely married too young. Besides, I would be entitled to a substantial percentage of his share of the partnership if we divorce."

Hound's instinct began speaking to him when Carol said she was divorcing Tim. He knew she was involved with another man, a man who likely saw her money potential as more appealing than her performance in bed. He decided to humor her and verify all his suspicions.

"Maybe we should talk more about this, but I don't wish to do it in a private place. If your mind is made up, then I don't know why you would want to talk to me anyway. All I'd do is try to convince you to reconsider. Tim is my partner. He wouldn't be if I didn't know him to be an honest and trustworthy man, an overall decent gentleman. There's not an abundance of his kind around. You'd do well to consider that."

Other vehicles were arriving to get fuel. Hound suggested he and Carol drive to the café for coffee and continue their conversation. She agreed it would be OK if they didn't arrive together. She'd been seated at a table in the back for about 10 minutes when he joined her. Only a small number of customers were there. None noticed or cared who the two people seated, drinking coffee and having a chat were.

"Hound, I want to know the best way to receive from the construction company what I'll be awarded in my divorce settlement," said Carol. "Best for me and the company. I don't want to cause you any headaches."

"You won't cause me or the corporation any headaches, Carol, because you won't get anything from the corporation. Anything you get will be based on Tim's personal salary. He'll take a huge cut in pay if you divorce him."

"What are you talking about? I would get half his share of the forty-nine percent split between him and his father."

"No, you wouldn't. Remember the paperwork you signed when I made Tim and his dad partners in the corporation?"

"Yes, but I don't remember what I signed."

"As a condition of me granting the partnership, you agreed to waive any claim to any portion of the corporation, or any of its earnings in the event of Tim's death or divorce from you."

"That's bullshit, Hound! It's not fair and you know it!"

"Maybe, but if you want to continue to share in Tim's success, then you should remain his wife. I'm certain that if he finds out you're in an adulterous relationship, then it will be Tim who files for divorce."

Hound decided to act on his instinct that she was in such a relationship. Also, he hoped her emotions would cause her tongue to slip and verify his suspicion, maybe even reveal the man's name.

"How did you find out about Eugene?"

"Just now, when you told me. I guessed he would be Eugene Miller, the attorney here in town. What were you thinking to tie up with that bottom feeder? I'm sure he plans to handle your divorce at no charge. The son of a bitch has his eye on the money he plans to get from the corporation."

"Eugene is a good man and an amazing attorney. Naturally, it's his responsibility to get as much money for me as possible."

"Has he asked and have you agreed to marry him after your divorce?"

"Actually, yes, we plan to be married."

"Maybe you should tell him right away about the papers you signed. He might change his mind about marrying you. He might decide not to be your attorney."

"I'll tell him. I'm sure he'll advise me there's a way around whatever I signed. Anyway, he loves me and would still want to marry me if there wasn't."

"Maybe, but would you still want a divorce?"

"Do you think I'd stay married to Tim only because of money?"

"Only you can decide that, but if you do, then being a faithful wife will be an ongoing requirement. If you can't do that, then I'll make sure he finds out what kind of wife you are."

"You won't tell him about me and Eugene, will you, if I proceed with the divorce?"

"No, you told me your plans in confidence, but I'll make sure you don't get money from the corporation."

"Like I said, Eugene will find a way."

"Why don't you let me come with you to talk to him? I'm sure if you do, he'll side with me."

"He wouldn't like it that I've told you about him and me."

"So what? He's going to find out anyway. I'm going to see him with or without you there."

"Why are you being so mean to me? I thought you were my friend too and would understand my desire to divorce."

"You have the right to do as you please, but not if it has a negative effect on my construction business. Besides, I plan to help Tim in every way possible. He's not only a trusted, loyal partner, but also a friend I value more than you."

Carol agreed for Hound to be present when she met with Eugene. The meeting took place in Eugene's office an hour later. He was surprised when Hound arrived with her. Carol introduced the two men and explained what was going on. Eugene wasn't pleased that Hound knew he and Carol were romantically involved but concealed his feelings.

"Hound, with all due respect," said Eugene, "there's nothing Carol could have signed as an independent party that would keep her from being awarded a fair share of her husband's share of the corporation. They were married when the partnership was formed, not after. That has great significance."

Hound presented his usual smile, the one he always offered before correcting someone in a mistake they had made.

"Well, even if you were right, Eugene, it would be years before a judge would render a decision in your client's favor. By the time one did, Tim Sanders would no longer be a partner in my business."

"What makes you think it would take so long to conclude the divorce?"

"Do you know anything about me?"

"As a matter of fact, I've heard a lot about you. I'm sorry to say it, but none of it has been good."

"Shit! You're referring to rumors and propaganda! I'm referring to the fact that I have enough money to keep your case from ever being litigated and never miss the amount spent to do so. Besides, the lawyers I would provide for Tim could do no less than ruin your reputation and get you disbarred. Of course, Carol needs to consider what effect exposing her infidelity would have on her reputation and how it would impact her parents."

"I'm not concerned with your threats, sir! You have no proof that infidelity is an issue. It would be hearsay against mine and Carol's denying rumors."

"I don't make threats, sir. I state absolute facts."

Eugene asked Carol to give him some time alone with Hound. She nodded and stepped out of his office.

"Hound, surely you'd consider a one-time, reasonable cash settlement for Carol," said Eugene. "She deserves at least that."

"Eugene, here's something for you to consider. If you bring the case, there will be consequences that will make you regret doing so. I'll do whatever is necessary to win. Again, that's not a threat, it's a God-damned fact. Good day, sir."

Hound continued to smile as he turned and left the office. He walked past Carol, still smiling, but saying nothing. She reentered the office to find Eugene seated at his desk with a concerned look on his face.

"What wrong, Eugene?" she asked."

"We can't win, not against a man like that."

"Can't we at least try?"

"Everything he said was true. Besides, even if it weren't, I don't plan to fuck with him. There just might be some truth to what I've heard about the infamous Hound."

"What have you heard?"

"Hell, the same thing you and everyone else has heard! He can kill and get away with it! If he has the balls to kill a judge and a sheriff's detective, he sure as hell would kill us!"

Carol left Eugene's office convinced she should abandon her plan to acquire any interest in the corporation through a divorce. She suddenly decided it would be best to stay married. Eugene had made it clear that their relationship had been a mistake and was concluded. Carol would waste no time in having another conversation with Hound to get his approval regarding her decision. She wasn't surprised to find him waiting for her in the parking lot.

"I've decided to give my marriage another try, Hound," she said as she stood next to him by his truck. "I hope you'll allow me to do that."

"Carol, there's nothing that would please me more. However, I'll present you with a choice. If you don't plan to be a good wife to Tim, then get your divorce as soon as possible. I'll pay you a sum of money that will support you for the rest of your life, but you

154

won't ask any type of settlement from Tim, ever. You'll disappear and never see Tim again, ever. If you stay with Tim and cheat with another man, then you'll earn a very unpleasant consequence. That is the choice you have to make, and be sure it's the right one."

"What consequence are you referring to?"

"You'll disappear for good."

Carol paused. She looked into Hound's eyes and instantly knew he was sincere.

"Hound, are you saying I would pay with my life?" she asked in a exited, breaking voice.

"Choose wisely, Carol."

Hound smiled and then got into his truck and drove away. Carol began to consider the old rumors about him, those that had become less spoken. However, they were still the topic of discussion from time to time by citizens of the community. She realized that he'd intended to verify the rumors to her, but in a very subtle manner. She now had to determine if the verification was a bluff or fact. As she remembered the look in his eyes when he presented her with the choices, her heart began to beat faster and it seemed hard to take a breath. Carol then came to believe the rumors were true. She would make her choice based on that belief.

Hound was driving back to the farm when Carol's car appeared in his rearview mirror. When she flashed her headlights signaling for him to pull over, he did. She pulled to the side of the road and stopped her car at the rear of his truck. He walked to hear what she had to say through the driver's side open window.

"Hound, I want to stay with Tim," she said, "if it's OK with you."

"If that's what you truly desire, then I'm happy to hear it."

"Thank you. I will stay married and honor your terms."

"I'm happy to hear that as well."

"I hope in time you will come to not think bad of me."

"We all make bad decisions, Carol. The only thing we can do is learn from them and go on living, trying to never repeat previous mistakes."

Hound returned to his truck and continued his drive. Carol turned her car around and sped away in the opposite direction.

Hound agreed to attend church with his parents on Sunday. He was surprised when members of the large congregation offered him a more friendly welcome than he expected. Tim had came come home unexpectedly to surprise Carol. They sat next to Hound and his parents during the service.

When the service concluded and all members had left, Hound, his parents, Tim and Carol were invited to the pastor's office for a brief visit.

"I'm so happy you came today, Hound," said the pastor as an opening statement. "It's good to see the man who built this church attend worship in it."

"Thank you, Pastor. I enjoyed it."

"We all have much to be thankful for in our lives. This church has been a blessing for all its many members. It has been a special blessing for me."

"I'm glad to hear that."

"I'd like to add how blessed I am to have Carol as my wife," Tim said as a jester of love and gratitude toward her.

Hound smiled at the comment, as did everyone else.

"Carol and I are also blessed to have met Hound. As a result, we now have a financial status that is abundant. God has truly been good to us in so many ways."

"God pours abundant blessings on the faithful," said the pastor.

"Yes, he does," added John and Linda, with Hound smiling and shaking his head in agreement.

Hound gave a quick glance toward Carol who was starring at him. He understood her smile that hid what she was feeling.

"You're a lucky man indeed, Tim, to have all that God has provided for you," said Hound as he returned Carol's smile. "I'm sure Carol feels the same way you do."

"Yes, I do," she said in response. "God only knows how much I appreciate his blessings."

Hound boarded his private jet at the airport on Monday morning and sat in the left pilot's seat. His parents watched as he sped down the runway and then took off on his way to Phoenix.

Maggie was anxiously waiting to greet him when he landed in Phoenix, which would be his only stop during the flight back to Montana. She presented him with a kiss on his cheek and a long, warm embrace when he emerged from the jet.

"Hound, it's wonderful to finally see you again," Maggie told him. "How have you been? I'm dying to hear all you have been up to!"

"You already know, Maggie."

"I'm not talking about that shit! I want to know about other things."

"We can talk during dinner tonight."

"Good idea. Let's go to my home and you can shower and rest a bit first."

"That's a nice idea, but I want to check on my estate. I'll shower and rest there, then meet you at your place around 8. Where shall we go for dinner?"

"At my home. I'm cooking for you tonight."

"Well, I appreciate that Maggie. What are we having?"

"It's a surprise, but I'm sure you'll like it."

"No doubt about that. As I recall, you're a good cook."

"I'm good at everything I do, Hound. You know that."

"I do know that."

"I'm still good in bed too."

"I don't doubt that either, Maggie."

"Do I still look good now that I'm thirty-seven?"

"You haven't aged a day since I first met you, Maggie. You're still one of the most beautiful women I've ever known."

Hound was being honest. The years he'd know Maggie hadn't changed her. This was amazing considering the stress she experienced as the result of the nefarious and very dangerous career she'd chosen.

"Maybe so, Hound, but I'm not the very most beautiful, right?"

Hound knew Maggie was respectfully referring to Rita.

"Yes, you're right, Maggie," he told her. "Rita was number one."

"Have you met anyone yet, Hound? You need to start living again. I hope you have."

"I'm dating Dobi, the woman in Montana."

"Is it serious?"

"Maybe it could be eventually, but I'm going slow. There's a lot to consider."

"Like how she would feel about your past life?"

"Maybe. I suppose so."

"You know it would be dangerous to tell her. Only those of us who shared in that life with you can ever know."

"I know, Maggie. Shit! How well I know."

"By the way, Hound, I have a letter for you. I was paid a good sum of money to personally deliver it to you. If you hadn't decided to visit here, I would have come to Montana."

"What's it about? Who's it from?"

"I have no idea. A stranger met with me and offered me the money to deliver it to you. He said his name was James Thomas Huntington and that he represented some very special people and knew we were close friends. I quickly realized that this guy was someone not to take lightly. He was very polite and proper. He was confident that I was the person to be trusted to put the letter in your hand. You are to read it when you're alone. He was adamant about that."

Maggie pulled the letter from her purse and delivered it to Hound. The name Hound was on the envelope, nothing else. Its thickness indicated that likely only one page of material, two at the most, were inside.

"Well, thank you, Maggie," said Hound. "I'll open and read this when I arrive at my estate."

"Will you tell me what's going on after you read it?"

"Maybe, maybe not. I don't know yet."

After Maggie left, Hound obtained the car he'd rented and drove to his desert estate. He knew he'd find everything in proper order. Maggie had taken it on herself to keep an eye on it for him.

17

Hound arrived at his desert estate around 11:30 that morning. The security guard on duty at the front entrance gate was delighted to see him again.

"Welcome home, Hound," said the guard. "It's good to see you. Are you here to stay for a while?"

"Thanks, pal," replied Hound. "It's good to be back in Phoenix. I've missed living in a warmer winter climate. However, I won't be here more than a day or two."

"Well, sir, it's already getting hot here. Today's temperatures are forecast to reach over one hundred degrees. A bit above expected normal for the first week of June."

Hound drove to his home and parked his car in the garage. He entered the house, set his luggage down and took a seat in a chair at the dining table. He looked briefly at the mysterious letter in his hand before opening it and beginning to read its content. There was only one page to read. The stationary was very elegant. It had a beautiful letterhead and the paper was of a type texture he'd never seen before. It had been written by hand in royal blue colored ink and in old English style lettering. Before he even started to read, his instinct told him that to do so might lead him into something he would prefer to avoid. But what if it contained information he wanted, even needed, to know? His eyes focused on the first line.

The letter read:

Dear Hound,

I hope you don't mind me addressing you by your nickname. It is my understanding that you prefer the name. I would have contacted you personally. However, such would not have been in mine or your best interest should what I wish to propose not be of interest to you. If such is the result, then you are not the man those whom I represent hope you are. Meeting you prior to establishing your interest would compromise the level of anonymity I need to maintain regarding the performance of my duties.

I represent the twelve wealthiest men in the world. Having followed your growth in wealth for several years, they believe you will be of equal status with each of them in the not so distant future. These men comprise the total membership of an organization. This organization has been in existence for a very long time. For all that time it has been kept a highly guarded secret. They have instructed me to interview you as a possible candidate to fill the position of the thirteenth and final member of the organization. With such membership comes great responsibility, but also power beyond what you ever thought existed.

Should you be interested in what has been told to you in this brief letter, then call me at the number included on it. However, be advised that should we meet, you are sworn to secrecy regarding any further information provided to you. Should you ever fail to honor that secrecy, then you will face harsh consequences. Also, you will be obligated to meet with these twelve men. During this meeting you will be told everything you need to know in order to make an informed decision to accept membership or not. Nothing more than your consistent silence will be required should you decline that membership.

Sincerely,

Sir James Thomas Huntington

Hound laid the letter on the table and then began to consider what he'd read. His intelligence and instinct both made him certain that the man who had authored it was sincere and to be taken seriously. Now he would rely on his intelligence and instinct to decide if he would meet with Sir James Thomas Huntington. He would rely on it further and with great care should he proceed beyond the first meeting.

Hound put all thoughts of the matter to rest for the time being. He took a long shower and then lay down for a short nap. His subconscious took command after he fell to sleep and he dreamed his destiny might be connected to a secret organization he yet knew little about.

Hound arrived at Maggie's home at 7:45 that evening. She greeted him at the door with a hug and a glass of expensive wine. She was dressed in an ivory colored dress that complemented her long dark hair and other attractive physical features. She was a beautiful woman. It was apparent she wanted to do all that was possible to accent it.

"You look wonderful, Maggie," said Hound. "I feel underdressed in these blue jeans and boots."

"I like to see you in tight-fitting jeans. Always have, always will."

Maggie handed him the glass of wine and asked if he was hungry.

"Yes, I haven't eaten since early this morning," he replied.

"Hound, you don't need to miss meals. That's not good for you."

"I don't miss many."

She had prepared an elegant meal. The main dish was one of his favorites.

"This dinner is fantastic, Maggie," he said. "Are we celebrating something I don't know about?"

"You being here, Hound. That's what I'm celebrating. It seems like old times."

"In some ways I guess, but not in every way."

"Yeah. A lot of water has gone under the bridge since then."

"A flood of water, Maggie."

"No shit! We've lived some exiting adventures, together and separate."

"We have."

"So, are you going to tell me what was in the letter?"

"Nothing but a lot of bullshit."

"Huntington didn't seem like a man peddling something that wasn't important for you to know. Shit! Like I told you, he paid me very well to make sure you received his letter and that only you read it."

"Maybe it seemed important to him, but I'm not sure it was to me, at least not yet."

"What do you mean?"

"Nothing, Maggie. Let's talk about something more significant and interesting."

Maggie understood he couldn't discuss the content of the letter, or just didn't want to. She changed the subject. There was something else to discuss that was important to her. Maggie was never one to beat around the bush. Regardless of what she wanted, she didn't hesitate to get to the point right away.

"Hound, you owe me a favor for helping you with your problem in Montana. Right?"

"Right. Do you need me to return the favor so soon?"

"Yes, if I can get the favor I want. Is there a limit to what I can ask for?"

"Considering all you did for me, then I suppose not. However, I'd prefer not to kill anybody that's not planning to kill me, or someone I care about."

"Hound, I know several qualified individuals to call on for such service. No, I want you to sleep here with me tonight and let me experience what we used to do in the good old days. However, only if you'll enjoy it even half as much as I will."

Hound's traditional smile came to his face as he looked across the dining table at her. The look on Maggie's face was one of embarrassment and vulnerability. These were emotions seldom if ever seen in her.

"Maggie, after all you did to help me out and all you want is for me to sleep with you is a splendid compliment to me," he said softly. "I'm happy to accept your invitation to spend the night."

"Only if you truly want to. I don't want your mind on Dobi, no regret in the morning."

"I understand."

When the act of intimacy between them began that night, Hound found it as satisfying as Maggie. She became completely uninhibited after realizing his performance was a result of being with her, absent thoughts of another woman. He was committed to her complete satisfaction before achieving his third and final climax. Maggie's was twice that number. There was no sexual position or act that wasn't provided by each to the other during the encounter.

"We're as good in bed as ever, Hound," said Maggie after the sex had ended and she lay in his arms, her head on his shoulder.

"I have to agree, Maggie."

"You're still the best lover I've ever had."

Maggie didn't expect a likewise response and didn't receive one. Happy with what she had at the moment, the thought came to her mind to say how much he was still very much loved. However, she allowed sleep to come, knowing he wouldn't offer the desired reply.

Hound awoke the next morning to find Maggie was already awake, smiling and looking at him.

"Did you sleep well?" she asked.

"Like a rock."

"Do you still like to complete you daily workout in the morning?"

"Absolutely."

"Good, we'll do it together, and then I'll fix a nice breakfast. I have a surprise for you after we've finished."

"What?"

"I don't want to spoil the surprise by saying anything more. I assume you're planning to visit the biker club today, right?"

"Right."

"Your surprise is there. I'll go with you to see it."

"Well, OK."

"We need to get there by noon, in time for lunch."

"Have we been invited to eat?"

"Of course."

"How did the club find out I was in town?"

"I called Bill when you left for your estate yesterday."

"Will Bill and Pony be there?"

"Hell yes. All the Phoenix chapter members will be there that can be."

Hound and Maggie arrived at the biker clubhouse at 11:45. It was overflowing with club members. Bill and Pony led a round of welcoming applause when the guest of honor entered. Hound said hello, shook many hands and got a lot of hugs from biker wives, mammas and groupies as he and Maggie made their way through the crowd to the bar where Bill and Pony were waiting to buy him a beer.

"It's good to see you again, Hound!" said Bill, offering a hand-shake and then a hug to him.

Pony did likewise after Bill's greeting.

"Damn! It's good to see you two outlaws again," said Hound. "It's good to see everybody that's here."

"We're glad to see you as well, Hound," replied Bill. "How the hell have you been? Fuck! Where have you been?"

"Living on a ranch in Montana."

"No shit! You bought a ranch in Montana?"

"Not until I'd been there awhile."

"Did you buy a big one?"

"I would say so."

"I guess Maggie told you about the surprise."

"Yep. What is it?"

"It's not a what. It's a who."

Everyone applauded and cheered when Bear stood up from where he'd been crouching behind the bar. Hound laughed and stepped back when his best friend sprang over the bar as if he were attacking. When Bear landed, Hound rushed forward and the two men embraced while calling each other a variety of obscene names that only the best of friends would tolerate.

"Bear, you are one crazy son of a bitch to be back in the States!" said Hound in a loud voice, but with a smile of delight. "The entire God-damned government is still looking to put you under the prison."

"Fuck it! I needed to see my biker brothers and get some made-in-the-USA pussy before I got completely addicted to that hot, wet South American snatch! The risk I'm taking by being here became completely worth it when I learned you were in town! Fuck! It's great to see you again, my friend!"

"Same here, Bear. How did you get here from Colombia?"

"I was smuggled to New Orleans on a ship delivering a load of quality coke. Maggie met me there and we flew here in her private jet."

Hound looked at Maggie.

"So, Maggie, you finally bought a jet," he said.

"I've had one for some time. I bought it from your company in L.A. Robbi and Bobbi gave me a good deal."

"I was never told."

"I told them to keep it a secret. I wanted to tell you the next time we got together. I could have said something yesterday, but I wanted to add to the surprise here. Robbi and Bobbi agreed that you wouldn't mind the secret."

"The three of you were right. I don't mind."

"I'll show the plane to you before you leave. You're a pilot now, so you can take it for a spin."

"If time permits, I might do that."

"It's not as big as yours, but just as nice."

Hound sat a table with Maggie, Bear, Bill and Pony. As they ate the splendid lunch prepared for them, they talked about happenings of the past. After a time, the present became the topic.

"Hound, do you ever regret retiring and getting out of the business?" asked Bear. "Everybody misses you, me most of all."

"You couldn't miss him more than I do," added Maggie.

"I miss you guys more than you could imagine," replied Hound. "However, not being able to see you on a regular basis is all I regret. I wish all of you would consider the money you've made in business with the cartel enough and quit while there's still time."

"Seems like you still believe we're headed for a bad end if we don't, Hound," said Bear.

"Bear, it's not just a belief. It's something that I know."

"Maybe you're right, Hound, but what choice do I have? I may never be able to return to the States. I'll be a wanted man for the rest of my life. I've accepted my fate to stay in Colombia under the protection of the Sanchez Cartel for as long as it exists."

"How long it will exist is something you should think about, Bear. It can't continue indefinitely. Carlos Sanchez won't always be alive, even if he survives to die of old age. Who will take over when he's gone?"

"He intends me to replace him."

"Come on, Bear! How long do you think that would last? You'd be a white American in charge of a Colombian drug cartel."

"You always said to never cross a bridge until you get there, Hound. I won't cross that one until I get there."

"I hope you live long enough to try crossing. I hope all of you do, because the odds are not in your favor."

"It's hard to walk away from the shit pile of money we're all making. You know that better than anyone."

"Bear, you know I got out as soon as I could. There were reasons why I couldn't leave. When I could, I did."

"True, but you left after becoming a multibillionaire."

"Yes, but that was in part the result of legitimate businesses I was creating and growing."

Well, I don't have the ability to own legitimate business in the States, or anywhere else. I'm a wanted man, remember?"

"You could join me in a new venture as a silent partner. Hell, Maggie, Bill and Pony too. We could all be partners."

"What kind of business?"

"Something you like that would make a lot of money. Each of you could choose one and partner with me."

After they had finished eating and sharing a long conversation with the others, Hound and Bear took a walk outside.

"How are things really going for you, Hound?" asked Bear.

"There's been a few bumps in the road, but things are OK. How about you, Bear?" I hear drug wars are getting more common."

"You know it, buddy! Every son of a bitch with enough money to buy a little power wants to become a drug lord. The Cubans have been competing in Miami for control and it's getting worse. If that weren't pain in the ass enough, other players are getting involved in Florida and in other high market areas of the country. For a long time, it was mainly Mexican cartels, but we're seeing more Russian and Chinese entering the game. God damn, Hound! You predicted years ago this shit would happen. How were you so fucking sure?"

"It was common sense, Bear. There's big money to be made in selling drugs. Greed is natural. Those who don't have money want it. To get it, the want-to-be bad guys have to compete with and take it away from the bad guys who have it. The result is drug wars. The guys who kill rather than get killed grow in power. They stay in power until they're killed and they will be sooner or later. The biggest threat is internal. There's always going to be a subordinate that wants what the boss has and is willing to try and take over. I had to deal with that in the past. You were involved the second time I had to put down a coup. Remember?"

"Hell yes! How could I forget?"

"Bear, if you stay in the business, sooner or later you're going to wind up dead or in prison. That's a God-damned fact. Get out and let me help you. I can hide you out of the country for as long as necessary. I'll form a corporation that can have a division anywhere you are. I'll invest the money you already have. You'll make more money as my partner and you'll get richer and richer, just like I do."

"Hound, I may take you up on that offer someday."

"Don't wait too long. Why not do it now?"

"I was born an outlaw, Hound. I don't know if I could stand to be otherwise."

"God damn it, Bear! That is pure bullshit and you know it!"

"Hound, you can be two different people. I'm not sure I could. You know that's true for Maggie, Bill and Pony too."

Bear changed the subject. He wanted to know what life was like on the ranch in Montana. Hound gave him an accurate and detailed description.

"So, Hound is a rancher cowboy now," Bear said and then laughed. "How long will it be before you get bored and try something new?"

"I have no problem with handling the business end of ranching, but I can't say I'm a qualified cowboy yet. However, I look forward to learning from all the men that work for me. I consider them very qualified."

"How are Sam and his men doing? Have they learned to be real cowboys yet?"

"No, but they'll get there. Bear, I read Sam as a man I can trust and who will make sure all his men can be trusted as well. Am I right? He's served me well so far."

"Sam is a biker brother I'd bet my life on under any circumstance. If he likes a man, then that man can trust Sam to be loyal forever. He'll make sure the man he pledges his loyalty to is equally loyal to him. Hound, he's among the very few men I know that I would not want mad at me. Sam is a tough, deadly and determined killer when circumstances call for such."

"I feel certain he likes me."

"Damn right he does. He's heard all about you from me, Maggie, and others who know your history. However, he for sure has formed a personal opinion of you. Anyway, if he didn't like, respect and trust you, he wouldn't have given up the life of an outlaw biker to become an outlaw cowboy. I'm sure you know he'll remain an outlaw regardless of the fact he's a cowboy."

"Yes, I know."

"Naturally, you hired him and his crew to perform other duties as needed."

"Yes."

"Hound, Sam is six feet four inches tall and weighs close to three hundred pounds. Was it hard to find a horse big enough for him?"

"Not at all. Horses come in a variety of sizes."

"My friend, have you heard from or have any information about how Carmella is doing?"

"No, Bear. I'm certain she's off the grid and wants to stay there. We need to let her."

"I know, but I can't get over that bitch. I loved her so much! You can understand that. I know you felt the same way about Rita. Right?"

"Right, Bear, but I starting to get on with my life without Rita. You have to do the same."

"I'll never forget Carmella, Hound."

"Neither of us will forget the first true love of our lives, but we have to deal with it and get on with living."

"How?"

"Close one door and open another so the next true love can come in."

"I'll never find a woman to replace Carmella."

"When you open the door, then maybe she'll find you, Bear."

"Have you opened another door yet?"

"I think so."

"Has someone that could replace Rita found you?"

"Maybe. I don't know yet, but I'm not looking to replace Rita, or my sons. I'm seeking a new start, at a new life."

Hound and Bear walked and talked for over two hours. They

would have visited longer, but Bear had to leave and return to Bogota. Hound and Maggie drove him to her jet. They watched the plane during and after takeoff until it was out of sight. Maggie could tell Hound was troubled.

"What's on your mind, Hound?" she asked.

"Maggie, Bear must never find out what really happened to Carmella. It would destroy him and it would be my fault."

"He won't. Baby, you were justified in killing her. She was responsible for the death of your family. She didn't give a shit about Bear and almost got him killed too. She was damn sure responsible for him being identified and wanted by the federal government. Hell! He will never be off the radar."

"Not as long as he's a major player in the drug business. I wish you and he would get the hell out of the business and accept my offer. I'm sick of hearing you won't because you're born outlaws, destined to remain so."

"Hound, Bear and I were born to be what we are. We can't change because we love what we do."

"More than you love your lives, your freedom?"

"I suppose enough to risk losing either, Hound. You're different from us in that respect."

"Smarter in that respect also!"

"Yes, probably that too."

"Hound, do you regret killing Carmella?"

"I find myself regretting all the lives I've taken."

"Did you really have a choice in order to survive?"

"I don't know. Maybe."

"You don't take chances based on maybe, Hound. That's how you stayed alive. It's how you became what you are now and what you will become. Your life will continue to evolve. Who knows what you will be five, ten, twenty years from now, but maybe is something you'll never base a decision on to get there."

"I guess you know me better than most others do, Maggie."

"You're damn right! I've learned a lot from you too. So has Bear.

Hopefully, we've learned enough to survive what you believe we won't."

"Maggie, I'll tell you one last time, and then never again! Nobody is smart, tough, ruthless or even lucky enough to forever beat the odds you and Bear face daily in the business you're in. I've always known that and got out as soon as I could. Fortunately, I got out in time. If you really believe what I taught you about maybe, then embrace my lead and follow it."

"I'll give what you've said careful consideration, Hound. I know Bear will as well."

Hound would do as he said and never ask Maggie or Bear to retire from the drug business again. He spent one more night in Phoenix at his desert estate. Maggie was there. She went with him to his nightclub. The many new employees had no idea who he was until the long-term veterans made them aware.

Hound took off in his jet the next morning. He would arrive at the Montana ranch in time to have lunch with several of the cowboys.

A paved runway and hangar for Hound's new jet had been built on a portion of land he'd purchased from Long's widow. Dobi was waiting anxiously for him when he landed. She welcomed him home with a passionate kiss and warm embrace.

"It's good to finally have you home, Hound," she said. "I hope you'll stay awhile before you decide to leave again. I've only seen you three times in the last three months. I miss you terribly when you're not here."

"I don't plan to be away again, at least for a while. How are things with the ranch?"

"All is well, Hound. How does it feel to be a pilot and fly your jet?"

"Good. I don't know why I waited so long to learn."

"When can I get a ride?"

"Whenever you want. Maybe we can take a trip somewhere, maybe have a vacation together."

"Oh, Hound, that would be wonderful!"

She drove him to the bunkhouse and joined him and the cowboys for lunch.

18

Hound had arrived back in Montana during the first week of June. The next day after his return, he was up early and began his five-mile run. Afterward, he went to the new barn close to his house and completed the rest of his workout in the gym he'd built inside. Pardner lay quietly watching. When he returned home, Dobi had slept later than usual and was taking a shower in the master bathroom. She laughed when he opened the shower door and came in. He was erect and she quickly became aroused at the site.

"Didn't you get enough pussy last night, baby?" she asked in a teasing manner.

"Of course, but that was last night. Are you in the mood?"

"Hell yes, I am now."

She wrapped her legs around his waist as he lifted her and put her back to the wall. He gently entered her and began to thrust slow and deep.

"I like fucking you in the shower, Hound," Dobi told him during breakfast.

"What do you like about it?"

"We don't have to take a shower after we finish."

"Is that all?"

Dodi laughed and threw a bit of biscuit at him.

"I like to fuck you at any time, at any place," she said, continuing to laugh.

"Lady, you've sure been talking dirty lately."

"I only talk that way to you, when we're alone. Do you mind?"

"No. Actually I like it."

"I know. All men do."

"Oh, and just how do you know that?"

"All women know that. Haven't all the women you've been with talked dirty to you?"

Hound began laughing with her.

"Yes, Maggie, I suppose they did."

Hound couldn't believe he had just called Dobi Maggie. He could tell by the look on her face that the atmosphere was about to change.

"Hound, why did you call me Maggie?" Dobi asked, feeling hurt and anger. "You once told me about a former girlfriend named Maggie. She lives in Phoenix. Is that the Maggie you were thinking of just now?"

"I wasn't thinking about her, Dobi. Saying her name was an innocent slip of my tongue."

"Did you visit Phoenix before you came home?"

"Well, yes, I did. I wanted to see some old friends and check on my estate and club there."

"Was Maggie one of the old friends you saw?"

Hound decided not to lie. He wasn't sure why.

"Yes, I saw Maggie, but a lot of other old friends as well," he answered.

"Did you sleep with her, Hound?"

"Why would you ask me that, Dobi?"

"My intuition is telling me you did! Am I wrong?"

"Dobi, I'm not going to answer that."

"You told me that you would refuse to answer, but you would never lie to me. Are you refusing to answer rather than lie or tell the truth?"

"I'm refusing because it's my right to. I don't feel it's worth answering."

Dobi got up and walked hurriedly to the front door. Hound remained seated at the dining table. When she reached the door, Dobi yelled that she knew the truth and left. Hound began to consider certain things. Maggie hadn't demanded that he sleep with her in return for the huge favor she'd granted him. She had only asked. He had wanted to spend the two nights with her. The reason for having that desire was still unknown to him, but surely it fulfilled some need. He realized he wasn't ready for a committed relationship. He also realized such a relationship was mandatory to keep things progressing with Dobi. He was uncertain about the future, but he knew his intimate relationship with her was over for now. How he ended his thoughts of the incident was that this was for the best.

Hound reminded himself of the letter from the mysterious man who had written it. He retrieved the letter from the safe in his bedroom and sat down to read it again. A decision to call Sir James Thomas Huntington needed to be made. Hound's intelligence said to forget the letter's content, but his instinct said otherwise. He went to the closest phone and dialed the number that had been provided.

"It's wonderful to hear from you, Hound," James said in a cheerful voice. "I've been anxiously waiting for your call."

"It sounds like you were convinced I would call, Mr. Huntington."

"Yes, I was, but you must call me James. Mr. Huntington is much too formal between friends."

"I didn't know we were friends? We don't know each other. We've never met."

"We've never met, but I know a great deal about you. I trust we'll become closer as time goes on and you learn more about me, and naturally, the men I want you to meet."

"What is the purpose for me calling?"

"To let me know if you'd like to visit with me in person and hear all I have to say."

"Do you want to tell me about the men you want me to meet?"

"Yes, Hound. That is the duty they've asked me to perform."

"OK, James. I'll meet and hear what you have to say, but I agree to listen and ask questions, nothing more."

"That's all that is desired from you at our meeting. Then, if you decide to except the invitation of my twelve employers to meet with them, during that time you'll be required to make some paramount decisions regarding what will be expected of you should you accept what will be offered."

"Where do you want me to come for our meeting, James?"

"I wouldn't dream of inconveniencing you with travel. I'll come to you. Your runway and hangar at the ranch will easily accommodate the aircraft I'll arrive in."

"How did you know about my runway and hangar?"

"Hound, I know a great deal about you, but those I represent know much more."

"OK. When would you like to come?"

"How does 9 a.m. the day after tomorrow sound?"

"That's fine. I'll be expecting you. I assume you know where I am."

"Of course. My pilots have already plotted a course and filed a flight plan. I look forward to meeting you in person."

"Same here, James. Do you like to fish? The trout are biting."

"Yes, I do. I'll bring my equipment."

"No need. I'll furnish what you need."

"Splendid! I'll see you day after tomorrow, Hound."

"OK. I'll look forward to that."

Hound had just completed his conversation with James when he heard a loud knock on the front door. Sam had come to deliver some news.

"Good morning, Sam," said Hound as he invited Sam to come in. "What brings you here?"

"There's been some trouble at my bunkhouse."

"What happened?"

"Me and one of my boys caught a couple of teenagers stealing personal items in the bunkhouse. We all left at the usual early time to begin work. Me and Curly forgot some personal equipment needed for work today, so we went back to get it. We caught the two young girls stealing all they could carry when we entered the bunkhouse."

"Girls?"

"Yeah, they're pretty hot looking little cunts too."

"What did you do with them?"

"Gave them both a good ass whipping and locked them in a closet. Curly stayed to keep an eye on the little bitches. I came to find out what you want to do with them."

"I hope you didn't hurt them, Sam."

"Both their asses are probably still smoking, but that's all. We might ought to get back there pretty soon. Curly prefers young meat when he can get it."

"How old are these girls?"

"Not younger than 16 or older than 18, maybe 19."

Curly was sitting in a chair watching the closet when Hound and Sam arrived. The captives were cussing like a couple of sailors, banging on the door with their fists and kicking it with their feet.

"Curly, tell me you didn't sexually assault either or both of them," Hound said calmly.

"Shit! No, but I was tempted."

"Just be glad you didn't."

"Why? Do you think a couple of burglars — thieves — would have called the law?"

"That's not it, dumb ass!" said Sam. "Hound would have dealt with you harshly!"

Curly was surprised at what Sam said.

"Is Sam right, Hound? Would you have been mad at me for fucking a couple of petty thieves?"

"I don't like bullies. A rapist is among the worst type of bully."

Hound didn't say more. Instead, he told Curly to let the girls out of the closet.

They stepped from the closet anxious, afraid and planning to run. However, when they saw Hound standing in front of them, they halted their attempt to escape. Hound politely asked them to take a seat at the long dining table so he could ask a few questions. They did as he asked.

"What are your names?" he asked.

"We ain't telling you shit!" yelled the tall slender blonde. "Just call the cops and let them get us out of here!"

"Nobody is going to call the cops, at least not if you settle down, be more respectful and cooperate by answering my questions."

"Fuck you! Our cooperation would include a lot more than that!"

"What do you mean?"

"You know damn well what I mean. That cocksucker over there, the one called Curly, told us that we'd have to fuck and suck our way around going to jail!"

"Well, Curly was only kidding, weren't you, Curly?"

Curly looked at Sam, who indicated with a nod that he should say yes. He looked at Hound, who was staring at him but smiling.

"Oh, hell yes," said Curly. "I was only kidding."

"Now, Miss, what are the names of you and your friend?"

Hound's voice and manner had a calming effect on the girl. She felt he could be trusted.

"My name is Kelly Wyman, "she said. "My friend is Stacy Bates."

"How old are you young ladies?"

Kelly laughed.

"What's funny, Kelly?" Hound asked.

"Shit! I don't ever remember anyone calling me a lady. I'm seventeen and Stacy is sixteen. Both of our birthdays are in July."

"Mine too. What day?"

"I was born on the twenty-fifth and Stacy on the twenty-seventh."

"I'll be thirty-two on the thirty-first. Looks like the three of us are Leos."

"Yes, looks like it."

Stacy remained still and silent during Hound's conversation with Kelly. She was shorter and was a redhead. Both of the girls were attractive. Hound sensed they were intelligent as well.

"Stacy, would you like to say anything?" asked Hound.

"I'd like to know what you're going to do with Kelly and me."

"Nothing, unless you ladies want a job on the ranch. Do you need a job? By the way, where do you go to school and what grades are you in?"

"We dropped out of school this year. I was a sophomore. Kelly was a junior."

"Why did you drop out?"

"Our parents were killed together in a car crash last New Year. They were drunk and driving home after a night of partying. My dad was driving, lost control of the car and hit a semi-truck head-on."

"I heard about that. Where have you been living, and how have you been buying food and other basics?"

"We lived together at my house until we couldn't make enough money to pay the rent and utilities. The only work we could find didn't pay enough to take care of the basics."

"Is that why you started stealing?"

"Yes, and other things."

"What other things?"

"Let's just say we did what was needed to survive."

"You sold pussy, didn't you?" said Curly, laughing."

"Curly, be quiet," said Hound. "Is that right, Kelly? Did you prostitute yourselves?"

"Only when we had to so we could eat and buy those basics."

"Where have you been living?"

"On the streets and in old vacant houses, barns, any such shelter we could use without being caught."

"Why not stay at the shelter in town?"

"We were afraid we'd be reported as underage minors and put in foster care. Stacy and I are like sisters. We didn't want to risk being separated. Besides, most foster homes are worse than the streets. Were you serious about having a job for us?"

"Sure. Do you have any experience working on a ranch?"

"Well, no, but we're hard workers and willing to learn."

"OK. You'll be doing some dirty jobs to start your learning, but if you want to learn how to be real cowgirls, then you can be taught by some damn good cowboys. You'll be paid based on what you know how to do, as you become able to do it. Your room and board will also be included."

"Where will we sleep?" asked Kelly. "Not in a bunkhouse with a bunch of cowboys who will try to fuck us at every turn!"

"Of course not, but you will take your meals with them."

"OK, then the job sounds good to me."

"What about you, Stacy?"

"Yes, me too."

"Well, all right then, but you have to agree to some conditions before I hire you."

"What?"

"Both of you go back to school and graduate, and no more prostitution or stealing. Add no lying. I don't like a liar."

"You must be Hound?" said Kelly. "The owner of all this?"

"Yep, but only part owner of The Double D."

"I thought so. You're everything we heard you were."

"That's good, I hope."

"Yes, especially the way you look."

The girls agreed to Hound's conditions.

"I need to inform Dobi, the other owner, about you two. She needs to meet you. Come on, we'll go see her now."

"She's not here, Hound," said Sam. "I saw her leaving, driving fast, as I was on my way to get you. I think she was pissed off about something."

"Maybe. Well, ladies, you can meet her later."

Hound had built a large bedroom and bath in the rear of the barn where he set his gym up. He did that just in case another

Boots came along. The girls met the requirements to stay there. He escorted them to the barn and showed them where they would be living. The girls were surprised and delighted with how big, modern and nicely furnished the bedroom and bath were.

"Does this meet your approval, girls?" Hound asked.

"It's wonderful," replied Kelly and Stacy agreed. "Who lived here before?"

"No one has ever lived here. You're the first. It was built in memory of a former ranch hand and special friend who lived in one like this before it burned in a fire."

"What was your friend's name?"

"Boots."

"Where is Boots now?"

"He died."

Hound sent word to all the cowboys that worked for him. He asked that they all meet him for lunch at the main and largest bunkhouse. Kelly and Stacy would be introduced at that time. After everyone had filled their plates and were seated and eating, Hound stood up to address them.

"I know all you cowboys are wondering who the ladies are that are seated next to me," Hound began, "and why they are here. This is Kelly Wyman and Stacy Bates. They have been hired to work on the ranch. They'll be bunking in the quarters at the barn and will take meals at the bunkhouse. Hud, they want to be cowgirls, top hands. I want them trained as such. They're to be treated like any other new hire regarding the work required for a day's pay. I don't expect any of you to go easy on them because they're young women. They need to endure the knocks it takes to be part of our team. However, they are to be given the respect due any woman hired to work here. Any sexual harassment, or other mistreatment from any of you, will result in your termination. There will be no second chances. In turn, they'll behave in a manner that doesn't provoke such treatment, or they will be terminated. I would hope that none of you would ever physically assault them. However, should it ever happen, then you will not like the consequences. Are there any questions?"

"Other than being fired, what are the consequences for the man that physically assaults a female hired hand?" Curly asked, with a smile that seemed to challenge the rule.

"I kill him."

Curly lost his smile. Everyone stopped eating and looked at Hound as they considered what he told Curly. One by one they began finishing their meal. After lunch, Hound left with the girls to drive them to Kelly's old truck that had been left hidden in a patch of trees and bushes on the side of the road that ran in front of the ranch's eastern border. They would return after accompanying Hound to buy clothes needed for their new job and basic personal items thy were short on. The money Hound advanced them for this would be paid back in reasonable amounts from each weekly paycheck.

The cowboys remained in the bunkhouse after Hound and the girls left. They conversed until their lunch break was over.

"Boys, I hope you'll abide by the rules Hound laid down regarding how those girls are to be treated," said Hud. "I agree with the rules and will enforce them."

"Do you agree with the rule that he'll kill anyone who physically assaults them?" asked Curly, smiling again."

"No, but that I wouldn't gamble on him not being serious. He'd have to enforce that rule on his own."

"Shit! I don't believe Hound would kill a man after stating he would in front of so many witnesses!"

"If I were you, I wouldn't bet my life on that, Curly," said Sam."

Curly had seen Hound's revenge before. He knew it was Sam's intention to remind him of that. Sam, Curly and the rest of the biker cowboys were riding alone, returning to work for the remainder of the day.

"Sam, I wouldn't fear Hound could do me in," said Curly. "I'd be ready when I saw him coming."

"You're a damn fool, Curly! You'd never see him coming! You need to understand that Hound is a man to never fuck with. I've heard many true stories about him from Maggie, Bear and others. Besides, I know how to judge a man's salt minus any stories. Hound is the only man I've ever met that would cause me to never challenge him. Fuck! Even if I bested him, having to live with the difference would be worse than death."

Curly and the others feared and respected Sam. That was why they followed him. They took what he said about Hound as absolute gospel.

The girls ate supper with the cowboys in the bunkhouse that evening. They wondered why none of them wanted to engage in a lot of conversation. It seemed being afraid to say the wrong thing was a concern. Kelly knew what was going on and decided to break the ice.

"God damn, guys!" she shouted, smiling. "Just because you can't fondle or fuck us don't mean you can't talk to us!"

The cowboys saw the reality of what she said and laughed. A friendly conversation resulted.

The girls were in their quarters that night getting ready for bed. They wanted to get plenty of sleep in preparation for their first day of work. Dobi hadn't yet returned after being gone all day. Hound decided to wait until the next day to tell her about the two new hands. He had a late supper and then sat visiting with Pardner for a time before going to bed.

19

Dobi didn't return the next day. She got home again the following morning. She noticed Hound's truck heading in the direction of the landing strip and hangar. She had planned to talk to him but assumed he might be leaving on a trip. She had no way of knowing that Hound was on his way to greet a mysterious visitor.

The jet carrying Sir James Thomas Huntington landed on schedule. Hound walked to greet James as he got off the plane. He extended his arm and the two men shook hands.

"Hello, you must be Hound," James said, smiling. "I would recognize you anywhere."

"Nice to meet you, James. How was your flight here?"

"Nice, but long."

"Where did you travel from?"

"From London. My home is there. However, I'm not there as much as I would like. As you might think, I travel a lot."

"Actually, I don't know what to think about who you are, or what you do."

"Of course, but that's why I've traveled a great distance to meet with you. I look forward to telling you everything you need and want to know about me. What will be most significant, however, is what you learn about the men I have come to represent."

"Yes, you're right."

"You certainly have beautiful scenery here."

"I agree. Have you ever been to Montana?"

"No. I understand you own eighteen thousand acres of quality ranch land, Hound."

"I own fifty-one percent of the three-thousand-acre Double D Ranch."

"Yes, I know that too."

"You seem to know a lot about my business here."

"Hound, I know a lot about all the businesses you own. A lot about you personally as well. That's why I'm here."

"Well, let's get your luggage and go to my home. I hope you'll be comfortable there during your stay."

"I will be leaving as soon as our business has been completed. That should be by late afternoon. The men who sent me to you will be anxious to hear what the outcome of our meeting was. They want my report to be in person. They insist on knowing as soon as possible."

"I suppose that means you won't have time to catch and eat a few of those trout I told you about."

"That's true. Perhaps you would extend me another invitation at a more convenient time."

"Perhaps. Are you hungry? I've had breakfast, but it wouldn't be a problem to prepare something for you."

"Thank you, but I enjoyed a nice meal before I arrived. Will we be afforded privacy at your home?"

"Yes."

James's pilots would remain with his jet until he was ready to leave.

"Have you ever driven in a pickup truck before, James?" asked Hound.

"I suppose I've been in all kinds of vehicles before, but yes, I have been in a pickup before. Why do you ask?"

"Your mode of dress and manner wouldn't make me think so. You strike me as a man that is accustomed to more elegant forms of transportation."

"Hound, I know you believe a book should never be judged by its cover. If I were to judge you in that fashion, then you would be seen as a common man. Handsome and charismatic, but common, none the less. We both know you are much more than that. So very much more."

As Hound drove James to his home, he sensed that James was likely the most intelligent human being he had ever met. There was no doubt that he was very wealthy. He also became convinced that whatever James had come to tell him would be the truth, but he was unsure if hearing that truth would be a good thing.

Once inside the large log home, the two men elected to sit at the dining table to have their visit. When asked if he wanted a beverage, James asked Hound if he had tea.

"I have ordinary black tea," replied Hound, "nothing fancy."

"The type you have is my favorite. May I have it hot?"

"Of course."

Hound made the tea for his guest and coffee for himself. When he returned from the kitchen with both, he sat across the table from James and the meeting began.

"Well, James, my time is yours. What have you traveled all this way to tell me? I'll sit here and listen until you've finished."

"Excellent. Hound, as I have already said, I am here on behalf of the twelve wealthiest men in the world," James began. "I have also indicated that makes them the most powerful men on the planet. As individuals they have substantial power, but that power has limits. As a group, combining all the wealth each has, well, their power is virtually without limit. These men comprise a secret organization whose membership is known only by them. They want to personally meet with you. The reason is for interviewing you as the possible thirteenth member of the organization, which for the many years of their existence has always been twelve. You may refuse membership after, but you're required to accept a meeting with them at a time and location they have already chosen, 9 a.m., July 31, on your thirty-second birthday. You will meet me in London on July 29. I will fly you to the location where the meeting will be held. After the meeting, I will return you to London and you will carry on with whatever decision you have made. Now, you may ask questions. I know you have some."

"You say that I'm required to meet with them," said Hound. "I was under the impression I had a choice."

"You had a choice until you invited me here to meet with and give you specific information. In doing so, you obligated yourself to take the next step."

"You didn't tell me that, James. Why?

"Hound, these men intend to meet with you. That's just a fact you must except."

"And if I refuse, what happens?"

"Consequences you don't want."

"What happens if I meet with them and decline membership in their secret organization, or did you lie to me about having a choice?"

"I told you the truth. You are required to hear what they have to say, and then you can accept or decline. However, you are forever sworn to secrecy about everything they tell you regardless of your decision."

"I suppose consequences would be imposed if I did otherwise."

"Hound, it would mean the death of your family, friends, everyone you are associated with or care about."

"James, I don't like being forced by threats to do anything."

"Do you believe what I am telling you?"

"My intelligence and instinct are both in agreement, so yes, I do."

"Good, then shall we meet in London on the twenty-ninth?"

"It would seem so. I'll be there."

"Excellent. Hound, I have enjoyed my time with you, but the purpose of our meeting has been completed. I must leave and deliver my report of its outcome to my employers."

"I'm sure they're certain I'll meet with them."

"Not at all. Perhaps if you were predictable when faced with a threat they would be. However, they know you are not motivated by threats."

"What do you mean?"

"You are a man without fear, but not without excellent insight and judgement. They were right about that and will be happy when it is verified to them."

"What makes them think I'm fearless?"

"They know many things about you. That you are without fear is one of them."

Hound drove James to his jet. They shook hands again and said goodbye. The jet took off and quickly vanished from site. He was angry that he'd been manipulated in such a manner but believed himself obligated, none the less.

Hound saw Dobi's truck parked at her house as he returned to his. He decided to stop and inform her about Kelly and Stacy. When he knocked on her front door, she didn't answer. He would wait still longer to provide her with the news.

It was in the early afternoon that day when he answered a knock to his front door.

"May I come in, Hound?" asked Dobi, unsure of the answer.

"Sure, Dobi, please come in."

He asked her to take a seat in the living room.

"What can I do for you, Dobi?" he asked.

"After what happened, I'm surprised to hear you ask me that, Hound. Don't you think we need to talk?"

"That depends on what you want to talk about."

"I want to talk about Maggie. I need to know why you slept with her."

"I never said I slept with Maggie. You did."

"Are you telling me you didn't?"

"I'm not telling you anything. I don't intend to have any further discussion about Maggie."

Hound saw Dobi was quickly becoming troubled. He was certain he knew why.

"You didn't come home last night," he said. "Maybe you felt like getting even with me."

Dobi began to tear a bit and her voice broke as she spoke.

"I spent the night with a man, Hound!" she said in an excited manner.

"OK, but why are you telling me?"

"Because it wasn't what I intended to do. I went to the Broken Spur and had too much to drink. I ran into an old boyfriend and went home with him. I was sure you had sex with Maggie and, well, maybe getting even was part of it, but I wouldn't have gone through with it if I'd been sober. You didn't sleep with Maggie, did you?"

"Like I said, Dobi, I won't discuss Maggie any further. However, let me ask you if the man you fucked last night played a major role in saving your life and your ranch?"

Dobi was beginning to cry.

"No, of course not! What the fuck does that have to do with anything?"

"Maggie did a lot to save us both. That's what!"

"Hound, I may have made a mistake about you and Maggie. If I did, I'm so sorry! You'll never know how sorry I am about being unfaithful to you! Please forgive me! Can you?"

"Forgive you for what? There's nothing to forgive. You wanted to do something and did it. If I wanted to fuck an old flame, then I would. I don't care to hear any more about it. Besides, the only reason you're confessing is because you know that I'd find out sooner or later."

"What happens now, Hound?"

"What do you mean?"

"What happens now between us?"

"You'll live your life the way that pleases you and I'll do the same."

"Can we start over, put all this behind us?"

"Sure, that's what I meant."

"Does that mean our relationship is over?"

"Let's take a time out and think about everything."

Hound politely escorted her to the door.

"When you find the time, look up the two new cowgirls I hired and introduce yourself," he said, smiling as he bid Dobi goodbye and shut the door behind her.

Dobi said nothing. She couldn't find the appropriate words to express what was on her mind and in her heart.

Hound had made a decision he felt was necessary. There was no way to know how the secret mystery meeting in London would change his life, or what path it would put him on. Whatever the path, it was likely that Dobi couldn't travel it with him or would want to.

The month of June passed quickly. It was now the second week of July. Operations were normal and business as usual on all ranch property. Dobi and Hound carried on a friendly business relationship, but it was strained at times. Hound stayed away from any contact with her a much as possible. She looked for every opportunity to meet with him, knowing he still cared for her, but unable to determine the reason for his reluctance to admit it. Not asking was the best thing to do. Dobi hoped that the wall he'd built between them would fall after a time and they could start over.

Hound was visiting with Casey at her home to discuss the sale of a number of cattle. She could have a very comfortable life of leisure from the money he paid her for Jack's property and the money returned to her that Jack had hidden. However, Casey chose to stay in her old home and run the ranch as Hound's second-in-command.

"So, Hound, I think it's a good business decision to sell the cattle at this time," said Casey. "What do you think?"

"Yep, I agree. The price is too good to refuse. I wish the buyer would take the whole herd at that price."

"That would be nice, but he doesn't have the money to buy them all, or the land to accommodate that many head of livestock. Hound, is there something on your mind that's troubling you?"

"I've got an important meeting to attend in a few days. I don't know how to prepare for it."

"Where's the meeting? What's it about?"

"It's not important. Never mind."

"OK, but if there's anything I can do to help, then all you have to do is ask. I hope you know that."

Hound looked at her for a moment and didn't respond.

"What are you thinking now, Hound?" she asked. "You seem to be in deep thought about something."

He smiled.

"I was wondering about something that's been on my mind since I first saw you," he replied.

"What might that be?"

"Casey, is your pussy as good as you think it is?"

The question was unexpected and caught her off guard. She wasn't sure if it was meant as a forward compliment or simply a rude insult.

"Well, you can bet it is!" she replied rather loudly and with conviction. "I've never had a man tell me otherwise!"

"I want to fuck you, Casey. How do you respond to that?"

Again, the question was unexpected, but one she easily and quickly answered.

"You son of a bitch! I've wanted to fuck you since the first time we met. I offered myself to you once and you weren't interested. I was convinced that was the end of it. What changed your mind?"

"It wasn't the right time then. It is now."

"I sure as hell don't know what that means, but who cares. Do you think you can keep up?"

"I promise to give you my best."

Casey smiled, took him by his hand and led him to the bedroom. She wasted no time in stripping to the nude, and then hurried to help him do the same. His large cock was fully erect when she finished. She took a few steps back to view him from head to toe.

"God damn! Hound, you are a magnificent hunk of man," she said, beginning to breathe harder. "Perfect in every way."

He kissed her passionately as he gently positioned her on her back in the bed and began what was needed to keep his promise. For the next hour he provided his best performance. He could tell from her verbal and physical responses that his promise was being kept. After her final orgasm, Casey was exhausted, but she knew he hadn't reached an orgasm.

"Hound, can you finish soon? I would welcome you to go for as long as you like, but I'm getting very sore and tender."

He stopped, kissed her passionately, and then rolled from atop her. He pulled her close beside him. She laid her head on his shoulder as she ran her hand softly over his chest.

"Did I keep up to your satisfaction, Casey?" he asked softly.

"Damn! I figured you to be a real stud, but shit! Not more man than I could satisfy. I'm sorry."

"No problem, it was my intention to make sure you were. That was most important to me."

"Well, you sure as hell did what you intended. I hope you'll give me a chance to do you the same courtesy soon."

"So, I'll get another invitation to enjoy some good pussy?"

"Hound, you have a standing invitation to fuck me at any time, just not for a day or so!"

They both began to laugh.

"Just to put your mind at ease," she said, "don't worry about Dobi finding out about this. I won't say a word to anyone, ever."

"Dobi and I aren't together now. If we were, then this wouldn't have happened. However, it might be a good idea to keep it between us so whomever you're seeing doesn't get upset and cause a problem."

"I suppose that's a good idea, but you still have that standing invitation. For what it's worth, I'd make you my one and only at any time you'd do the same for me."

"That's good to know, something to consider. I'll give it some thought."

"Good, I hope you do."

When he left Casey, Hound drove into town. He had an appointment with his good friend and attorney, Beth Weaver. After his meeting with James, Hound decided to have a will made to leave all his properties in Montana to Dobi. Stipulations were included that none of the pay rates and benefits being given to employees would be changed unless it would better them, or financial circumstances made it impossible to maintain such pay rates and benefits. He had already taken care of a will pertaining to all of his other interests in other states. When he arrived in Beth's office, she welcomed him in the usual warm and affectionate way.

"It's good to see you as always, Hound," Beth said cheerfully.

"Same here, my friend. I suppose you're still as busy as a bee."

"Hound, I can't seem to hire enough help to staff my practice. It's growing so fast."

"That's a good thing though, right?"

"Of course. You played a big part in getting the growth started. I'll never forget all you've done for me."

"I was glad to do it. Have you got my will ready for signing?"

"Yes, I told you it would be ready and it is."

Beth presented the papers on her desk and Hound began reading and signing them.

"Hound, can I ask you something?" said Beth.

"Sure, what is it?"

"Are you worried that something might happen to you?"

"No. Why would you think that, Beth?"

"Well, you contact me out of the blue to prepare a will for you within a couple of days. That just seemed to imply some sort of urgency."

"Not at all. I've been meaning to get it done for a long time. I plan to be around a long time. However, tomorrow is never guaranteed to anyone. Besides, I plan to start being away more and will be short of time to deal with such matters in the future."

"OK, if you say so, but don't be away any more than necessary. Everyone would miss you. How does Dobi feel about you being away more?"

"She'll be fine, staying busy taking care of the ranch, her vet practice and the charities she's overseeing."

Hound was concerned about the meeting in England he'd obligated himself to attend. He was confident that James had told him the truth about what he could expect, but not that James had been told the truth regarding the information he'd delivered. Hound decided to put all his affairs in order just in case the meeting resulted in truth not yet revealed.

After signing all the paperwork, Hound thanked Beth for expediting the will's preparation and left. His next stop was the courthouse for a meeting with the new judge in his chamber. A new sheriff and prosecuting attorney had also been elected. Hound had invited them to attend the meeting. They were waiting with the judge in his chamber when he arrived. Hound sat in a chair in front of the judge's desk. The sheriff and prosecutor were seated to his right.

"Gentlemen, it's good to see you," said Hound. "It's been a while since we were all together, and I thought it time to meet again."

"It's good to see you as well, Hound," replied the judge. "Do we have business to discuss, or is this to be a casual visit?"

"Casual. Since each of you was elected, I've never told any of you how proud I am for the honesty and integrity you all show in doing your jobs."

"Thanks, Hound. None of us would have our jobs if it weren't for your support during our campaigns."

"I was happy to do it. It was time for the change."

"Naturally, you realize the things you did behind the scenes to get us elected wasn't legal. How does that fit into our code of honesty and integrity?"

"Well, let's just say sometimes you have to be a bit bad to produce a lot of good."

They all smiled and nodded in agreement.

"Is that all you wanted to say to us, Hound?" asked the judge. "That you're proud of us?"

"Yes, and that I want you to never compromise who you are or the way you do your jobs. I may not always be around to keep an eye on you, but a lot of other folks will."

"What do you mean, you may not always be around? Are you going somewhere?"

"Well, I'm taking a vacation soon. I don't know how long I might be away. Hell! I may find a place to live that I like better than here. If I do, then I'll stay awhile."

"You have a lot to look after here, your large ranch properties, not to mention the bank and other business interests you own."

"Here, like everywhere all over the country, I have the right people to take care of my interests for me."

"Where do you plan to go first on this vacation?"

"England. There's someone I know there that I haven't seen or heard from in a long time. I need to tend to some business as well."

"Shit! Hound, you won't find a better life in either of those places than you have here."

"You're right, but perhaps a much different one.

20

On the morning of July 27, Hound was at home packing for his trip to London. Pardner seemed to know his best friend would soon be leaving. He sat and stared at Hound as though he could sense the deep thought his master was in.

Dobi had liked Kelly and Stacy since first meeting them. She made herself like a big sister to the girls. They also viewed her as a mentor. Both young ladies were making good progress to learn all aspects of ranching. Some of their work time was spent helping Dobi in her vet practice and at the shelters in town. Hound had asked all the women to have breakfast with him that morning. No one on the ranch knew he would be leaving the next morning and that he didn't know how long it would be before he returned, if ever. The ladies arrived on time at 8 a.m. Hound had a hearty breakfast prepared and waiting.

During breakfast, Hound announced his plan to be away for an indefinite period. He asked that Dobi and the two girls look after Pardner while he was away. They were happy to comply but not pleased with the news of his leaving. Dobi was very upset but didn't let it show. She would speak with Hound in private after breakfast when the girls had returned to their ranch work. When they had left, Dobi stayed to help clean up.

"What's going on, Hound? Why are you leaving? Where are you going?" she asked anxiously.

"I'm just getting away for a time. I'm not sure of all the places I might go, or when I'll be back, if I come back."

"God damn it! Hound, why would you not come back?"

"I don't care to say why, but you'll be in charge of all my business interests while I'm gone. I've informed all concerned parties that you'll be the boss until I return."

He handed her a copy of the will Beth had prepared. When she saw what it was, Dobi became frantic with concern.

"Hound! What the fuck is going on?" she asked at a level just short of a scream. "You think something is going to happen to you, that you might die!"

"Not at all, but it is a smart move to always have business affairs in order just in case."

"All right, then tell me why it's necessary for you to leave. Is it because of what happened between you and me, that I made a horrible mistake and slept with another man? Why can't you forgive me and let's start over? I would do that for you! Damn it! I'm in love with you now and forever. I can't believe your feelings for me are gone!"

"They're not, Dobi. What I have to do has nothing to do with you, or us, just me."

"You're not going to tell me a God-damned thing, are you?"

"No, it's best you don't know. Just promise to take care of things, especially Pardner."

She saw it was no use to beg him to stay, or for a reason why he was leaving.

"OK, I promise, but wherever you go, whatever you do, for as long as you have to be away, never forget that I love you. I'll be waiting for you when you get back. I don't care how long it takes. Will you call, or write to me?"

"If and when I can."

"Hound, can you ever forgive and forget the mistake I made?"

"Dobi, we'll have to wait and talk about that after I return. I can't answer you now."

"Then get your ass home as soon as possible. Can I stay with you until you leave?"

"Let's leave things the way they are for now, Dobi."

Dobi didn't want to hear that, but she agreed. Tears filled her eyes as she walked to the door and left.

Hound took off in his jet at 4 a.m. the next morning. He didn't want anyone present to say goodbye and see him off. Dobi was awakened by the sound of the jet engines in the distance and knew he was gone. She began to cry louder and longer than ever before.

Hound landed at a private airport on the outskirts of London. He had purposely arrived early in order to get some sleep after the long flight. Not knowing what to expect after James arrived to escort him to his next destination, he wanted to be rested and alert.

Hound's jet was parked in a hangar location that had been reserved for him, and then an airport employee showed him where he could shower and have a meal if he so desired. After he'd showered and had something to eat, Hound returned to the bedroom in his plane. He lay down on the bed and fell quickly to sleep.

Several hours later, he was awakened by the alarm clock at the side of his bed. James was due to arrive in an hour. Hound dressed in a country club casual attire, as James had suggested, and then went to the airport lounge to wait for James to arrive.

James arrived in the lounge precisely on time.

"Hello, Hound," he said with a smile. "I hope your flight here was good. You must have been tired when you arrived after piloting your aircraft all this way."

"I was tired, but I enjoy being a pilot, so I didn't mind. I got here early so I could sleep a bit before I met you."

"That's fine. However, you will have time to rest and relax when we reach your final destination. You'll be free to do what you like until you meet your hosts for dinner at 6 p.m. on the thirty-first. you will find many activities to enjoy until then."

"How far is this destination? Where am I going from here?"

"Actually, it will only require a twenty-minute flight in my jet to reach where you are going. You'll be a guest at the most beautiful estate in all of England.

Hound walked with James toward the waiting jet.

"I need to get my luggage," Hound told James.

"Leave your luggage; you won't be needing it. Everything you'll need is waiting for you at the estate."

"What about appropriate clothing attire?"

"Everything you'll need."

James and Hound took off in the jet, reached an altitude of only ten thousand feet, and then it began to descend. As the aircraft was on its landing approach, Hound looked out a window and saw a very beautiful, well-groomed landscape below.

"Is what I see the property belonging to the estate, James?" asked Hound.

"Yes, part of one thousand acres. The castle is located in the center of the property."

"An authentic castle?"

"No, a newer, much more modern and elegant version."

The aircraft landed and then taxied to the front of a large hangar. Estate personnel were waiting to begin making sure the time Hound spent there was the most enjoyable and memorable of his life thus far. A very beautiful young woman greeted him with an embrace and soft kiss on the cheek after he was off the plane. She was tall, slender and had an accent Hound knew was unmistakably British.

"It is a great honor and privilege to finally meet you, sir," she told him.

"Really? Why is it an honor and privilege, miss?"

"I have heard so many exciting and remarkable things about you; everyone here has. Sir, my name is Anna. I volunteered to be your concierge during your stay."

"Well, it's a pleasure to meet you, Anna, but my first request is that you call me Hound, not sir."

"If that is your wish, then it would be my pleasure, Hound. I have a car waiting to drive you to the estate residence. You can get settled in your room. Afterward, if you wish, I will take you on a tour of the grounds. There are many things available that you might enjoy doing during your stay."

"Like what?"

"Swimming, sailing, tennis, horseback riding, skeet shooting. There is also an indoor and outdoor shooting and archery range. Those are a few of the activities you might like."

As Anna escorted Hound to the waiting luxury car, James walked with them a short distance.

"Hound, I will now leave you in the capable hands of Anna. We won't see each other again until I return you back to London. Tell Anna when you're ready to leave."

"Won't that be after I meet with my hosts on the thirty-first?"

"If you wish, but you are invited to stay longer if you'd like. By the way, if for any reason Anna is not satisfactory as your go-to companion, then another will be provided."

James smiled, turned and walked back to his jet. It would return him to London where he would stay at his home until Hound summoned him. The driver of the car offered Hound a hearty welcome as he opened the door for him and Anna to enter the rear seat. Anna insisted that Hound enter first. He did and then she followed and seated herself only a few inches from him. Hound was impressed with the property's landscape he saw as the car moved at an average speed toward the estate home. When the home appeared in the distance, it truly resembled a large, magnificent castle.

"This is a most impressive place, Anna," said Hound as the car came to a stop in the driveway in front.

"Yes, it is, Hound, but wait until you see the inside of the castle and the rest of the property. There are only a few estates in the world that compare to this one."

"I'd bet there are eleven others that do."

Anna smiled, but that was her only response to his comment. The driver quickly exited the car and opened the rear passenger door. Anna walked with Hound to the front entrance where an older, very proper, distinguished and well–dressed gentleman was waiting to greet them. Anna introduced him as Andrew, the man in charge of all the estate's personnel.

"Welcome, sir," said Andrew."

"Andrew, our guest prefers to be called by his nickname, Hound."

"Very good, Miss Anna. It's a pleasure to meet and welcome you here, Hound."

"Thank you, Andrew. It's a pleasure to meet you as well."

Hound and Anna followed Andrew inside, down a long, wide foyer into a gigantic reception living area. Where the foyer ended, Hound saw a line of men and women dressed in different types of uniform apparel. As he proceeded down the line, Andrew introduced him to all the castle's staff. The chefs, kitchen staff, butlers and maids all did their best to make the guest of honor feel welcome and at home.

Hound looked in awe at the way the area he was in had been furnished. He could see at a glance that the furniture was very expensive. So were the paintings hanging on the walls and all the other items that decorated the room.

As Anna escorted him down a long wide hallway to a stairway leading to the level where his room was located, Hound saw even more valuable furnishings.

"Hound, you seem impressed with the way the castle is furnished," remarked Anna.

"Yes, what I've seen is breathtaking."

"I have to agree with you. The entire castle is furnished in a similar fashion, but no two items are the same."

"How large is this mansion, Anna?"

"I don't know the square feet. Under roof it has fifty bedroom suites, two libraries, three dens, one large main kitchen, two smaller kitchens, I can't remember how many pantries and storage rooms, and two laundries. There's an indoor gym that has a variety of exercise equipment; Olympic size swimming pool; jogging track; and tennis, racket and basketball courts. There's also a small movie theatre and bowling alley. There's a large main dining room and two others of a lesser size. In addition to the large reception and living area you were just in, there are two others of a lesser size. I can't remember all I've said. I hope I gave you a total description of the mansion's layout."

"Well, if you didn't it was close enough, Anna. How much do you know about the owner of all this?"

"I see him when I'm hired to be here, but he rarely interacts with anyone except Andrew and William, the gentleman in charge of all things on the estate, separate from the mansion. I'm not certain how much they know about him beyond. They've never said, and I haven't asked."

"How were you hired for your job?"

"I responded to an ad in the newspaper. I work on a call basis, only when I'm needed."

"Do you have a regular job?"

"I do modeling work, but I wouldn't say it's on a regular basis. When I do model, the pay is very good, so I don't need to work full time."

"Are you paid well when you work here?"

"To be honest, I make more when I'm called here than when I work equal time as a model. A lot more, and I'm paid very well as a model."

"That question was none of my business. I apologize for asking."

"It's fine, Hound. Part of my job is to answer your questions honestly. You're free to ask anything you like."

"How often are you hired to work here?"

"Usually whenever there is some type of important meeting that includes a party before or after."

"I assume very important guests attend those meetings and parties?"

"I'm sure they are."

"Do you notice that the same eleven men always attend, in addition to the other guests?"

"I believe so. Why?"

"I was just wondering. Did you ever have conversation with any or all of them?"

"No. I usually meet and converse with many, if not all, the other guests, but never them."

"Why not?"

"They, nor my employer, are ever present at the parties. I assume they only participate in the meetings conducted with the male guests."

"Are the guests always only male?"

"I've never seen a female attend."

"OK, then I assume you're not the only woman hired to entertain the guests."

"That's right."

"You're the only one here now because I'm the only guest."

"Well, yes, that's correct. I've never heard of a single guest ever being invited here before. You must be very special and important, or else the VIP treatment wouldn't be given to you. I was called to entertain only you. If those eleven other men show up, then that will indeed make you a very important guest. Can you tell me why you are here?"

"No, because I don't know. What does your entertaining of me include, Anna?"

Anna smiled. She had taken his question to be naïve.

"I'm here to provide any service that will add to the pleasure of your stay here, Hound," she replied, "but I'm sure you knew that."

"Yes, I suppose you're right."

"Then, why did you feel it was necessary to ask?"

"I was hoping I might be wrong."

"Why?"

"You're a very sultry woman. I would have enjoyed sleeping with you, but only if it was the result of a natural desire on your part to do so. I don't care to be intimate with a woman who has been bought for me."

Anna didn't expect his response and certainly not that it would be made in such a rude manner. However, it was her duty to overlook the comment as if he'd never made it.

"Hound, would you prefer I not be your liaison while you are here?" she asked. "Andrew can arrange for someone to be your guide if that's all you require. Someone you will like."

"No, I want you to stay, Anna. I didn't say you weren't liked; I only said I wouldn't sleep with you. With that settled, we should get along just fine."

"Well, if that's your wish, then I'm happy to comply, Hound."

"Those eleven men that always show up, from the way they dress, or by their physical appearance, could you tell where they might be from?"

"The owner of this estate seems to be the leader, so he is British. I know another is German and one is Italian. I'm not certain about the others. Why do you want to know? You're here to meet with them and my employer, aren't you?"

"Maybe, maybe not, but it would be a good idea if you didn't voice your curiosity to anyone."

"Of course. I'm smart enough to know that."

When they reached Hound's room, Anna unlocked the door and allowed him to enter first. It was a huge area. As expected, it was elegantly furnished. The private bath was as large as his bedroom in Montana. Anna led him into the spacious walk-in closet. There he found shoes and clothing for all occasions, each in his exact size.

"Does everything here meet your satisfaction, Hound?" asked Anna.

"How could it be otherwise? "

"I understand. Your host certainly intends to make sure you enjoy being here. It would be a dream come true to have, on a permanent basis, the lifestyle that has been provided to you during the time you're here."

"Indeed, a dream come true for most people, I suppose, but that kind of lifestyle doesn't come without a paramount cost to the individual who lives it."

"What do you mean?"

Hound remembered what James had said earlier, "with great power comes great responsibility."

"I don't mean anything, Anna," replied Hound. "I was just thinking out loud."

"What would you like to do now, Hound? We have some time before dinner is served. By the way, are you hungry now? Did you have lunch before your arrival?"

"I'll be fine until dinner. What time will it be served?"

"At the time you request."

"What time does my host usually dine in the evening?"

"I don't know, but he's not here now. I was told he would arrive late tomorrow night. I was also told he would meet with you during lunch on the thirty-first of July, the day after tomorrow. I'm afraid you're stuck with me as company until then, but as I told you, there are many wonderful activities to enjoy while you wait. What would you enjoy doing for the rest of the afternoon?"

"What are we having for dinner tonight?"

"Whatever you want."

"What is your favorite meal? I assume you'll be joining me for dinner."

"Of course, if you want me to. However, I will dine separately if you prefer to be alone."

"Don't be ridiculous. I would welcome your company and the good conversation. Now, what is your favorite meal?"

"I enjoy a nice steak with all the trimmings."

"Anna, so do I. It looks like enjoying a nice steak is something we have in common. I guess the first thing I should do this afternoon is inform the chef what to serve for dinner. Next, I would enjoy a tour of the estate grounds. I understand they cover one thousand acres."

"Yes, it is large. Where do you live?"

"On a ranch in Montana."

"That sounds exciting! Are you a real cowboy?"

"I'm only part cowboy, but the hired hands who work on the ranches are real cowboys — the best."

"You said ranches. Do you own more than one?"

"I own one that is fifteen thousand acres and fifty-one percent of another that is three thousand acres, but that's only in Montana. I have a corporation that owns ranches and farms all over the U.S. I'm not sure what the current number of acres all of them add up to. New properties are added from time to time that I don't find out about until I meet with the corporation's CEO."

"I assumed you were wealthy. That's likely the reason you were invited here. I've never seen anyone here that didn't look or act wealthy. However, you're different from the others I've met."

"How am I different?"

"Well, you aren't a snob and don't feel you're better than a commoner. If I had met you anywhere other than here, say in a café, or just on the street, I would have assumed you were simply an everyday, average, common man. Naturally, I'm referring to financial status. Nothing else about you is common at all."

"How so?"

"Your physical features and charismatic personality are the most alluring I've ever experienced. I can honestly say that I've never met a more handsome man."

"Well, Anna, if you mean that, then I'm very flattered."

"I assure I mean it, Hound. You don't feel like you're better than the rest of us because of that either. I would guess you own more businesses than ranching and farming?"

"You would be correct, but I don't care to discuss businesses. Let's speak with the chef about dinner, and then you take me on that tour."

"Of course, as you wish."

A car and driver were standing by to drive Hound on his tour. Anna was a perfect guide, giving details regarding the many things seen and places visited that afternoon. Whatever Hound saw was most impressive. All the land was beautifully landscaped, kept clean and well groomed. The maintenance and recreational equipment were the best money could buy. Every building was elegantly designed.

The tour lasted until 6 p.m., but Hound didn't see everything on the estate. There were simply too many places to visit in the length of time available. Anna told him she had made sure he was taken to all the best and most impressive sites.

"Well, what did you think of the estate property, Hound?" Anna asked after the tour ended and they were driving back to the mansion.

"I've never seen a more beautiful, impressive property."

"I have to agree, nor have I."

After arriving back at the mansion, Hound retired to his room to shower and dress for the dinner he had scheduled for 7:30. Anna had inquired how she should dress for dinner. He told her that casual and comfortable would be the attire. She smiled, nodded in agreement and said she would call for him at the door of his room to accompany him to the formal dining room at 7:20.

When they arrived in the dining room, Andrew, the chef and several house attendants were waiting to greet them. Andrew seated Anna at one end of the long table and prepared to seat Hound at the other end.

"Andrew, if you don't mind, I would prefer to sit across from Anna at the end," said Hound. "Conversation will be easier that way."

"Of course, if that is your desire."

"Andrew, have you and everyone else here had dinner?"

"No, we will eat later, after you and Anna have finished."

"What are you having?"

"The chef has prepared enough of what you ordered to include the staff."

"That's great. Then I'd like to invite you and everyone else to join Anna and me for dinner."

"Hound, that is most kind and gracious of you, but such would not be proper in that you are a guest of our employer. He would frown on us for accepting, but thank you for the invitation."

"Andrew, is it your duty to ensure my visit is as enjoyable as possible?"

"Yes, of course."

"OK, then I would greatly enjoy it if you and the others would join me for dinner."

"Andrew, if our guest desires it, then our employer would frown on your refusal to provide it," said Anna, smiling and nodding an approval of Hound's request.

Since arriving and first meeting Anna, Hound's instinct told him that she was more than she claimed or appeared to be. When Andrew didn't hesitate to agree with her, this was further evidenced. The staff was both surprised and impressed when Hound and Anna pitched in to help them bring all the food to the dining table and add the china and silverware needed to accommodate the additional dinner guests.

During dinner, Hound made it a point to make casual conversation with each individual and get better acquainted with them. They were all nervous at first. This was the first time any of them had been invited to socialize with a guest. Because Hound was the first single guest to ever be there, they assumed his visit held significant importance. This added to their nervousness. Knowing this, Hound set to the task of calming all apprehension. Soon the atmosphere was one of a relaxed and enjoyable dinner shared by friends. After dinner, everyone enjoyed another glass of wine and the conversation continued for another hour.

It was after 9:30 when Hound announced he would excuse himself and retire for the night. Anna escorted him to his room.

"Hound, you are indeed a remarkable and exceptional man," Anna said as they reached his room.

"I'm just a man, Anna. No better than most, but worse than some."

"The fact that you feel that way, considering all you've accomplished at soon to be age thirty-two, speaks volumes about you."

"You speak as if you know more about me than I thought, Anna."

"I was given a great deal of information about you, Hound. That's why I personally volunteered to be your go-to person while you were here. What I was told intrigued me and sparked my curiosity. I wanted to meet and spend time getting to know the man called Hound better."

"You're not simply a beautiful woman who's a model part time and part time escort for guests here, are you, Anna?"

"Actually, no, I'm not, but you sensed that, didn't you?"

"I suppose so, but I would like to know the truth about you and the complete reason you're here."

"All truth will be provided to you at the appropriate time. Don't concern yourself with such matters now. Have a good sleep. We'll talk more tomorrow. If you need anything before morning, just dial the number 2 on the phone in your room. That's the in-house number to my room, which is at the end of the hall."

"When will the appropriate time be?"

"When you have lunch with your host, day after tomorrow on your birthday. Incidentally, I hear he has a wonderful birthday present to offer you."

"Really, what might that be?"

"Never mind. I wouldn't want to spoil your surprise. Good night, Hound."

"Good night to you, Anna, if that's your real name. Is it?"

"Yes, it is, Hound."

Hound watched Anna as she walked to and entered her room. He knew she was aware his eyes were following her.

Hound was up the next morning at 6 a.m. He dressed in a set of the workout clothing that had been provided for him and went to the gym. He had just started his normal regimen when Anna arrived.

"May I join you, Hound?" she asked.

"Sure, I'd welcome a workout partner."

Anna stood looking at Hound's splendid physic. He had removed his sleeveless shirt and wore only lightweight gym shorts. She couldn't keep from admiring what she perceived his body to be, the epitome of physical fitness. His body was perfectly proportioned and muscular.

"Hound, how long have you been working out to have such a beautiful body?" she asked.

"A long time to achieve it and daily to keep it."

Anna was wearing a robe over her workout apparel, which was similar to his. When she removed the robe, it was his turn to admire her. He had assumed she possessed an attractive body, but the type clothing she had been wearing concealed that she also had for a long time been dedicated to having the best body possible. Her arms and legs where solid, revealing just the right amount of muscle. He noticed her breasts were larger than could be determined from the clothes she'd been wearing. He'd never seen a more fetching body since he saw Rita's for the first time.

"Do you like what you see, Hound?" Anna asked."

"Of course. It would appear you've spent considerable time working out."

"A long time to achieve it and daily to keep it. It would seem we have that in common. You look surprised."

"Well, I assumed you had a lovely body, but the clothes you've been wearing have kept the real truth hidden."

"One can never know for sure what's in a package until they open it and see what's inside."

"Well, I suppose you're right. Never judge a book by its cover."

"Right. I don't allow just anyone to know what's beneath my cover."

"If that's true, then you're not really employed here as entertainment for the guests, are you?"

"No, I'm not, Hound. Did you really completely believe I was an escort for hire, a highly paid whore?"

"No, not completely, but you tried hard to make me believe it. Why?"

"I wanted to see what your response would be believing I was hired to provide anything you wanted."

"You wanted to know if I would ask you to sleep with me?"

"Yes."

"Were you testing me for some reason?"

"I've said all that I'm permitted to about that and what my real function is here."

"Why?"

"Because your host doesn't want me to say more."

"So, you do work part time for my host, performing a special duty, or duties."

"No, I have a special duty full time."

Hound completed his usual workout which included a five-mile run. Anna remained competitive through its completion. After showering and dressing, they met for breakfast in one of the smaller dining rooms. Hound said he'd enjoy some skeet shooting and then some handgun practice on the firing range. During both, Anna again remained competitive.

"I can likely do as well as you at most things, Hound," Anna said, laughing.

"Can you piss in a beer bottle without letting a single drop miss entering the bottle?"

Anna began to laugh louder.

"No, I guess you'd be better at pissing in a beer bottle than me!"

They spent the entire day together. Time passed quickly and they both enjoyed their time together. They dined on oysters, lobster and a wonderful white wine that evening. After dinner, they shared another bottle of wine and discussed a series of topics and personal interests. At 10 p.m., Anna suggested Hound go to bed and get some rest. The next day would be a very important one for him.

"Shall we work out together again in the morning, Anna?" asked Hound.

"Yes, but let's sleep in a bit longer. We'll have time to exercise before you meet with your host for lunch at 1 p.m."

"OK, I can probably sleep a bit longer than usual."

This time Hound walked Anna to her room and said good night. This time she watched him walk to his room. He knew she was watching.

Hound was lying in bed, staring at the shadows on the high ceiling in his room. His mind was skipping from one memory to another regarding his current and past life. He still hadn't decided if being there had been based on a good decision or just curiosity. It didn't matter now. He was there and would see his visit through to whatever the result would be. He wasn't sure what the real purpose was for Anna being there. She'd become an unsolved riddle that kept repeating itself over and over in his mind, a piece he hadn't yet found the proper place for in the puzzle.

He closed his eyes in hopes sleep would come soon when he heard the faint sound of what he believed was a knock on his door. He waited to see if he heard it again. When it came, he hurried to the door. He hoped it wasn't Anna. It was.

"I hope I didn't wake you, Hound," she said in almost a whisper.

"It's OK. I wasn't asleep. Is anything wrong?"

"No, but may I come in?"

"Yes, of course."

Anna entered. She walked to the bed and sat on it.

"What can I do for you, Anna? Why are you here?"

She smiled softly at him and then stood up and removed her silk robe. She was wearing nothing beneath it.

"I want you to make love to me, Hound," she stated most sincerely. "I've never desired anything as much as to have you inside me."

Hound stood looking at her nude body. His erection bulged and showed itself above the waistband of his briefs.

"It would appear you desire the same as me," she said softly.

"Anna, of course I do, but I know little about you. I consider myself an intelligent man. I'm sure sleeping with you would be an extremely pleasurable experience. However, it could be a mistake that I would regret, we both would regret."

Hound always embraced what he learned long ago: if something seems too good to be true, then it usually is. He never dove into unfamiliar water without knowing how deep it was.

"Do you think my being here is some kind of test?" she asked.

"I really don't know what to think, Anna."

"I'm not testing, only being honest with you about my need and desire. I haven't been with a man in a long time. You're the first I've wanted since the man I loved died."

"I'm sorry for your loss, Anna. I too have felt the pain of losing a true love."

"Do you believe in love at first sight?"

"Well, yes, I suppose that's possible."

"Hound, I fell in love with you when we first met. I promise that is the truth."

"Anna, even if that's true, I'm not in love with you. Considering that, it would be taking advantage to have sex with you."

"God damn it! I know you can't be that honorable!"

"I never said I was honorable, but I do try to be. However, I often choose instinct and intelligence over honor."

"You're not going to give me what I want and need, are you, Hound?"

"No, but maybe we can address this again at a later and more appropriate time, when we both know how deep the water is."

"Be assured that I will never offer myself to you again. I feel so humiliated, Hound! How will you feel when you learn the water was safe and you didn't dive in?"

"That will be a regret I'll carry for some time. Will I see you for our workout in the morning?"

"Of course, if that's what you want. I still have my job to do as your concierge."

"Anna, I don't want you spending time with me if you don't want to."

"Are you serious?"

"Absolutely."

"Can I rely on you not to say it was my choice, rather yours because you desired more time alone?"

"Of course. You have my word."

"Is your word reliable?"

"I suspect that you know it is, Anna."

"Well, then I'll see you again when I see you. Call for me at any time I can be of service."

"OK, that's fair enough."

Anna put her robe on and left without saying more. Hound went back to bed. He gave due consideration to what had happened and then fell into a deep sleep.

21

Hound was up and in the gym by 6:30 the next morning. He trained especially hard and an hour longer than usual. Maybe that was because it was his birthday and he wanted to test himself to see if being a year older would prohibit him from lasting the additional hour. It was, however, more reasonable that he needed the extra time and exercise to help relieve the apprehension he was feeling about what to expect later in the day.

Normally, any degree of stress was foreign to him, but he was always a step ahead and had a plan to deal with the situation causing it. There was no way to prepare for want was unknown to him.

After his shower, he dressed and went to the kitchen to have breakfast. Andrew and the entire mansion were waiting there to wish him a happy thirty-second birthday. Hound was surprised to see Anna there, but he supposed appearances must be maintained. Anyway, he was pleased with the gesture offered by all of them.

"Thank you, Andrew," Hound said. "Thank you all."

"What will you be having for breakfast this morning, Hound?" asked Andrew.

"It's late, so I need to eat light. How about a bowl of oatmeal and some fresh fruit?"

"Certainly. Indeed, you want a good appetite so you can enjoy the gourmet meal to be provided at your birthday luncheon. Have you wondered why it will be a luncheon rather than dinner?"

"Not really, but you raise a good question. Can you answer it?"

"The guests that will be attending your luncheon are extremely busy men. It was simply not possible for all of them to attend a dinner, but all of them wanted to meet with you."

"The meeting will last longer than lunch, Hound," Anna added, feeling he should know the business with him wouldn't be rushed to a conclusion.

"How long do you think it will last?"

"It will begin during the meal, but continue until 6 p.m., if necessary. All the guests are scheduled to leave no later than that."

"Do you know how many guests I'll be joining?"

"The owner of this estate and eleven other men, but you were already convinced of that."

"I strongly suspected that but take nothing for granted. What's the required dress attire?"

"It's your birthday. I was instructed to inform you to dress anyway you like, to wear what you're most comfortable in."

"How will everyone else be dressed?"

"All will be dressed in formal attire, but not all in suits. Some will be wearing clothing that is fashion in the country they are from. However, you can be sure it will be formal."

"I think I'll wear the tuxedo I saw in my closet."

"Good choice. It was bought solely for you to wear if you wanted to dress equal to your host and the guests."

After breakfast, Hound announced he would take a walk outside the mansion.

"I should come with you," said Anna.

"If you want to, but it's not necessary. I don't plan on walking far from the mansion. Are you afraid I'll get lost?"

"No, but there's a small chance you might get shot."

"What are you talking about, Anna?"

"The estate security force is out in full number making sure all is secure for the guests' arrival."

"When did this force get here?"

"A specific number of them are always on duty. You simply haven't seen them because they didn't want you to. They've been providing for your safety and you didn't even know it."

"If that's true, then they'll know who I am, and that I'm not an intruder."

Anna walked to Hound and whispered in his ear.

"You're right, but I would enjoy your company," she said, "if you don't mind."

"Does that mean you're no longer mad at me?"

"I was never mad at you, Hound."

"Good, then I would welcome your company. Besides, it's your job to hang with me, right?"

Anna nodded and smiled.

"Yes," she replied, "and I don't want to disappoint my employer."

"I'm anxious to meet him and the other men as well. Is your employer a good boss?"

"The best, as long as I don't disappoint him."

Their walk lasted about an hour. Hound decided he would go to his room, relax for a time, and then dress and report to the large reception area at the entrance to the mansion. When the time came, Andrew assisted Hound to dress. He didn't need help, but it was a task required of Andrew.

At 1 p.m., Hound was waiting with Andrew and Anna in the reception area when the front door opened and two mansion butlers came in and walked through the long foyer. Six armed bodyguards followed them. Next came the twelve men Hound was there to meet. Leading the men was Sir James Thomas Huntington. Behind them came six more armed bodyguards. It was very apparent that all the bodyguards knew their business and were not men to mess with.

When Hound saw James, he couldn't keep from smiling and shaking his head.

"I'll just be damned!" Hound remarked to Anna in a low voice. "James is the owner of the estate, the guy you work for and the top dog of the group I'm to meet with."

"You're right about everything but one."

"What's that?"

"You're about to find out."

James reached Hound and shook his hand.

"I hope your stay thus far has been enjoyable, Hound," James said cheerfully. "Has my beautiful daughter and only child, Anna, been a proper host in my absence?"

Hound gave a quick glance at Anna, who was smiling with delight at how shocked and surprised he was to learn the only daughter had recently stood naked in his room, trying to seduce him.

"I couldn't begin to tell you what a fabulous host she has been, Sir Huntington," Hound replied, offering a forced grin.

"Hound, I know you're surprised to find out who I really am, but please continue to call me James. I'm sorry it was necessary to keep who I was a secret until now. I hope you understand."

"I do."

"Allow me to introduce you to my associates."

The eleven men stood in a line. One by one, they walked to Hound and were introduced to him by James. Afterwards, James walked beside Hound to the large dining room where lunch was ready to be served on time. Anna walked beside her father.

"Hound, we only have time during lunch and the afternoon to conduct our business, "James told him as they walked. "We have much to tell you, and I'm sure many answers to offer regarding the questions you'll want to ask. You'll remain here until tomorrow, and then you'll be taken back to London where you'll be free to return home or go wherever you wish. The offer that will be made to you this afternoon will require your best review and consideration before you accept or decline it. It is our hope that you can make that decision before my associates leave. We also hope that your decision will be to join us and become a member of our organization. However, if you require additional time to decide, then you will be given the month of August to do so."

"That is greatly appreciated."

The group arrived at the dining room. Only members were allowed to enter. Anna smiled at Hound and her father, and then turned and departed. Seating arrangements were standard and based on membership tenure in the organization. James was seated at the head of the table. As chairman of the organization, this was a seat symbolic of the most wealthy and powerful member. The position of chairman was also held by the member with the longest tenure. Even though all business decisions were based on a majority vote, the chairman most often was able to swing the majority to vote the way he wanted. James would remain in his position until he died, and then the next member with the most tenure would replace him.

Hound was seated at the opposite end of the table. This position had been reserved for the guest of honor. Only a new inductee to the organization was permitted to sit there. Hound was the first in the history of the organization to occupy the position that was not the son or close male blood relative of a former member. When a member died or became unable to perform his duties, it was his eldest son, if capable, who would replace him. If he had no son, then his closet male blood relative was acceptable. From the time the organization began, no membership position had ever been filled by anyone who wasn't a blood descendent of an original founder.

James gave Hound all this preliminary information after all servants had left the dining room and privacy had been established. The group began to eat, and James began to disclose what Hound had been invited there to hear. The meeting would continue long after everyone had finished eating. James and Hound would converse with each other during that time. The other men remained consistently attentive but silent.

"What do you have to say about what you've learned so far, Hound?" asked James.

"Well, I feel honored to be here with you and all the other gentlemen. It's obvious that I'm in the presence of extraordinary men."

"Yes, I would have to agree, but we believe you are an extraordinary gentleman as well. The things you have accomplished and the life you have lived before your thirty-second birthday is more than amazing. The members of this organization inherited their wealth and power, but you didn't. You earned yours. I will add it was not earned easily."

"What do you mean?"

"You paid a price at times, didn't you?"

"I suppose so, but I'm not sure to what times you are referring."

"Might it be possible that you may not have gained certain opportunities to advance so quickly regarding your wealth and the power that came with it if not for your relationship with many different, specific individuals at just the precise time in the history of your life?"

"I'm not sure what you're asking me."

"Of course you are, Hound. We know more about you than you yet realize. Your level of intelligence is as high as anyone here. It's at least equal to one that is present. It's higher than the others, but not mine. You know exactly what I mean. You are free to be honest with us. There will be no consequences for doing so. Besides, your honesty is required as a condition of your being here."

"Well, I would have to say that many things are possible but not probable."

Hound knew he needed to proceed with caution regarding his conversation with James. His host was indeed of a higher intelligence than he, but hopefully not significantly. He hoped his level of reliable instinct would level the playing field and that James's instinct wasn't superior to his own. He remained silent to allow

James to, hopefully, arm him with further information. He needed to know what was known about him and how much more was required before divulging more needlessly.

"Would you care to give some examples of the individuals you're referring to, name some of them?" asked Hound.

James had carried a file folder to the meeting. He opened it to reference the information inside.

"OK, why not," James replied. "Well, let's go back to the time you were conceived, and your destiny began, when an unidentified vagrant raped your biological mother when she was fifteen and she became pregnant with you. Next was John and Linda Williams, the farm couple who adopted you shortly after your birth. Carmella Vargas certainly must be included. How about Carlos Mendoza, Joann O'Malley and her father, Ken O'Malley, the Irish mob boss. Detective Karen Thibodaux and her father, Judge Robert Thibodaux. Also included on the list should be those associated with your time in the military. John Roth, your commanding officer during boot camp and Sergeants Jonas Hill and Jim Ritter, drill instructors. General Allen White, the base commander. In Vietnam there was Base Camp Bravo 127 commanded by Major Butch Tucker. Lieutenant Jeff Connors was there. I'm certain you remember him. There was First Sergeant Terrance Washington, and Privates Ed Holcroft, Bob Hayes and Tom Benson who were there also. Before we move on to Base Camp Delta 126 and Colonel Joe Westerman, General Hughes and sweet little Kim Li should be mentioned. After your return from Vietnam, there are many individuals worthy of mentioning, including but not limited to the following: Steve Cooper, the FBI agent who raped Joann O'Malley. I wonder who killed him? Charlie (Bear) Wyman, Bill Tillman, Pony Johnson, and so many other members of that notorious biker club. We mustn't forget Megan (Maggie) Mitchell. How about Roberto Sanchez and your second most loved wife, Rita Sanchez, and of course, your infant twin sons. The list is longer, but have I cited enough individuals that have influenced the direction your life has gone to make my point?"

Through his intelligence and instinct, Hound was convinced that offering complete honesty regarding all things during the meeting was the only choice available to him.

"Yes, James, I believe your point has been made," said Hound.

"Do you agree with it?"

"Yes, I have to agree."

"Good, now tell me if you believe that all that has happened to you in your life, all that you've done, experienced, the individuals I stated, and the role they played in your life, were all random, accidental coincidences?"

"I suppose my honest answer would have to be yes, James. What other explanation could there be? Do you believe otherwise?"

"Of course I do. All of my associate members do as well."

"Are you going to tell me what you all believe?"

"Yes, Hound, what we believe is why you were invited to come here and meet with us."

James became silent for a moment. Hound looked into his eyes and saw that what James was about to tell him was something he wasn't prepared to hear, much less quickly accept.

"Hound, since the moment of your conception, you were ordained to achieve a specific destiny," said James. "Absolutely everything that has happened in your life has been to prepare and lead you toward that destiny."

"What is that destiny, James?"

"To join us as the thirteenth member and help continue the work of our organization."

"What work is that?"

"Hound, in answering your question, it will require me to disclose information about our organization and its members. This information has been highly guarded and kept secret since the organization was founded. Usually, it is only after one becomes a member when he learns what I'm about to tell you. Hound, you are the first nonmember to be given that knowledge since our organization was founded many years ago. I want you to know that to reveal what you learn to anyone will result in your death, the death of all those who learn it from you, and the ones who may learn it from them, until the secret is once again secure. Do you understand and agree to the condition?"

"Yes."

James and the other men spent a moment looking at Hound in silence. Hound made eye contact with each of them briefly until James spoke again.

"Hound, is there anything you would like to ask before I begin?" asked James.

"Well, I'd like to know why you and these other gentlemen were looking at me so intensely just now."

"We want to make certain that you will believe and take seriously everything that is told to you here. I hope you will, because most, if not all, of what you'll hear will seem bizarre, ridiculous and impossible to accept as truth. However, all I'm about to disclose to you is the absolute truth."

"OK."

"As you have already been told, Hound, myself and the other men here are the twelve wealthiest in the world," James began. "Because we are and combine our wealth, we comprise the most powerful organization in the world. So great is that power that we can control and direct world events. We do that in order to maintain the proper balance of all things required to maintain who and what we are. That purpose is easily stated but is of gigantic complexity regarding the things which must be accomplished to maintain that balance. To state simply how we are able to accomplish all these things at any given time is to tell you we control the world's economy. Would you care to ask any questions before I continue?"

"Would you give me a few examples of what might be needed to maintain the balance you mentioned?"

"Some examples would include starting wars and determining how long those wars will last and who will win, getting ranking government officials placed in office, either by election in countries of democracy, or chosen as dictators. Hound, no one is elected to the United States Congress, Senate, or even the Presidency without our involvement."

"Did you influence the war in Vietnam and it's outcome?"

"Yes, of course. Hound, I'm sorry for all you experienced there. Would you like to make a statement about the war?"

At that moment, Hound felt intense anger over what he had been told. If it were true, then he felt contempt for all the men seated at the table. If not true, he felt the same contempt just because the statement had been made. However, he knew it was wise not to show how he felt, or at least to what degree he felt it. His concentration was broken when James spoke again.

"Hound, you seem to be somewhere else in your mind," said James. "Now, would you like to make a statement about the war?"

Hound decided to make an honest statement, believing such was expected of him and it would be a mistake to do otherwise.

"There wouldn't be any wars if those who started them had to fight them," Hound replied, "if they had to experience firsthand the horrors of combat."

James and the other members showed no sign of it, but Hound knew they weren't happy with his criticism.

"James, it's my understanding you required complete honesty from me. I saw many of my friends die for nothing in Nam. I killed a lot of enemy soldiers that wanted to live as much as my friends did. I could never take part in starting a war."

"Hound, all the members and myself understand why you feel that way. However, in time you will come to agree with the reasons the war was fought."

"Maybe, but I'll never understand why the war was lost. The Americans were never allowed to fight in a manner in which the war could have been won."

"In time, you'll come to understand and embrace the reason for the outcome of the war. Anyway, let me proceed in giving you the information you're here to receive."

"May I ask another question first?"

"Of course."

"Each time your organization does something to maintain the balance you mentioned, do you and the other members of the organization benefit financially? Do the wealthiest men in the world continue to increase their wealth? Will your sons or bloodline relatives start their reigns richer than you were when you began yours?"

"Hound, the answer to all those questions is yes, but you knew the answer before you asked."

A short break was called in the meeting. James stayed with Hound during it.

"Hound, it might be best if you didn't ask any more questions or make statements that could be taken by the members as demeaning or as a purposely intended insult," James told him, very sincerely. "Curb your honesty just a bit. The courtesy being extended to you does have its limits."

"Do you feel demeaned or insulted, James?"

"No, I want and appreciate your honesty. However, my skin is thicker than most, if not all, my associates."

When the meeting resumed, Hound sat prepared to remain silent through the completion of James's delivery of information.

"Hound, I know you're wondering why you, an outsider with no known bloodline ties, is being considered for membership," began James, "why the organization is in agreement to breach tradition and induct a thirteenth member. Hound, we believe it is your destiny to be one of us. Your level of intelligence, keen instinct, natural leadership abilities, superior business sense, and of course, your life experiences all perfectly meet the criteria for the member we seek. Very important is the fact we need a member that is a natural American citizen and is young enough to serve the organization for many years to come. We know you are loyal and honor your word once it is given. If you take the oath of membership, we know you would give your life before breaking that oath. Again, I'll state and it's very important that we all believe and agree that it has always been your destiny to be one of us. That's another reason we have been following your life for some time. Hound, that is all I will tell you now. It should be enough for you to make an informed decision whether or not to join us. I have presented a general picture of who we are and what we do. The ways in which we accomplish what we do, you will discover after you are formally made a member."

James then declared the meeting open to any questions Hound might have for any of the members and any they might have for him. He discovered as much as possible about the men who each came from a different country. He was able to learn only what they felt necessary at that time. That wasn't much. Fewer questions were asked of him. They already knew the things about him that were significant to their purpose.

It was 5:30 that afternoon when the meeting was adjourned. Each member shook Hound's hand and offered their sincere wish that he become a member of their organization. Their conversation was brief and soon they were on James's jet flying to London. There they would each board their own private jet and proceed to their next destination.

Hound went to his room to remove his formal attire and dress in something more familiar, casual and comfortable. He has just finished when he answered a knock on the door of his room. He suspected it would be Anna knocking. His suspicion was confirmed when he opened the door and Anna came in.

"The meeting lasted longer than my father thought it would, Hound," she said. "How did everything go? What did you talk about?"

Anna knew that the eleven men in the meeting were her father's business associates. She also was aware that the meeting was to convince Hound to become a fellow associate. However, she had not and would never be told the true nature of the association. Hound would be on his guard not to say anything that would change that.

"Believe it or not, I have never before been asked so many questions about farming, ranching, land development, real estate, nightclubs and the construction business," he told her. "I enjoyed meeting and conversing with all the guests regarding a variety of topics. It was more a get-acquainted meeting than anything else."

"Well, are you going to become an associate? You are, aren't you?"

"I don't know yet. I'll have to take some time and think it over."

"What? I would think you would jump at the chance to join them."

"Why?"

"Because doing so would make you wealthy."

"How do you know?"

"Hound! My father is very wealthy, and so are all his associates. It is more than reasonable to think you would become as wealthy as they are."

"Anna, I'm already wealthy. You know that."

"I know, but you're far from being as wealthy as any of them, especially my father."

"That may be true, but I have more money than I will ever spend. Why should I want more?"

"Power! You should want all the power you can obtain."

"Maybe, maybe not. I suppose power is good to have, but there's a limit to the amount of power any one man or association of men should have. The more power one has, greater is the chance one will abuse it."

"Have you ever abused the power your amount of wealth has afforded you?"

"Anyone who is wealthy has been guilty of that. The abuse will occur from time to time. However, I believe the abuse I've committed in the past was done out of necessity. I will commit it in the future for the same reason. I hope greed is never a reason."

"Are you saying it's impossible to be extremely wealthy and not abuse the power that comes with it?"

"I can't speak for all who are extremely wealthy, Anna, only for myself."

Hound wasn't being honest with Anna. He knew he was speaking for all extremely wealthy individuals. The greater the wealth, the greater will be the abuse that comes with it. That would be a fact he would give special consideration as he pondered whether or not to accept membership in the most powerful organization in the world.

James returned to the estate in time to have dinner with Hound and Anna. He asked to meet with Hound in private after dinner. There were a couple more important things he wanted to discuss before Hound left the following day. Anna was irritated that she couldn't take part in the private visit.

As soon as dinner was over, James escorted Hound to a den for their private talk.

"Hound, I don't suppose you're ready at this time to tell me you accept what the organization has offered?" said James.

"No, James."

"Well, I hope you're not going to decline the offer at this time either."

"Of course not, but I do require time to think about many things before making such an important decision, James."

"I understand."

"What are the other things you wanted to talk to me about?"

"Hound, do you truly believe the things I revealed to you in the meeting? Please be honest."

"I have to say that, in general, it all sounded like a script for a fiction novel, a wonderful story to read for an escape from reality. However, I'm convinced the information you gave me was true, perhaps with the exception that it is my destiny to join your organization."

"I know you feel a bit overwhelmed and confused, Hound. What you've learned would make anyone feel that way."

"It certainly changed my thinking about my life and the world I live in."

"I completely understand. However, the twelve men who control and manage the world believe it is your destiny to join them. Is it reasonable to doubt such men could be wrong?"

"I see your point, James. I suppose my decision will be based on if I agree or not with what they believe."

"What does your intelligence and instinct tell you?"

"That I should rely heavily on both of them. They will be greatly put to the test as I consider the organization's offer."

"Hound, just think of the positives being one of us would bring to your life!"

"Those things will require little thought and consideration, James. It's the negatives that concern me."

"What negatives?"

"The positives are beyond comprehension at this point, but so are the negatives. I'm sure the paramount level of wealth and power I've been offered doesn't come without a paramount cost."

"I told you great responsibility would befall you, Hound."

"I'm not concerned with responsibility. I shoulder much of it in my life. At times in the past I often thought I would perish from its weight. The price I'm talking about is still unknown to me. That won't be revealed until after I take the oath and begin my duty as a member. I feel certain once I become one of you, then I must remain so for life. Is that true? Will you at least confirm or deny that for me?"

James considered for a moment if he would provide an answer to the question.

"Yes, Hound, the only way to stop being a member is to become incapable of performing your duties or die," said James. "That's a price you'll pay for being one of us."

"What about the other costs?"

"I'm sorry, Hound, that's all I can tell you now."

"I would suppose the number and amount of the other costs would be determined by my conscious?"

James smiled but didn't answer. Hound knew James was affirming the assumption.

"Well, Hound, you have the month of August to make your decision," James told him. "I'm sure you'll make the right one. I suppose you'll be returning to Montana tomorrow. Of course you are welcome to remain here as my guest for as long as you wish during August."

"I think I'll accept your kind offer and stay a bit longer. Will you be here?"

"Unfortunately, no, I will be away most of the month, but I'm sure Anna will ensure your extended stay remains memorable. Is there anything I can do for you before I leave tomorrow?"

"Actually, perhaps there is. Joann O'Malley, my former wife, is now living somewhere in the London area. I haven't had any contact with her in quite some time and would very much like to pay her a visit, if she's agreeable. If not, then a phone call to her might do. I know she's married, but I don't know her married name, address, or phone number. Is there any way you could assist me in contacting her?"

"That's an easy request. I've been keeping an eye on her for a long time as part of my keeping an eye on you. I have a current file on her in my file safe. The file contains the information you need."

"I'd bet you have many files in that safe."

"Indeed, it's a very big safe."

James rose from his chair and walked to a wall in the den. He positioned his hand on and slightly moved a book in the library case that covered the entire wall. A door opened and James disappeared behind it. A short time later, he returned and handed Hound a piece of paper on which was written the information about Jo that he requested.

"Is that all I can do for you, Hound?" asked James."

"Yes, thank you."

"I'll be leaving early in the morning. I'll have breakfast with you before I do. Hound, I'll expect you to contact me with your decision on or before the first of September."

"You'll have it no later than that, James."

"Very good, Hound, at this time I'll bid you good night and go to my bedroom. I'll see you at 7 a.m. for breakfast."

"I'll see you then, James. Good night."

22

Shortly after James had left the next morning, Hound returned to his room to place a phone call to Jo. She was now Mrs. Jeffery Mills and lived on a small but very nice estate a short drive from London. Jeffery was the owner of a variety of successful businesses in the city. It was Jo who answered the phone. Her voice was easily identified. It sounded like the Jo he first met in high school, happy, full of life and free of past emotional problems.

Hound hesitated to speak. Jo said hello three more times and was about to hang up when he spoke.

"Hello, Jo," he said. "This is Hound. I hope you don't mind my calling you?"

She was silent for a moment.

"No, I don't think I mind," Jo said, "but after our last visit in Dublin, I never expected to hear from you again. How are you? Well, I hope."

"Very well, Jo. Thanks. How are you?"

"Hound, my life is good, very good."

"That's wonderful! I'm so very happy for you."

"How did you find me? How did you get my number? It's not listed."

"I was lucky to meet a gentleman who knew and gave it to me."

"What was his name?"

"I really don't remember, but he knows your husband and had this phone number. He also knew you and Jeffery had met in Dublin and that your maiden name was O'Malley."

"Hound, I know you remember the name of every person you've ever met. I assume you don't want to tell me who the gentleman was. I don't really care anyway. I assume you're in London. Are you?"

"Yes, I'm here on business."

"Legal business, I hope."

"Of course. All my business ventures are completely legitimate. They have been for a long time."

"I would make still another assumption — that you are doing well in those ventures."

"I make a good living."

Jo laughed.

"How wealthy are you now, Hound?" she asked. "Oh dear! I don't care and it's none of my business. I'm sorry for asking."

"Don't worry about it, Jo."

"Well, I'm sure you're doing well financially. How are the other aspects of your life? Did you ever get married again?"

Hound didn't want to reveal his marriage to Rita. He didn't want to answer the questions Jo was sure to ask.

"I'm not married, Jo," he told her. "It's doubtful that I will ever be married again."

"Is there a particular reason why you called me, Hound?"

"Only to see how you were. Like I said, I'm glad you're happy."

She paused her conversation for a moment.

"Jo, are still there?" he asked.

"Hound, would you like to come to my home for a visit while you're in London?"

"I would if that's something you want, Jo."

"It is. How long are you going to be here?"

"I was planning to be here for two or three more days, but I can stay longer if necessary."

"Can you come for lunch tomorrow, say about one?"

"Of course, but how will your husband feel about that? I'm sure you've told him about me."

"Yes, I told him all about you."

"Not everything, I hope."

"Of course not, only the things that were safe for him to know. Shit, he only knows the safe things about me. However, I don't mention you now. He knows how I felt about you and is insanely jealous."

"I don't want you to get in trouble if I come to visit."

"I'll be the only one here when you come. He'll never know."

"Jo, that doesn't sound like you, to sneak around and hide things from your husband."

"I know, but I want to see you. We may never have another opportunity to meet face to face. Do you feel the same?"

"Yes, Jo, I do."

"Good, then I'll see you at one tomorrow."

"OK. I'll be there."

Hound sat for a time after talking to Jo. He remembered his sixteenth birthday party back home on the farm, when they first met. He began to recall the events of his life that occurred after that. Jo had played a key role in setting him on the path that helped direct his journey to the point he had now arrived in his life. He began to consider what James had said in the meeting, that she and many other significant individuals had been put in his life to assist him in fulfilling his destiny. Could it be possible James was right? Had he never really had any other choice but to make the journey that ultimately led to where he was now? How many other such individuals would he meet as his journey continued? What was next after James and the other members of the organization? Hound wondered where he would go next on the journey.

When would it end and his destiny be revealed, how long until it was completed?

A firm knock on the door of his room interrupted Hound's thoughts. He knew it had to be Anna. He was surprised when he answered the door and found it was Andrew who was calling.

"Well, Andrew, what can I do for you?" asked Hound.

"Your presence is requested in the main living room, Hound."

"Why?"

"Anna is waiting there to introduce you to her mother, Diana, and a guest."

"Neither James nor Anna said anything about Diana. I assumed the mother and wife was no longer in the picture."

"Hound, perhaps Sir James didn't feel it was important regarding his business with you."

"I suppose so."

"How long shall I tell them it will be before you join them?"

"If I don't need to dress a certain way, then I can go now."

"Your attire is fine."

Hound walked with Andrew, who excused himself when they arrived in the large living area. Anna was seated and having a conversation with two other women. The older of the two was Anna's mother, an attractive, well dressed and groomed lady. She certainly looked years younger than her actual age of forty-five. Seated to the right of Diana was a young lady, age twenty-four. Her name was Sophia. Hound had never seen a more beautiful woman than Rita until that moment. So perfect were Sophia's physical features that Hound didn't realize he had paused his walk toward them. He seemed to be mesmerized by the sight of her. The three women clearly noticed his behavior and knew the reason for it. Diana was amused, Sophia felt complimented and delighted, but Anna's jealousy and envy peaked. She had already decided to do everything possible to win him.

"You must be our special guest who prefers to be called Hound," Diana said softly as she smiled at him.

Her voice broke what seemed to be a spell he was under. He walked to join the ladies.

"Yes, ma'am, I'm Hound," he replied, "but I don't know how special I am."

"Young man, you're special or James wouldn't have invited you here."

"Well, I've certainly been made to feel special during my stay."

"Hound, allow me to present Sophia. I've been visiting with her and her family at their estate in Italy. She's come home with me to meet you before you have to leave. I hope you're planning to remain here as our guest a few more days. That will give us more time to get better acquainted."

"Well, I'm flattered, but I don't understand why that would be important."

"We've heard much about you. Based on that, we want to spend time with you in person."

Hound looked at Sophia. Her smile indicated her agreement with Diana's statement.

"As a matter of fact, James wanted you to stay longer so you could get to know Anna better," said Diana.

"Really, why is that?"

"James will have to answer that when he returns."

"I may not be here when he returns. When will that be?"

"We never know how long my husband will be away, but I suspect the trip he's on this time will be brief."

"Hound, you agreed to extend your visit a few days, didn't you?"

"Yes, I did, but I don't know for how long."

"Is there some reason you can't stay until he gets back? Do you have pressing business that requires your presence?"

"No."

"Wonderful, then you can stay long enough to see him when he gets home."

"Maybe."

"You didn't know about me, did you, Hound?"

"No, neither James nor Anna said a word about you. I didn't feel like either wanted to offer any information, so I decided not to pry."

"James wanted you to be surprised when I showed up."

"Why?"

"Who knows why he does anything, Hound, but I'm sure he has a reason and will tell it to you."

Diana suggested she and Sophia excuse themselves and let Hound and Anna be alone to continue getting better acquainted. Sophia wasn't happy to leave so soon but did as Diana requested. It was apparent that Diana was a strong matriarch.

"Anna, would you mind telling me what's going on?" asked Hound.

"What do you mean?"

"It's obvious that your mother wants us to spend time alone together. Why?"

"Like she said, to continue getting better acquainted, Hound."

"OK, but why would she want us to be alone? We could get better acquainted without privacy."

"Hound, let's go for a walk outdoors and talk more."

They left the mansion and began to walk down the driveway. They walked a few moments before either spoke. It was Hound who began their conversation.

"Anna, are you ready to tell me what's going on?"

"Regarding what?"

"What significance are you in the reason for me being invited here?"

"To be offered a business opportunity by my father is why you were invited."

"I know, but I feel you're connected to the opportunity, if I accept it."

Anna paused and presented a brief but loud burst of laughter.

"What's so funny?" he asked.

"Nothing. Never mind, Hound. My father will be the one to answer any questions pertaining to business."

"So, you're not going to tell me anything."

"I can't, sorry."

"Is there anything you can tell me?"

"What do you want to find out? I'll tell you what I know."

"What kind of business does your father conduct with the members of the organization?"

"I have no idea. My father never discusses his business."

"How often do the other members come here for meetings?"

"At least once each year, but sometimes more often."

"Does anyone other than the membership attend these meetings?"

"You're the first that I'm aware of. Why?"

"I was just wondering. Never mind, it's not important."

"Hound, I was told you have a high IQ."

"I suppose so. How did you find out?"

"From my father. He has told me much about you."

"Why?"

"He said he wanted me to meet you, that you were an extraordinary man. I was most impressed with your great success as a businessman at such a young age, but your physical description was of equal interest to me."

"Does what you were told about me measure up to your expectations?"

"I knew you'd be extremely handsome, but you've surpassed my expectations in that area. Do you find me attractive as well?"

"Of course, very much so."

"I'm happy to hear that."

"Anna, is there anything more you can tell me about the organization?"

"Like I told you, nothing about their business. However, there is something unique that they have in common."

"What's that?"

"Each of them is married to a close female family member of another, usually a sister or daughter."

"That sounds like the marriages were arranged."

"They were."

"Why?"

"To keep members of their organization connected by family bloodlines."

Hound suddenly had a premonition that concerned but also angered him.

"Anna, what role, if any, does your father have planned for you regarding an arranged marriage?"

Anna smiled but wasn't sure how she should respond. She knew her father had reserved the proper time to answer that question. She decided not to answer and risk incurring her father's wrath.

"Hound, I don't know what my father plans to do about anything until he does it," she said. "If I have any role to play, then he will tell me when the time is right."

Hound stopped walking. His smile and cheerful disposition vanished, and he became silent.

"Would you agree to an arranged marriage, Anna?" Hound asked.

"I would have no choice, if I wanted to remain in good standing with my family and continue to enjoy the luxuries that I would otherwise lose. Naturally, I feel confident that my father would only ask me to marry a man that would appeal to and be compatible with me."

"What if a man was selected that didn't appeal to you?"

"I would have no choice but to marry him."

"So, you would marry a man you didn't want as a husband to continue living a life of luxury."

"Of course, but you understand it would be ultimate luxury."

"I suppose."

"It's just something women are expected to do, if they are chosen."

"I think arranged marriages are unfair to both the bride and groom."

"I can understand why you would say that. Sometimes that may be the case, but the benefits far outweigh the unfairness."

"I would never consider marrying a woman that I didn't love."

"Well, you should consider the possibility that you would grow to love her over time. Consider the beautiful and intelligent children she would give you. You would like that, wouldn't you?"

"I would assume maintaining a bloodline of male and female children is important for the arranged marriages to continue from one group of associates to the next."

Anna smiled but offered no response.

"I'm sure you, Sophia, Diana and all the other wives, sons and daughters of the associates know nothing about what business their organization conducts," said Hound. "However, you know it's important enough to do whatever is asked of you to support it. You like the lifestyle you have and want it to last. I can understand that, but probably more significant than that is the other consequences you might face should you refuse that support. If I'm right, if you can, then tell me."

"Hound, I have already told you all I'm permitted to say. Father will be the one to answer any other questions, if he chooses to do so. You sound as if you're considering not accepting the offer my father has made to you."

"So, you know the reason why I was invited here."

"Yes."

"Well, I haven't yet decided to accept or decline, but I suspect that when I learn all that will be required of me, the less likely I'll choose to become a member."

Anna stared at Hound. He saw she was disturbed by what he said.

"What's the reason for that surprised and concerned look you're giving me, Anna?" he asked.

"Hound, you were chosen by the organization to become one of its members. You have no choice; it has been made for you. That much I do know and will tell you."

"I was given a month to think about and make my decision."

"Yes, but everyone is certain you will agree to become a member. The month was simply a gesture of courtesy and respect."

Anna suddenly realized she had said too much. Hound could tell that she had become frightened due to the slip of her tongue.

"Oh my! Hound, it wasn't my place to tell you that! Please don't tell anyone that I did!

"Don't worry, Anna," he said sincerely. "I won't."

Hound changed the subject and began to tell her about Montana, his ranch and the cowboys who worked for him. She was interested to learn about what he told her. When they returned to the mansion after their stroll, Sophia and Diana were sitting in one of the smaller dining rooms having a cup of tea. Andrew met Hound and Anna when they entered the mansion and escorted them to the dining room.

Hound saw that Sophia was extremely upset. However, he made no comment of it. He now believed James wanted him to marry Anna as a condition of joining the organization. He now also believed that Anna was aware of this and agreed with her father's wishes. Maybe her earlier behavior of trying to seduce him and declaring her love at first sight was in part a test to determine how attracted he was to her. His instinct was telling him that he should have never accepted the invitation to come there. However, now he had to play his cards carefully and hope that James had been truthful about him having the choice to accept or refuse membership in the organization.

"Did you and Anna enjoy your walk, Hound?" asked Diana.

"Yes, it was very enjoyable."

"Sit down and join Sophia and me in a cup of tea."

They sat down. Sophia stayed a short time and then excused herself and went to her room.

"Hound, Andrew told me you plan to leave the estate tomorrow and travel to London," remarked Diana.

"That's right."

"May I ask why?"

"To visit an old friend."

"Of course, I remember now. James told me you wanted to visit your former wife. It's good that you remained friends. I assume you'll require the use of an aircraft to fly you to London and then back after your visit."

"I assumed someone would drive me."

"Nonsense. It's a two-hour drive one way. We have a small jet that can reach London in twenty minutes. A car and driver will be there to take you to your destination."

"That sounds wonderful. Thank you."

"Certainly. What time do you wish to leave?"

"By 10 a.m."

"The plane will be ready to leave when you are."

Hound visited a short time longer and then excused himself and went to his room. He had already planned to board his own jet and fly back to the states after his visit with Jo was completed. Fortunately, he had no luggage, so no one would suspect he had no intention of returning to the estate.

A short time after arriving in his room, Hound received a visit from Sophia. She didn't wait for him to ask her to come in, she just pushed passed him and shut the door behind them.

"Hound, you don't have to marry Anna!" Sophia quickly announced. "You can request someone else that meets the blood-line requirement."

"Sophia, I don't plan on having an arranged marriage to anyone!"

"Hound, surely Anna told you that marrying within the organization's bloodline is a requirement if you are to be a member."

Hound decided to seem uninformed in hopes he could get more information about his situation.

"Actually, Anna said she didn't know anything about requirements or conditions. She said James was the only one who could give me information about anything pertaining to the organization."

"She lied! Of course, there are many things that family members aren't allowed to know but arranged bloodline marriages is not one of them. She also knows that by accepting James's invitation to come here and meet the members, that you have been chosen and won't be allowed to decline membership. Did she tell you that?"

"No, she didn't. I suppose she was afraid of how her father would feel if she did. Why are you telling me? Aren't you afraid?"

"I suppose I am, but you won't say anything about what I tell you, right?"

"That's right, I won't. Tell me more about what you know."

"I know you can refuse to accept Anna as your wife and select another eligible woman from the family of any member."

"Like you, perhaps?"

"Yes! I would make you a better wife than Anna!"

"Sophia, if I ever marry again, it will be a woman I choose, not one that has been chosen for me."

"Hound, you may change your mind when James returns and informs you of the marriage requirement and that he wishes your choice to be Anna."

"Maybe, we'll see. Why would you want to marry me? You know nothing about me."

"I know enough. Besides, you're everything I want in a husband. You're handsome, intelligent and I'm certain a great lover. I don't want to be at risk of being chosen for some man I'm not attracted to. You and I would make beautiful children together. Do you agree?"

"What about love? Don't you want to be in love with the man you marry?"

"Yes, but I know we would come to love each other deeply in a short time. Hound, do you find me beautiful and desirable?"

"I have to admit that I do. Very much in fact, but I still want to be in love with the woman I marry."

"Hound, you will have to select me or some other woman who qualifies if you don't want Anna."

Hound smiled as he ended the conversation and escorted her to the door of his room.

"Will you think about what I've said, Hound?" Sophia asked as she prepared to leave.

"You can bet I will!"

After Sophia had offered her comments and left, Hound sat on the side of his bed to reflect on the things he had learned from her and from Anna. They both had delivered almost identical messages. Because they were so similar, he knew they must have contained some degree of validity. Knowing that further convinced him that he was likely once again in a pile of shit. This time the pile might very well be deeper than could have been anticipated and deeper than any he had ever experienced. The only option available to him now was to prepare for the worst, hope for the best and wait to see which it would be.

The next day Hound boarded the jet and took off for London. As told to him, a car was parked and waiting to drive him. The pilot who flew him there would be his driver. Hound spent a specific amount of time seeing a bit of the city so he wouldn't arrive early or late for his visit with Jo.

The driver waited in the car. Hound walked the distance from the driveway to the front entrance to the house. He rang the doorbell and waited. It was Jo who personally answered the door. Hound was surprised but delighted when he saw her. Jo appeared to be her old self again, both physically and emotionally. Her appearance reminded him of the time when they were most happy together. She was dressed in clothing intended to compliment her in every way. When Jo saw Hound, she smiled and asked him to come in.

"Oh, my darling, Hound, you haven't changed, even a bit since the last time we were together," she said as they walked to the living room and she showed him where to sit. "I'm thirty-eight now. How much do you think I've changed?"

"You look the same, Jo. You're still as beautiful as ever."

"Somehow, I feel like you mean that, Hound. Lunch is ready to be served. Shall we eat?"

Jo led the way to the dining room where a cook began to serve their meal.

"Jo, when you told me on the phone you were happy, I was happy for you," said Hound.

"Hound, I said my life was very good. I never said I was happy."

"I don't know what you mean, Jo."

"Well, I'm sure you enjoy a life of luxury, but are you happy? Is your life complete?"

"I would think there are things all people wish they had but don't. We make the best of what we have and remember things could always be worse. Maybe some things we want just aren't meant to be."

"Is to have someone that you truly love and returns that love not meant to be? I think everyone is entitled to love and be loved. Don't you?"

"I would think so, but don't you have that with your husband?"

"No, honestly I don't, Hound."

"Jo, I thought the reason you wanted to end our marriage was because of how you felt about Jeffery. That's what you told me."

"Yes, I remember."

"Did you lie to me?"

"I admit to stretching the truth a lot."

"Why?"

"Because what you once felt for me died. Things happened that made me worthless as a wife. I almost lost all touch with reality. Shit, I did lose touch. I went fucking crazy!"

"You were ill for a time, but you're well now."

"No, I'm better, but I may never again be the woman I was before those God-damned things happened to me! I wish I had remained the woman you loved and admired. Hound, you did once love and admire me, didn't you?"

"Yes, and I will always love and admire you."

"Not the same way you used to though, right?"

"No, Jo, I suppose not, but you'll always have a place in my heart."

"And you will in mine. Thanks for being honest. It makes my decision to marry Jeffery seem more justified. So, you're in London on business. With whom did you come to conduct business with?"

Hound didn't want to deny her an answer. She'd think his reason was to hide something nefarious. He didn't want her to think that. To name James as the person he came to see and not state particulars wouldn't breach his word to him.

"I've been the guest of a man named James Huntington at his estate for the last few days," Hound told her.

"Not Sir James Huntington, I hope!"

"Well, that's his title, but there may be more than one person with that title."

"The James I'm referring to is a very wealthy man. He owns a thousand-acre estate some distance north of London. His large mansion was constructed to look like a castle. Is he the man you came to transact business with, Hound?"

"Yes, Jo, he is. Do you know James?"

"Not personally, but rumors from people in high places say his wealth is greater than any individual in the country. I've always had a bad feeling about him."

"What is that feeling, your opinion of him?"

"Hound, I have nothing concrete to base this on, but I believe in my heart that Sir James is an evil man. Please tell me you aren't close to him in any business dealings yet! You're not, are you?"

"No, Jo."

"Then why are you here to see him?"

"James has proposed that we enter into a business arrangement. He told me that my financial success at such an early age greatly impressed him. That's what influenced his decision."

"What did he propose?"

"Nothing yet. He said we'd discuss it when he returned from a short trip he had to take."

"Hound, you should leave here immediately! Don't have anything to do with him in any way!"

"Are you telling me that based on nothing more than intuition, rumors you've heard about him?"

"Yes, but I know that I'm right!"

Jo was becoming extremely upset regarding her conviction about James. She seemed compelled to make Hound heed her warning. Based on what he knew at this point, he was inclined to think she might be right.

"Jo, please calm down," he said calmly. "You're passing judgment on James based on nothing more than a gut feeling about him."

"Hound, you're instinct about people has always been superior! What does it tell you about James?"

Hound knew his instinct had spoken volumes about James and the other members of the organization since his meeting with them. Now it was his intelligence and just plain common sense that motivated his decision to decline the membership that had been offered to him. It was that same intelligence and common sense that led him to suddenly realize a horrible truth. James and the other members were fully convinced that he would embrace his destiny to be one of them. James had told him he would have a choice to accept or decline doing so. That had been a lie told to ensure he would attend the meeting. Once there, all were certain, based on what he learned, that he would not hesitate to join them.

Hound realized that he had made a great error in judgment. He would not be able to simply leave and be done with the organization. He would return to the Huntington estate and meet again with James. Perhaps in doing so he could negotiate a way out of the situation he'd allowed himself to be put into. The sound of Jo's voice broke the deep thought she saw he was in.

"Hound, you left me for a time," Jo said loudly. "You were away in your thoughts. What were you thinking about?"

"About a lot of things, all at the same time."

"Are you returning to the States when our visit is over?"

"I may do that, Jo."

"So, you're going to take my advice."

"Looks like it."

"Did you enjoy your lunch?"

"Absolutely."

"Hound, how come you haven't married again, had some children?"

Hound's thoughts turned to Rita and his twin boys. He debated whether to tell Jo about them. He decided not to.

"I suppose it just wasn't meant for me to have a wife and kids, at least not yet," he replied.

"I wish we could have had a child. Maybe things would have worked out different between us."

"Yes, maybe so."

"How long can you stay here with me."

"How long do you want me to stay, Jo?"

"Long enough to do me a favor, if it's agreeable to you."

"I'd do anything in my power for you, Jo. What do you want me to do?"

"Do you still have any love in your heart for me, Hound, even the smallest amount?"

"Jo, I will never stop feeling love in my heart for you."

"OK, then I want you to make love to me. We may never see each other again. I want to experience making love to you at least one more time."

Hound saw Jo was sincere but was briefly at a loss of words to respond.

"Jo, what about your husband? How will you feel about being unfaithful to him after I leave?"

Jo sent the cook, who was also the housekeeper, home early. She led Hound to a spare bedroom that had never been occupied. He remained standing and silent as she slowly removed his clothing. He lay down on the bed and she began performing oral sex on him. He quickly became aroused. She removed all her clothing and lay on her back in the bed. She stopped him when he offered to reciprocate the oral sex.

"My darling, I want you inside me now," she said softly.

She positioned herself beneath him and then guided his erection inside her. As he began to move in ways familiar to her from the past, extreme desire and passion took control. She was once again enjoying the ecstasy of sex with the only man she had ever truly loved. Hound remained sensitive to her every desire and provided everything her cues indicated she wanted.

Jo had achieved multiple orgasms when she finally became still beneath him. He hadn't yet reached a climax. As he started to withdraw from her, she stopped him.

"Hound, you've surpassed your performance and attentiveness required to satisfy me," Jo said tenderly, "but you haven't yet reached a climax. Why are you stopping?"

"I thought you might be tired and maybe a bit sore, Jo."

"I want you to cum inside me as many times as you can and want to. I need you to do that, Hound."

He began thrusting again, slowly at first and then harder and harder until his first climax was achieved. He began again and again, finally finishing after his third. Jo pulled him close and as deeply as possible inside her each time.

Hound rolled from atop her. She snuggled close to his side and rested her head on his shoulder, with a portion of her face at his neck. She spent time softly kissing him there. She rolled to her back and placed a pillow beneath her hips. Hound knew what purpose she hoped that would serve. He didn't know how to feel about her intention.

"Jo, what are you trying to do?" he asked, believing it was still impossible for her to conceive. "Are you feeling OK?"

Jo burst out a short but loud laugh.

"Don't worry, Hound, I'm not losing my mind again," she told him, "but I hope to finally have your child."

"Jo, the doctors told us years ago that you could never conceive another child, remember?"

"Yes, I remember, but a doctor in Germany thinks he's repaired the damage done to my body when I poisoned the baby to abort it before we were married. I know you haven't forgotten that."

"Jo! Are you telling me the truth? Is it possible for you to conceive?"

"The doctor told me there was a reasonable probability that I could. I haven't been successful with Jeffery, but he may not be able to get me pregnant. I know you are. Besides, he's seldom at home at the precise time. Your visit occurred at the precise time."

"Damn! Jo, what possessed you to do such a thing? If you're successful, what will it do to your marriage? Think of how Jeffery will feel and what he might do!"

Jo didn't offer an answer to his question. She smiled and then pulled him close to her again. She wanted to know about his current life back in the States. He talked about his ranch in Montana and his friends there. She was delighted to hear of them all but asked more questions about Pardner than any other of the friends. They remained in bed talking until almost 5 that afternoon. Then he showered, dressed and prepared to leave.

"May I come to visit you at your ranch in Montana someday, Hound?" Jo asked as she walked with him to the front door.

"You're welcome anytime, Jo."

"Good, then I'll come when I can."

Tears had gathered in her eyes when they reached the door. She kissed him goodbye. As he walked to the car and driver that had been waiting all that time, she waved from the door and then closed it slowly.

The driver had nothing to say about the amount of time Hound had taken for his visit but did stop at the first bathroom facility after they left the estate.

23

Hound arrived at the Huntington Estate a little after 7:30 that evening. During his trip back, he wondered if returning was his best choice. Maybe doing as he had originally planned, to leave for the States after his visit with Jo, would have been better. However, if what he had been told contained even the smallest tinge of truth, then the choice he made was likely a wise one. He had confessed to James how bizarre what he told him was, but it was his instinct rather than intelligence that was motivating his decision to meet and discuss the matter further.

James had returned an hour earlier. He had dinner held until Hound returned and could join him, Diana, Anna and Sophia for the gourmet meal that had been prepared. Hound retuned from his room after a brief time to freshen up and the group seated themselves in one of the smaller dining rooms. Casual conversation began between everyone as they started eating the first course. It was James who focused the topic on Hound's long visit that day with Jo.

"I hope your visit with Jo today was all you hoped it would be, Hound," James said, seeming to be sincere.

"It was, thank you."

"Did you get the closure you wanted, Hound?" asked Anna.

"That's none of your business, Anna," James said in a commanding manner. "Hound doesn't owe any report. Hound, have you perhaps made a decision regarding the offer that was extended to you during your birthday luncheon?"

"No, James, not yet. I'm glad to have until September 1 to consider the offer. That hasn't changed, has it?"

"Of course not, but I was hoping you wouldn't require the time to say yes. I'm sure you realize the personal value the offer holds."

"James, may we have a bit more private discussion about that after dinner?"

"Certainly."

As soon as dinner was over, Hound and James made themselves comfortable in a den.

"OK, Hound, why don't you be completely honest with me about your concerns. What do you want to ask or tell me?"

"How honest can I be without appearing rude or disrespectful?"

"Are you saying that you're afraid to appear rude or disrespectful to me, Hound?"

"I suppose so, but you have been a gracious host. That's also a reason not to offend you, James."

"Hound, I will accept that statement, but we both know that you don't fear me. You don't fear anything."

"Why would you believe that, James, especially if I believe you and the other members of the organization are what you claim to be?"

"Because I know all about you. Even if you did believe we are what we say, you wouldn't be afraid. However, I feel you aren't convinced yet that you've been told the truth. If that's the case, then simply tell me. There are ways to provide the evidence needed to convince you."

"What ways?"

"What specific way would you require?"

"It would require more than twelve multi-billionaires to have the power your organization claims to have."

"Indeed, it would. However, I'm not at liberty to prove the combined or individual financial wealth of the members. Perhaps there is another way that would satisfy you?"

"I can't think of any right now, but I would like to ask you a question and get an honest answer."

"Ask your question. If I can give you an answer, then it will be the truth."

"Do I really have a choice to accept or decline the organization's offer?"

"Yes, you do. There's always a choice, Hound. Does that sound familiar?"

"I've embraced that belief for most of my life and quoted it many times. I've also embraced the fact that one should always consider the result of making a choice before making it. What will really be the result for me to consider if I want to decline membership? Was I told a lie about that, James?"

James gave some thought to the question before answering. He sat silently staring at Hound, deciding whether to answer truthfully.

"I have decided to be honest with you, Hound," James began. "I only told you a partial truth about your obligation should you attend the meeting. You were told that you could accept or decline, but if you decline our offer, then all that would be required was that you never reveal what you were told. All of that was true. However, I'll tell you now that should you refuse, action will be taken to ensure there's never a risk of your telling anyone. I'm sure you know what I mean."

"You're damn right I know, James! Why couldn't you just tell me that before I agreed to come here?"

"Because you wouldn't have come."

"James! That was a fucked up, shitty thing to do! You enticed me here to be forced into the service of your organization!"

"That's simply not true, Hound."

"How could your motive be different?"

"Like I said, Hound, we believe it is your destiny to join us. We were certain once you learned what the organization was about and all the benefits you would have as a member, then your choice could only be to become one of us. We never thought there was any chance you would refuse us. My God, Hound! I can't believe you would even consider refusing! You haven't, have you?"

"Damn it! You said I could have until September 1 to decide! Didn't that tell you I was uncertain?"

"Maybe a bit, but we were certain your answer would be yes. Again, why would it be otherwise? Now, tell me, would it have been?"

"Yes, James, I'm almost certain it would."

"You can't say for sure though, can you?"

Hound knew only too well what his response had to be.

"No, James, in all honesty, I was drawn by almost all I learned. Only one other thing I discovered caused me reservation."

"What? Tell me!"

Hound had to convince James that what he was about to say was based on his instinct and not what Anna and Sophia had told him.

"James, I'm not sure I will ever want to marry again," said Hound, "but if I do, the thought of an arranged and forced marriage isn't pleasing to me. I feel that would be required should I become a member."

James smiled. His other cues indicated that he believed the arranged marriage was the only objection Hound had to accepting his destiny.

"Hound, it's true. I would want you to marry Anna. That's another reason I petitioned for your acceptance as a member."

"Why?"

"Hound, I want a future heir to replace me in the organization, but I wanted a special kind of man to marry Anna and produce that heir. That man is you."

"James, I'm flattered, honored, but I can't marry Anna."

"Hound, what would be your objection to marrying my daughter?"

"Anna is truly a most beautiful and intelligent woman. I'm sure all things about her are superior, but I don't love her! What about love, James?"

"I understand how you feel, Hound. I felt the same way about Diana when we were married, and so did she about me. However, we now find ourselves deeply in love. It will be that way for you and Anna. She was chosen for you and you for her. I can promise you and her are perfectly compatible and will be ecstatically happy together. Besides, just imagine how beautiful and intelligent the children you have together will be."

"Yes, and their marriages will be arranged also."

"That may not have to happen, but if it does, only one child per a member's family are subject to an arranged marriage, a male or female offspring. Hound, you, your wife and all your children will live a life of absolute royalty and privilege. There will be nothing you want that you can't have or do. You will truly be one of thirteen kings in control of the world! Now, will you join us?"

Hound purposely took a moment, pretending to be in awe and having a catharsis.

"I accept membership in the organization, James," Hound said, displaying a convincing but false conviction.

"Splendid! See, we knew you would. We were right!"

They weren't right, but Hound had come to believe that to refuse membership would result in severe consequences of paramount proportions. He knew there would be no way to defend himself against them. His greatest concern was that these consequences would involve not only him, but those he cared about as well.

"James, just because I'm still curious," said Hound, "what was the way you were going to prove to me that your organization is everything you said it was?"

"Hound, I think you're convinced it is. You're instinct and intelligence has convinced you. I think you simply are eager to know everything, rather than just what you've been told so far."

"Yes, you're right. I want to know what you do."

"You will begin to learn everything after you take the oath and become a member. Hound, trust me, you have no idea what is in store for you once you become the first thirteenth member, when you finally begin to live your destiny."

"You make it sound like being the thirteenth member is some type of special honor, James."

"You'll have to wait until after you take your oath to know that, Hound. However, I will state one more bit of information. You will be surprised, delighted and honored regarding what being a member will do for you, especially in the future. Now, I can't tell you more."

"Can you tell me how long I have before all this begins? When must I take the oath you told me about? Where will I be required to live? Who will I be permitted to socialize, be friends with? Those are the kind of things I would like to know now."

James laughed softly.

"Hound, you can remain in Montana, or live anywhere you wish, have whomever you like as friends, do as you please. Nothing will change except you will keep the organization a guarded secret, be married to Anna, and your wealth will begin to increase at a planned rate."

"How?"

"The organization will assist in a variety of ways."

"How often does the membership meet to transact business?"

"You will attend meetings with me and the other members quarterly as standard procedure. When such is needed, any member can call for a meeting separate from those that are standard. The members take turns hosting the meetings at their private estates. You will be exempt from ever being a host."

"Why?"

"It will be better if you keep a bit lower profile. You should maintain the profile you have now as your wealth continues to grow."

"OK. When and where will I take the oath of membership?"

"Here at the estate on September 2. Afterward, you will be told all you are anxious to know about the organization. You and Anna will be married at the estate the next afternoon."

"What happens then?"

"You go on your honeymoon, of course!"

"Do we have a choice where to go, or has that been decided for us?"

James laughed again.

"Hound, you and Anna can go wherever you like," said James. "I think she wants to honeymoon in the United States. I know she wants to see your ranch in Montana as soon as possible and learn to be a real cowgirl."

"Surely, there's somewhere she would rather go on her honeymoon!"

"I don't think so. She has seen all the best things in the world, but never a real cattle ranch."

"Well, if that's what she wants, then it's fine with me. Perhaps I should return to the States tomorrow. I have much to do in preparation for her arrival."

"Yes, I'm sure it would be a shock to everyone there if you showed up with a beautiful new bride and they had no idea you were getting married. That's the preparation you mean, isn't it?"

"Yes, I suppose so."

"Are you worried about how Dobi will receive the news?"

"What about her?"

"Hound, we know much about you, remember?"

"I think Dobi will be hurt, but she'll survive. What choice does she have?"

"None. By the way, you will become complete owner of the three thousand acres that you are fifty-one percent owner of now."

"Dobi would not want that. She intends to buy my fifty-one percent back in as short a time as possible. James, I will not break my word to her!"

"You won't have to. It will be her desire that you own it all."

"I don't want anything bad to happen that would force her to make that decision."

"I know and nothing will. Her decision will result because of something she wants more than the ranch."

"What?"

"I've already told you more than I should. You will have to stop asking more questions. You can ask anything you want once you're a member."

"OK. James, will it be convenient for me to leave for London in the morning?"

"Hound, I would suggest that you stay as my guest a bit longer. Anna is anxious to spend time with you. You may have reservations about marrying her, but she has none about you. It would disappoint her greatly if you didn't stay longer."

"I see your point, James. I'll stay a couple more days."

"I feel a week would be best."

"I suppose you're right. I'll stay a week."

"Splendid."

When their meeting was concluded, Hound decided to go to his room. At the foot of the staircase, he found Anna waiting for him.

"Why are you going to your room now, Hound?" she asked. "It's still early. I would like to spend some private time talking to you."

"My room is private, if you'd feel comfortable talking there."

"That would be fine, but I would prefer that no one know. They might get the wrong idea, if you know what I mean."

"Sure, come to my room in five minutes. Make sure no one sees you."

Anna discreetly arrived in Hound's room and made herself comfortable in a chair. She didn't know it, but Sophia had been looking through the slightly opened door of her room and saw her sneak into Hound's room. This was disturbing to her.

"Well, here we are, Hound," Anna said happily. "What shall we talk about?"

"What do you want to talk about?"

"Where would you like to go on our honeymoon?"

"I'll leave that up to you. James told me that you've been everywhere in the world and seen everything worth seeing."

"Did he tell you that I hoped we could go to live on your ranch as soon as possible after we are married?"

"Yes, but are you sure that's where you want be on your honeymoon?"

"Yes, Hound! Please, if you wouldn't mind."

"OK, if that's what you want."

"Do you think I can learn to be a real cowgirl?"

"Sure. There are some experts working for me that can teach you all you need to know."

"I would like that very much, Hound. I want to learn and do everything to fit into your life, make you happy and proud to be married to me."

Hound sat looking at Anna and then he smiled. He was playing a game and hoping a month would give him enough time to devise a plan to remedy the situation he was in.

"Why would you think it necessary to do anything more than just be you after we are married, Anna?" he said. "Our marriage has been arranged. We don't have a choice. Why should we be concerned about being happy and proud of each other? All we have to do is be married."

Anna was clearly saddened by his remarks. He was testing her to see how she would respond but didn't enjoy hurting her feelings.

"I'm aware that you didn't have a choice about marrying me, Hound," she replied, "but I was given the opportunity to reject you as my husband. I wanted to be your wife, but not to treat you as a token husband and not to be treated as such by you. We can be a dynamic couple and be happier than either of us ever dreamed, if you will just give our marriage a chance. You had no idea how your life would change when you decided to come here, did you?"

"No, Anna, I didn't. I was told I'd have the choice to return to my former life if I didn't want what would be offered to me."

"Do you feel like a trap was set and baited with lies, that you wouldn't be here otherwise?"

"That's right, but I probably shouldn't have admitted that to you."

"Why not?"

Hound shook his head but didn't answer. He felt that trusting her with certain information would be a mistake.

"Do you feel I'm not to be trusted, Hound?" she asked. "Do you think I wouldn't keep what you say to me just between us?"

"Honestly, I don't know who to trust right now."

"I understand, Hound, but in time you'll learn that I can be trusted. Don't worry about anything you've said to me. It will not be told to anyone."

For whatever the reason, Hound believed what she had said. However, he would remain guarded with other things he was thinking. He certainly would remain silent about his desire to formulate a plan to separate himself successfully and safely from the situation he was in.

Getting free from obligation to the Sanchez Cartel was a lengthy and difficult process, but it was simple in comparison to escaping the organization that was coercing him to become a member. The benefits promised him were unbelievable, too good to be true. However, he was certain they were real. When something that was too good to be true was true, then having them would come at a huge price. It was this that concerned him the most. The wealth and power of the organization was so great that it could only have been achieved, grown and maintained by deeds that even he would find inconceivable and beyond repulsive. Of course, there was always a chance he was wrong. However, his instinct convinced him that he wasn't.

Anna remained in Hound's room for another hour before retiring to hers. They spent the time talking about a variety of topics. Hound made sure any further discussion regarding the organization was avoided. He spent most of the time answering questions about his ranch in Montana, being careful to avoid saying too much about Dobi.

24

Anna spent as much time as possible at Hound's side during the remainder of his stay. A good deal of that time was spent alone with him in his room. Not once did she indicate a desire to sleep with him. He was relieved, as he felt that would not be received well by her father should it occur and he find out. In addition to that, he knew having sex with her would only further decrease any chance of his being dismissed from his obligation to James and the organization.

Anna was a most desirable woman, but she couldn't compete with Rita. However, Sophia reminded him of Rita in many ways. Had he met Sophia under normal circumstances, he would have tried to develop a relationship with her. Diana was visiting Sophia and her family in Italy. Sophia had returned to the London estate at the invitation of Diana to come for a vacation visit. Hound wished she hadn't come. He knew she was attracted to him as well but had no idea just how much.

Anna was visiting Hound in his room late one afternoon. She decided to discuss something she felt was important.

"Hound, have you wondered why I haven't asked to sleep with you since the last time I tried?" she asked during a visit in his room.

"Not really. I felt you realized how it might affect your father, if he were to find out."

"That's not the reason, Hound. I made a vow to wait until after we were married. I want our first time to be as special as possible for both of us. I had been saving myself for marriage before I met you, and then I forgot myself for a time because I wanted you so much."

Hound was surprised and reluctant to believe her.

"Are you saying that you've never been with a man?"

"Yes, but you don't believe me, do you?"

"I would never call anyone a liar without knowing for certain they were. You told me you were in love once, but he died."

"I thought I was in love, but now I know different. Besides, I never had sex with him. Well, you'll know for certain on our wedding night. Hound, there's something you'll learn about me that should be important. I will never lie to you. Can I expect the same in return?"

"There will be things about my business that I can't talk about."

"Yes, I know. I'm referring to other things, especially those which will keep our marriage as good as it can be, the way I want it to be and I hope you do too."

Hound believed she was sincere regarding her honesty. This was in her favor. However, he was able to evade promising her the same.

Hound left the estate to return home early on a Monday morning. Anna flew with him to London on James's jet.

"I will be counting the days until you return for our wedding next month, Hound," Anna said as he prepared to board his jet in London. "The ceremony will take place on the second. I hope you will arrive at least a couple of days before."

"Yes, at least."

"Who will be the family members you bring with you?"

"I'll be alone."

"Don't you at least want your parents to attend? What about a best man?"

"My parents won't be able to attend, and James has agreed to be my best man."

Anna kissed and held him for a moment. He smiled and then turned and walked to board his jet that was fueled and waiting. He looked out through the left side window of the cockpit and saw her smiling and waving a final goodbye. He returned the smile and waved. Then he taxied the jet toward the runway for takeoff.

Hound's thoughts were focused on the controls of his aircraft until it reached a cruising altitude of thirty-two thousand feet and he set a course for New York. He would have some time now to consider his current situation.

He had expected to have a choice regarding membership in the organization, after learning all that it was about. Instead, he had found himself forced into membership, still knowing but a small bit of what he believed would be revealed to him. However, seeing only the tip of the iceberg had convinced him that what lay beneath the surface was a very monstrous, dark, nefarious and dangerous beast.

Hound was tired when he landed in New York City. He went straight to his hotel and ordered a meal to be sent to his suite. Shortly after eating, he showered and went to bed. After sleeping soundly for ten hours, he awoke to a new day.

He looked out his window and saw that a heavy downpour of rain was falling on the Big Apple. He opened the sliding glass doors leading onto the balcony patio and could see the frequent flashes of lightning and hear the rumbles of thunder that followed. He had planned to fly to his ranch in Montana and hoped the weather wouldn't delay his planned departure time early that afternoon.

Hound was hungry and decided to have a late breakfast in the hotel dining room. He was seated at a table next to a window in the dining room and was reviewing the menu when he was interrupted by a man who had arrived at his table and was speaking to him.

"Hello, young man," said the elderly gentleman. "Would you mind if I joined you for a meal?"

Hound looked up at the stranger. He was well-dressed, of

average height and weight, was holding an umbrella and appeared to be in his sixties. He had a full head of hair and a beard. Hound was quick to notice that both were as white as newly fallen snow and handsomely groomed in a conservative style. There was something about the man that made Hound feel comfortable with him.

"Yes, please join me, sir," replied Hound.

"Thanks. Young man, I always enjoy meeting new people and I hate to eat alone. My name is John."

"Nice to meet you, John. My father's name is John. So is mine, but I prefer to be called Hound, my nickname."

"OK. Hound, you have an unusual nickname, but I like it. How did you get it?"

After the stranger sat down, Hound explained how he earned the name.

"That's a wonderful story, Hound, said John. "I sense you don't live in the city."

"No, I live on a ranch in Montana. I was returning from London and spent the night here."

"I would bet you were in London on business."

"Well, yes, I was."

"I hope your business went well."

"Not as well as I had hoped for, but maybe things will improve."

"I believe anything can be made better when the right time to act arrives. One just has to be smart enough to allow the right time to arrive and know when it does."

"John, you may be right about that. It often takes a certain amount of time to figure out how to solve a problem."

"May I ask you a personal question, Hound?"

"I suppose so. What?"

"How big is your problem?"

"Well, considering all that I know at this point, I'd have to say it's paramount."

"Do you want to talk about it?"

"I wish I could, but I can't."

"Why not?"

"I won't tell you that either."

"I promise that no one will ever know but us if you want to confide in me."

Hound's thoughts turned to the possibility that John could have been sent by James to test him, to see if he would divulge confidential information to a seemingly honest and trustworthy elderly gentleman.

"John, did you approach me by chance, or did someone send you?" asked Hound.

"Hound, I'm simply a man who wanted some company to share a meal with. I felt you would be a good conversationalist. Who knows that you would be here that could have sent me?"

Hound considered John's question to be a good point. He had told no one of his plan to stay the night in New York City, or what hotel he would choose. However, he would not risk confiding his business with James.

"You make a valid point, John, but I never share my personal or professional business with a stranger," said Hound. "However, I will say that my instinct tells me that you're a good man, one of integrity, so I hope you're not offended."

"Of course not. I completely understand. One can never be sure who they can trust until it is proven to them. Perhaps you would allow me to tell you a story. All you have to do is listen and not respond unless you want to."

The waiter arrived at their table to take their food order. The conversation was paused and they both placed their order. Hound told John to proceed with his story, but John suggested they just have a casual conversation until they had eaten, and then he could tell the story without interruption.

Hound smiled and agreed.

During the time they waited for their meal to arrive and as they ate it, John talked about his experiences while living in the city. Hound talked about his ranch in Montana and had a lot of fond things to say about his friends there, especially Pardner.

After the meal was finished and the table was cleared, Hound ordered a refill of coffee for himself and John and then asked the waiter not to return as they wanted to have an uninterrupted discussion.

"John, I'm very interested to hear your story now," said Hound, "if you still wish to share it with me."

"I do, and may I make a request?"

"Of course."

"Hound, I would prefer not to be interrupted by any comments or questions until the story has been told."

"Certainly, agreed. Please proceed."

John smiled and nodded his head as a sign of his appreciation. He loosened his necktie, took a sip of coffee, relaxed in his chair, and then stared at Hound for a moment. A genuine expression of sincerity replaced his smile.

"Hound, I want you to imagine and envision a large, towering pyramid," John began. "Imagine this pyramid to represent the world. At its pinnacle is a group of men. They are the wealthiest men on the pyramid. They have combined their individual wealth into an organization that they are the sole members of. With great wealth comes great power. Their combined wealth has made this organization the most powerful in the world. Their agenda is to control and direct the destiny of the world and has been the goal of the organization since it was first formed hundreds of years ago. For all those years, the wealth and power of the organization has been transferred to blood relatives who are chosen by retiring members to replace them in the organization. Since its creation, wealth and power has increased from one generation to the next. As such, so has the control the organization has on the world. As we continue to descend by exact degrees down the pyramid, we will find individuals who by virtue of the organization's influence have also been placed in strategic positions and allowed to acquire their own specific wealth, status and power. As we further descend, we see other individuals assisted to gain wealth and power, but never more than those above them on the pyramid. To keep their financial status and their power, they all do as they are directed by the power just above them on the pyramid, which are all controlled by those at the pinnacle. Thus, it goes all the way to the bottom of the pyramid. While most, if not all, of these individuals are known for their wealth, position and power, those at the pinnacle remain shadowed in secrecy, but in command and control of all those they have empowered below them. Normal citizens all over the world simply are used as pawns in the organization's ongoing game of chess to achieve their goal to have global control of the world. Specific politicians on a state and federal level, including those in Congress, the Senate and indeed the President of the United States, are elected by the influence exerted by the organization at the pyramid's pinnacle. So great has that influence become that they contribute to who will be the dictators in non-democratic countries and top leaders in democratic countries other than the United States. The pawns who vote in democratic elections are ignorant to the fact that even they are influenced by the power of this secret group of men. In addition, they are oblivious to the fact that in the future their vote will count for nothing more than to appease their need and desire to feel in control of what type of government governs society. This secret organization and the men in it are evil by nature. They may never be eliminated, but they can be slowed in their progress. This will provide the people of the world an opportunity to finally see the truth regarding how society has been in a slow descent for the worst in such a discreet fashion that it has almost occurred, and a world dictatorship is on their doorsteps. When the time is right, it will be one man who defies the power of the organization and shakes that power to its very foundation. It will be a man that they bring into their organization believing he is something that he is not. It is the destiny of this lone, righteous rogue to buy a specific amount of time to allow all of humanity to wake to the truth. He will have no choice but to fulfill his destiny."

John paused and stood to stretch before returning to his seat. He remained silent, looking and smiling at Hound again, waiting for him to speak. Hound stared at John for a moment before he was able to speak.

"John, that was some story!" Hound finally said. "Where did you hear it, or is it something you just made up to entertain listeners?"

"I'll leave that for you to decide, Hound. Thank you for listening. What you choose to do with the information is also for you to decide. I'm certain your instinct and intelligence will lead you to the right decision. Now, enough has been said about such things. I have enjoyed our time together, but I must leave you now."

"Who are you, John? What are you really doing here?"

"I'm just a senior citizen who didn't want to eat alone and felt you would be good company and might enjoy my story. Did you?"

"Actually, I did, John. It was the best I've ever heard."

The old man stood up from the table, smiled, shook Hound's hand and then slowly walked away. Hound watched him until he left the dining room and vanished from sight. He was anxious to know who John really was and why he had arrived to tell the story. However, he felt John, like himself, might have had a good reason for not telling him. John showing up in such a mysterious way and the story he told were both bizarre, but he was becoming accustomed to those kinds of things happening. Still, the story caused him to consider and review some specific possibilities.

When Hound returned to his suite, the thunderstorm had ended, and the sun was beginning to break through the dissipating storm clouds. At 2 p.m., he boarded his jet and took off, heading for his ranch in Montana. During the entire flight, he couldn't stop thinking about his breakfast meeting with the mysterious stranger and the story he told. He was happy when it was time to begin the descent of his jet and the familiar Montana landscape came into view below.

Hound landed and taxied his plane to the front of the hangar. He chatted with employees as they moved the jet inside. No one had expected his return, so he wasn't met by anyone immediately. However, when the ranch hands heard and then saw Hound's jet approaching, Hud told Kelly and Stacy to go and welcome him home. They were working about a mile from the airstrip and hurried on horseback to reach the hangar. Hound was about to drive home in a ranch truck when he heard Kelly yelling his name and saw the two girls galloping their horses toward him. When they reached the truck, Hound got out to greet them.

"We didn't expect you to be back as soon as this, Hound!" Kelly told him in an excited manner. "Dobi said you might be away for quite a while, but I'm glad you're home!"

"Me too!" added Stacy. "Everything seems better when you're home."

Both girls gave him a big hug.

"Well, thank you, ladies," he replied. "I didn't think my time away would be short either, but my business was handled quicker than anticipated. I'm happy to be back. You ladies are looking good. Has everything been going well on the ranch?"

They assured him that all was well.

"How's Dobi doing?" asked Hound.

"She's been out of town on personal business for a few days," said Kelly.

"Really, what kind of business?"

"Nobody knows. She just told Hud to take care of things until she got back, if you didn't come home first."

"OK, but did she say where she was going?"

"Nope, she didn't. It seemed as if she needed to keep her plans a secret."

"Well, personal business is not for others to know."

"How was your trip? Did you have any fun, do anything interesting?"

"I suppose it was interesting, but not fun."

"Hound, you didn't spend time with any ladies while you were away?"

"Actually, I spent time with three women."

"I would guess they were beautiful."

"I suppose so."

"Well, then you did have some fun!"

"No, they were lovely, but they stressed me a great deal."

"What do you mean?"

"Never mind, Kelly. It's a tale I don't care to tell now."

Kelly and Stacy saw that his trip had not been enjoyable. He looked tired and troubled and didn't want to discuss it.

"I guess you'll be going home to get some rest now," Kelly remarked. "You look tired."

"Yep, that's exactly what I'm going to do. How's Pardner?"

"He's been well, but he's never happy when you're not here."

Pardner was lying beneath the large tree on the riverbank. He sprang to his feet when he saw his friend arrive in the truck. Hound walked toward the tree and was met halfway there by his dog. They returned to the tree. Hound sat down under it and Pardner joined him.

The dog sat still, looking at the curious expression on his master's face as Hound picked up a small stone and threw it into the slow flowing river.

"Well, Pardner, it seems like I've managed to fall into another huge pile of shit!" Hound said, thinking out loud. "Hell, pal, I didn't fall! I jumped in it! You're the only living thing that I can talk to about the Pandora's Box I've opened."

"What are you talking about, Hound?" came the familiar voice of Dobi, who was approaching from behind the tree.

Hound stood up and greeted her as she stepped into sight. She was smiling, but he sensed it might be forced, that Dobi was not in the happy mood she wanted him to believe.

"What is this about you opening Pandora's Box?" asked Dobi. "Your trip was shorter than I expected. Did something bad happen that caused you to cut your trip short?"

"No, I just completed my business sooner than was anticipated."

"OK, then tell me about the huge pile of shit you've jumped into, the Pandora's Box that has been opened."

"Oh, well, I was just thinking out loud about a bad business decision I made. It's really not worth mentioning. How are you, Dobi? I was told you were away on some business of your own."

"Hound, you don't make bad business decisions. However, I can see you don't want to tell me the truth, so I won't ask anything further about your trip. I'm glad you're back. To be honest, I was afraid you'd be gone a long time, maybe not ever come back."

Dobi paused briefly to hear what Hound would say next. He remained silent.

"Yes, I've been out of town on some business," she told him, "but it's necessary that I discuss the nature of that business with you. It concerns my forty-nine percent ownership of the ranch."

"OK, how does it concern me?"

"Some very strange things happened after you left, Hound. After considering everything, I think maybe they're good things for me. However, I wanted to talk to you about it before making a decision."

"OK, tell me what's going on."

"A couple of days after you left, I received a phone call from two separate individuals. One was from a company wanting to buy the ranch. When they were told I only owned forty-nine percent, they wanted to talk to me anyway. I went out of town to see them. I was shocked when they offered to buy my forty-nine percent for the amount they were prepared to offer for one hundred percent. The offer was a great deal more than one hundred percent of the ranch will ever be worth. I knew something was suspicious about that, so I asked why. They want the oil and natural gas that's on the ranch. I explained that you likely wouldn't agree to let them drill on the land. They said an offer would be made that even you wouldn't refuse."

Hound knew the organization was behind the offer made to Dobi.

"Yes, Dobi, I suppose that might be possible," Hound replied, "but why would you consider selling? You could probably make as much money from the mineral royalties as from selling your ranch. Of course, it would take some time. Besides, I thought you had planned to buy my fifty-one percent back as soon as possible. Don't you want the ranch to remain in your family as a tradition?"

"Yes, if the other call I received hadn't offered me the career opportunity of a lifetime and changed my mind!"

"What was the offer?"

"I was offered the position of Montana state veterinarian. Do you know what a great career status that would be?"

"No, but you would know that better than me. Anyway, why couldn't you accept the position and still keep the ranch?"

"My office would be in the capital city. I would have to live in Helena. A lot of travel will be involved as well. I wouldn't have time to even visit the ranch often, much less contribute my fair share of work to run it."

"You really want the position, don't you, Dobi?"

"Yes, but I don't understand why I would be selected for the position."

Hound felt certain the organization was behind this offer too.

"What were you told?" he asked.

"That my age, history as a vet, contributions in time and money to charities for the care of homeless animals, people and just overall citizenship to better my state was most impressive."

"I can understand that."

"Hound, you're really the person responsible for most of the things that I'm getting the credit for. Your money kept my practice going and built the shelters."

"So what? You made sure they were run properly. Anyway, how do I fit into your plans? If you want the position, then take it. I'm happy for you."

"I'm going to accept the position, but I wanted to offer you the opportunity to buy my forty-nine percent. I know you don't want the company that made me the offer for a partner."

"Well you're right, I don't, but you said they would pay you more than one hundred percent of what the ranch was worth. Will I have to pay that much for your forty-nine percent?"

"I would never be unfair and do that to you. All you need to do is pay me back the money I've been paying you monthly to buy the ranch back."

"Well, I appreciate your sense of fairness. When do you want to finalize all this?"

"As soon as possible. I start my position as state veterinarian on the first of next month. I need to be moved into my new home in Helena by then."

"Have you found a place to live already?"

"Yes, a beautiful new home on fifty acres. I want to keep my horses and have a place to ride."

"OK, we'll transact the deal tomorrow. I know Beth will fit us in for an appointment to get all the paperwork taken care of."

Hound noticed that Dobi had drifted into deep thought about something. He had a strong suspicion what she was thinking about.

"What else is on your mind, Dobi?" he asked, feeling it was time to clear the air.

She looked at him in a serious way and then spoke.

"You're not the least bit upset with my decision to take the position and move to Helena, are you?" she asked.

"Of course not. I want you to be happy, but I also hope you're sure this will make you happy."

"Hound, you really don't care for me in the same way that I do for you. Am I right?" I love you, but we can never be together, can we? You don't love me, do you?"

He had strong feelings for her but knew he couldn't say it. She must never know how he felt, or the reason why he could never act on his feelings. He would likely have to marry Anna and they would live together on the ranch. Dobi would be hurt and he could do nothing to prevent that. She would be moving to Helena and starting a new life. He knew it was for the best and hoped she would find happiness. Therefore, he would answer with a lie, one that he hated having to tell, but it was necessary.

"Dobi, I'm so sorry, but no, I don't love you," he replied.

"Is it because I slept with another man? Did you love me before I made that terrible mistake?"

"No, I never loved you, Dobi. I'm sorry."

The look that came to her face spoke volumes about the hurt she was feeling over his answer. She fought to hold back the tears. To her credit, she was successful in doing so.

"Thank you for your honesty, Hound," she said, smiling. "I guess I made the right decision about my future."

"Yes, probably so, Dobi."

She managed to wait until she was away from him before she began sobbing uncontrollably. Hound sat back down next to Pardner and began staring at the river.

"God damn the life I've been forced to live for so long!" he said in almost a yell. "Damn those who forced me to live it and hurt the hearts of so many good people that have had to suffer me!"

"Pardner drew close to him and laid his head in Hound's lap. It was although he was trying to comfort his friend the only way he knew how. Hound looked at him and smiled.

"I feel like you're the only one who would ever forgive me for all I've done and will do in the future," he said to the dog.

Pardner responded with a loud and long howl, as if to affirm Hound's statement.

"How about we catch some fish for supper, Pardner?" asked Hound.

Pardner howled again, seeming to understand and agree that fish for supper would be nice, and then he followed Hound to the house to obtain the needed gear.

Beth met with Hound and Dobi at 10 a.m. the next day. It was a little past noon when all the necessary paperwork was signed, and Hound became the sole owner of the Double D Ranch. He asked Dobi to join him at the café for lunch. She declined the invitation, saying she had made other plans. She asked if she could continue to live in her house until she was able to move into her new home near Helena. Naturally, he told her yes.

Neither Hound nor anyone else on the ranch except Kelly and Stacy saw Dobi very much for the rest of the time she lived on the ranch. Hound told them to help her pack and do other things in preparation for her move.

On the evening before she left for Helena, Dobi had supper with all the cowboys and girls in the large bunkhouse. The cook prepared a special meal for the occasion. Hound didn't attend. The goodbye speech she gave was heartfelt and received as such by everyone there. At 9 a.m. the next morning, she drove from the ranch. The large horse trailer carrying four horses was hooked to the rear of her truck. The moving van loaded with all her household belongings followed behind her. She didn't want to say goodbye to Hound, as it would be too hard. He and Pardner stood on a hill, behind a large tree, and watched her leave. They continued watching until she drove out of sight.

25

The next Saturday was a day the cowboys had been busy preparing for. It was rodeo time in Helena again. Cowboys and girls would be coming from all over the state and from other states to compete for big prize money.

With help from the cowboys and Dobi, Kelly and Stacy had become good at barrel racing and had entered the event. Kelly had suffered the scrapes and bruises of learning to ride saddle broncs. She hadn't yet perfected all the techniques needed to afford her a reasonable chance of winning any money, but she'd entered the event for the experience. She hoped to maybe get lucky and a few in the competition be unlucky.

The cowboys were proud of her courage but concerned for her safety. The broncs supplied for this rodeo were among the meanest and intense buckers to be found anywhere. Hound wasn't in favor of her taking such a risk, but like the cowboys admired her grit and determination.

Hound arrived at the bunkhouse on Friday morning to have breakfast with the hands and discuss the rodeo with them. They would leave after breakfast and travel to Helena and be ready to compete the next day. Every cowboy and girl had entered at least one event. Several had entered more. Sam and his crew had decided to ride a bull, saddle and bareback bronc. Like Kelly, they had been practicing and receiving instruction from their experienced ranch peers for some time.

"Sam, are you and your crew sure of what you're doing?" asked Hound as a big smile appeared on his face. "What you're going to ride is a bit different than a Harley."

"Fuck yes! Hound, we've become damn good cowpokes since we first arrived here. Hell, Hud and the rest of the boys think we might even win some money."

"That's right, Hound," said Hud as the rest of the hands nodded in agreement. "These motorcycle jockeys ain't half bad cowboys. Besides, even if they don't win any money, there will be plenty of women to comfort them. There's always more than enough willing ladies to go around at the big party after the rodeo."

"What party?"

"Helena always throws a big outdoor shindig at the fairgrounds after the rodeo. They build a huge wooden dance floor and hire a popular band to provide the music. We have to pay for our food and drinks."

"The party sounds like a lot of fun."

"Yep, you'll enjoy it very much."

"I don't think I'll be going."

"You have to go, Hound! The owner of the Double D needs to be there in support of all the hands entered in the rodeo who work for you."

"Hell yes! Hound if you ain't gonna show some balls and enter an event, then at least you can watch and cheer for us that do," Curly stated in a rude and challenging way. "Fuck! Everyday I see you doing those ridiculous exercise and running workouts to keep yourself in top physical condition, but you never use it for anything except to look good for the ladies."

Curly was seated next to Sam at the large table.

"Be careful, Curly," Sam whispered to him.

Curly was tired of taking Sam's word that Hound wasn't to be provoked. He had from the first time he met Hound been jealous and envious of him.

"What do I have to be careful of?" replied Curly in loud voice so all could hear. "Our boss only acts tough when he has tough men to back his play."

Everyone at the table became still and silent.

"Opinions are like assholes, Curly," Hound replied softly with a smile appearing on his face. "Everybody has one."

Pardner was sitting on the floor next to Hound's chair. He didn't like Curly's tone of voice and seemed to sense he was being aggressive toward Hound. He reared up on the side of the table and growled, showing his teeth to Curly seated on the opposite side.

Curly was convinced the dog was about to cross the table and attack him. He threw the steak knife he held in his hand at the growling dog. The point of the knife's blade hit Pardner in the front of his right shoulder and penetrated it about two inches. He yelped from the pain and then his paws slipped from the table. Hound laid him on the floor and pulled the knife from his shoulder.

The wound was determined not to be severe when pressure was applied to it with a cloth and the small amount of bleeding stopped. Everyone was standing in a semi-circle around Pardner, happy that he wasn't severely injured, except Curly, who remained seated in his chair.

Hound didn't say a word as his picked up the knife from the floor. He stood, turned and looked at Curly, who had retrieved another knife and was cutting another bit of steak. Hound began to walk slowly to the other side of the table. Curly chewed quickly and swallowed as Hound approached him. He stood up holding the knife in his hand.

"Mother fucker!" Curly yelled loudly. "Drop that fucking knife and don't come any closer! I'll gut you like a hog!"

Hound remained silent and kept coming. Curly looked into Hound's eyes and saw a man void of fear and filled with determination of purpose drawing nearer. He gave a quick thought to the warning Sam had given him about Hound. Curly felt the skin all over his body crawl. He had suddenly realized that he was about to die.

"Don't kill him, Hound!" shouted Sam as he hurried to get between the two men. "He's no match for you and not worth killing!

Hound stopped walking for an instant. Then, holding the knife in the same position as when he fought hand to hand with enemy soldiers in Vietnam, he moved forward again.

"If there was ever a man who deserved to die, this lowlife piece of shit is that man," said Hound in his usual soft and calm voice."

"Maybe so, but think of the consequences!" shouted Hud.

"Damn right! Think about what will happen to you!" added Sam. "Shit man! We all need you to remain as our boss. What would happen to the ranch if you weren't around?"

"We all need you, Hound!" yelled Kelly as she joined in to try and help. "Pardner needs you to be his best friend and take care of him!"

Kelly's remark about Pardner was what sparked Hound's decision to halt and consider her words. He dropped the knife and then looked hard at Curly.

"Get your worthless ass outside, Curly," Hound told him, still using that soft, calm voice. "I can't beat the hell out of you, but I can beat the shit out of you."

Curly, realizing he had no choice and thinking he might beat Hound in a fight where all things were considered fair, walked outside with Hound close behind. Everyone else followed them. Once outside and some distance from the bunkhouse, Curly turned and quickly charged his opponent. A second later, he was rolling on the ground trying to breath after being hit in the throat. Hound proceeded to give him the worst beating he had ever received or would ever endure again short of dying. His nose, both jaws, legs and arms were broken when the beating ended.

"You're going to the hospital where you will die or recover, Curly," said Hound. "If you recover, I never want to see you again. If I do, I'll kill you. Do you understand and believe me?"

The semiconscious man lying face up on the ground, suffering intense pain and looking at the blurred figure speaking, managed to convey his understanding and belief in a most convincing manner.

"Sam, Hud, get this son of a bitch to the hospital," Hound told them. "When he is able to travel, tell him to leave Montana and never return."

Sam and Hud hurried to rush Curly to the hospital. They were afraid he would die before they got there.

Hound looked at those who were gathered around. They were all standing silent, each processing the brutal beating he had delivered to Curly. They felt something was deserved but were relieved when Hound spared his life. However, everyone thought the intensity of the injuries Curly sustained from the beating seemed excessive for the crime. Besides, Curly might die from those injuries. It was Kelly who spoke first.

"Are you all right, Hound?" she asked. "Bad morning, huh, boss?"

"I've had better."

"No shit! So has Curly!"

"I need to get Pardner to a vet and get him checked out."

"Pardner is going to be fine, Hound," said Kelly, pointing to the dog who had walked from the bunkhouse and was limping to join the group. "He's not bleeding now, but a vet may want to use a couple of stitches to close the wound. Maybe some antibiotics would be needed as well."

Pardner arrived at Hound's side, licked his hand and sat down. Hound put the dog in his truck and drove to Dobi's former clinic. After he had left, the group returned to the bunkhouse to finish their steak and eggs breakfast before they departed for Helena.

The cook fixed everyone a freshly prepared meal to replace the partially eaten one that was now cold. As they ate and drank coffee, the ranch hands discussed what had happened. Everyone had heard how violent Hound could be when provoked. One of the cowboys remarked how the beating was more than what was deserved for what was done to Pardner.

"What would you do if Curly had hurt someone you loved?" Kelly asked the cowboy.

"I knew Hound was damn fond of his dog, but I didn't know he loved him!"

"Well, cowboy, you know it now. It's best you remember it too."

"Shit! No dog is worth damn near killing a man over!"

"Maybe, but like I said, it's best you remember that Hound would disagree. I think it's best for all of us to remember."

Dr. Susan Boseman now owned Dobi's former clinic. She had been a vet for a year and had worked for Dobi since graduating and receiving her license. She had arranged to buy the clinic when Dobi accepted the position as state veterinarian.

When Hound arrived at the clinic with Pardner, Susan was standing at the front desk, saying goodbye to a client. She had met Hound when she went to work for Dobi and had run into him numerous times in town while shopping for groceries and other things. She had always liked and respected him. She also believed he and Dobi were more than close friends and partners in the ranch. Susan quickly escorted him to an exam room and started to check Partner's injuries.

"This looks like a knife wound, Hound," she said.

"Yes, it is."

"How did it happen?"

"A ranch hand threw a knife at Pardner."

Susan knew how Hound felt about his dog.

"What did you do to the ranch hand?"

"He's no longer employed."

Susan stitched his wound, gave him an injection of antibiotics and then reported that Pardner would be good as new in a short time.

"I suppose you're looking forward to attending the rodeo in Helena, Hound, and the big party after," Susan said as they prepared to leave the exam room.

"I don't plan on going."

"Don't you want to see Dobi and take her to the rodeo and party?"

"Dobi and I have stopped seeing each other. I thought you knew that?"

"Yes, but I heard you were back together?"

"Where did you hear that?"

"Well, Dobi told me."

"I wonder why she would lie to you?"

Susan smiled and took a moment to answer.

"It's probably because I asked if she would be angry should I ask you home for dinner," she said. "It sounds like she feels like things can be worked out between you two. Is that a possibility?"

"No, it's not. Are you a good cook?"

"Sure, if you like chili, spaghetti or beef stew."

"I like all of them."

"Are you hinting that you would accept an invitation to dinner?"

"Of course. Why not?"

"How does tomorrow night sound, say around seven?"

"That's fine, but there's something I need to tell you before we confirm your invitation. You might wish to change your mind when I do."

"I don't like the sound of that, Hound, but please tell me."

"I would enjoy having dinner with you and some friendly conversation, but I plan to get married next month. I wouldn't want you to think we might ever be more than friends, not that I assume you would want more than that."

Susan was more than surprised at what he said.

"Who's the lucky lady?" she asked, trying to conceal her surprise and disappointment. "She's not from around here or she would have been announcing it all over town."

"No, she's not."

"Is that why Dobi gave up the ranch and moved to Helena?"

"No, she doesn't know about it. You're the first person I've told."

"Why?"

"I just wasn't ready to announce it."

"Why did you tell me, Hound?"

"Well, your dinner invitation was very nice and something I would enjoy. I could use some good company. I can see you're surprised, maybe shocked."

"Yes, I suppose, a bit. How long have you been engaged? It couldn't have been very long. You and Dobi broke up only a short time ago. Well, unless you were dishonest with her and unfaithful to your fiancée."

"No, I would never have done that to Dobi."

"I believe that, but it really would have been a trade-off."

"What do you mean?"

"Dobi slept with another man while you and her were together."

"How did you know that?"

"Everyone in town knew it. I thought it was the reason you broke it off with her. I'll never understand why she'd do that when she had you."

"She didn't have me, nor I her, not in that way. I wouldn't commit to the kind of relationship she wanted and needed."

"So, do you think she was maybe trying to punish you?"

"No, I think things just happen. People do things they're sorry for later."

"Well, I know she was sorry. How long have you known your fiancée?"

Hound didn't think it would be wise to tell the truth. It would only lead to more questions that he couldn't answer.

"I've known Anna for a long time," he replied. "We got together while I was away on my last trip and just decided to get married."

"I'm sure she is very beautiful and intelligent."

"Yes, very much so."

"Hound, I've wanted a chance to date you since we first met, but Dobi had you, or at least she said so. I don't think I could see you for dinner and not want to compete for your favor. I'd have no chance at winning, would I?"

On Hound's mind was the fact that by having been trapped into becoming a member of the organization, he had also been forced to surrender his ability to live the way he chose, a way that satisfied his needs and desires, rather than those of a brotherhood of men.

These men were or at least seemed to accept and even be happy with the deal, but he wasn't. For him, no amount of power through wealth was worth losing his freedom as an individual. It seemed as if he were being forced to sell his soul or die to save it. He remembered a scripture in the Bible that he had read and had discussed with his father. "What has a man profited to gain the world, but lose his soul," was the scripture that came to his mind.

"No, Susan, you wouldn't have a chance," he answered, "but neither would I, at least not now."

"What do you mean, not now?"

"Oh, nothing, I was just having a thought."

His thoughts had again focused on the ever so slight possibility that he might find a way to escape becoming a member of the organization. He didn't want to accept an arranged marriage to a woman he didn't love. He was certain that the duties he'd be obligated to as a member of the organization wouldn't make him happy. However, he was also considering the story told to him by the elderly man and who he really was. His thoughts were interrupted by the sound of Susan's voice.

"Hound, if you need to talk about anything, I'm a good listener and will keep it confidential."

Hound felt Susan was genuinely sincere in wanting to listen and help if she could. His instinct told him she was a woman who could be trusted. Unfortunately, he focused on the fact that there was very little if anything she could be told that wouldn't break his word of secrecy to James.

"Susan, I appreciate your concern and offer to be of help, but there's really nothing you can do," he told her, smiling. "Besides, it's my situation and I'll simply have to deal with it on my own, but thanks for offering."

"You're not in love with your fiancée, are you, Hound?"

He realized she had a keen instinct also.

"Why would you think I'm not?" he replied.

"You shouldn't marry her unless you're deeply in love and know for certain she's your true soulmate and feels the same way about you."

"You're right about that, Susan."

Susan looked at him for only a second.

"Oh my gosh!" she said loudly. "You're planning to marry a woman that you don't love! Why?"

"I never said that, Susan."

"I know, but it's true! Is she pregnant?"

"No, of course not."

"Then why?"

Hound knew it was time to leave. He told her goodbye and left the clinic with Pardner walking at his side. Other clients were waiting with their pets to see her. She asked them to excuse her for a moment longer and hurried outside to have a final word with Hound. She stood at the side of his truck as he prepared to leave.

"Hound, I know you don't want to tell me anything," she said, "but I'm here if you change your mind."

"Thanks, Susan, I appreciate that."

"I'd still enjoy your company for dinner, Hound. If nothing else, we can be friends."

"Maybe some other time, Susan."

"OK, I understand."

Hound drove slowly from the clinic's parking lot, turned onto the main highway and drove in the direction of the ranch. He began to think again of the many events in his life that had directed his journey to where he was now.

He had always believed he was headed toward a time and place when he would fulfill his destiny, but he never had a clue as to what it was. Now, he began to wonder if James and the other members of the organization were right, that his destiny would be realized as a member of something he wanted no part of. Perhaps it wasn't being a member that was his destiny, but rather the final part of the journey that would take him to its climax. He again remembered the story told to him by the strange, elderly gentleman. Hound greatly regretted not knowing who the man really was and that he didn't do more to find out.

Hound arrived home and he and Pardner went inside. It was during supper that evening that he made the decision to visit his family in Louisiana.

"Well, Pardner, I'm flying back home to the farm in Louisiana tomorrow," Hound said as if he felt the dog could somehow understand. "I need to visit with my parents and have an important conversation with my father. How would you like to come along? I know Mom and Dad would get a kick out of finally getting to see you. You look exactly like another dog I had as a friend in my younger years."

Pardner howled an acceptance to the invitation, as if he did understand.

"Yep, ole Hunter and I were best pals, just like we are," said Hound. "There will never be another Hunter, but never another Pardner either."

26

The next morning, all the ranch hands except those who were entered in the rodeo and in Helena were taking care of ranch operations. Hound thought he would make a stop in Phoenix on his way to Louisiana. He wanted to visit with Maggie, if she had the time. She was at home when he called.

"Damn! Hound, it's good to hear from you!" she said. "Are you well? Is everything OK?"

"I suppose things are as usual, Maggie. I was wondering if we could meet at my desert estate this evening for dinner and a visit. There's something I want to talk to you about."

"Hell yes! I welcome the chance to see you whenever it's possible. Shit! Have you gotten your ass in another crack and need my help to get you out?"

"No, I want to talk to you about something else."

"What time are you arriving? I'll pick you up at the airport."

"I've got a car rented and waiting. Just meet me at my estate around seven. I'll stop by the market and pick up something to cook for dinner."

"What can I bring?"

"Just yourself."

"How about I get there around six and help with the cooking? Then we'll have more time to talk."

"OK, I'll see you at six."

Hound took off from the ranch in his jet, climbed to his cruising altitude and then was given a direct course of flight to Phoenix.

Maggie arrived at Hound's desert estate a few minutes early. She spent a moment talking to the security guard at the front gate and then parked her car in the drive at the home's front entrance.

Pardner howled a signal of her arrival and Hound went to the door to greet his friend. He opened the door as Maggie was walking toward it. She hurried to greet him with a traditional passionate kiss followed by a lengthy embrace.

"God damn! Hound, it's so great to see you again!" she said as the embrace continued. "I'm happy you decided to come for a visit. How long will you be here?"

"Just tonight, Maggie. I'll leave to see my family in Louisiana tomorrow morning."

"That figures. You never stay long enough to suit me."

Pardner understood that Hound had a special fondness for Maggie and wanted to be introduced. He started to howl as evidence of this. Hound introduced him to her as if he were more human than canine.

Maggie knew how Hound felt about Pardner and took a moment to gently rub his head and pat his sides. The dog took an immediate liking to her.

Hound and Maggie took a seat in the living room for a time to visit before they started preparing dinner.

"Did you come for a visit because you wanted to see me, Hound?" she asked. "Or is there something you need me to do for you?"

"I told you that I wasn't in any trouble that required your help, Maggie."

"I know, but you said there was something you wanted to talk to me about. That usually means you need a favor."

"Well, I do. Actually, I need two favors."

"What?"

"I need you to retire from working with the cartel and come to work for me. I still want Bear to do the same."

"We've discussed that before, Hound. You know mine and Bear's answer is still no. What's the other favor?"

"I need you to use your contacts to find out as much as possible about Sir James Huntington from London, England."

"Isn't that the guy who paid me to deliver that mysterious letter to you?"

"Yes."

"Is he giving you problems? Why do you need to investigate him?"

Hound had to be careful not to give her more information than was safe.

"No, of course not, but I just want to know as much as I can find out about him, professionally and personally. I don't want him to know that you're the one trying to get the information."

"Not that he will, but why not?"

"I can't tell you that, Maggie. Just know that he can never find out. If you can't maintain your anonymity, then don't try to get the information."

"Sounds like this guy might not like being checked out."

"No, he wouldn't, Maggie."

"You're not going to tell me what was in that letter, are you?"

"No, I can't do that."

"I know you told me that you're not in any kind of trouble, but I sense that you are, and Sir Asshole Huntington is responsible. That's right, isn't it?"

"Maggie, please don't ask any questions. I can't answer them without putting us both at risk. Putting you at risk is why I don't want you to investigate him if he should find out about it. Trust me on this. I know what I'm talking about."

Maggie had no doubt that he was sincere and knew what he was talking about. She assured him that all needed precautions would be taken to ensure James knew nothing. If that wasn't possible, then she wouldn't proceed. They changed the topic of their conversation and went to the kitchen and began preparing dinner. They sat at the dining table after dinner sipping wine. Hound wanted to know how business with the cartel was going.

"Things aren't as simple and predictable as they used to be, Hound," she told him. "A lot more violence is necessary to deal with the competition. The major problem when you were in charge were the wars fought in Colombia to keep the Sanchez family in power. Those were violent and bloody, but business in the States remained easy to maintain. Naturally, there were times when specific interference had to be discouraged by violent means, but it was always handled without the violence being reported by the news as street wars. You predicted the time would come when that would happen, do you remember?"

"Yes, I do. Maggie, it will only get worse as time goes by. I know I sound like a broken record, but it's only a matter of time until you, Bear and many, maybe all, the biker club members wind up dead or in prison. There are some powerful competitors in the game now. They're gaining in power consistently. Not only are the cartels a threat, but law enforcement is going to continue putting you more and more at risk. Not only does the threat come from honest federal, state and local agencies, but the corrupt ones too. They are the worst risk of all."

"I suppose we'll just have to keep payoffs to them sufficient in amounts."

"Damn it! Maggie, very powerful men hiding in the shadows, unknown to anyone, are controlling the drug business worldwide. If it's decided by them that the Sanchez Cartel and those who are associated with it should fall and another replace it, then you don't have enough money to pay anybody off."

Maggie knew Hound had instinct about life that was reliable, but she felt the urgency and sincerity he was presenting meant there was more than instinct behind his warnings.

"Hound, what do you know that the rest of us don't?" she asked.

He had already confided more to her than was his intent. No more could be disclosed. He had already crossed a boundary that James could easily view as breaking the vow of secrecy.

"I can't say more, Maggie," Hound told her, "but please remember and heed everything I've told you."

"Why do you want me to find out all I can about Sir James? Is he connected to what you just told me?"

"Maggie, I simply want to know as much as possible about the man's character, business dealings and financial status. It doesn't mean he's connected to anything."

"Hound, I find it very unusual that you don't already know these things. You've always had the ability to read people."

"Yes, but I need to know if my instinct about this particular man is correct."

"What if I can't find out anything you need to know about him?"

"Well, then that will help to confirm that my instinct about him is likely correct."

"All right, I'll see what I can do."

"How long will it take?"

"Give me a week. I'll need to know as much as you can tell me about him to expedite things."

"I can give you the address of his estate in England and the names of his immediate family. That's all."

Hound provided Maggie with the information. He again stressed the importance of James never knowing she was investigating him. She was convinced of the certain danger implied and gave her word to not try if there was a chance he would find out. Hound changed the subject of their conversation.

"How's Bear doing these days?" he asked.

"He's busy taking care of business in Colombia. I think Bear has resigned to the fact he will never be able to safely return to the States without running the risk of being arrested and sent to prison."

"Do you think he would give up his association with the cartel in exchange for a clean criminal record?"

"I don't think he would. Besides, even it that were possible, he, like me, would never give up our business relationship and position with the cartel. You know we're born outlaws and are addicted to the money. Shit! Hound, Bear and I are both worth close to a billion dollars. We'll double that in a year."

"If both of you will come to work with me, I'll make sure you double it."

"Hound, even if we wanted to finally adhere to all your warnings, we couldn't accept your offer."

"Is that because you think the cartel will never allow you to resign?"

"Of course. That's right and you know it."

"If it were possible, then would you accept my offer?"

Maggie smiled.

"Hound, you've been making offers to Bear and me ever since you were allowed to resign from the cartel. My answer is still no, but thank you. I'm certain Bear feels the same way, but you can ask him."

"I plan to do that, Maggie. If I can convince him, then maybe he can help me convince you."

"Not likely, but I'd never say never. By the way, are you going to invite me to spend the night?"

"Would that be another favor for a favor, Maggie?"

"No, not this time. I want to be with you, but only if you want it too."

"Thank you. Maggie, would you like to spend the night and let me enjoy you sexually?"

"As always, my darling, you can enjoy me at any time."

Hound found his intimate time with her that night extraordinary. Sex with Maggie had always been a satisfying experience, but this time it seemed somehow even more so. The thought came to his mind that perhaps this was the last time they would see each other.

He attributed his thought to the fact he would soon be married and under a business as well as moral obligation to be a faithful husband. For a moment, a thought that Maggie might be close to meeting the climax of her career with the cartel crossed his mind, but it was quickly dismissed. He didn't want to consider that as a possibility.

The next morning, they said goodbye and drove from the estate at the same time. Maggie had much to do that day. At 8 a.m., Hound and Pardner took off from Phoenix. They landed in Louisiana in time to have lunch at the farm with John and Linda. John was waiting when they arrived at the airport.

"Hello, son!" said John as he shook Hound's hand and then embraced him. "It's wonderful that you've come for a visit."

"It's nice to be home again, Dad. How are you? How's Mom?"

"We're both well, son. How are you?"

"Pretty good, but I suppose things could be better."

John heard the concern in Hound's voice and saw it in his expression.

"What's wrong, son?" John asked. "Tell me what's going on."

"Not just now, Dad, but I want to talk to you about something before I leave. Now, I just want to rest a bit and enjoy being home."

"Fair enough, son. Just let me know when you're ready to talk."

Lunch was ready and on the table when they arrived home. Linda had prepared one of Hound's favorite meals. She rushed to give him a warm and welcoming hug and kiss on his cheek when he entered the house.

"Son, your father and I are so happy you decided to come for a visit," she told him. "How long can you stay?"

"Two or three days, maybe longer. It's good to be home and see you and Dad again."

"I hope you stay longer, son. It seems your visits are always too short."

During lunch, his parents updated Hound on everything that was going on in the community and regarding the corporation his father was in charge of. He wasn't surprised that profits were continuing to grow under John's leadership and dedication to the proper performance of his position.

"You're doing an outstanding job, Dad," Hound told his father. "I appreciate that, but it doesn't surprise me."

"Thanks, but I can't take all the credit. Hector plays a huge role in the continued success of your farming and ranching business."

"I know. Maybe you should give yourself and Hector another pay raise."

"Well, I already have."

Hound returned the smile given by his father when he spoke of the pay raises. Unlike Hunter, the dog Hound had as a boy, Pardner was accustomed to being inside the house whenever Hound was. John and Linda were happy to allow him inside. During lunch, Pardner sat quietly next to his master.

"Hound, I can't get over how much Pardner looks like Hunter," said Linda. "Does he bay, howl, as much as Hunter used to do?"

"Sometimes, when he wants to get my attention."

"Hunter did that too."

"Yes, he did."

After lunch, Hound asked his father to take a walk outdoors. John quickly agreed, thinking his son had decided it was time to have a private talk. They walked to the swimming hole and sat on the ground under the large oak tree near the bank of the creek.

"What shall we talk about, Hound?" John asked.

Hound was concentrating intensely and took a moment to answer. He wasn't yet sure he should reveal what was weighing heavily on his mind.

"Dad, naturally I came home unexpectedly because I wanted to see you and Mom. However, it was also because I wanted to discuss something with only you. I feel you're the only person I can trust to keep what I want to talk about just between us. Now, even though I know you will keep it a secret, I'm reluctant to give you some information."

"Why?"

Hound hesitated as he gave final consideration about placing his family at any kind of risk.

"To tell you what I need to talk about will put you and Mom in danger should certain people find out."

"Son, I realize you have a serious problem. If we're in no danger unless I tell anyone, then there will be no danger. I will keep our secret. You have my word. You could trust your mom as well. I hope you know that."

"I do, but I don't want her to worry, and we know she would. No, I want to keep it between you and me."

"All right, Hound, say what you came here to tell me."

Hound told John all that had happened regarding Sir James, beginning with the letter delivered by Maggie. John listened intently, saying nothing until Hound had delivered the complete story, all Sir James had told him.

"Well, Hound, that's quite a tale," said John when it was time for him to respond.

"Yes, it is. What do you think about it?"

"First, what do you think?"

"In what regard?"

"Do you believe any or all of what you were told by Sir James?"

"It seems too science fiction for me to believe, Dad."

"Well, then why are you discussing it with me, a man with much less insight and intelligence than yours?"

"My intelligence says it's impossible, but my instinct says otherwise."

"Son, your intelligence and instinct are so closely related that they provide a check and balance to each other. I believe if the two are in disagreement, then what you were told should be given due consideration."

"OK, but what does your check and balance tell you dad?"

"Hound, my level of intelligence and reliability of instinct is far below yours. If you think what was told to you has a probability of being true, then Sir James and the rest of the organization should not be taken lightly. If even part of what you were told is true, then, son, you're in a bad situation, a really tough spot."

"Yes, I know that."

"What are you going to do?"

"I don't know, Dad, at least not yet, but if what I was told was the truth, then I don't have a choice, do I?"

"Well, Hound, I've heard you say many times over the years that persons always have a choice, if they're prepared to live with the consequences of their choice."

"Yes, I believe that's true, but I'm certainly not going to gamble with the lives of the people I love and reject what I've given my word to do."

"I wouldn't either, son. I suppose what you have to do now is choose to believe what James told you was the truth or a lie. I wish I could decide for you, but the decision is yours alone to make."

Hound had not told John about the old man who mysteriously appeared to have breakfast with him in New York, or what he had said. As the conversation continued, Hound spoke of the incident. A curious look appeared on John's face. Hound sensed the discloser of the old man had triggered a thought by his father that might be of possible significance.

"What's on your mind, Dad?" Hound asked.

"I just had what might be called an unusual feeling, perhaps a premonition, even an epiphany regarding that old man. It's strange that such would come to mind so quickly."

"What are you talking about, Dad?"

"First, why did you really come here to tell me about James and the organization?"

"Like I told you, to get your opinion."

"Did you want my opinion regarding the truth or fiction about what you were told, or did you want my counsel regarding more than just that?"

"What else would I want?"

"Hound, you're too smart to need my review and consideration as to the fact or fiction of anything you learned after you met James and the other members of that mysterious organization. You've already determined that. Now tell me if it is fact or not. What do you believe?"

Hound looked at his father intensely. The expression on his face was one John had never seen before, one that indicated his son had a problem he didn't believe could be solved, a situation he wanted to correct, but couldn't.

"I wasn't told everything, Dad," Hound said, "but what I was told was the truth, I'm certain of it. I won't be fully informed until I take the oath and become a member."

"OK, then why did you really need to talk to me? What do you need and not have that you feel I do?"

"Dad, is it possible that these men, this organization, is evil as such would apply to the teachings of Christianity?"

"Based only on what you were told by James, I couldn't speculate an answer to that, son. However, the old man who visited you for breakfast might be the answer to your question. Who do you think he was?"

"I first thought he was sent by James to test me. He could have followed me from the airport to learn which hotel I was staying at."

"What made you think James may not have sent him?"

"It was the story the old gentleman told me."

"Exactly, Hound, and for some reason you felt he was telling the truth. Now, just tell me how you think this wise old man may be connected to your question about the organization being evil from the standpoint of Christianity."

Hound decided he wouldn't provide a truthful answer. It still seemed too bizarre to consider a possibility.

"Dad, you know I've never been convinced or even came close to supporting a belief in the Christian faith, certainly not like you and Mom always have."

"I know that, son. That has always been a great burden to your mother and me. However, we've always prayed and waited for God to wake you up. Maybe that's what's happening now, and you sense it."

"I can't say that's true at this point."

"Can you say it's not?"

"No, Dad, I suppose not."

"Hound, I'd like to be of more help to you, but maybe I'm not the best qualified to offer what you need. However, a man comes to my mind that likely can."

"Pastor Jim won't be able to help."

"I'm not talking about our church pastor. He's a very good and learned man, but you need something more."

"Who are you talking about, Dad?"

"Bobby Joe Homer. As a young man, he worked on our family farm for my father. Your grandfather believed BJ was the best example of a true Christian and had a better insight into biblical scriptures than anyone he had ever known. I was just a baby when BJ came to work. After I got older, I came to agree with your grandfather's opinion of him."

"How old is this BJ?"

"Well, he's at least in his eighties by now."

"Does he live around here?"

"No, BJ lives some distance from here, out in the swamplands. One day he simply announced his plan to build a cabin on a small tract of land he inherited from his family. He left the farm, built his cabin and has lived there ever since. I guess that would be around thirty-five years now."

"How long has it been since you've seen him?"

"Not for some time, but I try keep in touch by mail. BJ doesn't have a phone, or electricity, none of the modern conveniences. By boat is the only way anyone can get to his cabin. He uses his to reach a small marina every Saturday and then drives an old truck into the small town a few miles away to buy supplies, pick up his mail from the post office and visit with people he wants to associate with. The rest of the time he and his wife live like hermits deep in the swamp."

"BJ sounds like a unique fellow, but I really don't think he can be of any assistance to me, Dad."

"Maybe, son, but I think you should keep an open mind and go see him. What is that reliable instinct of yours telling you to do?"

Hound couldn't deny he was feeling compelled to go.

"OK, I'll go, Dad," said Hound. "I guess you'll be coming with me."

"No, son, I think you should go alone. I'll give you directions to the marina and the name of the man who can take you by boat to where BJ lives. Just tell them both that you're my son and that I sent you."

27

Hound was up early the next morning. He ate breakfast with his parents and then left to make the long drive to the marina. His father had written easy to follow directions on a piece of paper. Pardner wanted to go, but Hound felt it best that he remain on the farm with John and Linda.

It was a little past 10 a.m. when Hound arrived at the small marina located on the edge of what he saw to be a vast area of swamp. There was an old bait shop there where Hound's father said he would likely find the guide who would take him to BJ's cabin.

Hound walked by two Cajun men on his way to the bait shop. They were getting ready to head into the swamp to fish and likely hunt for alligator. The men paused the loading of their boat to take a long look at him. He smiled and said hello as he passed them. They said hello in return. One smiled and Hound saw the few teeth he had were badly stained as evidence of poor dental hygiene. The other remained straight-faced. He continued to stare as if he were trying to figure out if Hound should be welcome there.

As he approached the entrance to the bait shop, Hound saw it was much larger than it appeared from the side. Once inside, he realized the bait shop also housed a small grocery store and a somewhat larger beer parlor.

There was a middle-aged man behind the bar who had just served two male customers their first of several cold beers they would consume before leaving. Hound took a seat at the bar and said good morning to the men. The bartender asked what he wanted to drink.

"Sir, if you have it, I'll take a cup of freshly brewed coffee," Hound replied.

"Why don't you have a beer with us, stranger?" asked the bigger of the two male customers.

Hound noticed the sarcastic tone of the man's voice. He had realized strangers weren't welcome there.

"I enjoy a cold beer now and then," replied Hound, "but I'm not man enough to drink this early in the day."

"You don't look man enough to drink the coffee served here either."

"Really, why is that?"

"Have you ever had strong Cajun coffee?"

"Are you talking about chicory?"

"That's right, but really stout chicory."

"Yes, sir, I think so. It was so strong I shook like a dog shitting peach seeds until the effect of the caffeine wore off."

The man began laughing at Hound's remark.

"Yep, sounds like you've had real Cajun coffee," he said as the bartender poured Hound a cup of the coffee and joined in the laughter. "What's your name? Why are you here?"

"I'm Hound. It's my nickname. I'm looking for a man named Henry Breaux."

"What business do you have with Henry?"

"My father told me Henry could take me to see a gentleman named Bobby Joe Homer."

"Is that right? What's your pappy's name?"

"John William Smith. He and my mom live on a farm located about a three-hour drive north of here."

The man's attitude changed when he heard John's name.

"John told me he had a son that was called by the nickname Hound," he said, smiling. "So, you're the son."

"Yes, I am."

"Well, John has told us a lot about you, Hound. It's good to finally meet you. I'm Henry Breaux."

"Nice to meet you as well, Henry."

"I haven't seen John in quite a spell. How is he?"

"He's well."

"John is a good man. He, BJ and I have done a lot of swamp fishing together in the past. Why didn't he come with you?"

"I need to have a private visit with BJ and Dad was busy on the farm, so he didn't come. However, he wanted me to say hello for him and that he'd come for a visit soon."

"Hound, please excuse the rude behavior shown to you, but we're suspicious of strangers."

"I understand. No offense was taken."

"Well, BJ doesn't like unannounced visitors, but I'm sure he won't mind making an exception for John's son. I'll be happy to take you to his cabin as soon as I finish my beer."

"Thanks, Henry. I'll be pleased to pay you for your trouble."

"Bullshit! You ain't paying me a dime. Besides, I'm going right by his place on my way to check some holes I've got baited. That should take me a couple of hours. Will that give you enough time with BJ?"

"I would think so."

"Good. Then I'll pick you up and bring you back to your truck."

"Will my truck be safe here until I get back?"

"It will now that you are a welcome visitor."

Hound finished his coffee and talked with Henry and the other men until Henry sucked the last drop of beer from the bottle and said it was time to go. Hound walked with him to a long boat tied to the dock. They got in, Henry started the old outboard motor and they began the journey into the swamp.

It wasn't long before Hound realized how much he valued having Henry as a guide. He was already lost. As Henry navigated the boat from one narrow channel of water to another, Hound sat back and took in the scenery. This included a variety of wildlife, trees and vegetation.

"The swamp is actually a pretty place, isn't it, Henry?" asked Hound.

"Yes, it is, but you need to remember that most things in the swamp, including a lot of the vegetation, will either sting, bite or eat you. When I let you off on the bank where BJ's property begins, be damn sure you stay on the path until you reach his cabin. Even though you're on the path, be sure to keep an eye out for snakes on it and in low-hanging tree branches that you walk under. You're done for if a cottonmouth or rattlesnake bites you. Beware of gators too."

"Damn! Henry, you're a real pleasure to talk with, but thanks for the heads up."

"Yep."

"Are you sure BJ will be at home?"

"If not, then he'll be within the distance of my horn. I signal him that he has a visitor coming."

"What horn?"

"I made one from the horn I cut off a longhorn steer. It's great for calling in my Coonhounds."

"How many hounds do you have?"

"I have five of the best to be found anywhere. Your dad said you once owned a Bloodhound and that you got your nickname because of the dog."

"Yes, that's right."

"What was his name?"

"Hunter."

"That's right, your dad told me. I guess you miss Hunter."

"Yep, every day, but I have another hound now that looks just like Hunter. I've grown very fond of him, but there will never be another Hunter."

"What's his name?"

"Pardner."

"Hunter and Pardner, I like both names."

After about an hour boat ride, Henry turned the boat into a narrow waterway, slowed the motor and proceeded south. A mile distance later, he pulled the boat to a stop on the bank. He picked up his horn and blew it long and loud twice. It was a short time later that a similar sound was heard in the distance from the direction west, up the narrow path which began a few feet from where the boat was paused on the bank.

"Well, BJ knows you're coming, Hound," said Henry. "Start walking down the path. He'll meet you at some point."

"What can you tell me about BJ, Henry?"

"What did your dad tell you?"

"That BJ was well-versed in the Bible and that as a Christian, he was the real deal."

"John is right about that. However, I get the idea you're not convinced."

"To be honest, I'm very skeptical."

"Yep, we all are at specific points in our lives. I figure you're at a point in your life when you want and need answers that will support or dispel your skepticism. Is that why you're here?"

"I suppose it is, Henry."

"Well, after you talk to BJ, I hope you'll have the answers you seek. He's been like a teacher and preacher for most, if not all, of us who live around here for as long as he's lived in the swamp."

"So, you believe what he teaches and preaches is reliable?"

"Well, me and everyone else who has sought his counsel and advice have always profited by it."

"I suppose BJ is paid for his counsel and advice."

"Of course not. He would never take money for doing what God has ordained him to do. Hound, I think you're in for a big surprise when you sit down and visit with him."

Hound saw the great level of faith and confidence that Henry had in BJ. He didn't wish to say anything that would challenge that. The last thing he wanted was to offend the man that he needed to transport him back to the beginning of civilization after his visit with the man he had come to see. He began to question how a man of his intelligence and reason had been persuaded to come at all.

Hound got out of the boat and walked from the bank to where the path began.

"Don't forget to stay on the path, keep an eye on the ground in front of you and the limbs above your head," Henry reminded him, as he pulled away from the bank. "I'll pick you up in a couple of hours. I'll blow my horn to signal my arrival."

Hound waved a sign of understanding and began walking west, following the path. He followed Henry's advice and randomly slowed his pace to allow a snake enough time to slither off the path into the bushes. None were encountered in the tree limbs.

He had been walking about five minutes when he saw the figure of what appeared to be a young woman approaching from the opposite direction. Just before she reached him, they both stopped walking to allow a good size alligator to cross the path between them.

The woman looked to be barely in her twenties when she arrived to greet him. She was dressed in blue jeans with the legs cut off to a length above her knees. Her tight t-shirt had been shortened to reveal all her torso at just below her average size breasts. Her hair was brown, but it almost seemed black as it glistened in the sun shining through the tree branches. She smiled and revealed her perfectly aligned, pearl white teeth. Her complexion was dark, with unblemished skin. About five feet eleven inches in height, she looked like an athlete. Her body was firm with just the right amount of overall muscular definition. Her dark brown eyes carefully surveyed Hound from head to toe before she spoke to him.

"Hello, stranger," she said in a friendly manner. "My name is Cat. I'm BJ's granddaughter. Who are you?"

"I'm John W. Smith Jr., but everyone calls me Hound, my nickname."

"Cat is my nickname. It's short for Cathy. I know a John Smith who has a son called Hound. Are you him?"

"Yes, that's me."

"Well, Hound, I've heard a lot about you from your dad. How is John? I haven't seen him for some time."

"He's well. So is my mom, Linda."

"That's good. John used to come to visit and fish with Henry and my grandfather a couple of times yearly, but he hasn't come in a while."

"Dad has been really busy with work."

"Yes, I know. He told us in a letter that he was working for you."

"That's right. Well, it's nice to meet you, Cat. I hope all you have heard about me was good."

"It was. Your dad said you were a very handsome man. You are!"

"Thanks, Cat. You're pretty easy on the eyes yourself."

Cat thanked Hound for the compliment with a warm smile.

"Come on," she said. "I'll walk you the rest of the way and introduce you to my grandfather. He'll be waiting for you at his cabin."

"How far is it?"

"Not far, about a quarter mile."

They walked side by side on the path continuing to talk and get better acquainted. Hound had not expected a man held in such high esteem as a Christian preacher and teacher to be living like a hermit in an old cabin in the middle of a swamp, or to have such a beautiful granddaughter.

Cat told Hound that she was spending time with BJ before returning to LSU to begin working on her doctorate degree.

"I attended LSU in the past," he told her.

"Yes, I know. Your dad told me that you completed a graduate degree in an unbelievably short amount of time. He said you were very intelligent. John also said you were a brilliant businessman and very wealthy."

"I'm surprised he would tell you that."

"He probably wouldn't have if I hadn't asked."

"Are you getting a doctorate in business?"

"No, biology. I want a career working to preserve our swamplands."

"That sounds like a worthwhile career, Cat."

"Yes, it is. I will never be very wealthy the way you are, but there are things more important than money to me and my family."

"I understand and agree completely. When you begin your work, let me know if I can be of any assistance."

"How could you be of assistance?"

"I'm sure you could use some financial help from time to time."

"What do you mean?"

"Is there ever enough money available to get needed things done?"

"Why would you do that?"

"There are things more important to me than money too, Cat."

Cat smiled warmly at Hound for his gesture. She believed him to be sincere.

They continued their walk. Soon the path began to widen, and Hound found himself entering an area that seemed impossible to be found in the swamp. It was a beautiful landscape, covered in thick, manicured grass. A variety of colorful flowers and green shrubbery were growing in various, precise locations. Several large trees provided shade to certain areas. In the center of the five-acre property stood BJ's cabin.

Hound had expected to see a run-down, shabby dwelling that was surrounded by the same terrain he had seen since entering the swamp. What he saw was a lovely, good size, well-built and maintained log home. A large covered porch was on all sides. An elderly man about six feet tall, with a slender but muscular build and white hair was sitting on the front porch in a rocking chair.

When Cat introduced Hound to BJ, she included that he was the son of their good friend John Smith. Cat had stated that her grandfather was eighty-three. He looked several years younger. BJ shook Hound's hand and extended to him a warm welcome.

"Well, Hound, it's a pleasure to finally meet the son of my dear friend John," said BJ. "I normally don't receive visitors without prior notice, but you are welcome here."

"Thank you, Mr. Homer, it's a pleasure to be here. Your property and home are extraordinary."

"Thank you. Please have a seat in the chair beside me and we'll talk awhile."

Hound sat in the chair and turned it to face BJ. Cat took a seat on a porch step.

"I suppose it surprised you to see a place like this existing in the swamp," said BJ.

"Actually, I'm very surprised, but I'm also impressed."

"Have you noticed how cool it is in comparison to the heat and humidity you experienced during your trip to get here?"

"Yes, I was going to ask you how that's possible."

"I give the credit to Mother nature and just accept it as a natural event. I don't have to understand it, just appreciate it. You can go anywhere on my property and the temperature is cooler than it is when you leave its boundaries. There always seems to be a soft breeze blowing. I'm sure that helps. I suspect you have an important reason for wanting to visit me, Hound."

"I suppose I do, Mr. Homer, but I'm really not sure yet."

"Please stop calling me Mr. Homer. Call me BJ. Now, why have you come to see me?"

"I was told you are qualified as a Bible scholar."

BJ laughed.

"I have studied the Bible page by page, from cover to cover many times," replied BJ. "I would guess that my knowledge and understanding of it is as good as any common man's could be. Have you studied the Bible in length and in depth?"

"Actually, I have, but with all due respect, BJ, I've never been able to believe in anything that has never been proven to me."

"Hound, because something has never been proven, does that mean it's not true or doesn't exist? Is something impossible simply because it hasn't been scientifically verified?"

"I would have to say no, but probable is much different than possible."

"Your dad told me you are a very intelligent man, Hound. Is it true that you have a genius level IQ?"

"That's what the scores on an IQ test I took in the past revealed."

"Do you always rely on being smart to make important decisions?"

"I'm not sure what you're asking."

"Have you ever acted on a feeling to make an important decision rather than on your intellect?"

Hound didn't have to consider the question long to answer.

"I suppose I have relied on my instinct many times."

"How often was your instinct right?"

"One hundred percent, so far."

"Well, faith is having a good instinct that God and his word is real and true, even though it might not seem reasonable regarding the way of any intelligent man of the world today. Would you agree?"

Hound took a moment to consider the question.

"Maybe, but I feel instinct is closely connected to intelligence. You can't really separate them."

"You believe that the better the instinct, then the higher the intelligence?"

"Yes, I do."

"OK, then why have you come to me? I'm far from having your level of IQ, so your instinct should be superior to mine."

"Well, to be honest, I've come because my dad said I might profit from the extraordinary insight he believes you have. He said you were the best Christian he has ever known."

"So, have you come to me regarding spiritual matters?"

"Perhaps, I would like to hear what you have to say about some things that a Christian would say are spiritual."

"It's true that I have a strong faith and am well-versed in the scriptures, but if you are truly a non- believer, then why would you seek my counsel?"

"I suppose it was my dad's suggestion that I talk to you."

"Perhaps your dad thinks I can covert you. However, you may have more faith and a greater belief than you realize."

"I don't think so."

"Hound, why don't you just tell me how I can be of help. What did you come here to discuss?"

"Do you believe everyone has an ordained destiny?"

"Yes."

"Can we make the choice not to accept that destiny and choose for ourselves what we want it to be?"

"You're asking how far our free choice extends in regard to what God calls us to do. I believe those who are called have a choice. However, a select few are chosen to complete a specific destiny. Those few have no choice."

Hound noticed the deep conviction in BJ's voice.

"Do you believe yourself to be among the few that have been chosen, BJ?" asked Hound.

"I believe I have lived my life as God wanted me to. It might be that the climax of my destiny is to be here and provide you with what you came for."

Again, there was strong conviction in his voice, but Hound felt compelled to challenge the statement.

"Even if I were a believer, I could never believe that God would choose a man like me to achieve a destiny of such importance."

"What do you mean, of such importance?"

Hound knew he shouldn't answer that question.

"BJ, please believe me, I can't tell you that."

"OK, then tell me why God would never choose you for such an important destiny."

"I have lived a most sinful life, an evil life."

"God has chosen many who committed sinful and evil things to do great works for the benefit of mankind. Because you have done sinful and evil acts doesn't mean you are an evil person. God would never choose an evil person as a vessel. Do you know the difference between a person who does evil and one who is evil?"

"No, I don't think so."

"It would have to be a person that was qualified to receive God's forgiveness. Evil deeds can be forgiven. Evil persons can't."

"Would you explain what you mean?"

"Evil deeds committed willingly can be forgiven. Evil done willfully can't. Do you know the difference?"

"Yes."

"Have you done evil willingly, or willfully?"

"Willingly, but never willfully."

"I know that is the truth. Otherwise, you wouldn't have come here. Besides, I knew when I first looked in your eyes that you weren't an evil man. The eyes really do reveal what's in a person's heart and the condition of their soul."

They sat silent for a time just looking at each other.

"Is our discussion on this topic completed, Hound?" asked BJ.

"I'd like to ask your opinion about one more thing."

"OK, what?"

"Do you believe God would use a man like me for a purpose?"

"I can think of only one reason why God would want to do that."

"What would that reason be?"

"It would, for some reason, have to be a part of his divine plan."

Hound was paused by BJ's answer. He drifted into deep thought. The expression on his face revealed he was trying to put something very important into a proper prospective.

"What's wrong, Hound?" asked BJ.

"I was just reviewing and considering a story that was told to me by a stranger recently."

"Does the story have any significance to our discussion?"

"Well, I suppose it does."

"Can you tell me about the stranger and the story he told you?"

"No, but I wish I could."

BJ knew the discussion had arrived at its conclusion, but he wanted to present one last question to Hound.

"Who do you think the stranger was, Hound?" asked BJ.

"I have no idea."

"Are you certain of that?"

"Yes. BJ, who do you think he might have been?"

"What I think or believe about him is not important. It is up to you alone to find that answer."

"Yes, you're right. I understand."

"Hound, would you like to stay here for a few days? Maybe you'd benefit from a little rest and relaxation. I'm hosting a Cajun cookout this evening. There will be plenty of good food and music. You'd get to meet many of my friends and their families. They're nice folks."

"Yes, Hound! Please stay here for a while longer," said Cat. "We would have more time to get better acquainted. If you like to fish, then I can take you to the best areas in the swamp to catch some big ones."

"All you said sounds pretty good, Cat. I will stay a bit longer. BJ, are you sure I'd be welcome by all your friends?"

"Indeed, very welcome. If you're my friend, then you're their friend."

"OK, I accept your invitation. Thank you."

It was then that an elderly woman appeared from around the corner of the house. She had been tending to a garden on the rear of the property. She was a striking figure of a woman to be 79 years of age.

BJ introduced Lilly, his wife, to Hound.

"Will I be the only man at the cookout without a lady?" Hound asked jokingly.

"Not if you'll allow me to be your date, Hound," Cat said sincerely."

"Nothing would please me more."

BJ told Hound that there was a small guest house on the property that he could use if he preferred it over a guest room in the main house. Hound said he would prefer the guest house. BJ asked Cat to escort their guest to his quarters so he could rest a bit before the party started.

"BJ, I need to let Henry know that I'm staying," said Hound. "He's going to return and take me back to the marina."

"I'll let him know you're staying. He'll be able to get you back to civilization when you're ready to leave. He plans to attend the cookout. So, he's another person there that you'll know."

After Cat left with Hound to show him the guest cabin, BJ and Lilly began a conversation.

"There's something about Hound that leads me to like him, BJ," remarked Lilly.

"Darling, I feel the same way. However, I sense Hound is much more than what he appears to be on the surface."

"What do you mean, BJ?"

"I believe he is a very special man, destined to fulfill a purpose of extreme importance to mankind."

"What purpose?"

"I don't know, but I truly wish I did."

"Why do you believe that he has such a purpose?"

"It was something I saw in his eyes. I can't explain it, but I saw it."

"Your insight into others has always been reliable, BJ. So, you're probably right about Hound."

28

The guest cabin was located on the southwest corner of the property. It was a smaller version of BJ's log home. It had one bedroom that was separate from the kitchen, dining and living area, which all shared the open area in the front of the cabin.

"Do you like the cabin, Hound?" asked Cat after she had shown it to him. "Will you be comfortable here?"

"Absolutely."

"There's a well out back. You'll have to heat water on the wood stove for bathing. The outhouse is a short distance away, on the east side of the cabin. You'll find kerosene lanterns and candles in the pantry. There are no modern comforts here. I didn't think you would be comfortable with that."

"I will be fine, Cat."

"I just thought a man like you wouldn't."

"What do you mean?"

"Well, you're rich and used to the finer things in life."

"I consider this place an Eden in a place one wouldn't expect to find such. It reminds me of another place I called Eden in the past."

"Where was it?"

"Vietnam."

"I heard that you served in Vietnam. Was it bad there?"

"Yes, it was."

"Hound, how do you feel about your conversation with my grandfather?"

"Cat, BJ believes in something that I don't. However, I enjoyed our visit very much."

"What is it that you don't believe in?"

"God, the whole Christian thing. I would suspect you do, so I hope you're not offended."

"Hound, I consider myself a Christian, but I'm not offended. I have been around my grandfather all my life. As such, it would have been impossible for his belief not to have rubbed off on me. If you stay around him long enough, then it may rub off on you too."

"Maybe, but I don't think I'll be around him that long."

"Hound, your dad obviously believes in my grandfather's insight. That's likely why he sent you here. He felt you might find some answers that you were searching for."

"I suppose you're right, Cat, but I've found no answers yet, only more questions."

Cat smiled.

"OK, but maybe it's just not the right time for you to know the answers," she said. "Make yourself at home. Get some rest if you like. Folks will start arriving for the cookout later this afternoon. Join us whenever you like. If you want to look around, be sure to stay within the boundaries of the property. The grass is kept short so snakes and other dangerous creatures can be easily seen, but remember to look on the ground ahead while you're walking. We also get a gator as a visitor from time to time. Are you a good shot with a rifle?"

"Yes."

"OK, there's a loaded .30-30 Winchester in the closet. Take it along if you leave the cabin."

Hound stood in the door of the cabin after Cat left. He watched her go back to her grandfather's house and enter through the back door. He decided to draw water from the well and fill the galvanized bathtub located in a small shed built on the side of the cabin.

He allowed the cold water to sit and warm in the tub before he bathed. His shirt had become saturated from sweat during his trip through the swamp. The odor it was beginning to produce wouldn't be becoming at the cookout. After his bath, he drew more water and gave his shirt, socks and underwear a good rinse and then hung them on a clothesline to dry.

A cooling breeze entered and exited the cabin through open windows. Hound lay nude on the bed. He was thinking about all BJ had said earlier. He was amazed at all that had been said to him. However, he still wasn't ready to accept his host as being anything more than a very good man who believed the scriptures. Hound fell asleep and his thoughts turned to dreams.

When he woke, Hound could hear the sound of people speaking and laughing that was coming from a distance outside. He rose from the bed to find his clothes had been taken from the line, folded neatly and placed on the foot of his bed. Cat was likely responsible. That meant she had seen him naked as he slept. He grinned at the thought and that she had left a can of spray deodorant on top of the clothing.

It was around 5 p.m. when Hound left the cabin to join the crowd of at least one hundred people gathered a distance from the front of BJ's house. Cat saw him coming and walked to escort him the rest of the way.

"Was your nap restful, Hound?" asked Cat, smiling.

"Yes, but I didn't think I would sleep so long. It's rare that I can sleep during the day. I assume it was you who put my clothes on the bed."

"Yes, it was me. I hope you don't mind."

"Not if you don't. By the way, thanks for the deodorant."

"You're welcome and I didn't mind at all. I was able to satisfy another curiosity about you."

"Do I need to ask what it was?"

"I doubt it."

"Were you satisfied by what you saw?"

Cat smiled again and gave a short laugh.

"Not yet, but the evening is only beginning," she replied.

"My goodness! Cat, I thought you were a Christian!"

"Christians are still human, Hound."

They walked on and joined the crowd that was busy setting up the area where the cookout and other festivities would take place. Henry was talking to BJ. He waved, signaling Hound and Cat to join them.

BJ called all the guests together and introduced Hound as a new friend and special guest. Everyone as a group offered him a warm and friendly welcome. Hound asked BJ if he could help in preparing for the event.

"That's not needed. Cat, escort Hound around and help him get to know our friends and neighbors better," said BJ.

"Sure, Gramps. That's a good idea."

Hound was received in a friendly way by everyone, except for Joe Bradshaw. Joe was helping prepare the ingredients for shrimp gumbo, one of the foods to be served that evening. Joe saw Hound and Cat mingling with the crowd, stopping briefly to chat with individuals. He went to join them. Cat saw him approaching from a distance and abruptly began escorting Hound away in the opposite direction. Hound could tell something was troubling her.

"Where are you taking me, Cat?" asked Hound. "What's wrong?"

"Just keep walking, I don't want to be embarrassed by a guy I saw coming toward us."

Hound stopped and looked behind them. He saw Joe walking a fast pace to catch up.

"Is that the guy you're talking about, Cat?" asked Hound, pointing a finger at Joe.

"Yes. Come on, walk faster."

Hound refused to run from someone he didn't know and certainly didn't fear.

"Who is he, Cat? Why are we trying to avoid him?" asked Hound.

"His name is Joe Bradshaw. I made the mistake of dating him once. Now he says that he's in love and wants to marry me. I told him I thought he was crazy, and I didn't want to date him again. He's been a pain in my ass ever since. I certainly didn't expect him to be here."

"Was he invited?"

"Gramps must have invited him, or he wouldn't have come. Nobody comes here uninvited."

"Why would he be invited after you told BJ what had happened?"

"I never told him, not even that I had dated Joe."

"Why not?"

"Gramps would never have approved. I never wanted to date him anyway."

"Well, why did you?"

"Shit! I guess I just felt sorry for the guy. It got to a point when Joe was begging me to go out with him."

Joe caught up with them a moment later.

"Where are you going with this stranger, Cat?" asked Joe.

"That's none of your business. Why are you even here, Joe?"

"I came to be with you."

"Joe, I'm not interested. I've told you that so many times that I'm tired of saying it. Besides, Hound and I are dating steady now."

Hound looked surprised at her remark but didn't correct the lie. Joe was six feet, four inches tall and weighed two hundred eighty pounds. He fished, worked as a logger and hunted alligators for a living. His red hair seemed to move on his head when Cat proclaimed Hound her new boyfriend.

"I guess Cat didn't tell you, Hound, but she is my girlfriend," Joe said loudly. "I plan on marrying her."

"I'm sorry, Joe, but it seems she doesn't have the same plan in mind."

"Not as sorry as you're going to be if you don't get your ass away from my girl! Go back to where you came from. Your kind doesn't belong around here!"

Cat became furious. Hound remained calm.

"Joe, you're the one who needs to leave!" Cat shouted. "Gramps invited Hound to be here! He wouldn't like the way you're behaving!"

"I don't give a good God damn what BJ, you or anybody else thinks about my behavior. I'll tolerate this pretty boy staying until tomorrow, but he sure as hell ain't going to be your date, now, or ever!"

Joe had stepped passed Hound and was now face to face with Cat. His anger grew more intense and he began to curse at her. Hound spoke to him.

"Joe, I think it would be wise if you calmed down, stopped cursing and stepped back out of the lady's space," Hound said in a soft voice.

Joe turned quickly to face Hound. His fists were clenched as he prepared to attack. However, before he did, Hound delivered a swift kick to the large man's groin. Joe fell to the ground on his side. The pain from the kick was so severe he couldn't breathe. When he found his breath again, he began to vomit. It was so intense that some was discharged through his nose. Hound took Cat's hand and they returned to where the other guests were.

BJ, Henry and several of the guests had heard Joe's loud ranting and raving. They saw what Hound had done to quiet him. When Hound arrived at the group with Cat, he remained silent while she explained what had happened.

"It has always been difficult for Joe to control his anger," said BJ. "Cat, you should have known better than to date him. I'm not surprised that he wanted a lasting relationship. He's a lonesome man, easily encouraged and very possessive toward any woman who shows him any kind of attention. Hound, you've hurt him physically, along with his pride. I can control him during the time he's here, but when you leave, I would be very careful. Watch out for him until you're out of the swamp and on your way home."

"Why don't you ask him to leave, Gramps?" asked Cat.

"I won't do that unless he starts trouble again. I invited him here to participate in the festivities. Joe is one of our neighbors and part of the swamp family. Besides, everyone here will be staying overnight. It's too risky traveling in the swamp after dark."

"BJ, I'll also speak to Joe," said Henry. "He won't break any rules that we both tell him to follow."

"How do you feel about Joe staying, Hound?" asked BJ.

"I don't care one way or the other. It's your home, your decision as to who stays or goes."

"That's right, it is."

BJ and Henry went to check on Joe's condition and have words with him. He had crawled to a large tree and was sitting under it.

"How are you feeling, Joe?" asked BJ.

"That son of a bitch kicked me in the balls! It was a cheap shot!"

"BJ asked how you were feeling, Joe," said Henry, grinning. "Everybody knows where you got kicked. We saw what happened."

"My God-damned balls hurt something awful, but I'll be better in a while."

"Maybe, but you're going to walk funny for a couple of days."

"I'll be doing well soon enough to tear that bastard a new asshole!"

"I want you to pay attention and listen carefully to what I have to say, Joe," said BJ.

"It comes from both of us, Joe," added Henry. "Go ahead, BJ, tell him."

"Joe, you're considered to be a good neighbor and a friend to all of us," began BJ. "That's why I invited you here. Hound was invited as a special guest, so he is to be treated like part of our family. I didn't know you and Cat had a problem. She has explained it to me, making it clear that she doesn't have the same feelings as you. I don't want you bothering her or Hound any more. Now, I expect no more trouble out of you for the rest of your stay here tonight."

"She could have at least told me she and Hound were dating before I came here."

"She and Hound aren't dating, Joe. She met him for the first time when he arrived earlier today. She likely told you that to make it clear she didn't want to date you. You showed your ass to Hound for something he had nothing to do with."

"Well, I know she likes Hound, but if he's not dating her, then she might change her mind about me. However, I'm still going to get payback from him for kicking me in the nuts!"

"Maybe, but you're not going to do it on my property. Do you understand?"

"OK, BJ, I get it."

"Joe, I feel obligated to give you some good advice regarding Hound."

"What?"

"I've heard some stories about him. I believed a few of them. Others I had to question. However, after meeting and spending time with him, there are things about the man that I'm convinced of. I want you to know that he is fearless and more than able to defend himself. If you provoke him into a fight, then you will lose. Joe, Hound is no ordinary man. The main thing that you need to know is that he is deadly dangerous."

"I'm not afraid of that pretty boy!"

"That's fine, Joe. Good for you. I'm not saying you should fear him. Just don't provoke him. Have I ever been wrong regarding any advice given to you in the past?"

"Well, no."

"OK, then you better believe that I'm not wrong this time."

Joe agreed not to provoke an altercation. BJ and Henry helped him to his feet. He walked with them back to the area where the other guests were gathered. He was still experiencing a great deal of pain, so his walk was slow and with a pronounced limp.

Everyone had a wonderful time at the cookout and dancing to the Cajun music played by several of the guests. Cat kept close to Hound during the entire evening so Joe wouldn't be tempted to talk to or ask her to dance. There were no unescorted women there, but several of the wives and girlfriends of the other men took turns dancing with him. Even so, his eyes were always on or searching for Hound and Cat. He was furious to see them having a good time, but he knew it would be a mistake to break his word to BJ and cause any more trouble.

The food served included boiled shrimp, crawfish, fried fish and the gumbo. There was also corn on the cob, fried green tomatoes, okra, potatoes and beans. There was cornbread and soda biscuits with churned butter, home-canned fruits and preserves. One guest brought sorghum molasses. Another provided raw honey that he had robbed from tree hives in the swamp.

It was around 1 a.m. the next morning when Cat told Hound she was going to her room in the house and get some sleep. He walked her to the front door and bid her good night. He didn't expect the kiss she gave him, but he enjoyed it. Joe saw, but he didn't like it.

Hound remained with BJ and Henry as one by one all the guests put their bedrolls on the folding cots and went to bed. A line of kerosene torches surrounded the area where the guests would be sleeping. Several Coonhounds had been brought. As their owners went to bed, the dogs seemed to begin positioning themselves around the perimeter of where all the cots had been set up.

"BJ, what's going on with those dogs?" asked Hound.

"They're starting guard duty."

"Why?"

"Should a cottonmouth, rattlesnake or gator come close enough to present a danger, the dogs will sound an alarm."

"Well, that's really something. Are the dogs reliable?"

"Yep. All Coonhound owners who live in or near the swamp train their dogs in snake and gator patrol."

"How would these folks defend against a gator? They don't have any weapons."

"Yes, they do. You just haven't seen them. Every man here brought a rifle. There's a bright moon tonight, so you should be able to see well enough to get to your cabin safely. If you have to leave the cabin for any reason, then be sure to keep an eye on your surroundings. Be sure to shut the door and keep the Winchester handy."

"OK. Well, I think it's time for me to get some sleep. Thanks, for a great time. Good night, BJ. You too, Henry."

Hound began walking toward the cabin.

"BJ, I really like Hound," said Henry. "There's just something about him that rubs me the right way."

"Yep, I like him too, but I fear he's got a rough road ahead in his life."

"What do you mean?"

"Oh, it's just a feeling I have about him."

"From what I've heard, he's been on a rough road for a long time."

"I know, but nothing like the one he's about to travel. I hope the roads of the past have helped to prepare him."

"It sounds like you think your feeling is reliable, BJ."

"I believe it is."

"Then I wish him God's speed and help."

"Me too. He won't survive without it."

They talked a short time longer and then BJ went home and to bed. Henry went to his cot and quickly fell asleep.

Hound was lying in bed looking at the moonlight that was shining through a window. He had retrieved the Winchester from the closet and laid it on the floor next to the bed. It was about an hour later when he was awakened by the creaking sound of the back door opening. He jumped from the bed, grabbed the rifle, pointed it at the direction of the noise and made ready to shoot if necessary.

"Holy shit!" shrieked Cat. "Don't shoot, Hound. It's just me."

"Damn it! Cat, what are you doing here?"

"I wanted to spend some special time with you."

She smiled, took his hand and led him to the bed. She removed her clothing and lay down on the bed.

"Hound, have you ever had any Cajun pussy?" she asked, smiling softly.

"Not that I know of, but maybe."

"If you had, then you'd know for sure."

"Cat, I'm a guest here. Your gramps and grams would not take it well if I slept with you."

"I waited to come here until they were asleep. A hurricane couldn't wake them. They'll never know."

"We'll likely never see each other again after I leave, Cat."

"I know, but I'd like to spend as much intimate time with you as possible before you do. Now, are you going to fuck me, or do you think I'll be too much for you?"

"Cat, Christian ladies are supposed to resist such desires, right?"

"I am both a Christian and a lady, Hound, but I'm also a healthy, young Cajun woman with needs that can't be denied. Are you going to fulfill my need or not?"

Hound removed his under briefs and joined her on the bed. It wasn't long before neither were concerned about anything except enjoying and pleasing each other sexually. There was nothing sexual they didn't experience in the two hours they spent together. When Cat left close to 4:30 that morning to sneak back to her room in the main house, they had satisfied the needs of each other.

Joe had awakened from sleep in time to see Cat returning from her visit to the cabin. The rage that had filled him was intense, but he would control it and wait for a more appropriate time to unleash it and exact his revenge.

Hound went to bed and quickly fell asleep. At one that afternoon, he was awakened by loud knocking on the front door. Cat was yelling for him to wake up and come to the door.

"OK, but let me get dressed, Cat," he yelled in reply.

He rose from his bed, dressed quickly and opened the door. Cat greeted him with a smile as she came inside. She kissed him and then spoke.

"I assume you slept well," she said, "but it's afternoon and time to get up. We're going to have a meal before all the guests leave."

"What are we having to eat?"

"Eggs, potatoes, home-cured ham and homemade biscuits. Are you hungry?"

"Not really. I ate enough last night to last a day or two."

"You'll change your mind when you catch a smell of what's being cooked over an open fire."

"Maybe."

"Hound, I really enjoyed our time together earlier today."

"I did too, Cat. By the way, you were right."

"About what?"

"That I know for sure if I ever had any Cajun pussy. I know now that yours was my first."

Cat began to laugh, and he joined her in the laughter.

"Would you like some more of it?" she asked.

"As much as I can get, before I have to leave."

"I was hoping you'd say that!"

They walked together to where the guests were preparing to eat. They sat at a table with BJ, Lilly, Henry and his wife. Joe sat with friends at a table where he was facing Hound and Cat. His stare went unnoticed by everyone except Hound. His instinct was telling him that Joe felt he had a score to settle. "I hope I don't have to kill that son of a bitch!" Hound thought.

"What would you like to do this afternoon, Hound?" asked BJ.

"I have no idea."

"Cat said she promised to take you fishing while you are here."

"Yes, she did."

"Would you like to go early in the morning, Hound?" asked Cat. "We'll need to go and get back before it gets too hot."

"Sure, that sounds good. What time should we get started?"

"At first daylight."

"Can you guarantee that we'll catch some fish?"

"Yes, I'll take you to a spot called the blue hole. We'll pull some nice size bass out there."

Joe was able to hear every word of what Cat was saying. He planned to be waiting, hidden at the blue hole when Cat and Hound arrived. Hound knew Joe was listening and assumed what he might be planning.

All the guests were preparing to leave by three that afternoon. Before Henry left, he agreed to meet Hound in three days, at 8 a.m. and return him to the marina. That was as long as Hound felt he should stay.

Before Joe left, Hound looked to see what type of firearm he had brought. It was a 30-06 bolt-action rifle. It had no scope as such was not useful in most areas of the swamp. Hound was certain that all the swamp men had more than one firearm. Joe would likely use a weapon that no one knew he had, or one he could say was lost overboard from his boat in the past. Surely, he was at least that smart.

Hound gave consideration to his options and decided on what he believed to be the best. He decided to speak with Joe before he left. Neither Cat, BJ, nor Henry thought it was wise for Hound to confront Joe, but they didn't interfere. Joe was loading his boat when Hound Joined him.

"What the fuck do you want?" Joe asked in a loud, angry voice when Hound arrived.

"Joe, I would like to have a word with you in private before you leave."

"Mother fucker! You have nothing to say that I give a shit to hear!"

"How are your nuts feeling, Joe? I notice you're walking a little funny. Cat fucked me so much early this morning that mine are a bit sore too."

Joe's face turned as red as his hair. He was so angry that he couldn't speak. He began to shake all over as his rage reached its peak. He let out a loud scream. As he lunged forward, Hound once again delivered a brutal kick to the big man's groin. Once again, Joe fell to the ground in horrific pain. Hound rolled him to his back and delivered another even more brutal kick to the groin.

Joe rolled to his side and once again began to vomit. Hound picked up a heavy hammer that belonged to Joe, one he had used in helping set up the area for the cookout. He walked slowly back to where Joe was lying. He delivered a hard kick to the front of

Joe's face, rendering him unconscious. Hound then rolled Joe on his stomach and pulled his arms forward. He opened his hands wide and positioned them palms down on the ground. Using the hammer, he smashed the bones in Joe's hands and fingers.

Cat, BJ, Henry and several others who had witnessed what happened arrived from a distance of about fifty yards away.

"My God, Hound!" said BJ. "Why did you do this?"

"BJ, Joe attacked me. I defended myself."

"I saw Joe come at you! You had the right to defend yourself, but you carried that defense to far!"

"No, I didn't. I never leave an enemy at my back who plans to kill me. I'm a guest here, or I would have done worse. Anyway, now I don't have to worry about Joe bushwhacking me while I'm here. I figure he won't be able to hold, much less shoot, a firearm for quite some time."

"He won't be able to even wipe his own ass for quite some time! What made you believe he was planning to kill you?"

"Instinct, reliable instinct. BJ, I'm sorry for all of this. I wish that it could have been avoided. I'll understand if I'm no longer welcome here, and I'll leave right away."

BJ remained silent, looking at Hound for a moment before he replied. A couple of men were helping Joe, now conscious, into a boat to begin the long trip to a hospital. Joe couldn't walk. A quick inspection revealed that a rupture to his groin would be added to the list of his injuries.

"Hound, if it was anyone else but you, I would ask them to leave," replied BJ, "but my invitation for you to stay longer still stands. However, should charges be filed, you might want to consider getting out of the area."

"Thank you. I still accept that invitation. I'll take my chances regarding any charges Joe might file."

"Joe would never file charges. However, his injuries are serious enough that legal authorities might file charges. Hound, there's a chance Joe might be permanently disabled. He might even die."

"Joe will recover. He's strong, just not smart."

A short time later, Joe had been made as comfortable as possible in a boat and he began his journey to the nearest hospital. One by one, the other guests finished loading their boats and left. None of them spoke a word to Hound, but a variety of different expressions were on their faces as they looked his way before leaving. Henry was the last to leave. He reaffirmed when he would return to pick Hound up and deliver him back to the marina. Cat and Hound walked to the guest cabin. Before he left, Henry spent a few minutes talking with BJ.

"BJ, how do feel about what Hound did to Joe?" asked Henry.

"It was unfortunate, Henry. I hate that it happened, but I'm not sure that Hound didn't extend a courtesy to Joe."

"How do you figure that?"

"Hound might have been right about Joe planning to ambush him. I sense that Joe might be capable of such an act. If so, then Hound chose to disable, rather than kill him."

"Do you think Hound would have been the victor?"

"There's no doubt in my mind that Hound would have been the one who survived. I suspect he's killed many adversaries that were much more capable than Joe."

"Well, I sure as hell wouldn't want Hound mad at me."

"Nor would I, but Hound wasn't mad at Joe, that's why he extended the courtesy. He believed Joe didn't deserve to die. Hound has a code regarding such things."

When Cat and Hound arrived at the cabin, they sat beneath the shade of a tree. The conversation Hound had with BJ when he first arrived sparked her curiosity. There were things she wanted to know regarding the significance of Hound coming there. He had refused to answer certain questions that her grandfather asked. She hoped that Hound would confide more in her.

"Hound, do you trust me?" she asked.

"I suppose so, to a point."

"Only to a point, not completely?"

"That's right. I don't know you well enough to trust you completely."

"I see what you mean. However, that would indicate you have something to hide that could be harmful in some way if you told me and I told others. Otherwise you wouldn't feel the need to trust me completely. Am I right?"

"Cat, you should change the subject. I have nothing to say about my conversation with BJ. What you heard me say is all either of you need to know."

"OK, Hound, if that's the way you feel. What shall we talk about?"

"I feel I should apologize for what I did to Joe."

"No need. It didn't bother me. You may have been right about what he was planning to do."

"I was, but I'm sorry for having to make such a harsh spectacle of myself in front of you, your grandparents and all those other nice folks. I can only imagine what they must think of me. They came here as guests of a good Christian man and had to witness my heathen behavior."

"Swamp people have seen and done things as bad. There're not heathens and neither are you. You may be closer to becoming a believer than you realize."

"I don't think so. Why would you?"

"Why would a true atheist come here to seek counsel with an old man who is a devout Christian?"

"To hear what he had to say about specific things and how he would answer specific questions."

"Why would you think what he had to say was worth hearing, would benefit you?"

"I've always kept an open mind regarding the beliefs of others, even when they can't prove their beliefs are the truth."

Cat pointed across the waterway that separated the property from the vast swamp that lie beyond.

"Hound, you're a very intelligent man. Tell me what you see out there?" she asked.

"I see a marvelous work of nature."

"Indeed, but do you honestly believe that it is a result of natural evolution?"

"That seems logical."

"Hound, the swamp is an ecosystem that is in perfect and precise balance to support itself. The odds of such perfection occurring by random chance are astronomical. Those odds are enough to support the probability of a divine creation. It's the same for all systems all over the world. Consider how the position of the sun, moon, planets and stars are in a perfect and precise position as to support each other and how the earth is at a precise position among them to support all life forms. The odds of all that happening by chance are equally astronomical."

"You present an interesting theory, but it still doesn't offer any absolute proof to support divine creation."

"Hound, do you ever gamble?"

"What?"

"Do you ever play poker, blackjack, dice, slot machines, you know, like at a casino?"

Hound had to laugh at the question.

"Well, I haven't played blackjack for some time," he replied, "but I used to make a few bucks playing on a regular basis."

"Did you always win?"

"It would be impossible, unless I were somehow cheating to always win."

"What would the odds be that you would always win?"

Hound paused briefly and smiled.

"The odds would be astronomical," he said.

"Well, if you did always win, then would you have to agree that something more than skill or chance was responsible?"

"Yes, I suppose so."

"Hound, I believe that evolution occurs over time to change things that need to change in order to maintain the perfect balance of everything. It would have to be God in control of the evolution, or it would not be perfection."

"Cat, you have offered a good argument to support your faith. It isn't without merit and deserves consideration. However, I've heard similar arguments before. I still require better proof."

"Would you say that you're searching for proof, truth, and that's the reason you came here?"

Hound considered the question carefully and realized the significance of the answer he gave.

"Cat, I have to say that coming here may be the beginning of my journey to prove or disprove what Christians believe is real."

"Hound, God said if you will seek me, then you will find me. When the time is right, I believe God will reveal the truth of his existence to you."

There was something about her prediction that triggered his instinct, and it told him that she might be right. This caused him to feel a moment of strange anticipation that he soon dismissed.

"I would like to fix dinner here at the cabin this evening, just for you and me. would you like that, Hound?"

"Yes, that sounds good, Cat."

"What would you like?"

"How about something less traditionally Cajun?"

"How does a steak, baked potato, salad with homemade apple pie for dessert sound?"

"Wonderful."

"OK, I'll be back around 6 to start cooking. We need to get in bed early. Our fishing trip will begin at 4 a.m. tomorrow morning. You'll like the blue hole. It's a beautiful place. We can cool off in the water when it gets hot."

"What about gators and snakes? Won't it be dangerous to swim?"

"I think we'll be OK, but bring the Winchester."

"Don't worry! I will!"

Cat kissed him and returned to the main house. Hound watched her all the way there. He was growing fond of Cat. Hound had learned in the short time he had known her that she was a remarkable young woman.

29

They left at 4:30 the next morning on their fishing trip. The journey to the blue hole lasted about a half hour. Cat navigated the small boat through waterways that varied in width and depth. Finally, she turned the boat off the main channel into a narrow one. A quarter mile further and the channel ended at a small lake surrounded on three sides by land covered in a beautiful natural landscape filled with a variety of trees, flowers and green vegetation.

Cat slowed the small outboard motor and guided the boat to a landing at a specific area of the north shoreline. A portion of the area had been cleared and made appropriate for picnicking and overnight camping.

"Hound, we're here," said Cat. "How to you like it?"

"I don't think I've ever seen a prettier place in nature. It feels peaceful too."

"I thought you'd like it. I'm happy that you do."

"I do. Thanks for bringing me here. Who did the work to create the picnic and camping area?"

"My gramps and I did most of it, but we had some help from a couple of swamp families."

"I suppose a lot of swamp people come here from time to time."

"Yes, but Gramps doesn't allow that too often. He wants to make sure his property remains in a specific condition."

"BJ owns this lake and the land that surrounds it?"

"Yes, the lake and the land from the shorelines to about a quarter mile beyond on all three sides."

"I'm even more envious of BJ. He has more than one extraordinary property in an environment one wouldn't expect to find such."

"Hound, we can fish from the boat or from the shore. Which do you prefer?"

"I'd like to sit under a tree to fish, just relax and enjoy the surroundings."

"You said it was peaceful here."

"Yes, very much so."

"Do you find it as peaceful on the property where my gramps lives?"

"Of course."

"Why?"

"Would I be correct in thinking your life hasn't been very peaceful, that you're in need of peace for a while?"

He hesitated briefly.

"Yes, I suppose so."

"Maybe you'd benefit from being my gramp's guest longer than you have planned. I'm sure you could stay in the guest cabin for as long as you wanted to. I would love for you to stay longer."

"I would like to stay permanently, Cat, but what I want and what I can have are not the same."

"What do you mean by that?"

Hound knew she was still trying to find out more about what he couldn't tell her.

"I have business obligations and responsibilities that have

always dictated what I can and can't do, Cat. Now, I'm ready to find a tree and start to fish."

He found a tree, baited the hook on his fishing pole and cast it as far as possible out into the lake. Cat did the same and then sat down next to him under the tree. She felt that asking more questions would be a waste of time and might annoy him.

Within a couple of hours, the two of them had caught enough large bass to provide a feast for them, BJ and Lilly that evening. They secured their catch on a stringer and left it in the water. The temperature and humidity had risen quickly that morning. By 10 a.m., it felt like a hot steam bath in the swamp.

"Hound, let's go for a swim and cool off," said Cat.

"I'm not sure that's a good idea."

Cat knew his concern and smiled. She stood and removed all her clothing in preparation for a swim in the nude.

"Hound, don't worry. I've never seen a gator or snake in the lake," said Cat. "They don't seem to like the water."

"Why?"

"Have you noticed how clear the water is?"

"Yes."

"Gators prefer to hang out in water that isn't crystal clear. Besides, there are minerals in the water they don't like. Snakes don't either. It's just another natural phenomenon in the swamp. As a result, you're not likely to find a gator or snake on land surrounding a body of water like this lake. I've been swimming here since I was a young girl."

Hound took Cat at her word and they were soon nude, swimming and playing in the cool water together. Before they left around one that afternoon, they ate from the picnic lunch Cat had brought and spent plenty of intimate time under the shade of the tree. They would cool off in the lake after.

When they arrived back at her grandfather's home, they cleaned and filleted the fish to eat that evening. Hound visited with Cat and her grandparents until 9 p.m. and then announced he was going to get some sleep. It was a little after 10:30 when Cat arrived and joined him in bed.

"My gosh! Cat, I thought you got all the sex you wanted during our time at the lake earlier!" Hound said jokingly.

Cat pulled close to him.

"I was satisfied earlier, but that was several hours ago!" she replied seriously.

Hound had been a guest of BJ's for a week when he knew it was time to leave. Henry arrived at 7 a.m. on a rainy morning to transport him back to his truck at the marina. He had notified Hound's parents of his intention to remain as BJ's guest for the week and Hound didn't want them to worry.

"It's been a joy having you here, Hound," BJ told him as he prepared to leave. "Come back anytime. You're always welcome."

"Thanks. I appreciate that."

"You will come back and see us someday, Hound," said Cat. "You know I care for you."

"I'll come for a visit if and when I can, but my future is uncertain right now."

"I'm sure it is, Hound," said BJ, "but you'll figure it out."

Cat kissed him goodbye. As she held him for a moment in a warm embrace, she whispered in his ear that she loved him very much. He smiled and then he and Henry turned and began walking down the path to where Henry had left his boat. Before they were out of sight, Hound turned, smiled and waved a final goodbye to a family he would always remember as among the finest people he had ever known.

During the trip back to the marina and the beginning of civilization, Hound asked Henry if he knew how Joe was doing. Henry was reluctant to answer, but he told him that Joe had died from a heart attack during surgery to repair the injuries sustained from the beating Hound had given him.

"Son of a bitch!" Hound yelled loudly. "I meant to save Joe, not kill him!"

"I know that. Hound, you didn't kill Joe, a heart attack did."

Hound didn't respond. He remained silent for the rest of the trip. When they arrived at the marina, he said farewell and thank you to Henry, got into his truck and began the drive back to the farm. He knew his father would be waiting to hear how his visit with BJ had gone. John wouldn't be prepared for all he would be told. It had been reported that Joe had been injured in a boating accident. Therefore, Hound would be free of any legal charges and from any consequences. However, he would carry a feeling of guilt and regret always. Despite his intentions, the code he followed had been broken.

Hound arrived at the farm in the early afternoon. Pardner was lying under the oak tree in the front yard, close to the grave of Hunter. The summer harvest was almost over. Hector was away doing work on other properties owned by Hound's farming and ranching corporation.

It was a hot and humid day. John decided to quit work early and come to the house. He joined Hound and Pardner, who were relaxing in the shade. John was anxious to know if Hound's time with BJ had been productive.

"You were expected to see BJ and return home on the same day, son," said John, "but I can understand your desire to stay longer. It's nice at BJ's place, isn't it?"

"Yes, I wish my stay could have been even longer."

"That means he liked you. I'd bet you enjoyed his cookout party."

"There was a cookout and dance. I had a good time."

"Did you find answers to questions that were troubling you?"

"Dad, I don't know yet. I suppose time will tell."

"I wish there was more I could do to help you, son."

"I know."

John decided it was time to ask about the particulars of his son's visit with BJ.

"Son, will you tell me how your visit with BJ went regarding the private things we talked about?" asked John. "Those things that greatly concern you."

"Dad, you know I couldn't tell BJ everything that I confided in you."

"I know, but I'd bet he was able to figure out a lot, if not most, of what you didn't disclose."

"Maybe, but he never let me know for sure that he did."

"Naturally, he wouldn't. Did he provide you with anything that helped?"

"He provided a lot of things for me to review and consider, but nothing that I'm ready to embrace as true, nothing that hasn't always seemed more unlikely than reasonable."

"I'm sorry to hear that, son. I hoped what he had to say would give you some sense of direction. What will you do now?"

"What I feel is my best choice, given what my instinct tells me that choice is at this point."

"Hound, remember that there is always more than one choice."

"Dad, I said it was my best choice, not the only choice."

"Hound, knowing only the incomplete information about James, the other members of the organization and what they do should be enough to convince you not to have anything to do with them."

"It does, but they want me to join them and have told me what the consequences will be if I don't."

"That's why you feel it's the best choice to do so."

"That's right."

"Are you convinced they are powerful enough to administer those consequences?"

"Yes, I've already told you that."

"OK, but your current wealth and contacts makes you powerful too. That's a reason they want you to join them. Maybe if you decide to reject their offer, it would deter them from following through on possible threats made only as a bluff."

"These men don't bluff or make idle threats, Dad. I'm convinced of that. What I'd really like to know is why they want to break with tradition and make me, an outsider, one of them."

"Do you have any theories about that?"

"No, but if I knew it would be of great help to me. I won't find that out until after I've taken a very serious oath and become one of them."

"When you find out everything, then it may be too late."

"I know, Dad."

"Son, do you want my advice?"

"Of course. What is it?"

"Hound, I love you and it kills me to say this, but you should reject these men and if necessary, defend yourself against them to your last breath, if that is required. They and their organization are evil."

Hound decided the conversation needed to end.

"Dad, I don't believe in evil, not in the way you're referring. However, I do believe in bad things that people do. These men are capable of doing bad things to anyone they choose. Even if I could defend myself against them, I'm certain I would be unable to defend you, mom and all the other people that I love or care deeply about. It's for certain that all of you would be helpless to defend yourselves."

When John tried to continue the conversation, Hound declared it was over. He stood up and walked away in the direction of the barn. Pardner walked at his side. John realized it was of no use to try and change Hound's mind. He did, however, understand why he couldn't.

Hound entered the barn and sat on a bale of hay. He looked at the spot in the corner and told Pardner it was where Hunter used to have his bed. He began to recall fond memories of days long passed when he and Carmella would meet in the barn to spend intimate time together on bales of hay he arranged into a suitable bed. It seemed as though every fond memory of his growing up on the farm and in the rural Louisiana community came to mind.

Hound left the barn and walked to the swimming hole. He and Pardner sat under the large oak tree on the bank of the creek. A breeze began to blow. It crossed the creek and was cooling.

Memories that were darker began to replace the good ones. In his mind, he relived the day he killed Carlos Mendoza and could see him floating face down in the swimming hole. He heard the voices and saw the faces of all the others he had killed. Karen Thibodaux and her boyfriend, Carmella and her cousin, Judge Robert Thibodaux, Lieutenant Connors, Colonel Westerman and even the enemy soldiers in Vietnam and those in Colombia, Steve Cooper, Roberto Sanchez and his men, Ken O'Malley, the Irish mob boss in Florida, Cole Hanson, Jack Long and his men. He thought of his last victim, Joe Bradshaw, and then refused to search his memory for any others.

Hound wondered what his life would be like now, if he had simply allowed Carlos to live. It was for sure that single act of violence had set him on the path that led him to where he was now. He wondered if James had been right, that everything that had happened in his life was preparing him for membership in the organization. Would that lead him to the destiny he was born to achieve?"

Hound decided to take a swim in the cool water of the creek and clear his mind of all confusing thoughts. He removed all his clothes and entered the water. When he felt sufficiently cooled and refreshed, he returned to the tree and dressed. He walked back to the house and later enjoyed a nice dinner and conversation with his parents.

Early the next morning, Hound boarded his jet. With Pardner lying quietly just outside the cockpit, the jet took off for Montana. It climbed to a cruising altitude of thirty thousand feet and the course was set. Hound gave a final thought as to when he might see his parents again and to what life would hold for him as a member of the organization. His attention soon focused on flying the plane and on Pardner who was now sitting in the co-pilot seat.

When Hound arrived home in Montana, the first thing he did was to call Maggie and ask if she had gathered any helpful information about James. There was nothing out of the ordinary to be found anywhere. Hound agreed that Sam and his crew should return to their biker chapter and duties in the drug business. All of them except Curly would leave the ranch on the following day. He would leave as soon as he was released from the hospital.

Hound stayed on the ranch until he left for England. Hud would be left in charge of running ranch operations. Casey would handle the business end. Both would be reporting to Beth. Kelly and Stacey were put in charge of caring for Pardner until Hound's return.

On August 31, 1981, Hound said a final goodbye to all those who came to see him off. He boarded his jet, taxied into position, and then took off on his way to London.

To see what happens next, read the beginning of "God, the Devil, and Destiny" on the following pages.

God, the Devil, and Destiny

1

When Hound arrived in London, Anna and her body-guards were waiting to greet him at the private airport. She rushed into his arms as soon as he was off the plane. "I'm so happy to see you, Hound," she said. "You have been in my thoughts constantly while you were away. Did you think of me?"

"You can't imagine how much you were in my thoughts."

She took that to mean he missed and wanted to be with her. He didn't include how his thoughts of her were combined with his thinking about all things connected to the situation he was faced with.

Anna took his arm and told him that a helicopter was waiting to take them to the family estate. Once on board the luxury aircraft, the three bodyguards took seats in the main passenger cabin. Anna led Hound to the small private cabin in the rear.

"Do you like the helicopter, Hound?" she asked.

"It's very nice."

"It's the finest money can buy, my darling."

"I assumed that."

Anna laughed.

"What kind of helicopter do you have in Montana?"

"Well, I don't have one."

"Why not?"

"So far, I haven't needed one. I have my jet for long distant travel. I drive where I need to go locally. My ranch is only a few miles from town. I don't usually need to travel anywhere else, unless it's far enough to use my jet."

"Are there many fun things to do there, adequate places for me to shop?"

"Anna, the places to shop are adequate for what you will need. I fear you are in for a real culture shock. Living on a ranch will be much different than what you're accustomed too."

"How so?"

"The dress code is western boots and blue jeans. Most folks wear western hats, but some, like me, consider a hat optional."

"What do you wear when you go out for dinner at an exquisite restaurant?"

"Boots and blue jeans. There are restaurants where formal dress is worn, but not in the county where I live."

"What do you do for fun where we will be living?"

"Rodeos and the Silver Spur."

"What is the Silver Spur?"

"The best restaurant and dancehall to be found in Montana. I own it.

"Hound, will I like living in Montana?"

"I don't know, likely not at first, but I think it will grow on you."

"If it doesn't, can we live somewhere else?"

When he didn't answer, Anna changed the subject and pulled herself as close to him as possible.

A car was waiting when they landed to drive them to the estate home. The house staff and Anna's parents were waiting to welcome her and her soon-to-be new husband. Naturally, James was delighted to see Hound again.

"Hound, are you hungry?" asked James. "Would you like something to eat?"

"No, thank you, but I could use some sleep."

"Certainly. I know you're tired and ready to rest. Anna can walk you to your room. Will you be rested enough to join us for dinner at 7 p.m. this evening?"

"Of course."

Anna escorted Hound to his usual room. She stayed in his room only briefly, and then kissed him and left. He took a long shower and then began to unpack his luggage. He paused after removing the pair of matching, ivory grip, Colt 45 handguns from the smallest piece of luggage. He held them in his hands and thought of his best friend, Bear, who had given him the weapons. He returned the pistols to the luggage, placed it in a closet, and then lay on the bed in preparation for some sleep.

He had just closed his eyes when he heard a soft knock on the door of his room. He went and opened the door. To his surprise, Sophia had come to see him.

"Sophia, what are you doing here?" he asked.

"I wanted to see you."

She pushed past him and entered the room. He closed the door.

"I didn't know that you were still at the estate, Sophia," he said. "I thought you would be at home in Rome."

"I decided to stay until after the wedding. I will be the maid of honor. I wanted to see you before you were married."

"Why?"

"I know you don't want to marry Anna. I should be your wife, not her."

"Sophia, you know I have no choice but to marry her."

"I know, but you won't have to stay married to her. After James has the heirs he wants, then you can divorce her and marry me."

"I think you're wrong about how James would feel about me divorcing Anna."

"Maybe, but he will no longer control you in that way once you and Anna produce an heir. After that, as a member of the organization, you can marry any woman who has a bloodline tie to any member. You can marry me and produce the perfection in heirs, as many as you want."

"Sophia, you need to leave before someone finds out you're here."

"All the family is downstairs. They think that I'm napping in my room and you're doing the same. No one will ever know I was here, or what we did."

"Sophia, what are you talking about? What is it that you think we're going to do?"

"You're going to sleep with me before you do with her. I want to be first. Besides, you need to know what you have to look forward to with me even after you're married to her."

"God damn it! Sophia, what's wrong with you? I know you're not crazy!"

"I'm in love with you and will eventually have you for my own at any cost! Tell me that you don't want me and I'll leave."

Sophia removed all her clothing and walked to the bed. He viewed her body as perfection in every way. Again, he thought she was the only woman he'd ever seen whose physical perfection was equal to that of Rita. She lay on her back in the bed and beckoned him with a soft smile and tender expression. He joined her on the bed.

"Be gentle with me for a while, my darling," she said softly.

He did as she requested. She smiled and pulled him deep inside her as she surrendered her virginity. He fulfilled her every need and desire as he made love to her in all the ways that he knew.

When it was time for her to leave, she reaffirmed her love for him and that she would wait faithfully until they could be together again and again secretly until the time arrived when they could be married. Hound smiled but didn't speak. He opened the door and surveyed the hallway in both directions. All was clear. Sophia kissed him passionately and then returned to her room.

Hound returned to the bed and noticed the blood stains on the sheet. He removed and replaced it with a clean one. He took another shower and then returned to bed for some needed sleep.

"Well, fuck, here I am!" he said to himself in a low voice. "Chin deep in multiple piles of shit! I wonder if I can come out smelling like a rose this time?"

His instinct offered no clue to the answer. He soon fell to a deep sleep absent of dreams.

To be continued.

www.ingramcontent.com/pod-product-compliance
Lightning Source LLC
Chambersburg PA
CBHW020327180626
46812CB00001B/88

* 9 7 8 1 9 4 6 7 0 2 4 3 2 *